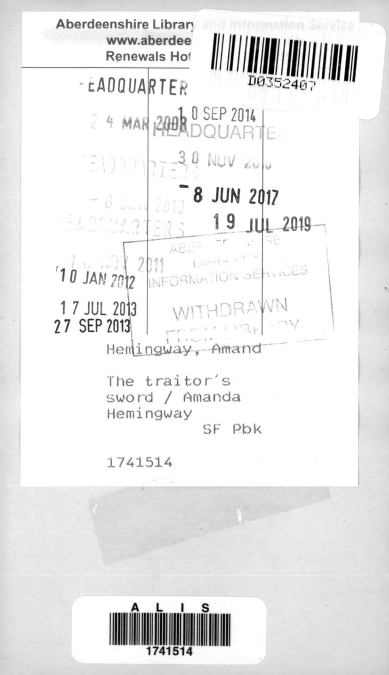

By Amanda Hemingway

THE GREENSTONE GRAIL

As Jan Siegel

PROSPERO'S CHILDREN
THE DRAGON-CHARMER
WITCH'S HONOUR

SANGREAL TRILOGY

II

THE TRAITOR'S SWORD

Amanda Hemingway

Harper*Voyager*
An Imprint of HarperCollins*Publishers*
77–85 Fulham Palace Road,
Hammersmith, London W6 8JB

www.harpercollins.co.uk

First published in Great Britain by *Voyager* 2005

This paperback edition 2006
1

A catalogue record for this book
is available from the British Library

ISBN-13: 978 0 00 715389 3
ISBN-10: 0 00 715389 9

Set in Sabon by Palimpsest Book Production Limited,
Grangemouth, Stirlingshire

Printed and bound in Great Britain by
Clays Ltd, St Ives plc

Contents

Battle

Not the blade
but the hand on the hilt

Not the prize
but the blood that is spilt.

Not the song
but the cry of the steel

Not the pain
but the ones who can't feel.

Not the fire
but the pulse of the heart

Not the fear
but the standing apart.

Not to weep
but the tears running red

Not to sleep
but to dream with the dead.

PROLOGUE

The Dead City

It began with a city, a city in another universe.

Nathan Ward dreamed of the city, as he had dreamed of other cities long before. Most people dream of other worlds, dreamworlds parallel to our own yet subtly different, where strange things are familiar and familiar things strange – the spin-off regions of the subconscious mind. But the worlds in Nathan's dreams were real, or seemed real, depending on the nature of reality. He went to the kind of school where teachers talked about philosophy and quantum physics, so he knew the chair he was sitting on was provably non-existent, and the entire cosmos was made up of particles too small to believe in, popping in and out of reality whenever scientists studied them too closely. (Sneaky things, particles.) Nonetheless, Nathan was a down-to-earth boy who had yet to find a magical country at the back of a wardrobe, so it was unnerving to find one in his own head. The previous summer he had almost got lost in such a dream, and had been unable to make his way back without help.

Sometimes on these journeys he was merely a disembodied thought; at others, as the dream grew more solid so did he, while his sleeping form would fade, even vanish altogether. He was a weekly boarder at Ffylde Abbey, sharing a dormitory with other boys, and a tendency to dematerialize in the night didn't always pass unremarked. Particles can get away with such behaviour more easily than teenage boys. At home his mother, his best friend, and the man he called uncle all knew of the problem, so there was no need to try and explain the inexplicable, but there were moments when he still felt unsafe. As if there was a hole inside his head through which his life and his very self might slip away. Dreams can too easily become nightmares, and when your dreams are real, the nightmares have teeth . . .

The strange thing was, when he dreamed of the city, he knew it wasn't the first time, though the earlier times were all but forgotten, immured in a locked cupboard at the back of his memory. The dream gave him a *feel* he couldn't mistake, like when you return to a place visited in early childhood. There's nothing you recognize, yet you know you've been there before.

There had been a city in his dreams many times in the past, the city of Arkatron on Eos – a city at the end of time, last stronghold of a high-tech, high-magic civilization in a universe that was dying. It had been a futuristic metropolis of soaring sky-towers and airborne vehicles that wheeled and dipped around them like giant birds, and a population mantled and masked and gloved against the poisonous sunlight – a science fiction city with a ruler called the Grandir – a ruler thousands of years old, whose face was never seen and whose true name was never spoken – a ruler who had once had a whole cosmos for his empire.

But this city was different. (In his mind, he called it a city, giving it the benefit of the doubt, though quite possibly it was only a town.) It sprawled over two hills, the higher rising into a bastion of rock with a grey-walled house perched on the top, built of the same stone and blending with it, so you couldn't tell where the crag ended and the house began. The lower hill was a hump-backed ridge crested with pointy gables and spiked with chimney stacks, but only one or two emitted a thin spindrift of smoke, and as his vision drew nearer Nathan saw windows without panes, doors ajar on empty halls, new grass growing over untrodden roads. It was a ghost town – or ghost city – except there seemed to be no ghosts left, only endless vacancy. There weren't even any birds.

In Arkatron, focus of a universe that was ending, the city thrived after a fashion, crawling with people and lights and life, yet here, though the universe showed no signs of imminent demise, the city was dead. A Marie-Celeste of a city, whose footsteps had barely faded and whose voices might have been stilled only a little while ago. It reminded Nathan of towns pictured in history books, the outer houses made of mud bricks and rickety timbers, with shaggy thatching on the roofs, the inner of stone and tile. The hilltop house was the largest, poised in the eye of the wind, weatherbeaten and grim, sprouting irrelevant battlements and tiny turrets as if it were trying to become a castle, though no one would be fooled. It had neither moat nor portcullis, and on one side a steep little garden sloped down to wall and road. As Nathan's thought winged earthwards he saw four children were playing there.

They might have been the only children – perhaps the only people – in the whole city. Three boys and a girl. The boys were fighting with wooden swords, banging their weapons on toy shields, shouting incomprehensible war cries. The girl was making mud pies. She looked about seven or eight years old and wore an expression of extreme concentration half hidden under the tangle of her hair. She reminded him a little of Hazel, his best friend, who often hid behind her hair, but whereas Hazel's was brown and straight this child's was blonde, dark blonde like wheat, and the tangle was rippled and crinkled into untidy waves. One of the boys came over, evidently to check on her, and she looked up with a sudden sweet smile which made Nathan think that when she was older, though she might not be pretty or beautiful, her smile would always win her friends. As in other dreams he could understand what the children said, though he realized afterwards that the language they spoke wasn't English.

'Let me play with you,' the girl said. 'I can fight too.'

'Swords aren't for girls,' the boy retorted. 'You might get hurt.'

'Have one of my pies, then.' The smile disappeared; her face closed.

'I don't eat mud and sand,' the boy said, half teasing, half scornful.

''Tisn't mud and sand,' said the girl. 'It's chocolate.'

''Tisn't chocolate, stupid.'

''Tis so.'

The boy opened his mouth to go on arguing, and then was suddenly quiet. Nathan found his gaze fixed on the mud pie, which was round and carefully moulded, and thought it did indeed look a lot like chocolate. There were even little flakes around the rim, like decoration . . .

'Chocolate,' said the girl with satisfaction.

A shadow swept over the scene, the advancing edge of a stormcloud. The boys ceased their game, staring upwards. A door opened at the top of the garden and a woman in a linen headdress leaned out, calling to the children to come in. There was a note of urgency or fear in her voice. The boy who had been quarrelling with the girl seized her wrist and pulled her towards the shelter of the doorway, though she seemed reluctant to go with him. A winged darkness swooped low over the city, swift as a sudden squall; on the slope a stunted tree twisted with the wind. There was a noise which might have been thunder or the booming of immense pinions. Whether the shadow was cloud or creature Nathan couldn't tell, but he felt the icy chill of its advent, and the wind that tried to tear the tree from its roots whirled his thought away, out of the city, out of the dream, into the gentle oblivion of sleep.

When he awoke he was in his own world, and the dream seemed very far away. Nonetheless, he thought about it, from time to time, all that day, and the next. It was the Easter holidays, and he was going to be fourteen, and he had to decide what he wanted, by way of a birthday treat. 'I want things to happen,' he said to himself, both hopeful and afraid, for things had happened to him the previous year, to him and to others – things both exciting and terrifying – and he knew that wishing for trouble is one way of inviting it in.

He said the same thing that evening, when his uncle (who wasn't really his uncle) came to supper.

'You sound like a child in a story,' said his mother, 'wishing for adventures. After last summer, you should know better. There may have been a kind of happy ending for you, but not for others. People died.'

'Of course I don't want anyone to die,' Nathan said. 'It's only a little wish. For my birthday.'

'When you're older,' Uncle Barty said, 'you'll learn that things happen without your wishing for them, all the time. You may even wish for peace and quiet one day. But you probably won't get it.'

Nathan said no more, quelled by the phrase *When you're older*, because he knew his uncle was older than anyone, and had seen more things happen than Nathan would ever dare to wish for. Bartlemy Goodman had the Gift, a strange legacy which gave him not only long life but other powers beyond the norm, powers which might have made him a sorcerer or a magus, though he appeared to use his abilities mostly for ordinary things, like cooking, and brewing home-made liquor, and herbal medicines. He didn't look at all sorcerous: true wizards should be lean and cadaverous, hook-nosed and long-bearded, but Bartlemy was fat and placid and clean-shaven, with a broad pink face, fair hair turned white with age, and mild blue eyes gazing tolerantly at the world. But Nathan had seen beneath the surface, though only a little way, and he never doubted his uncle's reliability, or his wisdom.

It was about a week later when he dreamed of the city again. It was just a brief glimpse of people piling bags and bundles into a cart, and the reins shaken, and the plodding hooves of a horse moving ponderously away. The girl was standing there – she was older now, almost his own age, but he knew her by her hair and the smile that gradually faded as she ceased waving and her hand fell to her side. The cart lumbered down the road and out of the city, heading along a sort of causeway across a low-lying country broken into many pools and water-channels which mirrored the grey pallor of the sky. Without her smile the girl's face looked grave and somehow resigned, as if she had seen many such departures. She turned and began to walk back up the road, until it narrowed into a steep path coiling about the hill, and then eventually became steps that climbed the last ascent to the house on the crag.

'This is *her* home,' Nathan thought, suddenly sure. 'Those boys were just visiting. She's the daughter of the lord or king or whoever it is rules this place.'

Her dress was patched with darns and her long hair looked as if it hadn't been brushed for a day or more but there was something about her, the gravity that touched a face which might have been merry, a hint of resolution or confidence, the assurance of a princess. A princess without crown or ermine, with no visible attendants and few remaining subjects, but a princess nonetheless.

When she reached the huge main door she opened it herself, without the aid of butler or footman. It must have been heavy since it took a strong thrust to move it. It creaked suitably, as such doors should, closing behind her with a reverberating thud as she went inside.

Nathan's dream followed her – into a hall that seemed to be hung with shadows, up stairs that branched and zig-zagged, along passageways and galleries with cold echoing floors and walls where threadbare tapestries flapped like cobwebs. At last she entered a room that was thick with books – books close-packed on regular shelves or piled in winding stacks or slithering earthwards like rows of collapsed dominoes. Nathan was reminded a little of the second-hand bookshop which his mother managed and where they lived, though this room was larger than his whole house, with a vaulted ceiling from the centre of which depended an iron chandelier festooned with dribbles of old wax, above a desk where an elderly man was bent over an opened volume, trying to read it with a magnifying glass. A window squeezed between two banks of shelving admitted a shaft of daylight which stretched towards the desk, picking out more books, and dust, and the man's hair which stood up around his head like a dandelion clock. Long strands of tallow trailed from the chandelier like stalagmites in a cave.

'Frim,' said the girl – the man looked up – 'the Hollyhawks have gone today, and old Mother Sparrowgrass and her boys. They wouldn't have told me, but I went to take them a cake, and there they were, all packed up and the cart rolling.'

'Deserters!' said the old man. 'What did you do?'

'What could I do? I wished them luck.'

'They deserve no luck,' said the old man. 'Running away. Bumskittles! They are your people.'

'They are their own people,' said the girl. 'What have I ever done for them?'

'Your best.' He reached out, squeezing her hand in his own thin, bony one, then patting it. He had a strange knobbly face with startled eyebrows, round inquiring eyes and a long nose that turned up at the tip. For all his age he had a quality of youthfulness which, Nathan reflected, few young people ever exhibited – he seemed vividly alive, curious, alert, exuding enough energy for a small mobile generator. 'Never mind,' he went on. 'The loyal and the true-hearted remain.'

'Only because they have no choice. Bandy Crow is a cripple; Granny Cleep passed a hundred and twenty last year. The Twymoors and the Yngleveres . . .'

'They'll not leave,' the old man said. 'They've always been faithful to your family. They won't abandon your father.'

'My father's sick,' said the girl, 'and growing sicker. I sometimes think the kingdom's been under a curse since my great-great-I-don't-know-how-many-greats grandfather first lifted the Traitor's Sword. And since I brought the Urdemons . . .'

'Don't be silly,' her mentor admonished. '*You* didn't bring them. They are drawn to acts of magic –'

'My magic.'

'You were a child, playing games of illusion. There's always been a little magic in your family; as magic goes, it's fairly harmless. You had no idea –'

'It's still my fault,' the princess insisted, brooding into her hair. (Like Hazel.)

'Babbletosh!' the old man said briskly. 'You take too much on yourself. Just because you're the princess, you think you can claim responsibility for everything? I never heard of such presumption. You're like a little girl who treads in a puddle,

8

and then blames herself for a flood. Utter foolishness! Isn't it?'

'Yes,' she said with a furtive smile. 'Sorry. It's only . . . Prenders told me . . .'

'That Woman,' her mentor said with unmistakable capital letters, 'talks a load of –'

'Frim!'

'Squiffle-piffle! That's all I was going to say. Doesn't know her coccyx from her humerus. Why, when everyone else leaves, she has to stay around . . .'

'She loves me,' the princess said gently. 'And Papa.'

'Overrated, love. People use it as an excuse for anything.' Absently, he stroked her hand again. 'Don't worry. We'll find a cure for the king – and then, so they say, the kingdom will be healed. Somewhere there'll be a formula – the recipe for a potion . . .'

'Then light the lamp,' said the girl, indicating an oil lamp on the desk, 'or you'll miss it.' She removed the glass chimney, struck a match and held the flame to the wick. The sudden glow flushed her cheek and spun a shimmer of gold from her hair. As the dream faded Nathan tried to fix the image in his mind, wanting to remember exactly how she looked, but of course, when he awoke, he couldn't.

It was deep night. He got out of bed and climbed up to the Den, his childhood retreat under the pitch of the roof. Through the skylight he saw a single star look down, watching him. But he knew it wasn't a star: it was a spy-crystal through which, in an alternative universe, the faceless ruler of Eos could survey anything in its range. Sometimes, when the world was ordinary, that knowledge seemed like a brief glimpse into madness, but not now, not tonight.

'Things are happening,' he thought, with a complicated shiver, reaching back into the dream. Something had been said, something significant – something which struck a faint chord of familiarity – but he was too busy trying to re-create the face of the princess, and he couldn't remember what it was.

ONE

Parents and Children

Bartlemy Goodman was home the night the burglars came. He usually was at home. For a man who had seen so much, and done so much, he now led a very tranquil life, or so it appeared, visiting the village of Eade mainly to see Annie Ward, who was widely thought to be his niece, and rarely venturing beyond Crowford. He was known to own the bookshop where Annie and her son lodged, and believed to be a collector, though no one was quite sure of what. The villagers accepted his unspecified eccentricities, and respected him for no particular reason, except that he appeared worthy of respect. It was a part of his Gift that he could pass almost unremarked in the local community, giving rise to no gossip, awakening no curiosity, though he had lived at Thornyhill, the old house out in the woods, since the original Thorns had sold up and all but died out generations before. Without really thinking about it, people assumed that the house had been bought by Bartlemy's grandfather, or some other elderly relative, and had passed on from Goodman to Goodman until it reached the present incumbent. They never wondered why each successive owner should look the same, or remain apparently the same age, around sixty; indeed, had anyone been asked, they would have sworn to little differences between the Bartlemys, to periods of absence following the death of one when another must have been growing up somewhere abroad. Nor did they ever wonder about the dog.

Every Goodman had had a dog, a large shaggy creature of mixed parentage and universal goodwill, with bright, intelligent eyes under whiskery eyebrows, and a lolling tongue. This one was called Hoover, because he devoured crumbs, and indeed anything else that came his way. The most wonderful cooking smells in the world would foregather in Bartlemy's kitchen, and the generosity of the leftovers made it canine heaven. Hoover had no reputation for savagery, welcoming every visitor, even the postman, with amiable enthusiasm, yet perhaps because of him the house had never been burgled before, except for the strange incident the previous year, and in that case the stolen object (which had belonged to someone else) had eventually been returned by Bartlemy himself, though no one knew how he retrieved it. The house was isolated, unprotected by alarms or security, and with the vague rumours that Bartlemy 'collected' it should have been an obvious target, yet until that night in late April the criminal fraternity had left it alone.

The burglars were two youths, as the newspapers would have called them, an Asian boy from Crowford who was only seventeen, and his sixteen-year-old sidekick, who was big and ginger-haired and not very bright. Getting in was easy: they broke a window, which was stupid, because the back door wasn't locked, and were just checking out the sitting room when the dog pounced. He didn't bark: it would've meant wasting time. Bartlemy came downstairs, wrapped in an enormous dark-blue dressing-gown with stars on it, to find the ginger-haired sidekick shivering in a corner while the other boy lay on his back with Hoover standing over him. He wasn't growling – he never growled – but the boy could see, behind the panting tongue and doggy grin, two rows of large yellow teeth which wouldn't have looked out-of-place on a wolf. There was a knife lying on the rug a little way away. Bartlemy picked it up by the blade. Afterwards, the boy puzzled over how the house owner had known to come down, when neither the intruders nor the dog had made much noise.

'This is – this is assault,' the youth stammered, keeping his voice to a whisper. 'I can sue.'

'I haven't assaulted you,' Bartlemy pointed out in his placid way.

'The dog –'

'He hasn't assaulted you either.' *Yet*, said the ensuing pause.

'We didn't mean no harm,' offered Ginger, between sullenness and fright.

'I'm sure you didn't. I'll telephone the police, and then you can sit down with me, and have a biscuit, and while we wait you can tell me what you *did* mean.'

The call was made, and somehow the boys didn't argue, perching nervously on the edge of Bartlemy's sofa and nibbling home-made biscuits while Hoover stood by, watching them in a proprietary manner. Ginger was known for beating up older boys, and the little Asian made up in aggression what he lacked in size, but they sat as quiet as if they were at a vicarage tea-party, and God was waiting with a thunderbolt for one of them to burp.

'Someone sent you here, didn't they?' said Bartlemy. 'What were you looking for?'

Mouths opened and shut, and Ginger choked on a biscuit crumb, but this time it was Ram who looked most afraid.

'No one sent us,' he said at last.

'It was your own idea?'

'Yeah. Yeah. I'm the one with the ideas.'

'Do you think it was a good idea?'

'No.'

'Are you sure no one sent you?' Bartlemy persisted.

Ram turned pale, and his mouth closed tight, and he looked almost relieved when the police arrived. He knew just how not to talk to the police. He'd sat through many interrogations, he was still underage, and insofar as it concerned himself he knew the law as well as any solicitor. But this man with his unruffled manner, and his alarming dog, and his calm blue gaze that seemed to see straight into your mind – this was something far more demoralizing than any bullying copper. Ram had a horrible feeling that given time – and a few more biscuits – he would have been telling Bartlemy things even his mother didn't know. He was secretly thankful to settle for the more familiar option.

Watching them go with a sigh, Bartlemy surmised that if they *had* been sent, Ginger, at least, knew nothing of it. He returned to bed, and in the half-hour before sleep considered possible lines of inquiry. A few days later, he telephoned an acquaintance in the CID.

Some months had passed since their last meeting, and Inspector Pobjoy had become Chief Inspector, helped by his recent arrest of a serial killer when most of his colleagues hadn't believed any murders had actually taken place. Bartlemy had been involved in that affair, which had been vaguely connected to the former theft at Thornyhill, and Pobjoy still darkly suspected that he knew many facts which had never emerged. There had been too many loopholes in the case, too many loose ends. Not that Bartlemy had ever been a suspect, though perhaps he should have been, caught as he was in the middle of things. However, Pobjoy was curiously glad to hear from him, and intrigued at the news of the attempted burglary, and he agreed instantly to come to Thornyhill for a cup of tea and an informal chat.

'You should lock your back door,' he suggested when they met.

'But if I did that,' Bartlemy said, 'people wouldn't be able to get in.' It was unanswerable. 'Anyway, they broke a window. That's the kind they were: crude, not very clever. The sort who would always break a window, if there was a window to break. I was rather surprised to find them so unsubtle. Kids like that usually give this place a miss. I would've expected any burglar who came here to be more . . . sophisticated.'

'Apart from that business last summer,' Pobjoy said – carefully, since he felt the subject required care – 'I notice you haven't really had any trouble here.' He added: 'I checked our records.'

'Naturally,' Bartlemy said. 'I assumed you would. No, we haven't had much trouble at Thornyhill. I prefer to avoid it, if I can.' He didn't say how, but Pobjoy, who was not a fanciful man, found himself wondering if the house had some intangible form of protection. Apart from the dog. He noted Bartlemy said 'we', perhaps including Hoover in the personal pronoun.

The canine hero of the recent burglary attempt was currently sitting with his chin in Pobjoy's lap and the classic please-feed-the-starving expression on his face.

'Which is why,' Bartlemy was saying, 'I was a little . . . disturbed by what happened. I can't help feeling there must have been something – some*one* – behind it. On the surface, there is nothing to steal here but books, some old but unremarkable furniture, and my collection of herbs for cooking.'

'The paintings?' Pobjoy asked, glancing up at a landscape in oils which seemed to consist mostly of gloom and a framed drawing so crowded with detail it was almost impossible to distinguish what it portrayed.

'Generally done by friends or acquaintances,' Bartlemy said

blandly. 'That drawing, for instance, is unsigned. Richard wasn't satisfied with it. Later, he went mad. People have sometimes been curious about my pictures, but their curiosity always seems to fade in the end.'

'You said "on the surface",' Pobjoy resumed, his narrow eyes narrowing still further, dark slits in the lean pallor of his face.

'I have a certain article concealed here,' Bartlemy explained after a pause. 'It was entrusted to me.' He didn't say *I am telling you this in confidence*. Pobjoy already knew that.

'The article which was stolen last year,' the inspector surmised. 'The so-called Grimthorn Grail.'

'Of course, it was never authenticated,' Bartlemy said. 'Technically, it's valueless. But I am concerned. I have lived here a long time, and no one has ever broken in until now.'

'Is it secure?'

Bartlemy smiled. 'No burglar would ever find it, I assure you,' he said. 'No *ordinary* burglar.'

Pobjoy let that pass. 'You think those boys were put up to it,' he summarized, 'by someone interested in the Grail.'

'It's a possibility I would like to check. You would know if there were any likely collectors in the market for such items.'

'Those kind of gentlemen don't usually have a record,' Pobjoy said with a trace of bitterness. 'Too rich, too influential. But – yes, I should know. I *might* know. I'll ask around.'

'Thank you.' He poured more tea. 'By the way, how is our murderer?'

'What? Oh – I don't know.' Pobjoy looked startled. For him, once a villain was convicted and imprisoned, that should be the end of the matter. 'We never found any trace of his accomplice – the woman who masqueraded as his wife.'

'I suspect,' Bartlemy said, 'she wasn't the kind of person

who would allow herself to be traced.' He was remembering a malignant water-spirit who had poured herself into the shape of a dead actress – a spirit now returned to the element from whence she came.

Pobjoy, who hated loose ends and didn't believe in phantoms, fretted at the recollection. 'Do you think she could be involved in this latest affair?'

'Hmm . . . I doubt it. Still, it is an idea.'

As he drank his tea, Pobjoy seemed to become abstracted. Once, he asked: 'How is . . . Mrs Ward?', hesitating over the inquiry as if it embarrassed him.

'She's very well,' Bartlemy said. 'You should go and see her.'

'I don't think . . . she wouldn't want . . .' Pobjoy's excuses faltered and failed; he looked around for a change of subject, but didn't find one.

'It's up to you,' Bartlemy said. 'Annie doesn't bear grudges.'

At one time, Pobjoy had wanted to arrest Nathan.

The inspector retreated into silence and stayed there, until Bartlemy began to talk of something else.

Nathan and Hazel Bagot had been friends from infancy, closer than brother and sister; they used to tell each other everything, but now they were getting older they needed their own secrets. Nathan didn't tell Hazel about the city and the princess (not yet, he said to himself, not till it becomes important), and Hazel didn't tell Nathan about the boy she was keen on at school. When they got together at the weekends and during the holidays, they talked about music and television and lessons, and feuds or allegiances with their classmates, and how parents never understood what it was like to be a teenager, because it must have been different for them. Hazel's bedroom had evolved into a kind of nest, lined with prints and posters, cushioned with discarded clothing, floored with crisp packets and CDs, where she and Nathan could curl up and listen to her latest musical discovery – usually something twangy and foreign-sounding and faintly bizarre – while she related how her father, who had left last year, wasn't allowed to come home any more because he'd tried to hit her mother again, and how her mother had a new boyfriend who was rather old and a bit dull but nice.

'They met through an ad in the paper,' Hazel said. 'Lots of people do that now. Has your mum tried it?'

'I don't think she's too keen on dating,' Nathan said. 'There was you-know-who last year – I'm not sure if he ever asked her for a date, exactly, but – well, obviously it didn't work out.' He didn't need to say any more. Hazel knew what he was alluding to.

'She must've loved your dad a lot,' she remarked. Nathan's father had died in a car accident before he was born, or so he had always been told. 'I mean, she's not forty yet and really pretty, but she hasn't had a proper boyfriend for years, has she?'

'No.'

'You wouldn't mind though, would you?' They'd been over this territory before, but Hazel thought it was worth checking.

'Of course not – as long as he was kind, and loved her. What about your mum's new man? Do you think it's serious?'

''Spect so. He brings her flowers, and that's always a sign, isn't it? She says he's dependable, which is what she wants, after dad. He'd never knock her about, or get drunk, or anything. He's sort of boring, but that's okay for her. She likes boring.'

'Have you talked to him much?' Nathan queried.

'Not really. He asked me about my homework once, but when I showed it to him he couldn't do it.'

'If you haven't talked to him,' Nathan said, 'you don't really know if he's boring or not.'

'You're being reasonable,' Hazel said sharply. 'You know I can't stand it when you do that. He – he gives off boring, like a smell. B.O. Boring Odour. He walks round in a little cloud of boringness. Please, *please* don't start being open-minded and tolerant about things. It's revolting.'

'When you shut your mind,' Nathan retorted, 'you shut yourself inside it. That's silly. Besides, I just said, give him a chance. You think he's nice, don't you? So he might surprise you. He might be fun after all.'

'Mum doesn't need fun,' Hazel said obstinately. 'She's my mum, for God's sake. I like him, okay? He'll do. I don't have to be thrilled by him.'

'Okay.' Nathan grinned, a little mischievously. Sometimes, he enjoyed provoking her. She was always too quick and too careless in judging people, and slow to alter her opinions, and he liked being the only person who could ruffle her certainties.

When he had gone she took out the picture she never showed anyone, cut off from the end of a group shot taken at the school disco. It was a picture of a boy with a fair childish face, wavy hair worn rather long (hobbit hair, said his detractors), blue eyes crinkled against the flashlight. He smiled less than his classmates and Hazel believed he nursed a secret sorrow, though she could only speculate what it might be. (Of course, he could have been merely sullen.) He rarely spoke to her, hardly seemed to notice her, but somehow that only made him more fascinating. He didn't have Boring Odour, she reflected – beneath their lack of communication she sensed the wells of his soul were fathoms deep. She stared at the photo for what felt like an age, racked with the pain of impossible longing, with anger at the hopelessness of it all, with shame because she would never be pretty enough to fascinate him in return. Her girlfriends all expected her to be in love with Nathan – Nathan with his dark alien beauty, his lithe athletic body, his indefinable uniqueness, charms she had known all her life and regarded with the indifference of familiarity – but she would only shrug at the suggestion, and smile, and hug the secret of her true affection to herself. She liked to be contrary, to keep Nathan as a friend – only a friend – and give her heart to someone nobody would suspect. Until the moment she dreamed of – the distant, elusive moment when they came together at last. The moment that would never happen . . .

Presently, she dived underneath the bed, groping behind the schoolbooks and sweaters and CD cases, and pulled out a carrier bag that chinked as it moved. The bag of things which had belonged to her great-grandmother, Effie Carlow, who was supposed to be a witch – the bag she had always meant to throw away, only somehow she hadn't got around to it. Hazel hadn't wanted to believe in witchcraft but she had seen too much of Effie not to know what she could do – at least, until she drowned. 'You too have the power,' the old woman had told her. 'It's in your blood.' The Carlows were offshoots of the Thorn family on the wrong side of the blanket: there was said to be a strain of the Gift in their genes, dating back to Josevius Grimling-Thorn, a magister of the Dark Ages who had reputedly sold his soul to the Devil. When Effie spoke of such things Hazel was frightened – frightened and sceptical both at once. (Scepticism was her protection from the fear, though it didn't work.) She had no intention of taking up her great-grandmother's legacy, of dabbling in spells and charms and other stupidities. But now there was Jonas Tyler, who wouldn't look at her, and the moment that would never happen, and maybe . . . maybe . . . among the sealed bottles with their handwritten labels was a love-philtre, or in Effie's notebook there was an incantation, something to make her irresistible, just to him.

One by one she took the bottles out of the bag and peered at the faded writing, trying to make it out.

Back at the bookshop, Nathan sat down to supper with his mother. In the summer months she tended to favour salads, but the weather was still vacillating and he noted with satisfaction that it was cauliflower cheese. 'You should have brought Hazel back,' Annie said. 'There's plenty.'

'I wasn't sure,' he explained. 'Have you met her mum's new boyfriend?'

'Yes.'

'She says he's nice, but boring.'

'He seems very nice, certainly,' Annie said. 'I don't know about boring. I haven't had much of a chance to talk to him.'

There was a brief interlude of cauliflower cheese, then Nathan resumed: 'Has Uncle Barty said any more about the burglary?'

'Apparently he called the inspector. You remember: the one from last year.'

'The one with the funny name?' Nathan said, with his mouth full.

'Pobjoy.' There was a shade of constraint in her manner. She hadn't completely forgiven the absent policeman for his suspicions.

But Nathan had forgotten them. 'He was clever,' he said judiciously, 'even if he did get lots of things wrong. I bet he guessed those burglars were after the Grail.'

'We don't know that. Anyway, Rowena Thorn has it, not your uncle.'

21

'She gave it to Uncle Barty to look after. The traditional hiding place is at Thornyhill: they once discussed it in front of me.'

'How do you know she –'

'I just know.'

Annie didn't argue any more. Even after fourteen years there were times when she found her son's alert intelligence disconcerting.

'The thing is,' he went on, 'they were just ordinary burglars, right? Not like the dwarf last time.'

'Mm.'

'So they wouldn't know about the Grail unless someone told them. It couldn't have been any of us, so they must have found out by magic.'

'They're just kids,' Annie said. 'I don't think they're the sort to use magic.'

'Of course not. It was somebody else, somebody who paid them to try and steal the cup. That's logical.' He added, with a creditable French accent: 'A kind of *eminence grise*.'

Annie smiled. 'You're a bit young to be turning into a conspiracy theorist.'

'Uncle Barty thinks so too,' Nathan pointed out. 'Otherwise he wouldn't have called the inspector.'

Annie's smile faded into a sigh. 'You wanted something to happen,' she said, 'and now it has. Can we just *try* not to let it grow into something worse? No more conspiracies, and spectres, and horrors. Not this time.'

'You talk as if it was my fault,' Nathan protested, referring to their adventures the previous year.

'Just don't *wish* for trouble,' his mother said without much hope. And: 'You will tell us, won't you, if you start having dreams again? *Those* dreams, I mean.'

He looked at her very steadily, and she was disturbed to

find his expression completely unreadable. 'Yes, I will,' he said at last, adding, to himself, fingers crossed: *When I'm ready*.

In her room that night Annie, too, took out a picture she never showed anyone. Daniel Ward, the man who was assumed to be Nathan's father. She had assumed it herself, until the baby was born. The face in the photograph was pleasant rather than handsome, fair-skinned, brown-haired, unremarkable. The eyes were a little dreamy and a secret smile lurked at the corners of his mouth. Even Nathan had never seen the picture; it would give rise to too many questions. Because there was nothing in genetics to enable two white Caucasian parents to produce a child so exotically dark . . . Annie herself had never really known what happened. In the instant of Daniel's death she had reached out for him, and a Gate had opened, and in death she had found love, returning to the world of life pregnant, and it wasn't until she saw the baby that she realized he couldn't be Daniel's child. He was the child of destiny, Bartlemy said, bridging the void between worlds; but it did not comfort her. One day, she would have to tell Nathan the truth – one day very soon – but she was still finding reasons to put it off. Keep him safe – keep him trusting – he doesn't need to know . . .

She put the picture away again, the looming dilemma clouding her mind, excluding any memories of distant happiness.

In his own bed Nathan lay with his eyes closed roaming the landscape inside his head, looking for the way through. It was there, he knew: he had found it once before, in an emergency, taking the plunge into another universe not at random but by his own will – though the act had frightened him and he hadn't attempted it again. But now curiosity – which kills even Schroedinger's cat – impelled him on, stronger than fear. He wanted to see the princess again, to explore the abandoned city and find out more about Urdemons, and why the people left, and the curse on the king . . .

He fell a long, long way, through a whirling dark pinpricked with stars. Then there was a jarring thud, and his mind was back in his body, but his body was somewhere else. Not the city on two hills with the Gothic house on top but another city, a huge metropolis with buildings like curving cliffs and a blood-red sunset reflected in endless windows and airborne skimmers and winged reptiles criss-crossing in the deadly light. He had landed on a rooftop platform in the shade of a wall, with a door close by. He scrambled to his feet, touched a panel – after a second the door opened and he slipped inside, escaping the lethal sun. He had forgotten the hazards of *willing* himself into another universe. Here was no misty realm of dreams and incorporeal being: he was almost solid, as visible as a ghost on a dark night, and this was Arkatron on Eos, the city at the end of the world, and there were too many dangers both known and unknown here to menace him. Worst of all, or so he thought when he looked down, he had ignored the first rule of dream-voyages – that you will find yourself wearing the clothes you slept in. It is difficult to feel brave and adventurous in pyjamas. (The previous year, he had got into the habit of going to bed in tracksuit trousers and a sweatshirt.) However, there was nothing he could do about it now.

He found himself on a gallery overlooking a hollow shaft, too deep for him to estimate how far it was to the bottom. Transparent egg-shaped lifts travelled up and down it, supported by alarmingly slender cables. He had assumed he would be in government headquarters, since that was where his dreams usually placed him, but nothing here looked familiar. A lift stopped close by, its door opening automatically even as a section of floor was extruded from the gallery to meet it. The lift was empty. Nathan took the hint, and stepped inside. A panel offered a wide choice of buttons: he pressed the top one. Being only semi-solid he had to press twice, hard. The door closed and the lift shot upwards.

He emerged onto another gallery, but this time he had to walk all the way round to find an exit, and when he pushed the door, it didn't move. He was too substantial to walk through it. He touched a square on the adjacent wall, but instead of the door opening there was a noise like a few bars of music – the kind of music Hazel would have liked, incorporating weird stringed instruments and very little rhythm. 'Of course,' Nathan thought, light dawning, 'it's a doorbell. This is a private apartment . . .' He wondered if he should run, but there was no point. His dream had brought him here, and he had no real option but to go on.

The door opened.

A man was standing there, a very tall man (all Eosians were taller than the people of our world) wearing a long white robe with a wide hood much looser than the usual kind. Under the hanging sleeves his hands were ungloved and his mask only covered three-quarters of his face; where it ended, just above mouth and jaw, his beard began, a thick white beard unlike anything Nathan had ever seen outside the pages of a book, forked and braided almost to his waist. He stared at Nathan in silence. Nathan stared back, forgetting how shocking his appearance must be to his host. No children had been born here for perhaps a thousand years, and though Nathan was big for his age, in this universe he was shorter than the indigents, slight of build and obviously youthful. His pyjamas were too small for him, stopping well above ankle and wrist – his body had a suggestion of transparency

– his face was naked. On Eos, it was rare for anyone to show their face.

When at last the man spoke, his words were strangely apposite. 'Well, well,' he said. 'What in the world are you? A holocast? – or not . . .'

As always, Nathan understood the language. 'Actually,' he said, 'I'm not really *in* your world. At least, I am, but –'

'But?'

'I'm *from* another world,' Nathan explained. His voice didn't sound quite right – eerily hollow and distant.

'So it's started, has it?' The man's tone sharpened. 'It's been long in the coming. The walls between the worlds are breaking down. Still, I don't quite understand . . . What would you want of me? Whoever you are.'

'I don't know,' Nathan admitted. 'My dream brought me here.'

'Your – dream? You mean, you are dreaming this? You are dreaming *me*?'

'Yes.'

'How very interesting. This couldn't be part of a spell – some leakage through a portal?'

'I don't think so,' Nathan said. 'If there's a portal, it's in my head.'

'Hmm.' There was a pause.

Then the man said: 'I am forgetting my manners. Won't you come in?'

Nathan followed him inside. The apartment consisted of a cluster of irregularly-shaped rooms connected with arched doorways and hung with diaphanous drapes. Furniture curved with the walls; a small fountain bubbled out of what looked like a crystal cakestand in the midst of the main room; the light was vague and sourceless. Stronger light was condensed into two or three pillars of clouded glass, and in the outer wall oval windows were covered with translucent screens, flushed red from the sunset beyond. 'My name,' said the man, seating himself, 'is Osskva Rodolfin Petanax. But perhaps you knew that already?'

'No,' said Nathan. 'I don't know anything very much. Is this part of the Grandir's palace?'

'If you mean the seat of government and residence of our ruler and his bridesister, then – no. We wouldn't call it a palace. This is accommodation for his senior advisers and others in the higher echelons of authority. I am a first level practor – if you understand what that means?'

'I . . . think so. A kind of magician?'

'So you do know *something* of this world. You have been here before.'

Nathan didn't comment. There was a niggle at the back of his mind, another of those elusive connections which he couldn't quite place. Whenever he sought for it, it slipped away into his subconscious, tantalizingly out of reach. He knew he was here for a reason – there was always a reason behind his dream-journeys – but he had no idea what it might be, and he felt like an actor dropped into the middle of an unfamiliar play, while the audience waited in vain for him to remember his lines. His host continued to study him with absorption but curiously little surprise.

'Have you met the Grandir?' Osskva asked.

'Not *met*, no. I've seen him.'

'Whom have you met, apart from me?'

Halmé, Nathan thought, but he didn't say so. She had concealed him from the Grandir; he could not betray her. And Raymor, her former bodyguard. And the dissident Kwanji Ley, who had stolen the Grail in *this* world, and paid with her life . . .

Now he remembered.

*'Take it,' she had said, giving him the cup, when she was
dying of the sundeath in a cave in the desert. 'To . . . Osskva
. . .'* Osskva!

'Who is he?'

'My father . . .'

Nathan sat down abruptly, holding his head in his hands.
When he looked up, the practor was standing over him. 'What
troubles you?' he said. 'What do you know?' His hood fell
back, showing hair to match the beard, long and white. Then
– perhaps to observe Nathan more closely – he took off his
mask. His face, like that of all Eosians, was disproportion-
ately long, at least to Nathan's eye, a structure all lean curving bones with a skin the colour of tarnished brass, contrasting
sharply with the hair and beard. Thick white brows swept
low over his eyes, which shone with a glint of pure amethyst.
The same shade as Kwanji's, Nathan remembered. There might
be many people on Eos called Osskva, but he knew his dream
had not deceived him. This was the one he sought.

Only he hadn't been seeking him. He'd been looking for
someone quite different. But the dreams, he now realized,
couldn't be controlled – or not by him . . .

'I once . . . met someone called Kwanji Ley,' he said.

'I see.' The man's face changed, his eyes hooding, as if he
did see.

'She asked me to find you.'

'Kwanjira. My daughter. Kwanjira the rebel.' Suddenly, he
looked up. 'Did you know she was my daughter?'

Nathan nodded, feeling uncomfortable, even though this
was a dream – or at least, a dream of sorts – waiting for the
question he knew would come.

'Is she dead?'

'Yes.'

'I've known it, I suppose – I've felt it – for months past.

We didn't keep in touch, but this time there was a different-ness to her silence. There is a point when you sense no word will come again. But . . . you are the word. A word that has come to me. Can you tell me how she died?'

'She was in Deep Confinement,' Nathan said, remember-ing the pale emptiness of the prison pits. 'She begged me to help her, to dream her out, and I tried, but you can't really manipulate the dreams. I messed it up. I left her in the desert – in the sun. She made it to the cave, but not in time. When I got back – when I found her – it was too late.' He didn't tell Kwanji's father what the sundeath had done to her. The guilt returned, like a sickness in his stomach, but Osskva made no move to apportion blame.

'She always wanted to change things,' he said with a curi-ous smile. 'The government – the magics – the fate of the world. In the cave . . . what was she looking for?'

'The Sangreal,' Nathan said, picturing the greenstone cup, held in Kwanji's ruined hand. 'She asked me to bring it to you. She thought you could perform the Great Spell.'

'Did she find it?'

'Yes.'

'Then she died happy. I couldn't do a Great Spell; I haven't the power. Even the Grandir may not have the strength for it, or our world would have been saved long since. Besides, the Cup alone is no use. It needs also the Sword, and the Crown. Once they were said to be in the cave, guarded by a monster of ancient days, but there are other rumours. I'd heard they were scattered throughout the worlds for safe-keeping, so they could not be brought together too soon, or by the wrong agency, lest the Spell of Spells should go awry . . . Yet you say the Sangreal was in the cave.'

'It was a mistake,' Nathan explained. 'It had been kept in my world, but someone stole it. After . . . after Kwanji died,

I wasn't sure what to do, but I thought it was best to take it back.'

'You did right,' Osskva said, 'I expect. Time will tell. If we have enough of it left. What about the sword? Was that stolen too?'

The sword. In Nathan's head, something else clicked into place. The princess had mentioned a sword, the Traitor's Sword . . .

With that question, that connection, the dream jolted. *Tell me about the sword,* Nathan wanted to ask, but the words wouldn't come out. It was like in an ordinary dream, when you try to speak but your vocal chords don't work, and everything slows down, and the person you want to speak to is receding, fading inexorably from your thought. He had felt insubstantial, a pyjama-clad teenage ghost, but now he was growing solid, and the world around him thinned, the world of Arkatron on Eos, becoming ghost-like while he alone was real. He heard the voice of Osskva, insect-small and faint with distance: 'Don't go. We have things . . . to discuss . . . Questions . . . answers . . .'

But he couldn't respond, and sleep swallowed him, plunging him back into the dark.

A few weeks after the attempted burglary, Chief Inspector Pobjoy called at Thornyhill again. 'Of course, they won't get custodial sentences,' he said, referring to Ram and Ginger. 'They're underage. Ginger has a record already, petty theft, petty assault, petty everything. Ram's been smarter: no previous, just a government health warning. The really interesting thing is their lawyer.'

'Dear me,' Bartlemy said, replenishing his guest's tea mug. 'I had no idea lawyers were interesting.'

Pobjoy didn't grin – he wasn't a natural grinner – but a

sharp-edged smile flicked in and out, quick as a knife-blade. 'Boys like that – backstreet kids, no dosh – they usually get whoever's on call that day. Legal aid, no frills. That's what they had in the past. But this time they get a Bentley among lawyers, top-of-the-range with power-steering and champagne-cooler. Hugh Purlieu-Smythe, legal adviser to the very, very rich. It would be a giveaway – if we knew who was footing the bill. Still, it *is* interesting, isn't it?'

'Indeed. Do we know who else this Purlieu-Smythe has represented in the recent past?'

'I've been finding out.' Pobjoy sipped his tea, nibbling the inevitable seductive biscuit. Sometimes he fantasized about what lunch or dinner might be like at Thornyhill. He was a single man living alone on a diet of ready meals, takeaways, and the occasional omelette, and the mere thought of such home-cooking must be put behind him, or it would seriously disrupt his professional detachment. 'He's done a few white-collar fraudsters – big city types who've brought their cash and their bad habits into the area in search of rural peace and quiet. Then there was that local authority corruption case – he was for the developer, got him off too. Grayling made donations to police charities – all the right people wined and dined – lent his Spanish villa to a lucky few. You get the picture.'

'Are you suggesting some of your colleagues could be . . . swayed by such things?' Bartlemy inquired gently.

'It wouldn't be anything overt,' Pobjoy explained. 'Just a general feeling that Grayling was a good bloke, one of the lads. One of the *chaps*, I should say. Wouldn't have thought he'd be interested in this place, though. Or that cup of yours.'

'It isn't actually mine,' Bartlemy murmured, but the inspector held to his train of thought.

'Grayling isn't much of a one for history and culture,' he

said. 'We're looking for the classic movie villain, right? Sinister type with very big bucks and an art collection no one ever gets to see. I have to say, most of the super-rich around here like to show off their paintings, at least to their chums; no point in having them otherwise. They collect for status, not pleasure. The Grail's a little obscure for them.'

Bartlemy made an affirmative noise.

'Myself, I've only come up against Purlieu-Smythe once before,' Pobjoy resumed after a pause. 'Another kid. Not quite like our Ram and Ginger, though. Poor little rich boy wanted for stealing a car, even though Daddy has four and Mummy two. Beat up a girl about a year ago, but someone talked her out of going to court. The boy's a nasty little psycho in the making. Not yet eighteen.'

'And the father?' Bartlemy queried. 'I assume it was he who employed the lawyer.'

'Respectable,' said Pobjoy. 'Squeaky-clean businessman, plenty of good works, pillar-of-the-community image.'

'Highly suspicious, in fact,' said Bartlemy with a faint smile.

Pobjoy read few novels, but he took the point. 'Real life isn't much like thrillers,' he said. 'Pillars of the community are usually stuffy, but . . .'

'Upright?'

'Yeah. Just one point: he's a publisher. Educational books, art, that sort of thing. He might have heard of the Grail.'

'His name?'

'I shouldn't be telling you that.'

Bartlemy offered the policeman another biscuit.

'Hackforth. Giles Hackforth. The company's called Pentacle Publishing.'

'A long-established firm,' Bartlemy said. 'Very reputable. So . . . we can infer that Hackforth is a cultured man, who might well have an interest in local antiquities, and the folk-lore that accompanies them.'

Pobjoy nodded. 'I'd say you were imagining things,' he went on, 'if it wasn't for Purlieu-Smythe. But lawyers like him don't do charity work. There has to be a connection with *someone*, and Hackforth seems to be your best bet. I don't see what we can do about it, though. Suspicion isn't evidence.'

'As you say. However, all information is valuable. Is there anything more you can tell me about him?'

Pobjoy hesitated. 'Your nephew, Nathan Ward . . .' There was a certain constraint in his manner. He was still uncomfortable at the mention of Nathan's name, not least because in his view any individual, once suspected, was suspect forever, and he found it hard to change his mindset.

'What about him?' Bartlemy's tone, as always, was mild.

'I heard he was at Ffylde Abbey. Scholarship boy.'

'Yes.'

'So's the problem child. Damon Hackforth. Should have thought they'd expel him, but apparently not. I expect Daddy's buying the school a new wing or something.'

'Ffylde Abbey is fundamentally a religious institution, remember. Perhaps they feel they cannot abandon the stray lamb – they want to bring him back to the fold.'

The inspector, cynical from experience, made a sound something like a snort.

'Don't dismiss the possibility,' Bartlemy said. 'I've seen things that would surprise you.' And, on a note of irony: 'You do not know the power of the light side.'

But Pobjoy missed the allusion. 'I ought to be going,' he said, finishing his tea. The biscuit plate was empty.

'Next time,' Bartlemy said, 'you must stay to lunch.'

* * *

Nathan was accustomed to his uncle's cooking, but habit didn't take the edge off his appetite. He, Hazel and their friend George Fawn were devouring roast lamb with teenage enthusiasm the following Sunday and talking about Jason Wicks, the village's aspiring thug, when Bartlemy inserted his question.

'Do you have any problems of that kind at Ffylde?'

'The teachers keep a close eye on things,' Nathan said. 'They try to stamp out bullying before it gets really nasty.'

'No school bad boys?' Bartlemy persisted. Annie looked thoughtfully at him.

'There's Nick Colby . . . he was caught insider-trading. He overheard his father talking about a merger and bought up shares for half the class.'

'Did you get some?' George asked, awed.

'He's the year below me.'

'Anyone else?' Bartlemy murmured.

'Well . . . Damon Hackforth, in the Sixth. He's been in trouble with the police. We're not supposed to know, but of course everybody does. There was a rumour he'd be expelled. He's always having long talks with Father Crowley. I expect they're trying to reclaim him – some of the monks are very idealistic.'

'Do you think they'll succeed?' Bartlemy asked.

Nathan made a face. 'Don't know. I've never really had anything to do with him, but . . . he gives off very bad vibes. You can feel it when he walks past. A sort of – *aura* – of anger and aggression. Worse than Jason Wicks. Ned Gable's parents know *his* parents, and Ned says they begged the school not to chuck him out. They must be pretty desperate about him.'

'They care about him, then?' Annie said, flicking another glance at Bartlemy.

'I expect so.' Nathan was still young enough to assume that parents generally cared about their children. 'He's got a sister who's an invalid. Ned says Damon's jealous because she gets all the attention. She's very ill – something they can't fix, where she just goes on and on deteriorating. Muscular dystrophy, maybe. Something like that. She's in a wheelchair. Ned says she's very pretty and clever.'

'How awful,' Hazel said, thinking of a girl who had everything she didn't, trapped in a wheelchair, wasting away.

'Awful,' Annie echoed, thinking of the parents, with their violent, mixed-up son and dying daughter.

'Stupid,' said George, 'being jealous of someone who can't even walk.'

'Good point,' Bartlemy said. 'Most of the unhappiness in the world is the direct result of stupidity – of one kind or another. Who's for baked apple?'

Afterwards, when Nathan, Hazel and George had left, Annie said: 'So what's your interest in this boy Damian?'

'Damon. Did I say I was interested?'

'You didn't need to say. I could see it.'

'I don't know that I am interested in him,' Bartlemy said. 'I might be interested in his father.' He told her about his conversation with Pobjoy.

'Is it going to start again?' Annie whispered. 'Like last year?' She was remembering a man with a crooked smile who had been nice to her – a thing made of river-water with a woman's face – a very old corpse in a white-cushioned bed. And the secret she had never shared with her son, the secret of his paternity . . .

'You'll have to tell him,' Bartlemy said, as though reading her mind.

'That's for me to decide.' Annie's tone was almost tart. 'He doesn't have to know yet. Perhaps he never will.'

'That's just it,' Bartlemy sighed. 'He *ought* to know. It's important. It may be relevant.'

'To what?'

'Trouble,' Bartlemy said. 'Like last year.'

TWO

Magic

As the light failed, Bartlemy moved round the living room, drawing the curtains. He was alone now except for the dog, who stood by one of the windows, staring through the latticed panes with cocked ears and a faint stirring of the hackles on his neck. When Bartlemy joined him, he thought he saw a movement outside – the branches of a nearby shrub twitched, new leaves shivered as if in the wake of something, but whatever it was, it had gone too swiftly for him to have even a glimpse of it. 'Something small, I think,' Bartlemy mused. 'Smaller than a human.' Hoover glanced up at his master, his shaggy face alarmingly intelligent. 'Well, well,' Bartlemy said. 'I see.'

When the darkness deepened he swept the hearth and laid a fire that wasn't made of coals. Presently, pale flames leaped up, casting a flickering glow that played with the shadows rather than dispersing them. Bartlemy threw a powder on the flames which smothered them into smoke. The chimney was blocked and the air in the room thickened, till the eyes of both man and dog grew red from the sting of it. Bartlemy began to speak, soft strange words that swirled the air and shaped the fume, sucking it into a kind of cloud which seemed to spin inward upon itself, until there was a shifting at the core, and the smoke cleared from an irregular space, and in the space was a picture. At first it looked like a television picture, only the definition was far better, but as it developed the perspective changed, until it was no longer smoke-deep but profound as reality, a peephole into another place. Sound followed image, and a draught came from it bearing the scent of roses. Bartlemy saw a woman in a garden cutting flowers. The garden was beautiful and the woman well-dressed, but when she lifted her head her face was pinched and sad.

Then the picture changed. Smoke-magic is wayward, unreliable; it can be encouraged but not controlled. The scenes that passed before him were fragmented, their meaning often obscure, with no logic in the sequence, no connecting thread – though Bartlemy knew that much later some connection might be revealed. After the garden the vision darkened. He saw a man whose hooked profile jutted beyond the overhang of his cowl, lit only by a furtive candle-glimmer, head bent towards another and whispering, whispering, while his auditor, a dwarf with more beard than face, listened with dread in the twist of his brows. Bartlemy knew this must be Josevius Grimthorn, ancient warden of the Grail, who had died fourteen hundred years ago, and his henchman (or henchdwarf), a creature long imprisoned beneath Thornyhill Darkwood, until Nathan and Hazel, exploring in the valley, had accidentally freed him. Then came the cup itself, a chalice of polished stone, glowing green in a dim recess, and what appeared to be a gallery of those who had sought for it. The Jewish collector, starving in Dachau – the grandson of an SS officer, drowning in a rainstorm – an old woman, older than she looked, tangled in river-weed – a greedy academic, clutching the wheel of a car, driven mad by phantoms who had eaten his mind. All insane, drowned, dead. And then those who had survived: Eric Rhindon, the purple-eyed exile from an alternative universe, Rowena Thorn, last descendant of a vanished family, Julian Epstein, the badger-haired man from Sotheby's – and Nathan, who had brought the Grail back from another world so it could return to Rowena, its rightful guardian. And now Bartlemy held it in trust at Thornyhill, the house where her ancestors had lived, until the moment came for which it had been made – whenever that moment might be.

There are three elements to a Great Spell: the female principle, the male principle, and the circle that binds. The Cup, the Sword, the Crown. Relics from a different Time, a different cosmos, forged endless ages ago and hidden away – the Cup in this world, the Sword and the Crown none knew where – guarded by alien forces – until in the city of Arkatron on Eos a ruler thousands of years old should find a way to complete the Spell and save his people from destruction . . .

But the smoke-magic could not pierce the walls of this world, nor reveal the purpose of the Ultimate Powers (if there was one). Bartlemy saw only the kaleidoscope of quick-change images, the clues that led and misled. A blue-eyed schoolboy with a soft mouth, and Hazel watching him, covertly, from behind her hair – a star that wasn't a star, looking down on Annie's bookshop – a phantom in a mirror, too vague to have form or face but slowly solidifying, gone before he could make it out. And then they were inside the bookshop, and a man with an anxious forehead was leafing through a book, a very old book with handwritten notes at the back, in an ink that wasn't black but brown with age. An ink, Bartlemy thought, that might once have been red. The man bought the book – Bartlemy heard Annie's murmur of thanks – and the picture followed him out of the shop, and down the street, and somewhere in the background there was a little sound like a sigh, the released breath of an archer who sees his arrow hit the bull's eye at last. But there was nobody there to breathe . . .

Lastly a dark figure in a dark room, long-robed, his back to the watcher, presumably Josevius again. He was dribbling powder through his fingers to form a magic circle – there was a hiss: '*Fiumé*!' and a gleam of fire ran round the perimeter. And then came the muttered rhythm of an incantation, and a slow pale form coalesced at the circle's heart. The magister, Bartlemy thought, summoning one of the Old Spirits – the Hunter, the Hag, the Child, the One We Do Not Name – in the deal which cost him his soul. But Bartlemy had used few fire-crystals, and as the last one crumbled to a smoulder the image faded into smoke. He unblocked the chimney, and the air cleared, and Hoover came and rested his chin on his master's knee.

'Well,' Bartlemy said, 'was that helpful, or wasn't it? Do we know anything we didn't know before? Or – at the risk of sounding like Donald Rumsfeld – do we only know things we don't know?' The dog made a whiffling noise. 'Who was the man in the bookshop? Would Annie have any idea? It might be worth making a little drawing, and showing it to her. It's a pity I'm not a better artist, but my creative skills are usually confined to the kitchen. Still, I can always cheat. Magic is about cheating, after all.'

Hoover gave a short, sharp bark.

'Yes,' said Bartlemy. 'I take the point. If I can cheat, so can others. I'll bear it in mind.'

He poured himself a glass of something that smelt of raspberries and blackberries, of cinnamon and cardamom, of Christmas cake and summer spice – but most of all of alcohol. When he had taken a sip or two he remarked with uncharacteristic force: 'I wish I knew what the hell was going on.'

Hoover thumped his tail by way of agreement.

* * *

The summer term had begun badly for Hazel. Maths, never her favourite subject, had taken a turn for the worse, and although Nathan usually helped her with it he was busy with his own commitments and somehow, when they *did* meet, they always had better things to talk about. George was quite good at understanding maths, but less good at explaining *what* he understood about it. Now, she was floundering in a quagmire of incomprehensible numbers, struggling with the feeling, long familiar to her, that there was no point in trying to think during lessons because it wouldn't get her anywhere, so she might as well give up before she started. Her own stupidity made her angry, and she turned the anger outward on others. She was used to the idea that Nathan was cleverer than her – Nathan was cleverer than *everybody* – but it was galling to find herself taking second place to George, whom she had always slightly despised, in a friendly sort of way.

But far more serious was the Jonas Tyler situation. Of course, he didn't *know* she liked him – they'd only ever exchanged a few words – she didn't want him to know, or anyone else – but that was beside the point. She'd seen him twice talking to Ellen Carver, not ordinary talking but the low-voiced, intimate kind of talk that people do when they are close to each other, and Ellen's friend Sarah said he'd asked Ellen out to a coffee shop. Jason Wicks, already six foot two, went to pubs and terrorized the older villagers of Eade by drinking beer on street corners and throwing the cans into people's gardens, but Jonas, though he probably drank beer, only did it in the privacy of his own home. Nonetheless, to Hazel a coffee shop represented a possible venue for seduction – the seduction, that is, of Jonas by Ellen, rather than vice versa. She spent her maths lessons brooding about it, and went home on the school bus sitting alone, wrapped in silence. Safe in the lair of her bedroom, she fought with frustration and inchoate rage, feeling herself ugly, undesirable, with a brain that wouldn't work and a body that let her down. She remembered her great-grandmother – Effie Carlow with her raptor's eye and witch's nose, living in an isolated cottage, frightening people, frightening Hazel, drowned in river-water after a spell too far. *You too have the power . . .* She didn't want to be like that, she didn't want to be old and mad and scary, dabbling in charms and cantrips and other illusions. But the thought of Jonas with Ellen was gall and wormwood to her – it seemed to her, in the blackness of her heart, that she had nothing to lose.

She got out the bottles she had already selected, Effie's notebook with its peely cover and scratchy writing, the beeswax candle she had bought the day before. Effie's notes said nothing about a candle, but Hazel felt it was appropriate. (In *Buffy*, Willow always lit candles when she was doing magic.) She ought to go into the attic – Effie had used the attic sometimes – but the lock was broken and anyway, she had once seen something there she didn't like. The bedroom was *her* place, private and secure. She wedged a chair under the door handle and cleared the dressing table by dint of shoving things onto the floor, fixing the candle in place in front of the mirror. Then she remembered the matches were in the kitchen and had to un-wedge the door to fetch them. Finally, she was ready.

She had drawn the curtains but it wasn't dark and the candle-flame looked dim and unimpressive, a tiny gleam against the many-coloured chaos of her room. The theme music from *Lord of the Rings* filled the background; she had hoped it would be suitably atmospheric. In fact, atmosphere seemed to be lacking. She read out the words Effie had penned, fortunately in block capitals for clarity, unfortunately in an unknown language with no guidelines as to pronunciation. Words – as far as she could tell – intended to summon a spirit to her assistance. There was something about drawing a circle, setting boundaries to confine the spirit, but the clutter of her bedroom offered little scope for magic circles, and anyway, she looked on this as a trial run, believing nothing would happen. She had faith in science, in Nathan's alternative universes, but not in magic, despite experience. Not in *her* magic.

Nothing happened.

She tried the words again, attempting a French-style pronunciation which seemed to go well with them. (Her French wasn't great but it was better than her maths.) Her voice sounded more confident now – if nothing was going to happen, it was safe to be confident about it.

The candle-flame stretched out into a thin spool of brilliance. The room seemed darker, even if it wasn't. Behind the flame, the mirror clouded. Hazel became aware of her heartbeat, pounding at her ribs. Thought stopped; she couldn't tear her gaze from the mirror. Mist coiled behind the glass, slowly resolving itself into a face – a face that wavered at first, as if unable to decide how it should look, then settled into a slim, pale oval, with silver-blue eyes and silver-blonde hair that fanned out in an intangible breeze. A face curiously resembling one on a magazine cover that stared up from the floor – but Hazel didn't notice that.

'You have called me,' said the face, in a voice that echoed strangely for a second, then grew low and soft. 'I have come.'

'Who are you?' Hazel whispered. She had once seen the spirit with whom her great-grandmother had had dealings – the same malignant water spirit whom both Annie and

Bartlemy had encountered – but it had looked nothing like this.

'I am Lilliat, the Spirit of Flowers,' said the face, and scattered petals seemed to flutter through her fanning hair, and pale blooms opened in a garland about her neck. 'What is your wish?'

'Do you – do you grant wishes?' Hazel stammered, doubting, incredulous, trying to quell the leap of hope inside her. She was no fairytale heroine, rubbing a lamp to get a genie. This was the real world (or at least, this was *a* real world) where rubbing a lamp gave you nothing but a cleaner lamp.

Lilliat laughed – a laugh as silvery as her hair. 'Sometimes,' she said. 'It depends on the wish – and the one who wishes. You are young for a witch, very young, but there is power in you. I can feel it. Green power, new and untried. Between us, we will try your power. What do you wish?'

'There's a boy,' Hazel said, too quickly, rushing into the fairytale before it could evaporate. 'I want him to – to notice me. To like me. Me and no one else.'

'Yes . . .' Lilliat closed her eyes, though it made little difference. The lids, too, were silver-blue. Sparkles danced on her eyelashes. 'I see him. He is dark, very dark, with hair as black as a crow's wing and –'

'Wrong boy,' Hazel said hastily. 'That one.' She pointed to the photograph which she had placed beside the candle.

Almost, Lilliat frowned. 'Show him to me.'

Hazel picked up the photo and held it out in front of the mirror. As Lilliat studied it the flowers at her breast seemed to wither, and the blue shadows on her skin deepened, and her lips grew pale. But when she spoke again the fairy colours returned, and there were wild roses in her hair.

'What is his name?'

'Jonas Tyler,' Hazel said, and somehow, saying his name made the magic real, and she knew she had taken an irrevocable step, though in what direction she couldn't guess.

'It shouldn't be difficult for a girl like you to enchant him,' Lilliat said sweetly. 'A girl with youth in her eyes, and power in her blood . . . Look at yourself!'

Hazel's face appeared beside her in the mirror – a different Hazel, beautiful and aloof, changed and yet the same, with her hair lifted off her face by Lilliat's phantom breeze and silver shadows on her skin . . .

There was a long pause. Then Hazel said: 'I found these potions –' she indicated the bottles on the dressing table '– I thought they might help. What do I do?'

Her reflection faded.

'What need of evil medicines?' Lilliat said. 'You have seen yourself – yourself as you truly are. I will do the rest.'

'*Thank* you.' Hazel felt grateful, hopeful, doubtful. Little showed in her face, but Lilliat saw it all.

'A favour for a favour.'

'What do you mean?'

'Don't you know the stories?' Her tone was still soft, still with an echo of silvery laughter. 'There is always a price. The mermaid who sold her voice to turn her fishtail into legs, the prince who toiled seven years to break a witch's spell . . . But what you ask is a little thing. The price will be small, no more than you can afford.'

'Money?' Hazel said. 'I don't have much money.'

Lilliat laughed again – laughed and laughed – and the flower-petals turned to bank notes which scattered around her like butterflies, and golden coins were shaken from the shower of her hair. 'Not money,' she said at last. 'Money is a humbug. I am not human.'

Suddenly, Hazel felt cold.
'What is the price?'

Nathan, back at school after the weekend, found himself wondering if his uncle's interest in Damon Hackforth had been merely idle curiosity. He wasn't sure – Bartlemy's manner was too subtle for him to be sure – but he was a perceptive boy, and he knew Uncle Barty wasn't idly curious by nature. When the opportunity presented itself, he encouraged Ned Gable to talk about his parents' friends.

'I *really* don't like Damon,' he said. 'You can feel the violence coming off him, sort of in pulses. Like a dodgy electric current.'

'He's dodgy all right,' Ned affirmed. 'Stupid, too. I mean, why steal a car when they've got five in the garage? His dad's got pots of money – he'd probably give him one for his eighteenth if he stayed out of trouble. He won't now, though.'

'What's his sister like?'

'Melly-Anne? I told you.'

'Meliane?' Nathan echoed.

'Melanie-Anne. They shorten it.'

'How old is she?' It was a starting point.

'She's quite old. Twenty-one or two. She's really nice. The Hackforths had a do there once, some charity thing, Mum made me go. Melly-Anne talked to me for ages – she was lovely. That was before she was in the wheelchair. At least a year ago.'

'What did you say was wrong with her?'

'Muscular dystrophy – multiple sclerosis – one of those diseases that's slow and fatal and can't be stopped. Beginning with M. Mum says old Hackforth's so desperate, he's trying potty cures now.'

'*Potty* cures?' Nathan said, bemused.

'New Age stuff, weird herbs, acupuncture, that kind of thing.' Ned was a shade impatient. 'Potty, poor sod. Still, you can't blame him. I mean, when you're desperate, really desperate, I suppose anything's worth a try.'

'Are you *sure* Damon's jealous of her?' Nathan asked. 'With her dying and all that.'

'He's warped,' Ned explained. 'You know? Warped inside. Like – like when you leave something out in the garden all winter, a rake or something, and the rain gets to it, and it goes all bendy, and you can't straighten it up.' It was a metaphor that might have surprised his English master, who rarely connected Ned with metaphors. 'That's Damon. He's bendy. They won't be able to straighten him. I expect he'll go to prison in the end.'

Nathan didn't say any more. The cricket season was under way, and there were important things to discuss. But he made up his mind he would tell his uncle what he had heard, just in case he wanted to know.

At night in the dormitory Nathan was torn between trying not to dream and the urge to revisit the dead city, to return to Osskva and say all that needed to be said, to see the princess again. (He didn't even know her name.) Somehow, he sensed that if he resisted the dreams would not come, but if his curiosity became too much for him then the dreams would take over, and his sleep would be no longer his own. He wondered if particles in physics experienced these dilemmas, or if they simply popped in and out of the world as a matter of course, because it was their nature. And he remembered a saying he had heard or read somewhere: 'Man is born to trouble as the sparks fly upward.' So he wasn't really surprised, the next night, to find himself back in the dream.

Not Arkatron: the other city. The city on two hills (he *must* try to learn some names). His awareness skimmed over the marshland, glimpsing the cloud-shapes sliding across the broken pools, breathing the foul-smelling gases that rose here and there in slow bubbles. The reed-beds were as tall as a child, and although he saw no living thing he caught the occasional whistling call of some solitary creature, probably a bird. Then he rose high over the city, circling the princess's house before plunging down into the narrow darkness of a chimney and emerging at the bottom slightly startled by the speed of his descent.

He found himself in a bedroom, or more accurately a bed*chamber*: it was too large, too full of shabby grandeur, to be merely a room. The ceiling was very high and the windows tall and heavily curtained – as in so much of the house, daylight was plainly unwelcome, forcibly excluded even when it had the chance to get in. There was a fourposter bed on a dais at the far end draped with still more curtains, layers of curtains, brocade frayed into threads and moth-eaten muslin, looped and scooped and tied with tattered cord. In the bed, supported on a lop-sided stack of pillows, was a man in a nightcap. He looked both fat and thin, his limbs like knotted pipe-cleaners, his rounded body smothered under a mound of rucked-up bedclothes. The rag-end of a bandage showed beneath the hem of his nightshirt. Another person stood beside the bed, holding a candle which dripped wax onto the coverlet. Nathan recognized him at once, even in the gloom – his dandelion-seed hair and elongated nose. The man from the library.

'You could do with some light in here, Maj,' he was saying. (*Madge?* Nathan thought.) 'Let me open the curtains – open the windows. Fresh air, that's what you need. Air and light!' He set down the candle, almost setting fire to the drapes, and went to the nearest window.

'It was Mrs Prendergoose,' the invalid explained. 'She thought the dark would help me sleep. Anyway, she says daylight is bad for the sick. And fresh air.' He sounded almost apologetic.

'Fiddle-fuddle! Twiddle-piffle! Woman's a fool. Nurse to the princess, indeed – Nell's so healthy she's never needed a nurse. Wouldn't have survived otherwise. Prendergoose couldn't nurse a sick rabbit – or cook one, come to that.' Daylight spilled in, revealing their surroundings to be even shabbier than Nathan had suspected, sombrely furnished and cobwebby about the corners. 'Did she give you lunch?'

'Beef jelly. She says it's very nourishing.'

'Probably right,' said the old man with an abrupt volte-face. 'Things that taste boring often are.' He came back to the bed, twitching aside both covers and nightshirt to expose a bulky mass of bandaging from calf to thigh. In the stronger light the invalid looked very ill. His face must once have been round and merry, but his cheeks had dropped to the jaw and his eyes sunk deep in their sockets. There were grey shadows on his skin, dark as bruises. His nightcap slipping sideways should have given him a comic look, but instead the effect was merely pathetic. Nathan noticed a tiny crown embroidered on it and realized who he must be.

He's the king. Of course. The king who's sick. Maj . . . your Majesty . . .

The old man undid the bandage. Nathan couldn't see very well but there seemed to be a long wound running half the length of the leg, imperfectly closed and seeping an evil ooze. The old man began to clean it, using a white cloth and water from a silver basin. Then he scooped dollops of thick paste from a jar and applied them to the infected area. 'Honey,' he muttered. 'Amazing stuff. Extraordinary healing properties. Intelligent creatures, bees.'

'It's awfully sticky,' the king pointed out. Some of it had found its way onto the bedding.

'It's supposed to be sticky. Change the linen later. Give the Prendergoose something useful to do.'

He covered the lot with padding and a fresh bandage, winding it round and round while the king, with a palpable effort, lifted his leg off the mattress. When it was over he fell back on the pillow-stack, his voice suddenly hoarse and faint. 'Frimbolus!' He seized the old man's collar, trying to draw him closer. 'Will I – will I ever be cured? Tell me the truth! How long has it been – ten years – twelve? What if I never get well again?'

Frimbolus detached the grasping hand and laid it gently down on the royal stomach, giving it a pat in the process. 'Ten years,' he said, in the tone of one who likes to get things right. 'Nellwyn was four when it happened. There'll be a cure – there's always a cure. Anyway, we have to keep trying – mustn't lose hope. Maybe the honey will do the trick. Magical stuff, honey. One of these days –'

'Will I live long enough to be cured?' the king said with a fretful movement of his head.

'Spineless guffle!' Frimbolus responded. 'You're the king, aren't you? Duty – responsibility – loving daughter – loyal subjects! No business to go dying on us.'

'How are my subjects?' the invalid asked, sounding very weary. 'They haven't seen me for so long. Do they still remember their king?'

'They're doing all right. The princess looks after them.' *He doesn't know*, Nathan thought. *They haven't told him about the people leaving.* 'Important thing is to keep your spirits up. They mustn't see you like this.'

'Spirits . . . up . . .' The king managed a smile, as though mocking himself, and then seemed to fall asleep.

Frimbolus emptied the basin out of a window, picked up the soiled bandages and left. Nathan tried to follow him, but the dream plucked him away, transporting him through a network of dim corridors where tapestries billowed in phantom draughts and embroidered horsemen galloped past him. Fireplaces yawned, dust sifted through the still air, pattering footsteps fled from him, vanishing into the muffling gloom of the house. Reality receded; the dream became surreal, the building a vast Gormenghast where his thought roamed endlessly, trapped as if in a maze, searching for something he couldn't find. Then suddenly there was an open door, daylight, normality. Another room, another scene. A room whose fourposter bed looked small and inviting, patchwork-quilted, its curtains sewn with silver stars, its pelmet carved with more stars and a crescent moon. There was a sheep-skin rug on the floor and a dressing-table with an oval mirror – a much bigger mirror than Hazel's, Nathan noted. It was the sort of mirror in front of which a queen might have sat, ermine-collared and velvet-gowned, applying her eyeliner or demanding verification of her beauty from some supernatural source. But the person sitting there had untidy hair and a darned dress and a smudge of dirt on her cheek. The princess.

He knew now her name was Nellwyn, Nell for short. Princess Nell. It suited her.

Behind her was the woman he had glimpsed once before, calling her and the other children in from the garden. Her head was bundled up in a species of wimple and her plump face was worn with time and worry. It was the sort of face that Nathan would have called *comely*, an old-fashioned word which in his mind meant homely, pleasant, almost but not quite pretty. It was marred by the worry-lines on her forehead and the pursing of her mouth. She was brushing the princess's hair, taking it a section at a time, dragging the brush through thickets of tangle while Nell winced and complained.

'Prenders, *please* . . . Ouch! Why can't I just leave it, like the other girls do?'

'You're the princess. You're not supposed to look like other girls.'

'Megwen Twymoor comes from one of our oldest families, so does Bronlee Ynglevere, and they don't have to spend hours brushing their hair. I know: I asked.'

'Megwen Twymoor looks like a gipsy, and Bronlee is barely six, so she doesn't count. A woman's chief beauty is her hair.'

'*I'm* not beautiful,' Nell said, pulling faces at the mirror. 'Anyway, there's no one here to see me.'

'That's not the point,' said her nurse (Nathan was sure that was who she must be). 'You don't want to get into bad habits.'

'I'd love some bad habits,' Nell sighed.

'One day you'll go away from here,' the nurse persisted, 'and then things will be different. You'll go to balls and parties, wear pretty dresses, dance with young men. Your hair will be threaded with flowers and pearls. If you would go to your mother's family –'

'I won't go,' the princess interrupted. 'We've been through this a hundred times. I won't leave my father, I won't leave Wilderslee. That's that.'

'Think again, mommet. This is no place for a young girl. I can look after your father. I asked him, the other evening, I said how would he feel, if you went away for a bit, just for a visit, met more young people –'

'You go too far.' Nell tugged her hair free of the brush and turned to face Mrs Prendergoose with an expression Nathan thought of as princessly. Proud, a little haughty, very grown-up. Her voice was quiet and cold. 'You had no business to discuss such matters with him. Whether I go or stay is not up to you.'

'But your father said it was a good idea, he said –'

'I am the princess, as you are always reminding me. I may not be princess of much, but it still counts for something. Princesses don't abandon the kingdom when things go wrong, they don't run away and go to balls when their people are suffering. Being a princess isn't about brushing your hair and wearing silk dresses; it's about duty and honour and love. I love my father, I love my subjects – those I have left, I'm *not going*. Don't *ever* presume to bring up the matter again.'

The woman looked slightly daunted, but still tried to protest. 'Who are you to talk of love? You know nothing about it. I've loved you from babyhood – I only want what's best for you. Who's turning you against me? It's that Frimbolus Quayne, isn't it? He's always been jealous of me – jealous of my position here . . .'

'You may leave now.'

'What about the Urdemons? They appeared first when you were a child, playing with magic. If you go, maybe they'll go.'

'*Leave.*'

Nell's face had hardened with determination. Mrs Prendergoose whisked round, dropping the hairbrush on the floor, and left on a flounce.

Alone, Nell picked up the brush, yanking in vain at her tangles. The hardness faded from her face; she looked confused, doubtful, on the verge of tears. 'It's not your fault!' Nathan wanted to tell her. 'Whatever's happening, it can't be your fault. Listen to Frimbolus.' She was surely too young, too brave, too good to be the cause of something evil. He wanted to reassure her so badly he thought he would materialize, but the dream-barrier held him back. Nell had set down the brush in frustration, murmuring a word he didn't recognize: '*Ruuissé!*' When she shook her hair it sparkled for a moment as if powdered with glitterdust, and the snarls unravelled by themselves, and the long waves rippled down her back as if they were alive. As the magic dissipated she swept the loose tresses over her shoulder and started to twist them into a thick braid.

Suddenly, the room darkened. The wind – or something worse than wind – screeched around the walls. The darkness pressed against the window, and in it there were eyes. Huge eyes full of a yellow fury, hungry and soulless. But the princess didn't scream or run. She jumped to her feet, knocking over the stool she had been sitting on, confronting the apparition. Her body shook with anger or fear or both. 'Go!' she cried. 'All I did was tidy my hair! *All I did* – Go, you foul thing! *Go!*' She thrust the hairbrush in front of her like a weapon, since that was all she had. For a second something like the muzzle of an animal was squashed against the pane, the mouth distended into an unnatural gape ragged with teeth. Then it seemed to dissolve, changing, becoming an ogre's leer with thick lips and warty snout, before it melted back into the dark, leaving only the eyes. They shrank, slowly, until the shadow swallowed them and they vanished, and the pallor of a clouded afternoon came pouring through the glass, bright as sunshine after the horror of the dark.

But the princess turned away, dropping on her knees beside the bed, her face in the quilt, sobbing not with relief but despair. Nathan struggled to touch her, to comfort her, but he could feel the dream fading, drifting away from him, and his will couldn't hold it, and he slid helplessly back into sleep.

'Do you recognize him?' Bartlemy asked, holding out a sketch which, despite his best efforts, made the average Identikit picture look like something by Rembrandt.

'Should I?' Annie said, clearly baffled by the artwork if not the question.

'I believe he bought a book from you, probably not long ago.'

Annie studied the sketch with a wry expression. 'I don't think . . .'

'I'm not much of an artist, I know,' Bartlemy conceded. 'Even with a little assistance, I'm not going to win any prizes. But I hoped there was enough of a likeness to give you some idea. The book might have been a description of local folklore, a history of satanic practices, even a grimoire. That sort of thing. Or so I suspect.'

'I sold a couple last month to a dealer,' Annie said, 'but that was on the Internet. I don't know what he looks like – we've never actually met.'

'This man came in personally.'

'Are you sure?' He nodded. 'I'm sorry, I can't recall anyone . . . like this. Not lately, anyway. I don't remember everybody who comes to the shop, but even so, it's a small place, most of my customers are regulars – collectors, enthusiasts, or just people who can't live without a book and find it cheaper to buy second-hand. I notice strangers. This man isn't a regular – at least, I don't think so.' Her faint grimace betrayed her doubts about Bartlemy's portraiture. 'If he came in recently, I ought to recognize him.'

'Never mind,' Bartlemy said. 'It's probably my drawing that's at fault. It isn't important.'

'Isn't it?' Annie asked shrewdly.

'I don't know,' Bartlemy admitted. 'That burglary attempt was . . . unusual. I'm not normally troubled by that sort of thing. I'd like to know what was behind it – if anything.'

'And this man?'

'A face in the spellfire. No more. He may not be relevant. He may be involved with something else, something that has little to do with us. Using smoke-magic is like surfing fifty

TV channels with no way of knowing which is which. Without reference points, you can't tell if you've got the programme you want or not . . .'

Annie smiled. 'That's a very modern metaphor,' she said, 'for such an arcane pursuit.'

'Magic isn't really arcane,' Bartlemy said. 'It's been around a long time, that's all. So has drawing – people were doing it on cave walls – but that doesn't make it arcane. And I'm better at magic than I am at drawing. Not much better, but a little. I prefer cooking to both.'

'Ah, but your cooking is definitely magical.'

'Not magic,' said Bartlemy. 'Just practice.'

After he went, Annie found the picture still on her desk. Perhaps he hadn't considered it worth keeping. She tucked it in a drawer, in case he should want it back, and sat down at the computer in quest of an obscure dictionary of wild flowers for a local botanist. The click of the door-latch made her look up, smiling on a reflex – but the smile cooled when she saw Chief Inspector Pobjoy.

She said: 'Hello. Can I help you?' in a tone that was strictly polite. She still wasn't prepared to forget his suspicions of Nathan.

Sensing hostility, his thin features grew a little thinner. 'Just passing,' he said. 'Since those kids broke in at Thornyhill, I thought I should keep an eye on things.'

Annie allowed herself to thaw a fraction. 'You must think we're prone to trouble,' she said.

'I think . . .' He checked himself. 'There's a lot I never learned about that business last year.'

'The accomplice,' Annie said promptly. 'The woman who pretended to be Rianna Sardou. You never heard any more about her, did you?' She herself knew the truth quite as well as Bartlemy, but it wasn't the kind of thing you could explain to a policeman. It occurred to her that it was unkind to mention it, but in view of Pobjoy's record she decided she didn't care.

'We're still looking,' he said, privately annoyed because he knew they weren't, and the fugitive would never be found. He felt he had lost control of the conversation, and told himself it had been a mistake to come in, succumbing to the urge to see her again. 'I wondered . . . It was a terrible experience for you. I hope you were able to get over the shock.'

'Shock?' Annie echoed blankly.

'Discovering the corpse. I've seen a few – I'm used to it – but it wasn't pretty.'

'I was all right,' Annie said. 'I'm tough.'

She didn't look tough, he thought, with her slight, compact figure, her soft short curls, the muted shades of her skin and hair. But there was a vein of strength under the softness, a core of something hidden – his detective instincts could sense it, even though it was out of reach.

He said awkwardly: 'I just wanted to be sure. You can get help with these things, but . . . I should've come sooner.'

'It doesn't matter,' Annie responded, confused by the pointlessness of the exchange. 'It was nice of you to bother. Er . . . about the burglary at Thornyhill: do *you* believe there was something behind it?'

He shrugged. 'Maybe. Could be just teenage youths going off the rails as usual. At that age, they think they can get away with anything.'

'Really?' Annie said, her hostility reviving. She assumed he was alluding to Nathan. 'I've always thought kids were a lot like adults, both good and bad, only braver – more reckless – more generous. Life hasn't yet taught them to be careful, to hold back, do nothing. Children are trusting and confident where people like me – and you – are cynical and afraid.'

'I didn't mean . . .' He wanted to apologize, but couldn't find the words. Instead, he said: 'I don't think you're afraid of very much.'

She stared at him, surprised and disconcerted. Before she could find something to say, another customer came in, and Pobjoy, with a mumbled goodbye, had gone. Annie, feeling the encounter had been oddly unfinished, returned to her computer screen.

But the wildflower dictionary was proving elusive and her mind wandered. She studied the latest customer, idly, conscious that she had come across him somewhere before though she didn't think it was here. He was a heavily-built man who looked as if he had once been heavier: his skin had that ill-fitting sag which occurs when someone has lost too much weight too quickly, and his jacket flapped around his midriff. His hair was thinning above an anxious frown; possibly he was unused to second-hand bookshops. Annie's routine *Can I help you?* made him turn, and suddenly she remembered.

'I've seen you before,' she said. 'At Ffylde. It must have been the carol service last Christmas.'

'Yes.' He didn't appear to consider it a talking point.

There was a short pause. 'What are you looking for?' Annie asked.

'A – a book. A book on pagan customs, magic rituals . . . A grimoire.'

Annie suppressed a jolt of shock. (After all, someone who wasn't traumatized by a dead body shouldn't be jolted by a request for a book, particularly in a bookshop.) 'At the back in the left-hand corner,' she said. 'Under Arch and Anth.'

As he moved away Annie opened the drawer, glanced down at the sketch, closed it again. Presently, the man came back to the desk carrying an old book with a stained cover which

Annie had bought in a job lot several months ago and never looked at properly. He gave her the money, clutching his purchase as if afraid somebody might take it from him, and refused her offer of a bag. She thanked him, making no further parent-to-parent overtures. When he had gone, she picked up the phone.

'Barty?'

'Yes?'

'Can you see the future in the smoke as well as the past?'

'Sometimes,' he said. 'But there are many futures. What you see may not always come true. The future can be changed, if you are resolute.'

Annie waved this irrelevance aside. 'A man just came in and bought a grimoire. I can't tell if he's the man in your picture – it could be a coincidence – but –'

'There are no coincidences in magic,' Bartlemy said. 'Did you get a chance to learn his name?'

'No,' Annie said, 'but I recognized him. I've seen him at Ffylde, at the carol service. He must have a son there.'

There was a thoughtful silence.

'What was in the book?' Bartlemy asked.

'I never really looked at it. Drawings I think – sigils and stuff. Incantations in Latin – you told me those don't normally work. Some hand-written notes at the back. I don't remember anything else.'

'A pity. Still . . .'

'If you had told me to check any grimoires in stock, I would have done,' Annie said with dignity.

'I know. Magic is invariably unpredictable. You'd think I would have learned that by now. But at least we have the link with Ffylde: that's something.'

'Do you think he's the father of that boy you were so interested in?' Annie inquired. 'The one who's always in trouble.'

'That,' Bartlemy said gently, 'really *would* be a coincidence.'

'Would it?' Annie said.

It was a couple of weeks before Nathan had the chance to tell his uncle what he had learnt about the Hackforths. 'Dear me,' Bartlemy said. 'I seem to have shown my curiosity very plainly. First your mother catches me out, now you. And I thought I was being subtle.'

'Oh, you were,' Nathan said. 'Hazel and George didn't notice anything. Mum and I are more observant – and we know you better.'

Bartlemy smiled. 'I must be more careful,' he said.

Nathan was sitting on the hearthrug in the living room where he had sat when he was a baby, while Hoover rolled onto his back to have his tummy rubbed. 'I ran into Damon the other day on the stairs,' he remarked. 'I mean, literally. He was sprinting down two steps at a time and he clouted me with his shoulder, I think it was an accident but I don't know. I sort of stumbled and said something – *Look out, look where you're going* – something like that. Anyway, he swore at me like it was my fault. A bit later he stopped me in the corridor. "You're the wonderboy, aren't you?" he said. "Keep out of my way." He looked like he really hated me. It was bizarre, I don't know why he should even know who I am – or care. He's four years ahead of me.'

'What did you say?' Bartlemy asked.

'Nothing. I was pretty surprised – and the whole thing seemed awfully silly. You know, as if he was the bad guy in a Western: *This school ain't big enough for the both of us.* Stupid.'

'Well done,' said Bartlemy. 'As Kipling put it: *If you can*

keep your head when all about you are losing theirs . . .
Restraint is a rare gift at your age.'

My head is the problem, Nathan thought ruefully. Aloud
he said: 'There must be something behind it. Are you going
to tell me?'

'Tell you what?'

'What you know – or guess.'

Bartlemy was silent for a long moment, considering. 'What
I know is very little,' he said. 'I wondered about the attempted
burglary here, that's all. I gather the two boys involved were
advised by a very expensive lawyer, the kind they wouldn't
get on legal aid. Among other people this lawyer has previ-
ously worked for Giles Hackforth, in a matter concerning his
son. The connection is very tenuous, you see. I'm trusting
you not to discuss this with anyone.'

'Not even Mum?' Nathan said.

'That's different. I wouldn't ask you to have secrets from
Annie.' Nathan looked a shade disappointed, possibly because
having a secret from his mother was, in his view, the benchmark of maturity. 'Since we're being so frank, have you had
any significant dreams lately? I've noticed a certain . . . restlessness in you. Maybe it's your age. You don't have to confide
in me if you don't wish to.'

'There was one,' Nathan said slowly. He explained about
Osskva. 'And . . . I've had a few dreams about another world.
Not like Eos. More . . . like some period from history.
Mediaeval, I suppose.' He didn't intend to mention the
princess.

'Hmm.'

'Uncle Barty, do you think I have these dreams because I
want to, or because something else makes them happen? Or
– are they just random?'

'*Do* you want to?' his uncle inquired.

'I – yes, I do. It's frightening sometimes, but in a stimulating way – an adventure. With this new world, I want to know it better, find out more. Like when you visit another country –' Annie had taken him twice to France, once to Holland '– only another universe is a million times more exciting. I mean, *anyone* can go abroad.' He grinned, looking suddenly very young.

'Indeed,' Bartlemy said, 'but remember, any dream you have is not a sight-seeing trip. I believe there is a purpose behind your wanderings, though I am not yet sure exactly what it is. Does this new world seem to have any connection with the Grail?'

'No,' Nathan said, 'but they talk about a sword. The Traitor's Sword.'

'Ah,' Bartlemy said. 'Well, dream carefully.' It was not the first time Nathan had been told that. 'Take the precautions I taught you. Keep the Rune of Finding in your room, and drawn on your arm. Use the herbal mixture I gave you which helps to bring the spirit home. Don't get lost.'

'I won't,' Nathan said confidently.

'He is always confident, Rukush,' Bartlemy told the dog when he had gone. 'I hope he is careful too . . . The sword. Well, well. There is a pattern developing here. The Grail relics – if I can call them that – were evidently hidden in different worlds, and it seems to be Nathan's job to retrieve them. At least, that's what it looks like. He's clearly on the trail of the sword now. But who gave him this task, if anyone did? The Ultimate Powers? Those who maintain equilibrium throughout the multiverse rarely involve themselves so personally. Or could the knowledge of what he has to do have been born in him, part of the heritage of two worlds? Maybe *this* is the special destiny for which he was created. After all, I've never heard of any other mortal – and few immortals – able to move so easily between universes. Objects – occasionally; but not people. People are too perishable. And what of the Grandir of Eos? This evidently fits in with some long-lost plan one of his forebears made to save a dying cosmos, but . . . Yes, that's the trouble. *But*.' He added with a sigh: 'I wish Annie would tell Nathan the truth about his conception. The time is coming when that information may be essential for his safety.'

Hoover looked at him with an expression both alert and meaningful.

'All right,' said Bartlemy. 'I'll talk to her.'

But Annie, when the time came, proved more recalcitrant than ever. 'It isn't just that he doesn't *need* to know,' she said. 'I think it might be safer if he *didn't*. Suppose I tell him his real father could be a – a being from another universe, a superhuman entity who impregnated me for a mysterious purpose? At least, I expect so, since he obviously didn't do it for fun. Anyhow, that may explain to Nathan why he can dream himself into other worlds, but then he'll start agonizing over his destiny, and all that sort of thing, when he should be agonizing over exams – he'll worry about the father thing – it could distance him from his friends. I don't mean it would make him conceited, but it isn't good for any boy to be told: *You're special. You aren't like the others. You have a Destiny with a capital D.*'

'I wasn't going to tell him any such thing,' Bartlemy objected.

'I want him to be just a normal boy,' Annie went on. 'The adolescent years are difficult enough, without adding other-worldly complications. I know we can't stop the dreams, but as long as his – his journeys stay in dream-form they're manage-able. He still sees them as a kind of storybook adventure, not the main focus of his life. Let's keep it that way.'

'You want Narnia to stay in the wardrobe,' Bartlemy said. 'But Narnia was the kingdom of childhood; when the children grew too old, they weren't allowed to return any more. The universes in Nathan's head are rather different. The signs show his dream journeys are intensifying, not diminishing, as he grows up. Without the knowledge he needs, you may endanger him.'

'Do you think I haven't thought of that?' Annie said. 'I think of it all the time. It's bad enough worrying if your children are out at night – what they're doing, who they're with, all the usual – but I have to worry when Nathan's home in bed. Barty, I don't know if I'm right – maybe I'm just a coward about telling him the true story – but I think he's better off dreaming in ignorance. Once he gets it into his head he's carrying some huge doom on his shoulders, the weight of it could crush him. Let him walk lightly for the moment. Let Narnia stay in the closet where it belongs. We don't know who his father was, or what he intended.'

'There are indications –'

'We *don't know*. We're just trying to – to second-guess fate. My recollection of . . . what happened . . . is closed. Maybe that's deliberate, to protect me, or Nathan. Anyway, I won't tell him until I *know* it's necessary – if it ever is.'

'By then,' said Bartlemy, 'it may be too late.'

Annie averted her gaze, and he said no more, sensing the muddle of her thoughts – hope, doubt, dread – unsure of his own arguments, or if he was in the right at all.

Later, left alone, Annie's mind returned to that sealed door in her memory, and what lay beyond. The anger she had never told rushed through her like a bushfire, so she was shaking with the force of it. She had passed the Gate between worlds – the Gate that opened only for the dead – in a moment of selfless love, seeking one who was gone, and in that moment another had taken her, violated her, sending her back with his seed in her womb and his lie in her heart. It had been thirteen years before she could open the door even a crack and let a fragment of memory through – thirteen years of wondering and secret fear, searching in vain for Daniel in her son's face and form. Now, whenever she dared to think about it, the anger leaped from a flicker to a flame, all but consuming her. Perhaps that was the real reason why she avoided telling Nathan – because she was afraid he might see it, and misunderstand, thinking it was directed at him. Or because her anger was a thing so deep, so private, that no one must know it was there – no one must see her damaged, betrayed, revengeful – until the moment came when she could let it out, and it would rage across the barriers of the worlds to find the one who had done this to her.

She wondered if other victims of supernatural impregnation had felt the same. Rosemary with her baby, Leda, ravaged by a swan (she had often wondered about the technicalities of that). And Mary, who had been honoured and over-whelmed, according to the Bible – but then, Annie reflected, the Bible was written by men. Maybe she too had known that instant of raw fury because her body had been used without her permission, invaded by a superior being who thought he was above the rules, and humans were his creatures, to do with as he pleased. Annie had been brought up a catholic, and, like anyone who lapses from a stern religion, God was real to her, both her Father and her Enemy. Her relationship with Him was Freudian, a matter of love and hate, and some-how the God of her childhood mingled with Nathan's pro-genitor, and their betrayal was as old as Time. Gods demanded constant worship and sacrifice, but what did They do for mere mortals? As far as she could see all you got was forgiveness for the fate God Himself had dished out to you, and that only if you were lucky. She lost herself in imaginary conversations with Mary, and in the end found she was trying to pray for the virgin mother with her lost innocence, because the reflex of prayer is strong in the human spirit. But she didn't know Whom she could pray to, because with God beyond the pale, there was Nobody left.

The next day, when Nathan telephoned from school, she asked him: 'Are you dreaming again? About – another world?'

'A bit,' he conceded after a pause.

'Take care,' she said, 'won't you?'

'Yes, Mum. There's no danger, honestly.' Except the Urdemons . . .

But Annie knew without being told that there was always danger, and it wasn't in Nathan's nature to take care.

THREE

An Entanglement of Clues

At Crowford Comprehensive, Hazel saw Jonas Tyler and Ellen Carver talking in the corridor after English, and her heart quailed.

'Don't know what she sees in him,' another girl said, but Hazel knew, and gloried in the knowing, because seeing something in him was her secret, and even Ellen Carver would never see what she saw. The hidden sorrow that he bore, the mystery behind his infrequent smile and the blue of his eyes. (He smiled more often when he was talking to Ellen, but Hazel told herself that was forced.)

Back at home she looked again at Effie's notebook, and the hand-labelled bottles, but still she hesitated. There was a poem she vaguely remembered from an anthology she had read with Nathan when she was a child, the usual sort of nursery doggerel, but the underlying horror in it had made a strong impression on her. In it there was a woman or girl, sitting alone and lonely, wishing – and a body came in to join her, piece by piece, starting with the feet and working up. But at the climax of each verse 'still she sat, and still she sighed, and still she wished for company'. When all the body was there, something unpleasant happened to the girl, Hazel couldn't recall exactly what, except that it was nasty. Perhaps she got eaten. Anyway, she couldn't help feeling she was in a similar position. *Still she sat, and still she sighed, and still she wished for company* . . . Fairytales, cleaned up for Victorian consumption, might tell you that if you rubbed a lamp you would get a genie who would obey your every command, but Hazel knew better. Wish-fulfilment always had its price, and the price was always more than you wanted to pay.

She didn't trust magic, even if it worked (especially if it worked). She didn't trust Lilliat, with her silver-blue eyes and the unnatural breeze in her hair. Lilliat had called her price trivial, but in her heart Hazel knew what was being asked of her, and it was too much. Even for the infrequent smiles of Jonas Tyler. Besides, what was the point of attracting him by magic? One day the magic would fade, and there would be no reality underneath. Or so she told herself, struggling for rationality. (But *one day* was in the future, and for a teenager the future was too remote to touch the urgency of present desire.)

Still she sat, and still she sighed . . .

She wished for Nathan, to take her mind off things, but Nathan wasn't there.

The evenings were growing longer now, and she went for a walk in the woods by way of distraction, because there was no witch paraphernalia out there to tempt her. When she was much younger and her father was still at home she used to run to the woods to be alone, sometimes climbing a tree and staying up there for hours, wrapped in the quiet and the privacy of her leaf-bound world. Now she was older and her father had gone she preferred her bedroom, but that day the lure of the woods drew her back. She found her favourite tree and scrambled up into the branches, just to prove she still could. And then somehow it was easy to lapse into her former quiescence, back against the tree-trunk, legs crooked, pulling the hush of leaf-murmur and wind-murmur around her like a cloak. She felt her self merging with the self of the tree, becoming bark and root, sap and acorn, reaching deep, deep into the darkness of the earth, listening to the sound of growing, and burrowing, and the tingle of new life uncurling and groping towards the light. And then she was stretching up to the sky, straining with twig-tip and leaf-tip to reach the sun. She didn't know that this oneness with things was a part of the power she feared to indulge; all she knew was that it made her feel peaceful, and somehow complete. The tiny denizens of the tree-tops came close to her, untroubled by her presence; a squirrel scurried over her thigh.

Presently, she saw the woodwose.

She had met him once or twice before, but only with Nathan, who had been his friend from infancy. She knew he was very shy. He was a stick-thin creature only a few feet high, with a pointy face all nose and the sideways eyes of an animal. His voice was as soft as a rustle in the leafmould; his movements altogether noiseless. She didn't hear him approach; rather, she became aware of him, one twig-pattern among many, perched on a nearby bough, watching her. Perhaps he had been there all the time.

It was a long while before he spoke.

'Tell Nathan . . .'

'Yes?'

'*He's* here. Hiding in woods, skulking behind bushes. Spying on the house where the wise man lives. He kills rabbits with slingstones and eats them. I don't know what he wants, but he won't go away.'

'Who?' Hazel asked, quiet as a breath.

'*Him*. The hairy one from down in the valley, where the old *old* house used to be. You let him out, you and Nathan. He stole the thing, and ran away, but he didn't go far. He sleeps in a fox's hole, down in the Darkwood. I think he strangled the fox. Tell Nathan.'

The dwarf, Hazel thought, remembering the curious little man she and Nathan had inadvertently released from his underground prison – someone who, Bartlemy claimed, might once have been the assistant to Josevius Grimling-Thorn. He had stolen the Grail, and thrust it back into its native world, though no one knew why.

'I'll tell him,' Hazel promised.

The woodwose gave a tiny nod of acknowledgement. 'He likes to know . . . everything that happens here,' he elaborated unexpectedly. 'I watch. I listen. I wait for him. He doesn't come now for many months, but I'm still here. Tell him . . .'

'He has to go away to school,' Hazel said. 'Even at weekends he has homework, rugger matches, cricket matches, stuff like that. He can't always find time for everyone.' She hadn't seen so much of Nathan that year, and although she knew it wasn't his fault the woodwose's words stirred a tiny niggle of resentment. Woody, Nathan had told her, had been his playfellow when he was little more than a baby, an imaginary friend who wasn't imaginary, tugged from some lost universe in childish innocence for companionship and games, unable to return to wherever he had come from. We're Nathan's closest friends, Hazel thought, and now we're both neglected.

She said: 'I'll come back. If you like.'

Woody considered her offer in silence. 'Do you have Smarties?' he asked at last. 'Nathan used to bring Smarties.'

'I can get some,' Hazel.

Nathan hadn't dreamed about the princess for nearly three weeks, and he was desperate to find her again, to help her or merely to see her – there was little help he could offer in his insubstantial dream-state, but he was sure that soon he would begin to materialize, because that was the pattern his dreams had followed in the past. He saw Hazel that weekend only briefly, pleading homework and tiredness. She told him about Woody and the dwarf, and he was pleased she had formed a bond with the woodwose; somehow, it excused him from having to spend precious time with either of them. Not that he saw it that way – his dreams filled his thought, and he wasn't seeing anything very clearly. He tried to help her with her maths, but, sensing his reluctance, she made less effort, and in the end he gave her the answers without an explanation, taking a shortcut because he was in a hurry to leave.

'I need an early night,' he said.

'Are you dreaming again?' she asked – like Bartlemy, like his mother – picking up the meaning behind the words.

'Yes.' He didn't temporize, not with Hazel. 'I'll tell you about it another time. I don't know enough yet. It's a new place, a new world . . .'

'Can't you dream me with you?'

'*No.* I mean, it would be dangerous – you could get trapped there – and anyway, I don't have that much control.'

You could if you wanted to, Hazel thought, suddenly convinced of it, and when he had gone she sat for a long time, her mind stuck on a single thought, going nowhere.

Nathan, meanwhile, went to bed early and, inevitably, couldn't sleep, let alone dream. He didn't want to risk probing the frontier of his own volition – it might only transport him to Eos – so he sat up reading till the words ran together and he hoped exhaustion would take over, slipping across the borderland into slumber only after what seemed like hours of weary wakefulness. Even then, he woke again after a short period when his dreams were commonplace and unmemorable, slept and woke and slept again. And now, at last, his sleep was deep enough, and the portal in his head opened, and his soul poured through.

He dreamed. Not of the princess as he had wished, nor of the city on two hills. He dreamed of the Grandir, the white-masked ruler of Eos: broken visions of him all jumbled together. The Grandir in his semicircular office high above the city, gazing out between the screens at the panorama of sunset, the western sky all fire and blood, and to the east the light reflected in a million windows, so the city sparkled like a monstrous piece of jewellery. A mounted xaurian flew past, unusually close, its hooked wingspan slicing the image in two, its bluish body turned to mauve in the glow. Then the scene changed, and the Grandir was in his secret chamber where the star-globes floated in darkness, compressed spheres of inter-dimensional space existing both in that world and in others, projecting onto the ceiling, as on a screen, glimpses of alternative universes. One of them hung in the sky above the bookshop, a star hidden among the stars, watching over Nathan and his mother – or spying on them. And then the Grandir was walking down a corridor towards a door marked *Danger* – it slid back automatically and there was the underground laboratory, and in a huge cage to the right was something so horrible Nathan drew back, not wanting to see it, feeling the horror of it from a distance and struggling to pull out of the dream . . .

Everything changed. He was in a grey daylight room plentifully layered with dust and shadows – the cleaners had obviously gone with everyone else, taking their brooms and brushes with them. On a table by the window was an enormous open book, the reader's place marked with a spoon. Nearby, someone silhouetted against the light was pouring things from one bottle into another, from bottle to jar, from jar to bowl. Occasionally, the mixture thus produced would change colour, or give off a tiny puff of purple smoke, or the sound of birds singing, or an eye-watering variety of smells. A diminutive oil-lamp with a naked flame, currently pale green, stood to hand; every so often the man would lift bottle or jar in a pair of tongs and warm it over the flame, whereupon the contents would bubble, or steam, or scream, until removed. As Nathan drew nearer he saw the man had a fluff of thistledown hair and very mobile eyebrows that soared in excitement and plunged in doubt according to the progress of his experiments. Frimbolus Quayne.

Nathan was eager to talk to him but it was no good; though his sinuses smarted from one of the smells he still felt hopelessly insubstantial. Nonetheless, when the door opened he drew back instinctively into the shadows, well away from the window. The woman who walked in – or rather, bustled; she was the sort of person who bustled a lot – was the princess's nurse, Mrs Prendergoose.

She started to speak, but Frimbolus held up a hand. 'Hush, woman! I am doing something very important. It needs the utmost concentration . . .' He held a glass jar over the flame and carefully added a single drop of liquid from a phial which smoked. Inside the jar, there was a small – a very small – explosion. When things settled down, what remained appeared to be fluid, lime-green and phosphorescent. 'Blinkus!' Frimbolus swore. 'Ah well, I didn't really think it would work. But it was worth a try. Madam, what can I do for you?'

Mrs Prendergoose didn't look as though she liked being called Madam – clearly she felt it had offensive undertones – but she got straight to the point. 'I want to talk to you,' she said, 'about the princess.'

'What about her?'

'She's not a child any more, she's a young lady –'

'Dear me, is she?'

'– and a pretty young lady, too, or she would be, if she got the chance to prettify herself a bit. Instead – look at her! Her dresses are all in tatters and we can't get the material here to make new ones – her hair's always in a tangle no matter how hard I brush it – she sits around in the gloom all day worrying about Urdemons and the state of the kingdom when she should be choosing her gown for a party – she never gets to meet anyone or go anywhere . . .'

'What do you suggest we do to remedy these ills?' Frimbolus inquired.

'She needs to get away – right away. She could go to her uncle, the duke of Quilp, or those cousins in Marplott – she stayed with them a few years back, and there wasn't any trouble then.'

'Trouble?'

'You know what I mean, don't pretend you don't. There wasn't none of this business with magic and monsters that's driving the poor child out of her mind –'

'I thought you said she wasn't a child?' Frimbolus interrupted.

Mrs Prendergoose ignored him. 'I'm not saying it's her fault – she's the sweetest thing in nature, just growing a bit obstinate – but it wasn't till she started playing around with magic that them Urdemons turned up: you can't deny it. There's got to be a connection, hasn't there?'

'Oh yes, there's a *connection*,' Frimbolus said, with a wealth of sinister meaning. 'That doesn't mean it's cause and effect. You've been stuffing her head with notions of self-blame, haven't you? Telling her *she's* the plague-carrier, the imp among cherubim? Thyrma Prendergoose, if this kingdom was properly run I'd see you executed for treason! As if Nell doesn't have enough to bear, without shouldering a load of guilt that doesn't belong to her!'

'How dare you!' The nurse was shaking with anger. 'How dare you talk to me of – of treason! I *love* the princess, and if you did you'd want what I want for her. If she went away all this magical nonsense would stop –'

'How do you know that?'

'The magic's *here*, bad magic, it's common knowledge. Or it would be, if there were any commoners left. The king's sick, the family's cursed – cursed with that evil sword they've been hanging on to for centuries – a sword that jumps up all by itself and stabs people. A sword like that, what do you expect? That's where all the bad magic comes from. I won't have my Nellwyn spending her whole life under a cloud. If she could get away from the sword, she'd get away from the curse. She could have a normal life, be happy . . . That's all I want for her.'

'I believe you,' said Frimbolus rather surprisingly. 'That's what I want for her too. But running away won't solve the problem. In any case, she won't do it. She *is* a princess, Prendergoose, a true princess, and that means more than you know. She's brave and generous and kind and as true as steel – that's what makes her a princess, not a sparkly crown and a ball dress. She won't leave her father or Carboneck –'

'She would if you told her to,' the nurse interjected. 'She reckons a lot to what you think.' The admission was grudging. 'If you said she ought to go, she'd be off quick enough, for certain sure.'

'Well, I can't,' Frimbolus said, not mincing words. 'Anyhow, you're wrong. This is *her* place, you stupid old fussbucket. *Her* kingdom, *her* people – or what's left of them – *her* problems to solve. Nothing you or I or anyone could say would make her budge. Now, if you've nothing more to complain about I'd be grateful if you'd go away and leave me to get on with my work.'

'Don't you go name-calling with me –'

'I said: *Go away!*'

Pointedly, Frimbolus returned to his experiments. The nurse stared impotently at his back for a few moments, sniffed angrily, then left. Nathan moved out of the shadows towards the old man, wanting to see what he was doing . . . and Frimbolus wheeled round, stared straight at him, and demanded: 'Who – and what – are you?'

'You can see me!' Nathan gasped, or tried to, but only a squeak of sound came out.

'What's that? Speak up, phantom, or be off with you! There's a high level of magic in here; stray spirits tend to show up. I noticed you hovering in the background when I was talking to the Prendergoose. Felt you peering over my shoulder just now, too – gives me a prickle up the spine, having a spectre right behind me. Who are you and what's your business here?'

But Nathan's essence in that world was still too flimsy for him to make himself heard. He thought of trying some sort of sign language, but he didn't know how to convey the message *I want to help you* in gestures, and he visualized his spirit enacting a kind of ghostly charades, and knew it would be ridiculous. He spaced his hands and shook his head to show his quandary even as the dream receded, and the room blurred, and the last thing he saw was the perplexed expression on Frimbolus' face.

He awoke the next morning feeling anxious, though he wasn't sure why. The hint of danger to the princess? – but that was nothing new. His own hazy materialization? Then he remembered. The Grandir's laboratory, and the thing in the cage which he hadn't been able to see – the thing whose proximity had filled him with a cold horror, so the mere recollection of it made him shiver. In a cage in that same laboratory the Grandir had kept the gnomons – creatures whose substance was fluid and whose collective mind was under his control, equipped with hypersenses and able to move between worlds. They were invisible here except as a stirring in the leaves, or the patter of following feet on an empty road – but their pursuit was relentless and when they caught someone they would enter his brain, twisting his thoughts, draining his very self, until he was left a drooling imbecile. They were the guardians of the Grail, intangible yet deadly. Suddenly, Nathan found himself wondering if the sword was similarly guarded, and by whom – or what.

He would have to talk to someone about it.

That day was Sunday, and Annie was going to tea with Bartlemy. Nathan excused himself, saying he needed to visit Rowena and Eric in Crowford to do some historical research. He didn't want to explain further at this stage, and Annie didn't ask questions, merely adjuring him to phone first and make sure they weren't otherwise occupied. Nathan went out after breakfast to play football with George and some of the village boys, and Annie sat contemplating a plan she had been making and leafing through a book. It was more of a tome than a book, leather-bound, with gilded lettering on the cover and beautiful illustrations inside shielded with tissue paper. It was called *Magical Herbs and Their Properties*, and she'd acquired it the previous week. Maybe it was the book which had given her the plan. She knew things were happening, probably bad things, and although she worried about Nathan, and told him to be careful, it didn't occur to her to take her own advice. Annie would never have claimed to be adventurous – indeed, she thought of herself as peace-loving, even rather timid, a quiet sort of person who liked a quiet sort of life. But last summer she had nearly been killed at least twice, she had hit Lily Bagot's husband over the head with a saucepan and attacked a psychopath with a hairbrush – not to mention discovering a decayed corpse without screaming, or being sick, or suffering post-traumatic stress. (She had *felt* sick, very sick, but sheer determination had kept her stomach under control.) Now, she wanted to know more of what was going on – there were things she had to find out if she was going to protect Nathan, or at least help him – and her plan was only a small plan, risk-free and relatively innocuous.

She had scanned a few websites, identified a photograph, found an address in the telephone book. A rather affluent address, in the village of Willowdene, about half an hour's drive from Eade. She left a note for Nathan – *Gone shopping* – after all, she would have to shop on her way home – and set off in her car with the book on the seat beside her.

The car was a fairly recent acquisition, a new look Volkswagen Beetle, second-hand but little used, sprayed a beautiful primrose yellow – Annie found, slightly to her surprise, that she adored it. She still wasn't sure how she had managed to afford the expense, but Bartlemy gave her a salary for running the shop, and as they lived on the premises she paid no rent, and somehow there was always a little over. The car number-plate started with SBL so she christened it Sybil, and treated it like a favoured pet.

In Willowdene – one of those rambling villages with no real centre or even a main street – she had to ask the way twice before finding the house she wanted. It was a big house some distance from its neighbours, evidently a barn conversion – or, to be precise, several barns – with old beams, and new windows, and an apparently limitless garden. She turned into the drive and pulled up just short of the front door, feeling suddenly pushy and vulgar, like a social climber using a tenuous connection to try and shin a few rungs up the ladder of class and wealth. The fact that she wasn't anything of the kind made her feel only a little better. She rang the doorbell, wondering if they had a butler. 'If there is one,' she thought, 'I'll run away.'

But the woman who answered the door definitely wasn't a butler. She wore tracksuit trousers faded from much washing and a shapeless sweater, no outfit for a butler or maid. Her haircut was expensive and her face very tired, and Annie instantly felt sorry for her.

'Mrs Hackforth?'

'Yes.' The woman didn't look hostile, or wary, or even interested.

'I'm Annie Ward. I think we've met at Ffylde Abbey – my son's there, he's some years younger than yours. I run a second-hand bookshop in Eade. Your husband bought a book from me recently, a grimoire, and I thought if he was collecting that kind of thing . . . I've had this in, a few days ago,' she flourished *Magical Herbs*, 'and I was over this way anyhow, so I thought – I wondered – if he might like to look at it.' Never a good liar, she was stammering by the time she finished this speech and conscious of a rising blush, but Selena Hackforth accepted her errand without question.

'Thoughtful of you.' The phrase was automatic. 'My husband's out at the moment but he should be back shortly. Would you like to come in? I'm afraid . . .' She didn't finish the sentence.

Annie followed her into the house and was promptly mobbed by a couple of retrievers who slobbered enthusiastically over her. 'Sorry – they're a bit uncontrolled,' Mrs Hackforth apologized, roused to faint animation.

'That's all right,' Annie said. 'I love dogs.'

She could see no sign of any offspring, though the distant twitter of a television came from some far-flung corner of the house. They went into a palatial kitchen, all stainless steel and stained wood, and her hostess made coffee in a complicated piece of equipment which seemed to take much longer than a cafetière. It was clearly a struggle for her to maintain even the most desultory small talk, though she did say: 'Call me Selena.'

Tentatively – in view of Damon's reputation – Annie brought up the subject of Ffylde, and what a good school it was. 'My son's a scholarship boy,' she explained. 'Otherwise I could never afford it. It's a wonderful opportunity for Nathan. Of course, I think he's very bright – very special – but I daresay all mothers say that.' She wasn't being tactful, she realized, but at least she might provoke some reaction in the other woman.

'I suppose so.' For a minute, an expression lingered on Selena's face that was beyond tiredness, a bone-deep, soul-deep fatigue – a weariness of life, a dreariness of spirit. 'Damon – my son – is a bit . . . *difficult*. Teenage stuff, the psychiatrists say. But then, psychiatrists are like mothers: they always say that.' A flicker of dried-up humour lifted her mouth. 'Let's be honest, *difficult* isn't the word.' For the first time, she looked directly at Annie. 'He's a thief, a liar, a vandal – a monster. My daughter is chronically sick and my son is a monster. Three cheers for motherhood.'

Dear God, Annie thought, overcome with pity. And my only problem is a son who pops into other universes in his sleep . . .

'Damon hates the people he loves – he hates himself – the only thing he doesn't seem to hate, oddly enough, is the school. Father Crowley has been wonderful; even Damon respects him. My husband's with him now. They should be here very soon.'

Annie stood up abruptly. 'I – I'm sorry,' she said, genuinely guilt-stricken. 'I'm intruding. I'd better go.'

'No – please.' Just as Annie was feeling like an impostor, her hostess had become anxious to keep her there. 'It was really kind of you to bring the book. I don't know if you realized, but Giles is a publisher: he has a genuine love of books. He's been collecting this sort of thing lately – antique volumes on magic and so on. I know he'll want to see this one.'

'I could leave it with you?'

'Have some more coffee.'

Annie accepted, feeling she should, wanting to abandon her researches but aware that she was trapped in the role she had created for herself. 'Has your son – has Damon always had problems?' she inquired, fishing for diplomatic language.

Selena shrugged. 'Not really. Not that we noticed. As a little boy he was naughty but not wicked. It's a teenage thing – it always is, isn't it? The psychiatrists say it was triggered by his sister's illness destabilizing his environment – he'd always been very fond of her but suddenly he became jealous. It showed in irrational tantrums – violence – it was as if he was possessed.'

'The catholic church believes in possession,' Annie said. 'Does Father Crowley . . . ?'

'This is the modern world,' Selena said. 'They don't use the word except in horror films. All we know is the abbot seems to be the only person who can ever get through to Damon.' She looked up at the sound of a car outside. 'That must be them now.'

Annie, increasingly uncomfortable, wasn't certain whether she should expect the teenage monster as well, but only Giles Hackforth and Father Crowley came in, fetched to the kitchen by Selena. If they had suspected her of vulgar curiosity or subversive investigation Annie would have been horribly embarrassed, but their unquestioning acceptance of her motives augmented her sense of guilt. This was a family in desperate trouble, and she was being nosy. She wasn't happy about it.

Giles was vague, mumbling something about her kindness, but Father Crowley leafed through the book with genuine interest. He was a man whose personality made him appear taller than his actual height, with a lofty nose and a face at once grave and graven, deeply lined with both humour and thought. Silver hair retreated from a high forehead, and he had the keen grey eyes of popular cliché – not merely keen-sighted, Annie felt, but keen from a profound wellspring of inner keenness, as if he had just discovered a formula for making the world a better place, and was eager to put it into action. She always thought he looked much more like a wizard than Bartlemy.

'This is good of you,' he told her. 'A lovely book – absolutely

81

lovely. Look at the delicacy of these drawings.' This to Giles, or possibly Selena. 'You shouldn't miss the chance to acquire this.'

Annie was forced to mention a price, which she kept low, but Giles insisted on overpaying her. Afterwards, rather to her surprise, Father Crowley asked for a lift: 'I know it's a little out of your way, but I would welcome the opportunity to talk to you about Nathan.'

Annie couldn't have refused even if she had wished to.

The priest was dressed in civilian clothes, apart from his dog collar, but a very long raincoat flapping around him in the wind gave the impression of monkish robes. He admired her car, arranging himself comfortably in the passenger seat – 'It's larger inside than out, like the Tardis' – and they drove off towards Ffylde.

'Nathan hasn't done anything wrong, has he?' Annie demanded without preamble.

'No indeed. On the contrary, an outstanding pupil. Many of our boys are *not* academic – at the school we like to focus on developing the individual in whatever way is best suited to him – but Nathan is exceptional. I wanted to take the chance to tell you so. I don't know if you've thought ahead as far as university, but he's definitely Oxbridge material. He seems to be particularly good at history and the arts, though he's strong in the sciences too – and, of course, a talented athlete. It's just that lately he seems a little . . . abstracted, at times. Less attentive in class, though it doesn't affect his essays. I gather he went through a similar phase last summer, though it wore off.' He paused, allowing Annie the chance to say something. When she didn't, he went on: 'It's a difficult age. The urges of the body can often outweigh every stimulus of the intellect. Perhaps there's a girlfriend?'

'No,' Annie said, adding, scrupulously: 'Not to my knowledge.' She was concentrating on her driving, unable to find an appropriate response beyond what she had already said.

'I understood there was someone called Hazel . . . ?'

Annie was startled. 'You're very well informed!'

'I make it my business to be. These boys are in my care, after all. Nathan has talked about her.'

'She's his friend,' Annie said. 'That's all. They sort of grew up together – a brother-sister situation. I'm quite sure that hasn't changed.'

Father Crowley nodded. 'You would know,' he said. 'You're a perceptive woman.'

And then: 'I'm told he's been having disturbed nights. It's unusual for a boy that age not to sleep well –'

Annie's hands jerked on the wheel; involuntarily, she swerved. Fortunately, they were on a quiet country road with no other traffic in sight. She mounted the verge and braked sharply, breathing hard.

'Mrs Ward –'

'Sorry. Sorry . . .'

'I didn't mean to alarm you. These are minor worries. I'm sure Nathan's perfectly healthy.' He had a deep, resonant voice, as if there was a tiny echo somewhere in his throat. Annie should have been soothed, but she wasn't.

'Insomnia isn't a serious problem,' Father Crowley continued. 'It was simply that – last year – his absence from the dormitory was noted, no doubt to go to the bathroom, and I believe he asked about sleeping pills once. It concerns me a little. I will watch to see if it recurs.'

Annie pulled herself together as best she could. 'Thank you,' she said.

'There. Are you all right now? You mustn't drive on till you're ready.'

'I'll be okay.' The engine had stalled. She re-started it,

slowly, annoyed to find herself trembling with the aftermath of shock.

'Tell me,' said the abbot, 'does Nathan dream vividly?'

Nathan was talking to Eric Rhindon in the apartment above the antique shop where he lived with his new wife, Rowena Thorn. Rowena, a grey-haired woman of sixty-odd, long widowed, whose recent marriage to an impecunious asylum-seeker had stunned her entire acquaintance, was out at a weekend antiques fair. Eric, a former Eosian, had been accidentally pitchforked into this world (by Nathan), and had adapted with unexpected ease to what was, for him, a low-tech, low-magic, quasi-primitive society. He was seven feet tall and a couple of thousand years old, with a long, curving face, wild dark hair and deep purple eyes, and an outlook on life permanently coloured by watching the early *Star Wars* trilogy shortly after his arrival here, and believing it was a factual account of a more civilized past.

Nathan was telling him about his latest dreams, and the mention of the Sword.

'The sword of *stroar*,' Eric affirmed. *Stroar*, Nathan knew, was a metal peculiar to the world of Eos, super-strong and harder than steel – but he always thought of the artifact as the Sword of Straw. 'Is very powerful weapon, but cursed. The first Grandir who made the three – the Cup, the Sword, the Crown – he was killed by friend, best friend, with the sword. His blood filled Cup.' The definite article came and went in Eric's speech. 'He saw it before, with aid of force, but could not avert.'

'Why not?' Nathan wanted to know.

Eric shrugged, a lavish shrug of huge shoulders. 'His fate to die. Must accept fate.'

'Did his friend hate him?'

'I not know. Maybe. The story is old, old even in my world. Details forgotten. Maybe there was a woman.'

'Could it have been a sacrifice?' Nathan suggested. 'Perhaps the first Grandir *ordered* his friend to kill him, to – to empower the three. It could have been a sort of preliminary to the Great Spell – the one the present Grandir has to perform, if he can work it out.'

'Good idea.' Eric brightened. 'Much force in lifeblood. Is new thought, but good. Maybe Grandir not murdered at all.'

'You said once, the sword moved . . . by itself?'

'Is legend, but make-believe illegal in my world, so could be true. Three kept in cave for thousands of years, but last Grandir move them, hide in other worlds, away from people who try to steal them and make Great Spell themselves. So Sangreal in this world, sword and crown –' He made a broad gesture signifying that their whereabouts was open to conjecture.

'Away from the neo-salvationists,' Nathan agreed. 'Like poor Kwanji Ley.'

'But even in other worlds, three need protection,' Eric went on. 'We know last Grandir send gnomons to protect Sangreal.' Nathan shuddered, remembering. 'In one legend, ancient spirit imprisoned in sword so only one person can lift it, or member of one family – Grandir's family. Spirit very powerful, very angry – not like to be trapped in sword. When wrong person touch it, spirit take over, stab him.'

'What kind of spirit is it?' Nathan asked.

'Something very old – from the Beginning, when universe in chaos. Before humans learn to control force, it is free, wild. Many spirits on different planets – some move through space. You would call them – spirits of element? Weather spirits, spirits of water, fire, rock . . .'

'Elementals?' Nathan hazarded. 'We have them here, Uncle Barty told me, but I don't think they're very powerful. He says they're all instinct, no thought.'

Eric nodded enthusiastically. 'But early ones have power. Men get power, fight them, subdue, make them sleep forever, but a few survive, learn to think like humans. Those ones most dangerous. But Grandir stronger than elemental; they say, he fix one in sword, use many spells. So no one can touch sword till right person, right time.'

'The Sword in the Stone,' Nathan said dreamily. 'Except this one is more likely to be the sword in the foot.'

'If you find this thing,' Eric said seriously, 'you not pick it up. I not want you hurt.'

'Maybe I could muffle it in cloth,' Nathan said. 'Or wear gloves.'

'You think people not try that?'

'Yes, I suppose so. Anyway, I may not need to pick it up. I mean, I know I had to find the Grail, but I don't know about this. Perhaps it should stay where it is.'

'Is better, yes.' Eric, who was partial to coffee, got up to make some more.

'Does the legend say anything about a princess?' Nathan inquired cautiously.

'A *princess*? No. Why you ask?'

'Oh, I don't know. There are always princesses in these kind of stories. I thought it would make a change from diabolical spirits and stuff.'

Eric looked at him out of gemstone-bright eyes that were suddenly very shrewd. 'I have bad feeling about this,' he announced.

At tea with Bartlemy, Annie told him about her investigations. 'I don't really think Father Crowley knows anything,' she said, 'but he's awfully perceptive. Actually, he reminds me a bit of you. Only –'

'Thinner?' Bartlemy said.

'Yes.' Annie smiled. 'More like a real wizard.'

Bartlemy laughed. 'And the Hackforths?'

'They just seemed so . . . sad. It's a dreadful situation. I can't believe Giles could be doing anything really evil – he's just suffering.'

'He's vulnerable,' Bartlemy pointed out. 'He could be used.'

'Mm. Selena – his wife – thinks Damon could be possessed. At least – she said he was *like* someone possessed. Is that possible?'

'It depends. Possession is very rare. A spirit can easily inhabit an inanimate object, but to take over a living person, with a soul, that person must invite it in. Like hypnosis: you can't be hypnotized to do anything you wouldn't do of your own free will. Nobody's mind can be controlled by another, magically or otherwise, unless, in some way, they allow it. It's one of the Ultimate Laws, as old as Time. Few people are stupid enough to invite possession.'

'Damon's a teenager,' Annie reminded him. Almost a joke, and wasted without Nathan to object to it.

'Nonetheless . . .'

Bartlemy suggested she stay for supper, and she rang Nathan on his new mobile to tell him to join them. (The phone had been a fourteenth birthday present, on a Pay-As-You-Go deal which he had to fund from his allowance.) Over the meal, Bartlemy steered the conversation back to the Hackforths, and Father Crowley.

'He sees things,' Nathan said. 'Everyone respects him. He knows stuff about all the boys, and nobody can work out *how* he knows it.'

'He certainly seems to know a lot about you,' Bartlemy said thoughtfully. 'Or guess.'

'I can't think where he got that business about me not being

87

there in the night. Ned Gable noticed, but he wouldn't have told anyone else, I know he wouldn't. He's not the tale-telling type.'

'A good headmaster should be omniscient about his pupils,' Bartlemy said.

'The worst thing about all this,' Annie remarked, 'is that you start suspecting everybody, just on the strength of some perfectly innocent inquiry. It's a lot worse than the trouble last year. We have too many clues, and no crime. Well, only a burglary that went wrong. What's the collective noun for clues?'

'Like a gaggle of geese?' Nathan was intrigued. 'How about – a muddle of clues?'

'An entanglement,' Bartlemy said. 'At least for the moment. Have you found out any more about this new world of yours, or would you rather not say?'

'There's a city,' Nathan said, 'called Carboneck, or Wilderslee. I think one's the city and one's the kingdom, but I don't know which is which. Most of the people have left, and the king's an invalid. He picked up the sword, and it bit him – stabbed him, I mean – and now the wound won't heal, and everything's under a curse.'

'Stories don't change,' Bartlemy sighed, 'wherever you are. Does this king have a daughter?'

'How did you guess?'

'They always do.'

Before they left, Nathan remembered to mention Hazel's meeting with Woody, and how he had told her the dwarf was still hanging about. 'He can't get the sword,' Nathan said. 'But he might still be after the Grail, if he knows or suspects you have it.'

'The dwarf is another clue,' Annie said, 'but to what?'

'Some time,' Bartlemy concluded, 'I shall have to talk to

him. When he's hungry enough, he'll come here.'

'He kills rabbits,' Nathan offered, 'but Hazel didn't mention if Woody said he cooked them.'

'I must prepare a wild rabbit stew,' Bartlemy said, 'and leave the kitchen door open. True dwarves have an excellent sense of smell.'

'Perhaps he likes them raw,' Nathan suggested. 'Like Gollum.'

'Gollum never had my cooking,' Bartlemy said tranquilly.

Remembering the omniscience of Father Crowley, Nathan knew he mustn't dream when he was at school. If he didn't let his mind dwell on Carboneck (or Wilderslee), if he focused on maths, history, cricket, if he fell asleep without thinking of the princess, then perhaps nothing would happen. But maths was sines and co-sines, which bored him, and history was the agricultural revolution (dull), and even cricket allowed too much time for his thoughts to wander in the wrong direction. And in bed, with the lights out, when there was nothing to get in the way, the princess's image rose up before him – not the most beautiful of women, he knew that, but somehow irresistible, if only to him. His memory of her was elusive, details came and went, he could never quite form a complete picture, but that simply made her more tantalizing, more enchanting, more special. He wasn't in love with her – well, not very much – but he knew he had to help her, and even the Traitor's Sword seemed only an adjunct to her story.

Inevitably, when the dream carried him back to Carboneck, he realized at once that he was in trouble.

He was visible. Not a solid being but a misty, ghost-like creature who would have to hide from general sight, more substantial than he had been in Frimbolus' workroom but still far from real. And of course, he was wearing pyjamas

– the curse of travellers in other worlds, from the children who followed Peter Pan into Neverland, to Arthur Dent on his galactic voyages. He wasn't particularly fashion-minded but he *really* didn't want to meet the princess for the first time as a pyjama-clad spectre. 'I am the ghost of Christmas Past,' he said to himself with a sigh, surveying hazy legs in trousers that were just too short. He was in an alleyway, it was twilight, and at least there was no one about. He began to walk uphill, hoping he was headed for the royal house.

After about twenty yards he found himself crossing a wider street, with light spilling from a half-open door a little way in front. A boy and a girl were standing in the light, deep in talk. The boy was maybe a couple of years older than Nathan, with lank black hair, a very thin face, and sombre shadows under his eyes.

The girl was Princess Nellwyn.

Nathan got as near as he dared, hoping he blended with the softness of dusk, before slipping into the lee of a wall.

'You shouldn't have come,' the boy was saying. 'It gets dark early; there may be demons out.'

'I'm not afraid of them,' Nell said staunchly. 'Anyway, I had to.'

'We could've collected the physic in the morning –'

'Bronlee needs it now. I saw how ill she is. Frim – Dr Quayne – said she should have the first dose tonight. It'll bring the fever down and help her sleep without the delirium.'

'I'm grateful,' the boy said, sounding curiously reluctant. 'Very grateful. But you shouldn't have taken the risk . . . I'll take you home.' Nathan thought he didn't sound especially keen, though the distance couldn't be far and Nell's company was surely desirable.

'This is my city,' the princess said. 'Nothing can hurt me here. Don't you remember I'm a witch?'

'Mud pies into chocolate,' the boy grinned. 'I remember.' And suddenly Nathan realized he was the same one who had taunted her in the garden, when they were both much younger.

'I can turn a nightscreech into a heartsong, and Urulation into a lullaby,' she declared. 'You needn't look after me, but *I* might look after *you*. If you insist on tagging along . . .'

He hesitated, but courage or courtesy won out. 'Wait a moment,' he said shortly. 'I'm coming.'

He went inside, reappearing a few minutes later wearing a cloak with the hood thrown back and carrying a staff or walking stick with a spiked tip and a solid metal knob by way of a handle.

'It's all right, Rosh,' Nell said, eying the stick dubiously. 'I think . . . I'd be better alone.'

He ignored this, and they set off up the road together with Nathan following, keeping to the shadows. His progress was complicated by the fact that Rosh in particular looked round frequently and once grabbed Nell's arm, telling her, in an urgent voice: 'There's something there!' However, when questioned, he couldn't say what, or who, and Nathan, ducked into the slot between two houses, took care not to show himself. After that he was more cautious, staying well back from the pair, though it meant he couldn't hear what they were saying. But he didn't think they said much. The empty silence of the city was overpowering, swallowing some sounds, magnifying others, the kind of silence where you felt you were living in an echo chamber, and if you burped, or breathed too loud, or thought too loud, the silence would hear you.

They stopped a few yards from the palace gate. It was much darker now, a deep blue evening like a Dulac painting, with a single lantern burning outside the wall; it's yellow glimmer might have been the only light in the city. The countless vacant houses changed with the growing night, becoming mysterious, crowded with shadows and potential. Nathan felt uneasy at the idea of those dark spaces waiting and watching behind him. But close to the light, the two he followed seemed relieved. He heard a murmur of words, saw Rosh, apparently on impulse, seize the princess in a clumsy embrace, still clutching his stick, pressed against her back. Nell gave a yelp of surprise, and then Rosh bent his head and kissed her.

He was flung back so violently, and with such force, he seemed to fly through the air, ending on the ground some yards away. A glitter of sparks in his wake betrayed the magic in Nell's thrust. 'Roshan!' she cried, panting slightly. 'How dare you! I mean, how – how *could* you? We're supposed to be *friends* – I've known you all my life –'

He was trying to stand up, hampered by his cloak, which appeared to have become twisted in his fall. 'Friends grow up,' he said, with a huff in his voice. 'Things change. That's how it's supposed to be.'

'Imbecile!' said the princess. 'Not between us. Have I ever said anything's changed?'

'You're a girl – you're quite pretty – well, not bad – and . . .'

'So you kissed me because suddenly you've noticed I'm a girl and I'm *quite pretty*?'

'Um . . . no . . . er, sort of . . .'

Wrong answer, thought Nathan, with a certain malicious satisfaction. *All* the wrong answers.

The princess was well away into a savage denunciation of Roshan's manners (lack of) and intelligence (ditto) when Nathan became aware of something else. A soft, slithery noise from further down the street – a noise with undertones of squelch and a suggestion of weightiness – a thickening in the darkness there – the impression of something large and bulky heaving itself slowly towards them. The watchful silence of the city altered, focusing on the unseen approach. Rosh and the princess were still arguing, oblivious to what was coming. *You used magic*, Nathan was thinking. *The Urdemons come when you use magic* –

He wanted to shout a warning but somehow his voice stuck in his throat.

Then they saw. It drew nearer to the light, humping itself awkwardly across the ground, a dim slug-shape with a head – or where a head should be – rearing up to six feet or more, dragging behind the dark gelatinous mass of its body. It had no face or eyes, but a mouth-hole gaped suddenly, jagged with teeth, and the light shone down the endless tunnel of its gorge. Rosh picked up his fallen staff and pointed the spiked end, perhaps unaware that he was backing away. The princess stood stiffly in its path. She didn't move – perhaps she couldn't. Nathan looked round for a weapon, but there was nothing to hand, and he was probably too insubstantial to hold one. Briefly, he noticed that he was glowing faintly in the presence of magic as he had done in Frimbolus' work-room. He thought: *I'm dreaming. I'm not solid. If the worst happens, I'll wake up.*

Then he ran out in front of the princess.

He heard a gasp which might have come from Nell, but he wasn't looking at her. The Urdemon towered above him like a giant bloated worm, its ragged maw stretching wider, wider . . . A sound came from it like the roar of a hurricane, like the shrieking of a hundred banshees – the Urulation. Nathan clapped his hands over his ears. The mouth came swooping down towards him, jaws distended to swallow him whole. This was a moment when you needed an elvish star-glass, and words like *Elbereth! Gilthoniel!* – but the only such words he knew were those he had heard his uncle utter, long before, to dismiss a spirit from the magic circle. He took his hands from his ears and reached out as though pushing the monster away: they shone pale and transparent against the blackness of its gape. '*Vardé*!' he cried, in the language of spellpower. '*Envarré*! By the cup and the sword and the crown, begone!' His voice sounded different from usual, clear and strange, like a voice from another plane, another world.

There was a horrible moment when he thought nothing would happen.

Then the Urdemon flinched as if from a sudden cold, its body arched backward – shuddered – and the whole towering mass began to collapse like a blancmange in an earthquake, quivering, flailing blindly from side to side, dissolving inward with a series of hideous glooping, gurgling noises, until there was nothing left but a viscous black puddle which shrank and shrank to the size of a droplet. A bubble heaved, burst with a tiny plop! – and it was gone.

Nathan, turning, saw the princess staring at him as if he were a ghost – which of course he was. She was obviously frightened, but she managed a smile, her lips moving on a phrase – probably *thank you*. But just when he wanted it most the dream was leaving him, slipping away, and all the princess would see was a phantom in pyjamas too small for him who faded into the gloom without a word, leaving her alone in the dark with Rosh . . .

Nathan was flung back into his own world so rapidly he woke with a jerk, starting up in bed and looking wildly round as though he expected the princess – or the Urdemon – to be there still. But the dormitory was dark, and everyone slept, and he lay down again with his heart pounding and his head in a tailspin.

It was some time before he could sleep again.

FOUR

A Feast of Slugs

Bartlemy spent much of that week reflecting on the dietary habits of dwarves. They were meat-eaters by repute; in fact, it was said they would eat animals no other intelligent lifeform would touch, including weasel, rat, water-vole, badger – the whole cast of *Wind in the Willows*, Bartlemy thought – lizard, and toad. The rarity of certain types of newt in the British Isles was attributable to the number of indigent true dwarves who survived here until the late Middle Ages, according to some Gifted historians. They didn't enjoy fish or greens, but ate root vegetables like potato, swede, and carrot (all dwarves have good darksight, which may be the origin of the popular myth about carrots) and used wild herbs for flavouring. They were not fond of fruit but liked nuts and honey, and – rumour again – made various kinds of bread more remarkable for toughness and durability than appetizing breadness.

In between periods of reflection, Bartlemy cooked. He cooked with the window open, and the kitchen door, sending delicious smells wafting across the garden towards the woods – smells of potatoes roasting, or baking in their jackets, and onions softening in butter, and venison stewing in wine, and wood pigeons in honey, and wild rabbit with prunes, and stuffed dormice, and other unusual ingredients which had not found themselves on the menu since the days of ancient Rome. Sometimes, he glimpsed eyes watching from the bushes, dark strange eyes with no whites – the eyes of the werepeople – but he never tried to ensnare the watcher, merely waiting for him to emerge, whenever he was ready. Hoover (and Annie) dined on exotic leftovers, but the dwarf did not come.

On Saturday Nathan and Annie came to supper (what they ate they weren't sure and didn't like to ask, but it tasted wonderful), and Nathan told his mother and uncle about the Urdemon.

'Do you have to be so reckless?' Annie demanded, feeling proud and terrified in equal measure.

'Interesting,' Bartlemy commented, as always. 'Clearly, the creature – like you – wasn't fully substantial. The two of you met on the same plane – and words of power seem to work anywhere. The language of magic is multiversal. Even so, you aren't Gifted in that way, so . . . Someone or something looks after you, as I've said before.' Nathan looked a little crestfallen, but Bartlemy concluded: 'That doesn't diminish your courage in confronting the thing, you know.'

'Just don't *rely* on supernatural protection, for God's sake,' Annie said. 'It may not be there next time.'

'The Urdemons turn up when the princess does bits of magic,' Nathan went on, 'but I can't believe she's summoning them. I thought it might have something to do with the sword. Supposing they guard it, like the gnomons guarded the Grail?'

'I should have thought that was unlikely,' Bartlemy said. 'These Urdemons appear to be native to . . . Wilderslee, did you call it? The sword – if it is the one we want – comes from Eos. And it has its own inhabitant, remember, or so they say. Of course, if whatever dwells in the sword is a spirit of similar type, then the Urdemons might well be drawn to it. But it would have to have a very potent aura indeed to wield such a powerful attraction.'

'Eric said the thing in the sword was an elemental, primitive but very powerful. The Grandir imprisoned it there by magic, a long time ago.'

Bartlemy considered this. 'The Urdemons, too, would appear to be elementals, chaos spirits who have no real form of their own but borrow the attributes of beasts, birds, weather, even humans, depending on their mood. However, even if they *are* drawn to the demon of the sword, you said they only appeared in the princess's lifetime, which makes them fairly recent arrivals. A summons is indicated, and for a summons, there must be a summoner.'

'The princess would never –'

'I didn't say it *was* the princess. She could be an unwitting catalyst. Whoever called them might have bound them to her without her knowledge.'

'That's *wicked*,' Nathan said, using the word in its literal sense. 'She feels so guilty . . .'

'You know how she feels, do you?' Bartlemy's innocent blue gaze held the suspicion of a twinkle.

'I – yes.' Nathan missed it. 'Who would do that? Could it – could it be the Grandir?'

'Difficult. A spell of that kind would require something belonging to the princess – a shoe, a glove, best of all, a lock of hair – and that would be hard for him to obtain. Besides, what motive could he have? The sword already has a guardian. The object of this seems to be to empty the city and isolate the king – possibly to obtain the sword. After all, many people were after the Grail – and the sword, too, is a thing of great power.'

'First we have an entanglement of clues,' Nathan said. 'Now, it's a – what's the collective noun for villains?'

'Think of one,' said Bartlemy.

'A congregation,' Annie suggested, her mind running on clerical matters since her encounter with Father Crowley.

'Cynical,' Bartlemy murmured.

'A slugfest,' Nathan said. 'How do you like that? A slugfest of villains.'

'What's a slugfest?' Annie asked. 'A feast of slugs?'

'I suppose so. It's a good word for villains, anyway.'

Annie turned back to Bartlemy. 'Have we come to any conclusions?' she said.

'One or two,' Bartlemy said. 'A smatter of conclusions, if we're collecting collectives.' He was looking very pensive.

When Annie and Nathan had left he found a bowl, filled it with beer, and put it out in the garden. A couple of bits of plank made a gangway up to the rim. The following day he collected the contents, marinaded them for a further twenty-four hours in a concoction including some of his rarer herbs, and on the next evening he was ready. He fried them in a light batter, spiced and seasoned according to a recipe long forgotten, and left the results in a bowl on the kitchen table, covered with a cloth. Then he went into the living room and sat for a while, sipping a glass of his favourite dark red liquor. No noise came from the kitchen that a human might hear, even a Gifted human, but when Hoover cocked his ears Bartlemy got up. For all his size he could move as quietly as a cat. He went to the kitchen door and looked in.

The dwarf was there. He was eating, not greedily, as might have been expected, after long incarceration and subsequently living wild, but slowly, savouring the delicacy. He had seated himself on a convenient stool which put him at the right height for the kitchen table; Bartlemy had left it there deliberately. He was very hairy, with barely a sliver of forehead squeezed in above his eyebrows and a beard that sprouted, like whiskers, on either side of his nose, spreading across his cheeks and bristling out from his jaw. It was a black beard, streaked grey with age and green from his outdoor existence. The hair on his head stuck up in spikes, gelled with mud or sweat or a combination of both. His clothing was so patched and re-patched, so mossed and grimed, it was hardly recognizable as clothing at all. He smelt something like a fox, and something like a badger, and a lot like a dwarf who hadn't taken a bath for several centuries.

Bartlemy smiled at him, but his visitor looked as if he didn't remember what smiles were for. 'Would you like a beer?'

There were two tankards on the table, a bottle placed nearby. Bartlemy poured, and drank from one of the tankards. Presently, the dwarf pounced on the other and drank too.

'You are welcome to my house,' Bartlemy said formally.

The dwarf gave an abrupt nod. After a minute or two, he seemed to recall the right response. 'Thank 'ee.' His voice was a guttural croak, rusted from lack of use, his accent ancient and strange.

Bartlemy waited, drinking his beer, while the other continued to eat. Eventually the dwarf spoke again. 'It's an age and an age since I ha' tasted that dishy. Comes good, to taste it agin. A mem'ry of home.'

'Where was home?' Bartlemy asked.

'Long gone. My people – long gone. How long? How long since the old spellcracker shut me up?'

'About fourteen hundred years.'

The dwarf stopped eating and sat for a while in a sort of frozen stillness. 'Evil,' he said. 'He was evil, and all his works. He would talk to me like a friend – he didna ha' too many o' those – but he bound me like a slave. I was ne'er free to leave, and when I told him . . . He wa' messing in other worlds, d'ye ken? No the magic places here but *other worlds*, beyond the Gate, beyond the Margin o' Being. D'ye ken?'

'Aye,' said Bartlemy, slipping absent-mindedly into the lingo of the past.

'May the Dark have him!'

'It has. He died in a fire, when his house burned to the ground. It must have been about the time he imprisoned you.'

The dwarf cackled suddenly. 'I set the fire!' he declared. 'I took the cup, d'ye see? It was a cursed thing, full o' blood though none had done the bleeding, and I took it to be done with it, but he caught me and buried me in the ground, buried me alive wi' locks and bars and cantrips to keep me there. He'd put out the fire wi' a Command, but water's better nor magic for that, and fire's a creepy, sneaky creature. Ye think it's dead but it's still breathing. Wants only a draught and a spark. I hope he died screaming.'

'Probably,' said Bartlemy.

The dwarf returned to his dinner. 'O' course,' he remarked, 'if the Magister had lived, he might ha' let me out. He wasna pity-full, but he needed me. Or he might ha' left me there. The spells rotted, but iron held me. I couldna dig. It was a long dark while just for sleeping and thinking . . . That boy, what does he want wi' the cup? What do they all want wi' it? It's accursed, evil. You tell them.'

'Why is it cursed? Did the Magister tell you about it?'

'Listen . . . The Gate is for mortal men, not for the likes o' me. Ye ha' the Gift, I ken, so ye know. Werefolk don't die like men, we sleep, we wither, but we canna pass through, and men shouldna, until their time. Then there's no returning, or none that we wot of. But the Magister, he got the cup from someone on the *other side*, d'ye see? That's power, deadly power, and when I saw it first, it were blood to the brim, and we all know the meaning of that.'

'The strongest spells use blood . . .'

'Aye, and it were a spell – a spell to open the Gate, to bring two worlds thegither. I wouldna be part of it. There are barriers ne'er meant to be broken: it's a forbidden thing. We ha' world enough here to keep us all. But now . . . I'm fourteen centuries out o' my time. No folk left, no Magister . . .' He shivered, half missing the master who had subjugated him. Even slavery can be a safe familiar thing.

'I meant what I said,' Bartlemy reiterated. 'You are welcome to my house. My name is Bartlemy Goodman. Will you tell me yours?'

'Thank 'ee, Magister Goodman. I am Login Nambrok. I must go, I'm thinking, but . . . this is a rare kitchen ye keep here. I ha' forgot how good food noses, when it's cooked right well.'

'Come again,' Bartlemy said. 'The door is always open.'

The dwarf got to his feet, leaving an empty dish. 'One sma' thing,' he said. 'Wi' those fatworms –'

'Yes?'

'A wee tippit more salt?'

Nathan was more eager than ever to see the princess again, hoping that this time – despite the risks – he would find himself rather more solid, existing on her plane instead of the Urdemon's. But he didn't dream on Friday or Saturday, and by Sunday night he was growing desperate. Though his dream-journey at school that week had had no awkward consequences the idea of midnight dematerialization in the dormitory was always hazardous, and he had been hoping to dream at home. He didn't like consciously reaching for the portal – it never worked out the way he wanted – but he felt he had no choice. In bed he closed his eyes and turned his mindsight inward, roaming the dim canyons inside his head until he found the place where everything blurred, a patch of wrongness on the walls of his very self. He focused his thought there, pushing his way into a barrier of nothingness – and then there was the tunnel through space, the planetscapes wheeling away from him, the distant swirl of stars. He arrived – unusually – with no sense of impact, but almost immediately he realized why. He wasn't solid or even ghost-like, merely an awareness moving through the gloom of an unfamiliar place. It didn't look like Arkatron or Carboneck, or anywhere he had been before. It was just darkness, with the dim curves of walls, hollows and openings gaping and closing around him. I'm underground, he guessed, but not in a building, nor in the desert cave on Eos where the Grail had once been concealed. Man-made caves, perhaps. A troglodyte colony . . . Then there was light ahead of him and he emerged into what seemed to be a vast natural cavern.

The vault of the roof soared far above, dripping with stalactites, pale green and faintly luminous, pointing downwards like a thousand spears. They were mirrored in a wide pool which stretched down the centre of the cavern; beyond, the walls were coved and ribbed, folded and fluted into fantastic sculptures, lit by pale lamps glowing through thin veils of stone. At one point the wall drew close to the pool, and there was an archway into a lesser chamber, through which Nathan could see a huge rock with a flattened top, like an anvil, and the orange smoulder of a fire in a brazier. A man was working there, a giant of a man – Nathan had no standards of comparison, but somehow the man's giantness was obvious – wearing the sort of clothing that might have been protective or merely ornamental, all layered leather and rippling mesh. He had the lean curving features of an Eosian, with a jutting hook of a nose, jagged cheekbones, and eyes glittering darkly under hooded lid and craggy brow. The man was honing a piece of the same greenish stone as the stalactites, shaping and polishing it using some sort of automatic chisel. The tool glowed blue at the tip and emitted a faint humming noise; sparks trailed from it as it travelled over the stone. *It's the Grail*, Nathan thought. This is the first Grandir, and he's making the Grimthorn Grail. Nathan's dreams had often jumped about in time, but he had never been carried so far into the past. But it isn't *my* past, he reflected; it's theirs. Now, it's my present. A teacher at his school had said Time was like a vast level plain, and we were moving across it, on a road with no turnings to right or left, no going back. But when you blunder into an alternative universe you could wind up anywhere on the plain, anywhere on the road. This wasn't what Nathan had hoped to find, but he forgot other considerations in fascination at the Grandir's task.

He used several chisels to carve the snake-patterns round the rim of the cup, each with a different-coloured glow, a different pitch of hum. Nathan had no idea how long it took – perhaps days, or even weeks – he was too busy concentrating on the process, watching the skill of the craftsman-wizard with complete absorption. When the cup was finished he placed it on the anvil and spoke in a clear, cold voice, words Nathan could not understand, yet he knew they were words of power. The Grandir drew a circle round the cup and enclosed it in a cone of flame, chanting all the time, and lights strobed over it, and there were whisperings, and mutterings, and a dark smoke whirled around it and was sucked into the very stone. The Grail changed, becoming opaque, and the fires and lights vanished, and the whispers were stilled, and it stood alone on the anvil, a cold, inanimate thing. The Grandir picked it up, carried it to the pool, and bent down to dip it in the water. When he lifted it, the cup was full to the brim, but the water inside had turned red.

The vision shifted, cavern blurring into cavern. Time must have passed, though Nathan had no idea how much. Now the wizard was working on the sword, beating out the metal, which was a silvery colour with a strange bluish lustre. *Stroar*, Nathan thought, wondering if it was an element, like iron, or a compound, like steel. Eric had told him once it was the strongest metal and could be tempered until it was sharp enough to slice through a hair on water. The Grandir had acquired a huge stone wheel which seemed to turn automatically, and he used it to refine the blade, while fire-flecks spurted and the grating of metal on rock made Nathan's teeth ache. The Grandir paused every so often to test the edge on his finger, drawing blood, but it was a long while before he was satisfied. Then he laid it on the anvil and performed the magic rituals, only this time the flames danced up and down the blade, turning from orange to blue, from blue to white, and were drawn into the metal, until the sword itself was flame. This time the mutterings had a tinny sound, and rose to a shrill crescendo, becoming the hiss of rapiers that cut the air, the scream of weapon on weapon. There was something wicked in the chorus, a kind of glee, like the voice of a thousand swords, crying out: *You made us to kill. We kill. With or without you, we kill.* The Traitor's Sword, Nathan thought – the Sword of Straw. He hadn't seen the elemental being imprisoned in the blade – it was the last Grandir, not the first, who had done that – but the sword had been from its forging blood-hungry, spellbound to kill.

When it was ready the Grandir took it and dipped it in the pool, and the drops that ran from the blade were dark as rubies, uncoiling into a dull stain on the surface of the water.

The scene changed. Nathan's consciousness seemed to flick into darkness for a moment, re-emerging at a later point in time, and in a slightly different part of the cavern. He was close to the anvil, watching the Grandir placing an iron circlet there, held in a pair of tongs and glowing orange from the smelting. It was shaped like a conventional crown, but the Grandir began to beat out the points, turning them into multiple spikes which he bent and twisted into a form that appeared random, though Nathan was certain there was a specific purpose in the design. He was reminded of the serpentine incisions round the cup, only this pattern was spikier, adorned with thorn-tips which the sorcerer chiselled to needle-sharpness. An iron crown, Nathan said to himself, a crown of thorns. *A crown of thorns . . .* It shone ice-blue in the magic, and shadows from every corner of the cavern were drawn into it. The Grandir lowered it into the pool with the tongs, and the water hissed and steamed around it. When he lifted it out it was cool. He placed it on his own head, and blood ran down his face from the thorn-tips, though Nathan didn't think they cut his skin.

Another man came into the cavern, a man only a little less tall than the Grandir, with a physiognomy in whose narrow curves there was a trace of what might have been cruelty. His expression changed when he saw the crown.

'What have you done?' he demanded. 'Romandos –'

'Do not use my name so carelessly, even here.' Their speech sounded faintly archaic to Nathan's ear. 'Who let you in?'

'The guards know I am your friend; they would not refuse me. But – that monstrosity you've made – a parody of the crown of ancient kings . . .'

'No parody,' said the Grandir. 'The first rulers of empire wore a wreath made from the thorn-trees of Callidor, to show they were strong to bear pain and the burden of leadership. Only later did the crown become a thing of mere beauty, a symbol of power and vanity. This is a true crown: iron to repel evil spirits, thorn-twined in the form of the king-wreaths of old. You cannot make a Great Spell with a common ornament.

Great Spells are woven from truth, and pain, and blood.'

'Lifeblood . . .' said the other, and Nathan wondered if his dark pallor was fear, or eagerness, or a little of both.

'Indeed, but not yet. All I know is merely a foreseeing. The time will come – maybe in a thousand years, maybe in a hundred thousand – but it *will* come. The sacrifice is preordained. Our universe cannot endure forever. The Great Spell will transform the very cosmos –'

'The sacrifice,' the other repeated. 'It is expedient for us that one man should die for the people.'

Nathan thought he had heard that phrase used somewhere before, and wondered if it was multiversal.

'One man must die to save the world. It is always the way.'

'And he who performs that Spell will wield unimaginable power . . .' Nathan could almost hear him thinking, the wheels turning in his head.

'And bear unimaginable responsibility.' The Grandir removed the crown, replacing it on the anvil. 'Whoever he is, he must go into the Spell with a heart of ice and a will of iron, or it will destroy him. The corrupt cannot perform such magics. Remember that, Lugair.'

'Real power is for the chosen few,' Lugair murmured, but he looked sideways at the Grandir out of narrowed eyes.

'This is the last of three,' Romandos continued. 'They will be kept safe all down the ages, until the hour of doom. It is fated. When the end draws near, the three will be united in the circle of power, and the blood of the Grandir will release the Spell.'

'So the Grandir – the last Grandir – will be the sacrifice?'

'I did not say so. I said the *blood* of the Grandir, not his life.'

'But only lifeblood can activate a Great Spell. That we all know.' Lugair was frowning.

'The answer will become clear, in time. There are many things even I cannot discern for now. Foresight gives you only a glimpse of the road ahead.'

'I see,' said Lugair, and once again he gave Romandos that sidelong look, which made his face slanted and sly.

Nathan had become so absorbed, he had forgotten he was dreaming, forgotten that, though invisible and intangible, he was a part of the scene. Suddenly he noticed he was floating over the pool, and below him the surface was broken by spreading ripples, as if his unseen essence had disturbed the water. He hoped no one would perceive the phenomenon, but the Grandir had turned to stare intently in his direction, and then he lifted his hand and spoke a word of Command. A lance of darkness stabbed towards Nathan, catching him in the chest like a punch from a fist of steel – hurling him across the barrier between worlds, out of the dream, out of time . . .

He was lying in his own bed, winded, gasping, feeling rather sick. It took some while to wear off.

Back at school, Nathan was increasingly aware of Damon Hackforth, elbowing him in the corridors, watching him from the edge of the cricket pitch or behind the wire around the tennis court. The older boy was good-looking in a sullen sort of way which went down well with susceptible girls, but Nathan was increasingly troubled by his aura of suppressed violence and the obsession in his gaze. Even Ned Gable remarked on it. 'Don't know why he's so interested in you,' he said as they finished batting for the afternoon and went in for tea. 'He always seems to be around lately, staring at you in that broody way. You don't think he's keen on you or something, do you?'

''Course not,' Nathan responded. 'He's not gay. Anyway, he doesn't look at me like that.'

'Mm. Looks sort of menacing, if you ask me. Maybe he's got a fixation on you.'

'What kind of fixation?'

'Like . . . you're really clever, you're great at sport, you don't have a sister whom everyone thinks is wonderful. Maybe you're the person he wants to be.' This was deep thinking for Ned, who had been much impressed by a programme on Freud which the class had seen recently. 'Like, you're his – his alter ego. You've got the talent and the personality that he thinks he should have. You're his *him*.'

'That's idiotic. I'm four years younger. Nobody could be that stupid.'

'Your being younger might make it worse for him,' Ned said profoundly. 'More galling.'

Nathan dismissed the notion, but later that week he was emerging from the library after some research for history when he found himself face to face with Damon. It was nearly suppertime and he was late, and suddenly there seemed to be no one near them. The library door swung shut; its only occupants were far away beyond the hush of book-laden shelves. If Nathan called out, he wasn't sure they would hear. The empty corridor stretched away towards distant windows filled with evening sunshine. The other boys must be already in the dining room: there were no footsteps in hallway or classroom, no scurrying down the adjacent stair. The whole abbey was mysteriously transformed into a place almost as vacant and as quiet as the dead city.

And in the midst of the quiet Damon Hackforth stood there with a look of ugly satisfaction on his face. There was malice in that look, and hatred, and a sort of gloating because he had caught Nathan alone at last, and he was bigger and stronger, and there was no one at hand to intervene.

He wouldn't really hurt me . . . would he? Nathan thought. He wouldn't really be that dumb . . .

But Damon didn't look as though intelligent thinking was a factor in his life at that moment.

'The wonderboy,' he said. 'The scholarship kid who thinks he's smarter than everyone else. I've been watching you: you know that? Fancy yourself, don't you? Shane Warne on the cricket pitch, Federer on the tennis court – and then you're back in the library like a good little swot. Little swot, piece of snot . . . A jumped-up Paki brat thinking you can outdo your betters –'

'For heaven's sake,' Nathan reacted without reflection, 'not that old-fashioned race-and-class stuff. That's *antique*.'

Damon's hand shot out, lightning-fast, seizing him by the throat.

'Don't you *dare* talk back at me! I'm older than you – I'm better than you – I'm *worse* than you. Do you understand? You're the good boy, I'm the bad boy. In the real world, good boys always lose.' (Which real world? Nathan wondered, in a tiny detached corner of his mind. *Probably all of them* . . .) 'Go on, squirm. Squirm like a rabbit. You can't get free. Soon, you'll whine and whimper like the pathetic piece of *nothing* you really are. The others'll see you: no more wonderboy – no more Shane Warne, no more Federer – just a snivelling little rabbit. I'm going to make you *cry*, Nathan Ward.'

'Crying doesn't matter.' Nathan's voice was hoarse from the grip on his windpipe. 'Only people who are too heartless or too thick never cry.'

He knew he was afraid – he could feel the cold tension of it in his limbs – but under the fear he was thinking, thinking. *He's broader and heavier than me, but not much taller – only an inch or so. He's awfully fast – but so am I. Could I break that neck hold?*

Damon was laughing – the laughter of someone whose idea of a joke is another person's pain. 'New Men cry: is that it?' he jeered. 'You'll still be the wonderboy – you'll still be the hero – even when I've reduced you to a sobbing jelly. Why don't we find out?'

The blow took Nathan in the stomach. He was against the wall – he couldn't dodge or move with it. His body tried to double over even as he struck out at Damon's other arm with his left hand while his right managed a hit on the advancing chin. Then everything became very muddled. He'd been in a few fights before but both muscles and brain seemed to know instinctively what to do. Concentrate on punching your opponent in his weak spots – don't notice the blows you take yourself. The knack is to tap into that forgotten core of anger, not the anger of the mind but the rage of blood and bone, the generic rage left over from the first cornered beast, the first hunted thing to turn and fight against impossible odds . . . Nathan was fourteen against eighteen, lighter and slighter than Damon, but he was fit and focused, strong for his age. Baffled by a fightback he hadn't expected, Damon grew more vicious, hitting wildly, desperate to hurt, to punish, to crush even as he felt himself losing his edge.

It was over very quickly. Suddenly there were people there, hands pulling them apart, the stern voice of Father Crowley admonishing them. Nathan didn't feel his bruises twingeing until he moved, but he saw the blood running from Damon's nose and the swelling of his lower lip. He tried not to be too pleased about it. Later, he found his mouth, too, was split, though he couldn't remember the blow.

'Are you going to tell me what happened?' Father Crowley asked, in the private sanctum of his study.

'I can't,' Nathan said, uncomfortably. He liked and respected the abbot and didn't want to let him down.

'Of course not. The moral code of all schoolboys – the eleventh commandment. Thou shalt not tell tales. Among adults, that rule only operates in the gangster world. Interesting, isn't it? The Italians call it *omertà*; it protected the Mafia for centuries. You might want to think about that.'

'Will I be expelled?' Nathan asked, imagining Annie's reaction. His status as a scholarship boy had never been mentioned except by Damon, but he knew it made him vulnerable. He had to be, not just the best at study and sport, but the best-behaved, in order to justify it.

'No. Not this time.' Father Crowley looked grave, as befitted a headmaster under the circumstances. 'You have no record of fighting, whereas Damon . . . Well. Enough said. I will talk to him when the infirmary have finished patching him up. You seem to have given a very good account of yourself.' Was there a glimmer of approval behind his gravitas?

Nathan hesitated, then said: 'Can I ask you something?'

The abbot's eyebrows lofted.

'How did you get there so fast? One minute there was nobody about, then – there you were. I . . . sorry. I was just wondering . . .'

'You do a lot of wondering, don't you?' The glint in the keen eyes might have been amusement. 'I gather you are known for it in class. The boy who always asks questions, when everyone else has nodded off. Keep wondering: it's healthy. As for me . . . I make it my business to know everything that goes on in this abbey.' There was an echo of Bartlemy in the words. 'Remember that, next time you contemplate getting into a fight.'

Nathan nodded mutely, thinking: *He still didn't tell me . . .*

'Now, seat yourself in that armchair, and I will have someone bring you a cup of hot chocolate. You don't appear to be badly hurt but your body needs sugar after physical and emotional trauma. Perhaps a teaspoonful of cognac would not be excessive.'

'Thank you,' Nathan gasped, astonished and pleased. The chair in question was deep and comfortable, the hot chocolate, when it arrived, rich and brandy-flavoured and subtly spiced. A palate trained by Bartlemy detected cinnamon and possibly nutmeg, though he thought there was something else as well, something he couldn't identify. They really are alike, he mused, meaning the abbot and his uncle. They ought to meet some time. Father Crowley had left him alone and the drink made him feel warm and drowsy. Heavy curtains shut out the night; a log smouldered in the grate, touching the room with the flicker of firelight. Nathan was aware he had missed supper and it must be nearly bedtime, but he didn't think he should leave without permission. Inevitably, he dozed off.

When he opened his eyes, it took him a few moments to work out where he was. Of course – Father Crowley's study, with the night shut outside and the flame-flicker on the walls. But the fire was too bright, roaring away in an open stove, the room too large and too hot, the windows uncurtained against the dark. The pulsing firelight and the glow from a couple of hanging lamps was reflected in the sides of copper-bellied pots, in suspended cauldrons and vast ceramic tureens, all long unused and unscoured, tarnished green with age or black with the grime of kitchen smokes and steams. There were potagers which could have supplied whole banquets with soup, racks of knives in every size, from the toothpick to the hatchet, dressers filled with teetering plate-stacks and the dull sheen of unpolished silver. But there was little food around, and the only aroma of cooking came from a small pan on top of the stove in which something bubbled sluggishly. Mrs Prendergoose, enveloped in a large apron, was sawing crookedly at the hulk of a loaf. The princess, her disorderly locks tied back with a strip of velvet, paced up and down in a restless manner which surely couldn't come from simple hunger, and Frimbolus Quayne peered critically into the pan, his fluffy hair quivering in the heat of the oven-draught. Nathan, lurking in a corner, felt both solid and visible.

I shouldn't be here, he thought. I'm at school, I'm in the abbot's study. If he comes back . . .

But at least he wasn't wearing pyjamas.

'How *can* he be worse?' Nell was saying. 'The honey's helping – you said so. Kern Twymoor went all the way to the Deepwoods for it. He got it from a wild bees' nest near the lavender fields, just like you asked. He swore to me it was pure –'

'Nothing wrong with the honey,' Frimbolus said. 'Everything wrong with his diet. Call this broth! It even *smells* watery. Here, woman –' to Mrs Prendergoose '– let me spice it up a little.'

'It's good and healthful. If it was too thick he wouldn't get it down. I'm not having you adding them hot peppers to it!'

'At least they'll wake him up! Don't worry, Nell: it's probably just a touch of the grippe. He needs better food to build up his strength, such as it is. You too.'

The nurse bridled. 'If you can tell me where we'll get it –!'

'There's some cured venison from the last hunt,' Nell offered.

'Too rich for the king.'

'Potherguffle!' snapped Frimbolus. 'He needs too rich. Better than too poor. Take me to the pantry, Prendergoose; show me what you're hiding. I bet you've got a secret store big enough to fatten up an army.'

'I have to plan for the winter –'

'It *is* winter, flubberbrain. Spring isn't due for a month.'

'I meant *next* winter . . .'

He herded her out with much argument and flapping of hands while Nell turned back to the pan, sniffing gingerly and adding something from a small jar. Nathan stepped out of his corner and came to look over her shoulder. Thinking of the smells that permeated Bartlemy's kitchen, he remarked: 'It isn't very appetizing, is it?'

She jumped, dropping the jar. Nathan, with a speed honed on the cricket pitch, fielded it neatly – a memory that would later give him more satisfaction than his confrontation with the Urdemon.

'Who – who are you?'

'I tried to help you, the other day, with that demon thing.' It couldn't be too long ago.

'You were a ghost – I could see right through you – and you *shone*.' She touched his arm, sending a strange warm shiver through him. 'You're . . . *normal* now.'

Nathan held out the herb jar, fishing for something to say, unnerved to find himself at a loss. He'd spent so much time longing to be able to talk to her – he'd never been tongue-tied in his life – yet now, all he could think about was the soup.

'Your nurse isn't much of a cook, is she?'

'She does her best.' Nell's tone was chilly. Evidently the right to criticize was reserved. 'How do you know she's my nurse? Who *are* you? How did you get here – in my kitchen?'

'My name's Nathan.' The easiest question first. 'I know you're Nell. I mean, you're the princess, but – may I call you Nell?'

'No.'

'Why not?' He was jolted.

'Because I'm the princess. Only my friends get to call me Nell. You're a complete stranger.'

'I suppose Roshan calls you Nell – that guy who tried to kiss you?'

'You've been spying on me!' She was drawing herself up, growing mysteriously taller. She only reached Nathan's shoulder but somehow she managed to look down on him.

'Not exactly. It's a bit difficult to explain.'

'*Try.*'

She *would* have to be a princess, he thought, the romance of royalty evaporating fast. She's used to giving orders, even if there's no one left to give them to. She's probably arrogant and spoiled and –

'Well?'

'I come from another world. I don't know why I'm here, except that it may have something to do with the Traitor's Sword. I dream myself here – I'm dreaming now – and I seem to get more solid as I go along. At the beginning I was invisible, sort of floating around, observing, then the other time I was like a ghost, and tonight –'

The princess's lips had thinned; her eyes would have flashed if eyes were actually capable of flashing. 'I never heard such a load of –'

'Potherguffle? Twiddle-twaddle?'

'– thank you, all of those – anyway, I never heard such a load of it in my entire life! You must think I'm a child or an imbecile, expecting me to swallow fairytales like that! I *know* about magic – I know what it involves – and it doesn't include people popping by from other worlds, in or out of dreams, or being invisible one minute and then ghostly the next and then turning into flesh-and-blood for no reason –'

'I don't think it *is* magic,' Nathan said. 'Not that kind, anyway. It's more like . . . particle physics.'

'What's that supposed to be?'

'Everything in the world – everything in all worlds – is

made up of very small particles which can move in and out of reality, so maybe . . . Look, I don't really understand it myself, so I can't possibly explain it. The point isn't whether you believe me or not, the point is that I'm here. And I must say, I would've expected a princess to have better manners.' He felt he had scored there, and was tempted to remind her that he had saved her from the Urdemon, but refrained nobly.

'I have beautiful manners,' Nell declared, slightly on the defensive. 'You gave me a shock, that's all. Appearing out of nowhere right behind me . . .'

'So you admit I appeared out of nowhere?'

'That was just how it looked. You were probably hiding. We don't keep the doors locked. Anyone could sneak in here.'

'There isn't anyone,' he pointed out. 'Nearly all the people have left.'

'For someone from another world,' she said tartly, 'you know an awful lot about this one.'

'I told you, I observed. Why did everyone go? Was it because of the Urdemons?'

'Mostly. My father's sick – that started it – people thought it was the curse of Carboneck starting again, and they began to leave. Then the Urdemons came, out of the marshes, and on the stormwinds. I don't know if they actually hurt anyone – they were just like hideous phantoms – but some children disappeared, maybe they ran away, and everybody said it was demons, and they were frightened. So more people went, and more, and life got harder for those who stayed, and there were no butchers or bakers or tailors, and not enough people to bake and sew for, and so it went on. The city emptied, and my father got sicker, and the Urdemons are getting bolder and more solid – like you – and the marsh has spread, so we're isolated, and . . . I don't know what to do.' She had forgotten both anger and disbelief in her explanation; she was looking at him differently, her expression hopeless, doubting, almost pleading.

'It isn't you,' he said, responding to her thought if not her words. 'It isn't you bringing the demons. I asked my uncle about it – I hope you don't mind – he's kind of a wizard, he knows about these things. He said someone could be doing it *through* you, using you as a catalyst. You couldn't summon demons without realizing it. I think there has to be some sort of conjuration . . .'

'Thank you.' Suddenly she smiled, or started to smile – that smile which had charmed him when he first dreamed of her, was it weeks or months before?

And on that thought he *felt* the dream, shivering around him, beginning to dissolve. He tried to call out *Can't stay*, and *I'll be back*, but even as he spoke the princess was gone, and the firelit vault of the kitchen, and he tumbled into waking at the sound of his own voice, back in the abbot's study. Father Crowley was bending over him, looking mildly concerned.

'You missed supper,' he said. 'My fault, I'm afraid; I should have woken you. Are you hungry? Perhaps just a quick snack, and then bed.'

Nathan thanked him, suppressing relief. Obviously he hadn't been found (or not found) absent in slumber, dematerialized from his snuggle in the armchair. He was taken to the dining room and fed soft-boiled eggs and toast, and went to bed but not to sleep, the fight forgotten except when his bruises called it to mind, his thoughts only on the princess.

Father Crowley sat in his study for a long while, surveying the empty chair. 'Most intriguing,' he murmured. 'A boy who falls asleep, disappears, and then – reappears, still asleep. I have heard of spirit-voyages in dreams, but I never before came across someone who took his body with him.

Fascinating, absolutely . . . fascinating. Ah well. In due course, I will know more.' He closed a file with the name Damon Hackforth on the cover, and drummed lightly on it with his fingertips.

Somewhere in Thornyhill woods, Hazel was sitting in the crook of a tree, feeding Smarties to the woodwose.

'I like the green ones best,' he said. And, after a long pause: 'Which do you like?' Hazel had only eaten one.

'Whichever.' Leaving the Smarties to Woody, she twiddled a broken twig between her fingers. 'I'm not hungry.'

'You are unhappy?'

Hazel shrugged, moodily. 'A little. There's someone I like, and he . . . likes someone else. That's life, isn't it? Only I can't help wondering how it feels, to be the sort of person who always gets liked. You see them around, those people – there's one in every class – and while everyone else is doing the liking they're always on the receiving end, being liked. They get to be with whoever they want – they get to pick and choose – they get to dish out hurt like it's nothing, like they're giving away chewing gum.' She added bitterly: 'She's not even all that pretty.'

Woody was concentrating on trying to unravel the meaning of Hazel's speech. It would have been perfectly clear to another teenager or pre-teen, but to a woodwose it was complicated. 'People who are liked,' he repeated. 'You mean . . . people like Nathan?'

'Oh . . . no, not really. Well, sort of. Nathan's different.'

'*I* like him,' said Woody. '*You* like him. But he doesn't spend much time with us any more.'

'I suppose . . . it's a point. But Nathan's not . . . he's not *smug* about it. And he wouldn't hurt anyone, not intentionally. Ellen Carver's so kind of glossy and pleased with herself.

She expects all the boys to like her, and so they do. And the girls like her because they're afraid of being left out.'

'But you don't,' Woody deduced.

'No I don't. I'm not going to be blackmailed into liking her because I'm scared of being out of step. Anyway, nobody knew why she wanted Jonas – he's not, like, the best-looking boy in the school – but now she does, that means all the others do too. And it used to be just me. They don't know why he's special – they're just following the fashion.'

'Jonas is the boy you like,' Woody said slowly, working it out, 'but he doesn't like you back.'

'He doesn't get the chance,' Hazel said.

After a minute, she went on: 'I haven't told anyone – not *anyone* – except you. I suppose . . . telling you doesn't seem to count. Because you're a woodwose.'

'Secrets!' said Woody. 'I like secrets. Nathan and I used to have them.'

'You mustn't even tell Nathan,' Hazel adjured, suddenly anxious. 'Promise me.'

'He doesn't come any more,' Woody said. 'How did you say it? I won't get the chance.'

Thoughtfully, Hazel picked up the Smarties again, selected a green one and gave it to him. 'I wish I could make them all green ones,' she said, 'just for you.'

'That would not be right. It is good to look for the ripest nut on the bush, or the juiciest of the blackberries – to taste, and smell, and find the best one. If all are best, there is no fun. But . . . it's kind of you to think of it.' He reached out, touching her with a timid fingertip. 'You are a kind person.'

If he had been human, Hazel would have been embarrassed. But he was a werecreature, so the compliment didn't bother her. She even forgot to pull her hair over her face. There was a silence while her thoughts wandered off along a different tack, temporarily abandoning her own affairs.

'Where do you come from?' she asked.

'The woods. Always woods. I am a woodwose.'

'*These* woods?'

'I don't know. Maybe not. Nathan thinks he brought me here, when he was very small, so we could play together. He dreamed me, and brought me here. To be his friend.'

'Could he dream you back?'

'I don't think so. We don't know where I must go back *to*. But I am happy here. These woods are beautiful. There are bluebells in spring, and small flowers that creep along the ground, and birds to sing to me, and squirrels to chase, and hollow logs to hide in. I used to show Nathan . . .' He stopped, or ran down, his pointy face showing no expression.

'Are you the only woodwose?' Hazel said.

'Yes.'

'It must be lonely, to be the only one of something. D'you think there were others, where you came from? Can't you remember?'

He made a strange twitching movement which might have been a shrug or a shiver, or a little of both. 'Perhaps. Sometimes I dream too. I have seen my face in water – a reflection – and there are other faces like mine, voices like mine, hands touching my hand. The trees are bigger than here, and there are more colours – autumn is more gold, and more orange, and pink and purple too – and the birds are like flowers, and the flowers like birds, and the woods seem to go on forever. But I do not dream like Nathan – my dreams have no power – and when I wake up they are gone. The colours and the flower-birds and the woses like me – all gone. Perhaps it is just a dream, a wish. Not true at all.'

This time, it was Hazel's turn to reach out, folding two of his twiggy fingers in hers. 'I heard, everything is true somewhere,' she said. 'Nathan told me that. They teach that kind of stuff at his school, not just maths and English and things. It might be physics, or it might be philosophy. If it's physics, it's real. I'm not sure about philosophy.'

'Are they very wise at this school?'

'That's the idea,' Hazel said.

'So Nathan will grow to be wise too?'

'S'pose so. At any rate, he'll grow to be educated.' Which is more than I will, she thought, at my present rate of progress.

There was a silence while Woody tried to figure out the meaning of *educated*, and Hazel tried not to think about her maths homework. Since they were both people comfortable with silence, it extended a long time without awkwardness.

Eventually, Hazel said: 'Have you ever told Nathan about your dream?'

'No. I did not want him to think I was unhappy.'

'Maybe you should. It might help him to find the place. He might remember dreaming of it himself.'

'*No.*' Woody sounded suddenly agitated. 'It's a secret – another secret. You have a secret with me, I have one with you. A secret for a secret. I keep yours, you keep mine. It is a pact.'

'All right,' Hazel agreed. 'I won't tell if you don't want me to. But I still think you should consider it. Nathan may be one of those people whom everybody likes, but he isn't selfish about it. He'd help you to go home if he could. I know it.'

'Here is home now,' Woody said, and wouldn't change his mind.

As Hazel headed back to her own house her thoughts reverted to Jonas and Ellen Carver. *She* had been the first to like him, the first to see mystery behind his reserve and charm in his rare smile, but now he was going out with Ellen all

121

the girls admired him. He himself was changing, becoming more outgoing, smiling more often in the sunshine of so much approval. No one said he had hobbit hair any more. But it's all false, Hazel thought. One day the fashion will move on, and he'll be out in the cold again, and then he'll recognize *my* feelings, and he'll know they're different and sincere, and he'll turn to me.

But one day seemed a very long way away.

In the bedroom she barricaded the door and lit a candle in front of the mirror. Then she spoke the words, words she knew by heart now from long reading and thinking on them. Though she didn't realize it her voice had grown, in hunger and in power; the accent she had never learned came naturally this time. In the mirror her face altered, paling into beauty, her features melting into the slanting silvery lineaments of Lilliat, Spirit of Flowers.

'You have called me,' she said, 'at last. Are you ready to pay the price?'

'I am ready,' Hazel said.

FIVE

Damon

Annie noticed the cut on his mouth, and some of the more obvious bruises, when Nathan came home the next weekend. She demanded an explanation; he refused to provide one. 'You've been bullied,' she said. Nathan, to her knowledge, had never been bullied, though he had stood up to bullies before now, but such bruises meant fights, and fights meant bullying. 'I won't allow it! I'll go to the school – I'll speak to the abbot –'

'Mum, *please*. I haven't been bullied – someone sort of tried, but it was a one-off, he won't do it again. And Father Crowley knows about it.'

'If you told Father Crowley, then you can tell me.' Idiotic to feel a pang of jealousy, to fear that his headmaster might feel a closer bond with her son than she did.

'I didn't tell him – I didn't tell anyone – he just knows. It's nothing to worry about, honestly. I can deal with it. I'm old enough to deal with things myself; I don't need you coming the protective mother all the time.' That was a mistake: he knew it as he spoke. Annie was rarely angry but her face flamed with embarrassment and indignation.

'*Coming the protective mother*? When I let you wander off into other worlds, and – and chase thieves, and outface monsters . . . I can't stop you doing those things, but what happens to you at school is still in my remit. You're fourteen, you're a child, and I'm your only parent. *I'll* decide what you deal with and don't deal with. Just tell me who did this to you . . .'

'I can't.' His face had stiffened with obstinacy.

'You mean you *won't*! In that case, you're – you're grounded. For the weekend. In fact, until I say otherwise.'

'*Grounded*? Mum – you've never grounded me. I didn't know you even knew the word. Have you been watching some teen TV soap?'

Annie wouldn't dignify that with a response. She was hanging on to her spur-of-the-moment act of discipline with the doggedness of someone who wasn't sure she was right. Nathan was forbidden to play football with George or meet up with Hazel, and when Annie went to Thornyhill Manor for dinner he stayed at home. The atmosphere in the house was taut and twangy, like an overstretched elastic band, both mother and son unhappy, but too proud, too pig-headed, or simply too confused to make a move towards reconciliation.

'I don't know what's come over her,' Nathan told Hazel, by phone. 'I mean, *grounded*. As if I was a silly kid.'

'She's never done that before.' Hazel's tone was oddly distant. 'Why did she –'

'Oh, there was some trouble at school. Nothing I couldn't handle – well, nothing for Mum to handle. I'll tell you about it some other time. The thing is, I can't see you. Not this weekend, maybe not next. It's like I'm in solitary, no visitors allowed.'

'You could sneak out,' Hazel said. She had been grounded, and had sneaked out, at regular intervals throughout her childhood. 'I always did.'

'I don't want to do that. My mum's not like –'

'Like mine?'

'Your mum's great – really great – but she's different. She's sort of tried to be strict, and failed, and made rules for you to break – that's how your relationship works. But my mum didn't make any rules, except about good manners and things. Generally, she let me do what I wanted – she trusted me. Now, it's like she doesn't trust me any more. I don't know why – but she won't get that trust back if I slip out the instant she leaves.'

'You could slip back in again a bit later,' Hazel said. 'Then she wouldn't know.'

'I can't lie to her. We don't do that. I'll have to talk her round. It may take a little while, that's all. Sorry I can't see you.'

'Doesn't matter.' The distant note had never quite left Hazel's voice.

'Are you all right? You sound a bit – aloof. You're upset with me, aren't you?'

'I'm fine. Everything's fine. You don't have to see me if you don't want to.'

'That isn't it, and you know it. I'd come if I could. Is there something you want to talk about?'

'No.' Hazel was feeding her own resentment, telling herself he was doing it on purpose, staying away from her because he couldn't be bothered to come. Opting out of their friendship. Which meant she didn't owe him anything any more – neither affection nor loyalty.

She hung up.

Nathan was left to brood on the fact that one row sparks off another – one ruptured relationship leads to another rupture. Like a row of dominoes, falling each against the next until the whole line lies flat. For a minute he was frightened, wondering if his powers of persuasion were equal to mending matters, and whether any other friendships would hit the floor, now the dominoes were falling. He felt himself losing hold of his life, sensed it slipping away from him, unravelling in the wrong direction while he stood by helpless, unable to call a halt. He wasn't someone who needed to be in control of family and friends, but he'd never felt so *out* of control before, never seen his homeworld spinning away from him while an irresistible current swept him somewhere else – somewhere he didn't want to be. It was almost as if reality had become the dream, and as in his dreams he was subject to the whim of chance or fate, and must go where he was led.

Uncle Barty will fix things, he thought with a sudden rush of thankfulness. *He'll make Mum come around*.

But when Annie got back it was late, and nothing was fixed.

Left to make his own entertainment for the weekend, Nathan did his homework, read several vintage novels from the bookshop, watched some largely mindless television, and thought a great deal about the princess. He went early to bed, but without physical exercise he wasn't tired, and he lay sleepless a long while, re-running his conversation with Nell in his mind, trying to prepare what he would say next time – if only next time would come. He even attempted to turn his thought inward and find the portal, but he couldn't seem to concentrate. Little sounds from outside distracted him: the distant rumble of lorry or Landrover, a sudden shout from someone on a path nearby, the cry of a barn owl flying past on its way to the river-meadows. He heard the pipes gurgling as his mother used the bathroom before going to bed, and waited for the night-silence to settle in, the silence of a sleeping house in a quiet village where, even on a Saturday, nothing much happened when the pub had closed. (Of course, last year there had been three murders and a robbery, but that, as everyone had told the police, was exceptional, and resulted solely from a recent influx of Londoners. Londoners, as the whole village knew, were immoral types capable of anything.)

It was midnight now, the witching hour – he could see the luminous dial of his bedside clock – but the silence felt wrong, the night felt wrong, tense and stuffy. Or maybe the wrongness was in him. Nathan got up, as quietly as he could, and made his way to the den where he, and Hazel and George had had their headquarters for so many years. They didn't go there very much now. It was a sort of secret room under the slope of the roof, fine for three children but constricting for growing teenagers. Nathan bent down to climb in, using a torch to see his way. There were still three mugs there, dusty from lack of use; he ought to remove them. He lifted the skylight and scrambled up to sit on the sill, looking down over rectangular slices of garden, and the path beyond, which local people called a twitten, then more gardens, more houses, a single lamp in the lane, and after that the darkness of the fields and the remote gleam of the moon on the river. The River Glyde, which flowed down the valley to the sea.

> *Cloud on the sunset*
> *wave on the tide;*
> *death from the deep sea*
> *swims up the Glyde.*

That was what a spirit had said, summoned to the magic circle by his uncle the preceding summer. The Glyde might only flow into the Channel, narrow and far from deep, but all seas interconnect, and Nenufar the water-phantom, the shapeshifter, the forgotten goddess, had come from the caverns far beneath the ocean, hungry for the Grail and its power. So three had died – old Effie Carlow, drowned in the river (or possibly Hazel's attic); stranger still, the German visitor, drowned in the wood in a shower of rain. And the woman whose corpse Annie had found, laid out in a white bed, with her face shrivelled to the bone and her hair spread across the pillow. And on that thought, Nathan abandoned resentment, resolving to talk to Annie, to make things right, somehow, anyhow. She was just having a brief attack of standard parenthood, but she wasn't a standard parent, she'd always been different. She'd resisted a psychopath, and defied the water-succubus, not to mention knocking Dave Bagot unconscious with a saucepan. *She's the best mother in the world*, he thought with a sudden warm rush of feeling, *the best in all the worlds*. And on that realization the tension went out of the night, and he knew that now he would sleep.

But before climbing back through the skylight he glanced up, involuntarily, and saw the star that didn't belong, watching him. The Grandir's star, hanging both in the sky above his house and in a tower room in Arkatron, a pale, unwinking point of light, like a sentinel keeping guard. But guarding what? The Grail perhaps – that made sense – but why watch over him? Why him? It was one of many questions he had yet to answer, a fragment of the puzzle that still didn't fit, whichever way he twisted it.

He closed the skylight and came down from the den, the momentary warmth gone from his heart, leaving him tired and empty.

He slept.

He was falling . . . falling . . . His ears popped and his head felt squeezed and his stomach was left far behind. It was not a pleasant sensation. He fell and the world fell with him . . . Then it stopped, allowing his insides to thump back into place, leaving him breathless and slightly sick. He didn't know if he was visible or not, it was too dark to tell, but a little way ahead there was a light, and he moved unsteadily towards it. Glancing back, his sight adapting to the gloom, he saw he had emerged from a lift-shaft (the lift needs some work, he thought) into a passageway that looked vaguely familiar. He had seen it before, with more illumination though not much. Now, there was only a single light above the laboratory door, its angled ray striking the warning sign. *Private – No Unauthorized Entry*. Cautiously, he pushed the door open and slipped through.

The laboratory was poorly lit by a grey glimmer which seemed to come from the ceiling; its sole occupant, far away down the other end of the room, appeared unaware of Nathan's entrance. Whatever he was doing absorbed him to the exclusion of all else. Nathan found it odd that the door wasn't locked, but perhaps there was some scanning device which had failed to register his shadowy, semi-spectral figure. He crept nearer, screened by a workbench, moving softly on bare, insubstantial feet. It was the Grandir, of course; not Romandos, the first, but *the* Grandir, the last Grandir – he who had set the star above Nathan's house, who controlled the gnomons that guarded the Grail, who was striving to complete the Great Spell his predecessor had begun uncounted millennia ago. Nathan wondered if the cave of the green stalactites was still there, then realized it mightn't have been on Eos – Eos was simply the one uncontaminated planet remaining in a universe that was poisoned, the final retreat of a people who had once ruled an entire cosmos.

He risked a quick look above the bench, and saw with a kind of shock that the Grandir was not masked. It was the first time he had seen the man's face, and he found it strangely disturbing, like seeing your headmaster naked. He received a fleeting impression of dark alien features, a sweep of black hair falling over the brow, the echo of a resemblance to someone. Halmé perhaps, his sister and lover, wedded to him by family tradition – Halmé who was so beautiful that few were permitted to look on her. But no, it was someone else, someone seen more recently. Romandos . . . no. No, it was Lugair – Lugair with his slanting glance and the trace element of cruelty about his mouth. Nathan ventured another look. In the Grandir's face, slyness had become calculation, cruelty, the coldness of detachment, but the resemblance was there, like a distant ghost infesting his features. Nathan wondered what his name was. Even Halmé had never used it, calling him only by his title. In the dimensions of magic a name could give you power over a person, or so Nathan had heard; if you were Grandir of a whole world that power might be deadly. Evidently this ruler was more prudent – or more distrustful – than Romandos long ago.

He was doing something with the sword – the Sword of Straw – which he had placed on a circular plinth in the space beyond the work benches. The wicked-looking blade appeared as sharp and bright as it had done when Romandos first tempered it so many ages before. As Nathan watched, a white spotlight shone down on it, perhaps from a source on the ceiling, fixing it in a pool of radiance. Beyond, the laboratory seemed to grow darker. Nathan was suddenly aware of the cage nearby, a cage he had seen in another dream – seen and feared. The front was glass, or some similar material, and there was a blur of darkness pressed against it, a darkness which seemed to pulse somehow, emitting a sense of tormented life. And at the core of the darkness there were two ragged ovals, like holes cut in a blanket, only red.

They swam against the glass, moving when the Grandir moved, following his every gesture. The pulse seemed to be centred in them, making their redness throb. The rage and menace that they exuded was so strong Nathan was amazed the Grandir did not appear to feel it. He found he was trembling from the impact of it – or his own horror – but he couldn't drag his gaze away. He sensed that whatever was imprisoned in that cage was akin to the Urdemons, in some remote way, but whereas they were creatures of fear and illusion, whose substance was fluid, this thing was real and terrible. It might have no shape but the spirit that looked out of those two red holes was as potent and savage as a volcano.

He missed what the Grandir was doing, until a sudden flare of light caught him off guard, irradiating the whole room. For an instant, shadows chased past him and fled, leaving him exposed – he hoped the ruler wasn't looking his way. Then the dark rushed back, so he was temporarily blinded, and when he looked again the Grandir was standing over the plinth, his arms spread and his eyes almost closed, speaking words of power to bind both spirit and sword. Nathan didn't understand the words but he sensed the meaning, sensed the vein of fear underlying the elemental's fury. The spotlight had become a thick white tentacle of brilliance reaching out from the sword-hilt, groping across the ceiling towards the cage. The searching end opened like lips, made of light, which seemed to suck at the surface of the glass as it crawled down to the imprisoned spirit. The Grandir's face was bubbled with tiny sweat-beads, but no effort showed in his voice: it remained strong and cold. The incantation culminated in two words, spoken so sharply they cut the air: *'Enfia! Nimrrassé!'* The glass shattered.

There was a moment when the blackness appeared to boil outwards into the room. Then Nathan blinked – or the world blinked – and it was gone. The shimmering tentacle flexed and bulged; the inky vapour was drawn down it – seething – struggling – red eyes flared and vanished against the sides.

The light closed after it, shrinking to a thread, dissolving into the hilt even as the flames of the first spell had done when the weapon was forged. But there was a difference. When the last of the light was swallowed up the sword quivered, as if trying to leap off the plinth. A chill gleam that came from nothing in the room ran up and down the edge of the blade. The Grandir seized the hilt with both hands – as he lifted it there was a snarling noise and for a second it seemed to fight his grasp. Nathan thought he saw the twin flickers of red moving down the sword like reflections in the metal.

The power of the sword was joined with a new power, an otherness, confined within it, resisting and using it, evil within evil, hot rage in cold. Nathan backed away, filled with a skin-crawling dread which he couldn't quite explain. It wasn't simply the terror of the ancient spirit, but something about what the Grandir had done, something he couldn't pinpoint, a perception just beyond his reach. Romandos' magic had been fascinating and fearful, but there was a fatality about this like the long shadow of doom. He remembered his first vision of the Grail, and the dreams that had followed, not otherworld adventures but nightmares of horror and blood. Cup and sword – two elements of the Great Spell – a spell to save a universe. He was driven to seek them out – but why the baptism of fear?

He had reached the end of the bench. He could dive for the door, but without the spell to divert him the Grandir would be almost certain to notice it opening. Nathan crouched in the gloom, waiting. Soon, he thought, the dream must end, but it didn't. He began to feel stiff and slightly cramped even in his insubstantial state. Peering out, he saw the Grandir sealing the sword in some kind of scabbard, made of what looked like leather and stamped with letters and symbols in red. The hilt too was covered; heavy fastenings clicked into place. Nathan retreated back under the bench.

In the cage opposite he noticed a small creature with silvery fur and large eyes, watching him. He was worried the Grandir might register the direction of its gaze, but evidently the animal was too insignificant to attract his attention. Nathan thought it looked sad, trapped in this laboratory of magic and science, the intended victim of some future experiment. He decided that when the Grandir left he would find a way to let it out, and the idea distracted him from both the sword and the dream, so he forgot his restlessness, scanning the cage for any sign of a lock or key panel. And inevitably, once he ignored the dream it crept up on him, and he didn't even recall the moment when sleep stole him away, leaving the unknown animal to its fate.

Oddly enough, when he awoke in the morning, that was the part that troubled him most, pushing away his fear of the Traitor's Sword.

Gathering nettles in the churchyard at midnight? Hazel stared blankly at her spirit-mentor. It was the ultimate cliché of witchcraft.

'There aren't any nettles in the churchyard,' she said. 'It's very well maintained. Anyway, I'd be bound to run into the vicar. He prowls round at night looking for bats and owls – at least, that's what he *says*. Mum thinks he's into wildlife, but *we* know –' she meant her generation '– he's hoping to catch someone at it on a tombstone. In any case, you said we wouldn't really need potions.'

'*I* don't need them,' Lilliat said, her silver eyes slanting narrowly. '*You* do. I have watched you. You believe in the old ways – your great-grandmother's ways – not the potion, but the pain. There must be pain. You must pluck the nettles with your bare hands, and suffer –'

'I've done lots of suffering,' Hazel said crossly. 'The whole point of magic is that I don't want to do any more.'

'It's a question of tradition,' Lilliat sighed. 'Your power is founded on such things. Old wives' tales, superstition, stories . . .'

'I know the story about the nettles,' Hazel said. 'It was in a book Nathan showed me when we were kids. Anderson or Grimm. There was a girl whose brothers were turned into swans by a wicked sorceress, and she had to weave them shirts of nettles to undo the spell.'

'It is a good story,' Lilliat said. 'A story of love, and suffering. Where there is love the true heart must bleed.'

'Forget it.'

'Oh very well. But these little rituals are important – *you* attach importance to them – and if you don't believe, the magic won't work.'

'I'll believe,' Hazel insisted, doggedly.

'You have spent your whole life trying not to, telling yourself it was all fantasy and falsehood. But now you *want* to believe, because you need the magic – because there's no other way. But maybe you've denied the power too often and too long. Without pain –'

'No nettles,' Hazel said flatly.

Lilliat smiled her faint, sweet smile. Hazel thought there were freckled foxgloves at her breast, and yellow celandines, also called aconite, starred her hair. 'Nonetheless,' she said, 'there are things we *will* need. A token from the boy you love – a torn fingernail, a lock of hair – and something from the girl you want him to forget.'

'DNA,' Hazel said. 'Is *that* how it works?'

'It works from the heart. What is DNA?'

'I can't remember what it stands for,' Hazel said, 'but it's like, the formula for who you are. That's how Nathan explained it to me. It's in every bit of you – hair, nails, spit. Every cell of your body.'

'I do not want spit,' Lilliat said distastefully. 'Still, you may say it's this DNA which we need, if it pleases you. I also require something from your friend.'

'Why?'

'There was a price. We agreed. Do you remember?'

Hazel shrugged, a twitchy, uncomfortable movement.

'*Do you remember*?'

'Yes. All right. I'll get a – a token from him too. But we have to do the love-spell first. If it doesn't work, then no price.'

'Foolish child!' The words were soft, teasing or mocking, light as flowerdust. 'I have told you, it will work – *if* you believe. It is a matter for you, not me – something between you and your heart. There can be no power where there is doubt. But I must have the tokens – *all* the tokens – before we start. That is my only condition.'

She made it sound like a trivial thing, a minor detail, but Hazel wasn't deceived. 'Would a piece of clothing do?' she asked.

'Only if it has been long in their possession, and is much worn, and unwashed, and impregnated with their spiritual aura.'

'I should think it would be,' Hazel muttered, 'if it's never been washed.'

'I will know if you try to cheat me,' Lilliat went on. 'That would not be wise. The price of my enmity is far higher than that of my friendship.'

Hazel nodded. Nettles, she thought. There are always nettles, one way or another.

'I won't cheat,' she said.

* * *

At school on Monday, Nathan kept a wary eye out for Damon
Hackforth. He wasn't afraid of another face-to-face encounter,
but he didn't want his masters to get the impression he was
the type who got into fights all the time: it might still damage
his chances of keeping the scholarship. It didn't occur to him
that few teachers would suspect a younger boy with a record
of good behaviour of picking fights with an older (and larger)
boy who was already a known trouble-maker. But although
he looked over his shoulder more than once that day he didn't
see Damon until he was summoned to Father Crowley's study
just after lunch.

Damon was there, ensconced in the comfortable armchair
where Nathan had slept – and dreamed – the previous week.
I met the princess in that chair, Nathan thought, and found
himself resenting its present occupant for reasons which he
knew were illogical.

'Sit down,' Father Crowley said, indicating the upright chair
by the desk.

Nathan sat.

'I have asked you here,' the abbot went on, 'because I will
not tolerate fighting in this school. If you want violent exercise you have rugger, a game you both play, though happily
not against each other. That is the only violence that is permitted here. I could talk to you about God, and the Christian
ethos – I am, after all, a priest – but neither of you has yet
shown the greatness of spirit that would enable you to turn
the other cheek. Few men ever do. Christianity is an ideal;
we must all fall short. However, ordinary people have to find
a way to live in peace with one another, if the world is to
survive. Ffylde Abbey is a microcosm of the world – if either
of you know what a microcosm is.'

'Very small universe,' Damon said unexpectedly. 'From the
Greek.'

'That is the literal meaning. Well done: you obviously haven't wasted *all* your time in lessons. To be precise, microcosm is a very small *version* of the universe. In the larger world, nation squares up to nation, but in the main they prefer to avoid war, since it is costly in both money and lives, and generally detrimental to society.'

'Like President Bush?' asked Damon.

'The exception that proves the rule.' The abbot was unperturbed. 'Fortunately, in Ffylde Abbey *I* am running things, not President Bush, and I do not care for war, whatever the reason. Nor do I allow any scope for terrorism. In a universe on the scale of this school, these things are far more manageable. Think of me as a very successful world dominator with the power to crush ruthlessly any individual with military ambitions.' Was it Nathan's imagination, or did those keen eyes bore into him a moment too long, and with a hidden meaning? 'While I cannot compel you to turn the other cheek, I do insist on your shaking hands. A small gesture, but significant. Any resumption of hostilities will be . . . frowned upon. Do I make myself clear?'

The boys nodded. Father Crowley snapped his fingers, and they stood up instantly, though Damon looked unnerved by his own instinctive obedience. At a word from the abbot Nathan extended his hand. The other boy stared at it for a second as if it were an alien object, then took it in his own. There was a second when his grip was tight and hard – a fraction too tight, squeezing Nathan's fingers. Nathan expected him to look sullen and reluctant, but his face was oddly blank. He let go and took a step backwards.

'That will do,' said the abbot. 'Thank you, Nathan; you may go.'

As the door closed behind him, Nathan saw Damon resuming his seat in the armchair, almost as if he belonged there.

'What happened?' Ned Gable asked, at the first available opportunity. Summonses to the abbot's study were rare.

'We shook hands.'

'You and Father Crow–'

'Me and Damon.'

'You're kidding! I bet he was furious. You put up a bloody good fight – if it had gone on a bit longer you might have beaten him. I bet he was chewing his own liver. Having to shake hands with you –! The abbot must really know how to turn the screw on him. Did he give you a pep-talk about Christian forgiveness and all that?'

'Not exactly. He talked a bit, but . . .'

'What about?'

'World domination.'

'You're kidding!'

'You know Father Crowley. He wouldn't trot out all the routine godspeak like – like it was a formula to make things right. He doesn't do that. He always says stuff you don't expect. But . . . I think he *does* have a lot of influence with Damon. A lot. Damon didn't want to shake hands with me, but he did. He didn't even look pissed off about it.'

'He's got a real complex about you,' Ned reiterated. 'Didn't I say so all along? He won't like being made to shake hands, whatever the abbot said. He'll go away and brood about it and he'll end up hating you even more. In fact . . . I don't think you should be left alone. We'll have to organize a body-guard –'

'You're nuts,' Nathan said with a quick grin.

'Who was right last time? Didn't I tell you he'd start something? *Didn't I?*'

'Okay,' Nathan conceded, 'but I'm not having a body-guard, and that's that. I'd look a complete dork. Anyway, I don't think he'll do anything now the abbot's warned him off. And he must be starting his A-levels soon.'

'He's started,' Ned said. 'He walked out of English Lit last week. I heard Mum telling Dad about it after *his* mum told her. He doesn't care.'

'He's not thick,' Nathan said, recalling the Greek origins of *microcosm*. 'He must care about something.'

'Getting back at you!'

That's Jason Wicks talk, Nathan thought. Damon isn't another Jason Wicks.

Surely the whole business must be over now.

Despite Nathan's rejection of the idea, Ned marshalled several of his classmates into a sort of informal protection unit. As a good rugger player and top-scoring batsman Nathan was always popular, but the fight had made him something of a hero, and as the word spread most of the class rallied round. Undercover Intelligence reported that Damon had various exams that week, though it was unable to verify whether or not he actually sat them. He was observed hanging around in the corridor near Nathan's lessons in an off-hand manner which was immediately labelled sinister, and once overheard interrogating a younger boy on Nathan's whereabouts. A blitz mentality developed, and Nathan found he couldn't even go to the loo unattended. Two or three boys would be waiting nonchalantly outside, or would knock on the door and hiss conspiratorially: '*Are you all right*?', as if fearing he might have been mysteriously spirited away. ('But then,' Nathan reflected, 'I *do* get spirited away sometimes, only not, I hope, in the loo.') Ned, who was a James Bond fan, insisted on checking his bedding every night for scorpions.

'Where on earth would Damon get a scorpion?' Nathan demanded. 'This is England.'

'You can buy tarantulas in pet shops,' Ned said. 'Harry Kassim's got one.'

'There you are. You should be looking for a tarantula.'

'Scorpions are cool,' another boy said. 'Spiders are so last-year.'

'I thought the one in *Return of the King* was pretty good,' someone offered.

'Oh, pur-lease! It was prancing around like something out of panto – *Look behind you!* – and there wasn't enough yukky stuff when it got stabbed. There should have been lots of fluorescent green goo bubbling out.'

'It was better than the ones in *Harry Potter*. They all ran around like they were clockwork.'

'10p in the forfeit box for mentioning the H-word!'

Settling down at last in his tarantula-free, scorpion-free bed, Nathan only hoped their zeal wouldn't disturb their sleep. If they woke in the night and saw him gone – off on some dream-voyage in Eos or Wilderslee – there would be panic.

But the boys slept the night through, and Nathan's dreams roamed no further than his own head.

By Friday, the bodyguard had begun to lose enthusiasm. Nathan left cricket practice slightly early to be ready for Annie, preoccupied with what he would say to her – how to apologize without actually telling her anything, how to restore their relationship to its normal easy-going status. (He thought of it as easy-going; Annie was the one whose efforts made it so.) He was mildly relieved to find he had lost his usual foot-pads as he went into the cloakroom to change. It was empty: those not on the cricket pitch had already left. There was a soft sound behind him – he started, turned. Something struck the back of his head, and the world went out.

He came to himself with the vague idea that this was a particularly unpleasant dream-journey – the inter-cosmic equivalent of a bad trip. He felt sick, his head throbbed, and the darkness muffling him was tangible and coarse and smelt of stale wool. He tried to move and found his wrists and ankles were tied. The surface on which he was lying was smooth and hard and trembling with subterranean vibration, seriously aggravating his nausea. Between the pulses of headache, recollection trickled back. *Not* a dream after all, which was a nuisance, since – unless he could fall asleep – dematerializing out of this mess wasn't an option. He had evidently been hit on the head, tied up, and bundled in a blanket in the back of some vehicle. Curiously, his first thought was: *This is ridiculous.*

The sound of voices very near at hand quashed any lingering doubts about the identity of his kidnapper.

'I know the way.' Damon Hackforth.

'It's miles from anywhere.' Another voice, unfamiliar and faintly downmarket. 'You missed a turning . . .'

'I missed it because it was the wrong one.'

He's *kidnapped* me, Nathan thought, his mind reeling – a mistake, since his body was reeling too. He must be mad. He'll be expelled – arrested – he's totally off his trolley. Sheer incredulity blanked out any thought of fear. Schoolboys didn't go around kidnapping each other, not even in the inner cities, let alone in a superior private school in the heart of the Sussex countryside. It just didn't happen.

Everything happens somewhere . . .

He had never been too sure about that theory, but right now it held up. Everything happens somewhere, and for the moment, somewhere was here.

There were two other boys with Damon, certainly not pupils from Ffylde. The one who had spoken before sounded nervous, asking questions and attempting argument, though with little success. Then there was another, with a strong southeast cockney accent, who spoke rarely and in monosyllables, possibly through gum. The muscle, Nathan deduced. Listening for names, he heard Damon call the first one Ram, while the strong silent type appeared to be Ginge. Something clicked in his brain. Weren't they the two who had tried to burgle Thornyhill? Nathan's heart leaped with momentary excitement. So Uncle Barty had been right – there was a definite connection between the failed burglary and the Hackforths.

But why would Damon be after the Grail – and how would he know about it, or where it was?

'Check on our passenger,' Damon ordered. Obviously he was driving.

Nathan closed his eyes hastily as the blanket was pulled back for a few seconds.

'He's still out.' Ram. 'You hit him too hard. Supposing he's hurt bad? I'm not going down for GBH.'

'Don't be such a weasel. You won't go down for anything so long as you do what you're told.' Damon was clearly enjoying being the boss.

'Why do we have to bring him along anyway?'

'We need him. I explained all that, cretin. He'll know where it is.'

'He won't tell *us*.'

'I hope not. I'm looking forward to squeezing it out of him.'

For the first time, Nathan experienced a twinge of dread. With his hands and feet bound, he couldn't put up a fight. And if Damon was mad enough to kidnap him, he might be mad enough to use torture . . . Suddenly the situation, fantastic and unbelievable though it was, didn't seem quite so comic-opera any more.

He must listen, learn, *think*. If only his head didn't hurt so much . . .

'I don't want to be part of this!' Ram was saying. 'I don't do violence.'

'Of course you don't. Ginge does the rough stuff, right?'

A suitable grunt from Ginge.

'Ginge does the punching, you do the talking. Only this time I talk, I punch, you both shut up and follow orders. Clear?'

'Don't want to go back there.' An unexpected contribution from Ginger.

Back where?

'You're pathetic.' Evidently this was a favourite insult of Damon's. 'An old man and a dog, and you're wetting yourself. Some tough guy. The dog isn't even a Rottweiler, just a rat-eared mongrel, half Battersea Dogs' Home, half Wookie. You're scared of your own fart.'

'Ginge once bit a Rottweiler,' Ram volunteered. 'You didn't see this dog. It don't act like it's trained, more like . . . like it thinks. You know, *really* thinks. Like a human.'

'What would you know about thinking?'

So we're going to Thornyhill, Nathan assimilated with a pang of relief which he knew could be premature. Uncle Barty and Hoover would be more than a match for Damon, with or without the tentative support of his henchmen. And he – Nathan – was supposed to reveal something, at a guess the secret hiding-place of the Grail, after some appropriate physical pressure which Damon plainly intended to enjoy. Only Bartlemy had never shown him where the Grail was kept, so he couldn't give it away, which was a good thing but might prove painful.

Despite the discomfort of his position, Nathan's headache was easing. He was young, fit and resilient; even under the present conditions, his body was able to recuperate. He wondered briefly what he had been hit with, but decided it wasn't important. What mattered now was to get free, if he could. But his wrists were bound too tight – it felt as if they had used tape – and he didn't want to wriggle too much and attract the attention of the three in the front. He felt it would be best for now if they thought he was still unconscious.

'Don't know why you and your dad are so set on this cup thing,' Ram was muttering. Nathan ceased his futile struggles to listen. 'If it's really well known it'll be bloody impossible to fence.'

'Dad isn't selling, he's buying. He thinks it's the Holy Grail – he's gone completely nuts on the idea. He believes its magical powers'll cure my sister. Ever since she got ill he's got more and more desperate –' the constriction in his voice betrayed suppressed emotion, but Nathan wasn't sure which emotion it was '– now he's gone soft in the head. He's stuffed himself so full of fairytales he's seeing elves in the bath. Stupid old bugger. If the doctors can't help her the bloody fairies won't. She's dying and that's that.'

He *does* care about her, Nathan thought. Somewhere deep down . . .

'You never know,' Ram said. 'I mean, that house – it's a spooky kind of place, right? The old man – he's spooky. All fat and soft-looking, but spooky underneath. Like the dog.'

'Forget the dog. I can deal with it.'

'Anyway,' Ram resumed, 'if you don't believe in the Grail stuff, why pinch it?'

''Cause Dad'll pay. I told you, he's buying.'

'Yeah, but – you're his son . . .'

'I'm not dumb. He won't know it's me. I'll do it anonymous – over the phone. He'll never know.'

'How much you gonna ask for?' Ram's brain was evidently beginning to work.

'You'll get a thousand apiece. That was the deal.'

'Not sure that's enough. If your dad's desperate like you say, you can ask him for a lot of dosh. A hell of a lot. Ten grand, twenty – fifty. Maybe even a hundred. I reckon we deserve a bigger cut.'

'You'll get what you're given and be grateful for it. Now shut the fuck up.' Earlier, Damon had sounded on a high, but from the first mention of his family his mood had darkened. Nathan sensed him walking an emotional precipice, inching closer and closer to the edge. He didn't like to think what would happen when Damon went over.

'I reckon you owe someone.' Ram's instinct for danger seemed to have temporarily shut down. 'If you needed the money for something legit, your old man'ld give it to you. 'Course he would. He's your old man, isn't he? I reckon you owe someone big time. What is it – crack, charlie? You a gambler?'

Damon stamped on the brakes with such violence Nathan was thrown against the seat-backs so hard he nearly cried out.

'*Leave it.*' Damon's voice had sunk to a hiss. 'Mind – your – own – business. Understand? You get a thousand each. No questions. Final.'

The silence crackled. Presently, they drove on. Nathan was remembering rumours floating round at school, drifting down from the sixth via someone's brother's friend of a friend. Rumours about internet poker. Ram got it right, he thought. I bet it's gambling. He felt a germ of pity for Damon, who, he suspected, loved the sister he envied – the sister who was dying by degrees – and was caught in a dark tangle of his own making, lashing out in vain like a tiger in a net. But a netted tiger can be deadly, if you get too close . . .

A few minutes later they slowed and turned, bumping along what Nathan guessed to be a lane or track. Then they stopped.

'Right,' said Damon. 'Let's get him out, and wake him up.'

'Where is he?' Annie demanded, fighting to keep the panic out of her voice. 'Last week he came home with bruises, and now he's disappeared. Where's my son?'

'I'm sure he's here somewhere.' The teacher spoke in his best parent-soothing accents. 'It's a big school. He may have popped into the library to check up on something – got lost in a book. Nathan's a great reader.'

'*I know.*' Annie spoke between clenched teeth – a difficult feat only achievable under extreme stress.

'He'll turn up shortly. He might have stopped to have a chat with one of the weekend boarders – begun playing some computer game, maybe. We do allow them on Friday and Saturday evenings.'

'I've been waiting three quarters of an hour . . .'

'Boys that age have no sense of time.'

'He doesn't answer his mobile . . .'

'We insist they're kept switched off in school hours.'

'I want to see the abbot.'

A little later she was talking to Ned Gable and the bodyguard.

'We were playing cricket,' Ned said. 'Nathan went off a bit early to get changed. He wanted to be on time for you. When we went into the cloakroom he'd gone, so we thought . . .'

'Yes, I see.' The boys looked uncomfortable and anxious. Annie was conscious of a rising fear. 'What's wrong?'

'We were worried about him,' said one of the others. 'There was someone who – who kept watching him. It was weird. We should've stayed with him.'

'Who?' Annie asked. 'Who kept watching him? Was it Damon Hackforth?'

There was a moment of hesitation before the schoolboy *omertà* started to fall apart.

'Was it Damon Hackforth who beat him up?'

At that, several boys began to speak at once. Ned Gable came out on top. 'He didn't beat him up, honestly. Nathan put up a bloody good fight. Damon looked much worse than him afterwards – didn't he?' There was a general assent. 'We think that's why he's been acting strange – Damon, I mean. He wants revenge. He's got this kind of fixation on Nathan, not gay or anything, but, like, jealousy, only more Freudian, because Nathan's the person he wants to be . . .'

'Do you think Damon's kidnapped him?' someone piped up.

'Not without help,' opined another boy.

'Preposterous suggestion!' said the teacher.

'I want the abbot,' Annie reiterated. '*Now.*'

In the time it took to locate Father Crowley, she was phoning Bartlemy.

With parents coming and going to collect their children, nobody had paid any attention to the little delivery van (it belonged to Ram's father) which had pulled up near the cloakroom exit at the back of the school. It had been cruising in the vicinity each evening since Wednesday; Ram's father thought he was using it to run errands. Those who had noticed it drive away assumed it was a legitimate part of the scenery. The school was always taking delivery of something or other. By the time the police were called most of the potential witnesses had gone and Annie, going quietly frantic, found herself confronted with a uniformed officer who took it for granted she was as wealthy as the other parents and her son had been kidnapped for ransom. The idea that the perpetrator might be another boy he, like the teacher, dismissed out of hand.

When DCI Pobjoy arrived, assigned to the case because of

his background knowledge of the family, Annie greeted him like a relieving force. Bartlemy, after brief consideration, had said he would await developments at Thornyhill, and the abbot, though both kindly and competent, assured her it would prove to be a storm in a teacup. Pobjoy listened to her, issued orders, mobilized searchers.

'Don't think it's a sicko,' the uniform asserted, on the side. 'Kid's fourteen but big for his age – too big to be snatched without a struggle – looks pretty mature, too. Sickos go for the baby-faced ones. Don't see how it could be one of the other kids, either. If you ask me, they're after a ransom, and grabbed the wrong boy. Some of the parents here are rolling in it. If you ask me –'

'I didn't,' said Pobjoy. Previous experience with the Wards made him disinclined to leap to conclusions of any kind. Besides, he knew Damon Hackforth's record.

He turned back to Annie.

'Try not to worry. We'll find him.' And then: 'I'm sorry, I have to ask you this. Has Nathan ever run away or just vanished for a while before?'

'No!' Annie protested – then checked herself.

Could he – could he somehow have fallen asleep, slipped into another universe, got lost between worlds? It *had* happened once, but Bartlemy had helped to call him back. Surely though, he wouldn't fall asleep straight after cricket, in the school cloakroom, when he was supposed to be going home . . .

'No,' she said resolutely. 'He's never done anything like that.'

Pobjoy saw the doubt writ clear in her face, and wondered at it.

They set Nathan with his back against a tree, Ginger and Ram holding him on either side. Damon had wanted them to tie him there but they hadn't brought any rope and their supply of tape was running out. Nathan thought of calling for help: he knew Woody would come to him, but the wood-wose would be too timid to do anything, too physically fragile even if he made the attempt. Nathan felt frightened, and angry with himself because he was frightened; fear was debilitating, shaming, it made you stupid. Whatever followed, he mustn't *show* fear, he mustn't let Damon see his weakness. Part of him still didn't quite believe this was happening – he was here in Thornyhill woods with his wrists and ankles taped together, while a boy he barely knew stood in front of him, sleeves rolled up to show unexpectedly brawny arms, one sporting a tattoo of a phoenix in flames, the other a plain metal bracelet, both prohibited at Ffylde. He was lighting a cigarette with peculiar care and drawing heavily on it, so Nathan saw the glow at the tip intensify to a red smoulder.

He'd tried talking to Ram and Ginger, telling them they were fools to go along with this – though he suspected Ram at least knew that already – but Damon's influence over them was too strong. Once the cigarette was going he shook the match and tossed it into the leafmould. A tiny thread of smoke drifted up from the spot.

'Stamp it out,' Nathan said, fleetingly distracted from the dangers of his own position. 'You could start a fire.'

After a stunned moment, Damon burst out laughing. 'Listen to him! Even now he has to be the virtuous little goody-goody! *Stamp it out – you could start a fire.*' He mimicked Nathan's tone in a baby-voice which didn't work. 'Well, why not? Let's start a fire. Let's watch the pretty woods burn . . . and burn . . .' He struck another match, holding it so the flame lengthened to a yellow tongue.

'If you do that,' Nathan said, suddenly angry, really angry, with a tight, black anger that swallowed fear, 'I'll see you dead.'

Something about his words made an impression, though he wasn't sure what sort. 'Then tell me,' Damon said, 'where's the cup? Where does the old man hide it?'

'I don't know.'

'Not even to save the pretty woods? How green they are – how lovely and green. Shall I turn them black and charred? Shall I fry all the squirrels and the rabbits and the other cute little woodland creatures? Shall I barbecue Squirrel Nutkin and Peter Rabbit and Mrs Tiggywinkle and all?'

'The courts don't like arson,' Ram muttered. 'We'd go down for a century.'

'Shut up.' The match burned down to Damon's fingers, and he dropped it with an oath, but it went out. Despite his situation, Nathan felt relief ooze through him. No more smoke came from the other one. 'All right, enough games. Let's get on with it.'

He drew on the cigarette again, tapped the excess ash from the tip. Then he opened Nathan's shirt.

Nathan thought: *He doesn't mean it. He won't really do it* – until he looked into Damon's eyes and saw the darkness there, and the gleam within the dark, the edge-of-madness gleam of someone who has gone beyond reality.

Damon pressed the cigarette against his chest.

The next few minutes were something that, all his life, Nathan preferred to forget. He tried not to scream – heard his breath hissing between gritted teeth – but he couldn't help himself. Even when the cigarette was removed the pain didn't stop. The tip had gone dark but Damon inhaled and the circle of smoulder revived, winking at him like a tiny eye of fire. Then more pain. Behind the pain, small cold thoughts ran through the part of Nathan's mind that was still *him*. Woody would hear his cries – he might go to Bartlemy – but how long would it take? How long did he have? How far would

Damon go? He kept asking about the cup, but Nathan didn't think he really expected an answer. He managed to say: 'I don't know', and 'I wouldn't tell you if I did', a pointless gesture of defiance which he realized, even as the words came out, would only make his tormenter angrier and more cruel. Ram and Ginger seemed very far away: he and Damon were enclosed in a cell of pain, one enjoying, the other suffering, bound together in a hideous intimacy.

At one point Nathan's eyes watered with the pain, and Damon saw, relishing it, mocking his tears, but at least he didn't beg, if that meant anything. He knew it wouldn't do any good.

Eventually, Ram said: 'He don't know shit. He'd of told you if he did. We ought to get on with the job.'

'This *is* the job,' Damon said. 'Part of it.' He was smiling a strange, shut-lipped smile.

'Someone might come – or hear him.'

'Who?' Damon looked contemptuous.

'Blokes walking dogs – people like that. It's *daylight*. Let's dump him and go.'

'Ram's right. We oughta get out of here.' Ginger. Out of the corner of his eye, Nathan saw he looked very pale, his acne scars standing out as bright red flecks. He might hit people and bite Rotweilers, but he didn't do slow torture.

Reluctantly, Damon allowed himself to be persuaded. 'Okay. Tape his mouth and stick him in the van.' And, to Nathan: 'I'll get back to you later.'

'We don't want to hold onto him, do we?' Ram protested. 'He's no more use to us.'

'We can't let him go,' Damon said coolly. 'Not after this.'

'But . . . you can't mean . . .' Ram faltered, running out of questions. Afraid of the answers.

You can't mean murder, Nathan thought, somewhere behind

the fog of agony. Ram had let go of him and he sagged forward, supported only by Ginger and the tree. Damon wouldn't really do it – would he? But it happened – he had heard of cases – he wasn't sure if they were fact or fiction – boys killing other boys out of sadism, savagery, experimental cruelty. He had a sudden fleeting vision of the court case – Damon's parents and sister – cameras – interviews – hate mail and headlines and public opprobrium. It made him feel vaguely sick. But despite the nausea – despite his fear and pain – he thought once again: *This is all so stupid.* It might yet be a thought to die on.

Damon had opened the back of the van and taken something out. A long zip carrier, meant for a pair of skis, only what was inside didn't seem to be ski-shaped. He unzipped, and took it out. A shotgun.

'Where did you get that?' Ram's voice was rising to a squeak. 'You said it was your sports gear. You didn't say –'

'It's my father's. He has a licence for it.' Damon broke the gun in an expert manner and loaded both barrels with shot from his pocket. 'This'll fix the old man. *And* his dog.'

Nathan's heart chilled.

'I don't like it,' Ginger said. 'I don't do guns.'

'You won't be using it. Shove the half-breed in here for the moment and let's get moving.'

They sealed his mouth with the rest of the tape and pitched him back in the van, slamming the doors. He heard the rustle of dead leaves and the crack of twigs as they retreated. Heading for Thornyhill Manor. For Uncle Barty and Hoover. With the gun. Nathan wriggled round and kicked against the doors, hoping against hope that someone would hear. Woody . . . but how could a woodwose get into the van? A stray dogwalker . . . Anyone. His nausea worsened but he knew, if he threw up, he would asphyxiate. The pain in his chest ate into him.

No one came.

SIX

The Love-Spell

In the living room at Thornyhill, Bartlemy extinguished the spellfire and sat down to wait. He had seen only glimpses, but it was enough to tell him to expect visitors, enough to make him deeply and quietly angry. He couldn't remember being angry for a long time, a hundred years or more. He could still be shocked, once in a while, for all his experience – disgusted, mildly surprised, but not angry, not that dreadful rocky anger that shakes the heart and has to be cooled and checked lest it overrule the head. 'It's because I love the boy,' he said to Hoover. 'And Annie. I love them both.' And he knew that *love*, too, was a word he hadn't used or thought in even longer, maybe centuries. Time had made him compassionate, tolerating and understanding human foibles, and he was always kind, but detached, faintly aloof, a being apart from the rest of mankind. Until now.

Hoover didn't thump his tail in agreement as he would usually have done, or pant, or loll his tongue. He stood by the kitchen door, ears cocked, looking somehow different from his normal self, less doggy, as if something feral in his ancestry had come to the fore, a trace of wolf, jackal, hyena. His face seemed wilder, his mane more shaggy, his stance alert, poised for movement – or attack. Maybe it was only the late

153

sunlight streaming through a nearby window that turned his brown eyes to yellow flame.

Bartlemy gave him a nod and he slipped out through the kitchen so swiftly he was gone in a breath, his big paws noiseless on the flagstone floor.

The old man waited.

Presently, he saw a shadow flit past the window – a rather clumsy flit, with much hesitation and looking-over-the-shoulder. Ram, he thought. A two-pronged invasion. Or probably three, with Ginger going round the other side. If his rate of approach was anything like Ram's, groping forward while glancing back, they would collide head-on at the rear door. Damon, on the other hand . . .

The knocker sounded at the front. Three loud knocks, sharp and imperative. Bartlemy rose, and went to open the door.

The spellfire hadn't shown him the gun.

There was a face at the window of the van, glimpsed as a mere flicker at the tail-end of Nathan's vision. A face that darted into view and then vanished, darted and vanished again. Not Woody – a swarthy, wrinkled, whiskery face, almost like that of a small animal, shaggy-browed and warty-nosed, with a bristle of hair on the top. Nathan tried to make some sound apart from kicking but all that came out was *Mm . . . mmf . . . mmmf*. The watcher – whoever he was – appeared to have gone, and Nathan was filled with a despair so intense it was almost worse than the pain. But only for a minute or two. Then someone leaped on the bonnet, darkening the windscreen, and there was a whirling motion and an impact which shattered the glass into a web of tiny cracks. Fists or feet punched the fragments inward, and a dark small figure ducked through the gap and sprang nimbly into the back of the van. The tape was ripped from Nathan's mouth; a knife hacked at his bonds.

It's the dwarf, Nathan realized, even before he looked round. Of course . . .

He tried to say *thank you – please – hurry –* but the words didn't come out right. The skin around his mouth smarted and the burns on his chest seared into him. Then his arms and legs were free but so cramped from long confinement he could barely move. He managed to open the rear doors and half stumbled, half fell onto the ground.

'You maun just sit there a wee while,' the dwarf said in his strange guttural brogue, assisting Nathan to heave himself into a sitting position propped against a wheel. He wore a few ragged garments which matched the leathery texture of his skin and the wiry thicket of his hair. His short knife was thrust through the knotted thongs that provided him with a belt; also the axe which he must have used to break the windscreen. The rank-fox-and-unwashed-dwarf odour hung around him like a miasma.

Nathan had never been so glad to see anyone.

'Thanks,' he said, more coherently this time. 'I don't know why you –'

'Ye ha' no cause to thank me,' the dwarf interrupted. 'I were merely returning a weal for a weal. Ye set me free; I set ye free. My folk dinna care to be indebted.'

'Well . . . thanks anyway. But I must get moving – I must get to Thornyhill. They've gone there now, and Damon's got a gun.' He was massaging his legs as he spoke, trying to kick-start his circulation with fingers still partially numb.

'A gun? What is 't?'

'Like a bow and arrow, only nastier. Much nastier. It fires lead pellets, incredibly fast. They plough through you, ripping holes in your body.'

'Men are iver fixing to come up wi' new ways o' killing,' the dwarf said philosophically. 'I wouldna worry about the old one, if I were you. I reckon he's well accustomed to taking care o' hissel. And there's the hound. I doubt there's many would get past him.'

It was a long speech for Nambrok, but Nathan wasn't reassured. 'You don't understand,' he said. 'There's no magic that stops a gun – not that I know of.' He scrambled to his feet, leaning against the van, then lurching a few steps forward. 'I ought to call the police, but I haven't even got my mobile. I *must* get there.'

'Mebbe I'd best help ye a ways,' said the dwarf, winding a sinewy arm around Nathan's waist, which was as high as he could reach.

Together, the unlikely pair tottered off through the woods.

Bartlemy glanced down at the gun, and then up into Damon's face. Like Nathan, he saw the darkness in his eyes, a cloud obscuring rational thought, and in the dark the glint of something not normal, not human. Behind, in the house, he heard voices, and the approaching footsteps of Ginger and Ram.

He said: 'Dear me.'

Damon raised the gun, sighting down the twin barrels, high on power, on brutality, on his own inner blackness. He was riding his madness like a wave-crest, all restraint abandoned, surfing the flood-tide of a glorious dark freedom. He could do anything – hurt, maim, kill – it didn't matter any more. There were no rules to hold him back, no whispering of conscience, no nudging of future guilt. In the shadows of his mind he fondly imagined the monster he had become was his true self.

'Give me the cup,' he said. 'I know you have it. Get it for me.'

'Where's the dog?' Ram quavered, from the rear. 'I can't see it.' He was looking round nervously.

'Never mind the bloody dog,' Damon snapped. 'If I see it, I'll blow its head off. Stop whining.'

'Ah, but you won't see him,' Bartlemy said softly.

'Why not?'

'He's behind you.'

Damon spun round, but too late – the teeth had already closed on his calf. He tried to swing the gun – aim it – but it was no longer in his control. Bartlemy had seized the muzzle in a grip that did not belong to an old man and wrenched it effortlessly from his hands. He saw blood running from the dog's jaws – his blood – and doubled over, grunting with pain. 'You didn't – warn me!' he accused Ram. 'Stupid c–'

'I didn't see it!' Damon's henchmen were retreating rapidly, into the house. 'It came from nowhere!'

'He does that,' Bartlemy acknowledged, shooing them negligently into his living room. And to Damon: 'He has a very strong jaw. Don't struggle: he could break your leg. The hyena's bite is the most powerful in the dog world, but I assure you my friend here can match it. Possibly there is some hyena in him. Are you in pain?'

Damon's breath hissed in answer.

'Good,' Bartlemy said tranquilly. 'You need to feel pain. You need to know what it's like to be on the receiving end. That is your first lesson.' The dog bit deeper, teeth touching bone. 'Rukush! That will do. Where is Nathan?'

'The woods . . .' Damon squeezed the words out. He was white and sweating.

'He's in the van!' Ram piped up. 'We parked along a track about half a mile away. Damon made us tie him up, but it wasn't our idea. None of it was our idea.'

'But you went along with it, didn't you?' Bartlemy said in the same gentle tone. 'Very well, Rukush, go and find him. I can handle things here.'

Hoover released the leg and sprang off through the trees. Damon crumpled where he stood.

A short while later he found himself, like others before him, in Bartlemy's living room. The gun was propped up against the wall, but no one made any move to retrieve it. Bartlemy had cut off the torn section of his trousers, bathed his wounds, and anointed them with a lotion which produced a sensation not unlike burning, for a minute or so. Damon screamed. As Bartlemy applied a bandage he said with an attempt at bravado: 'My father will sue you.'

'I don't think so.' Bartlemy was unruffled.

Ram and Ginger had obeyed the old man as if mesmerized, and now sat on the edge of the sofa, awaiting in suspense whatever might happen next. A newly-developed instinct told them it might include biscuits.

When Hoover returned with Nathan (the dwarf had vanished back into the woods) there was more bathing and anointing, this time with a lotion that anaesthetized pain. Nathan found himself looking at his late opponent (he didn't count the other two) with a curious lack of hate. Damon sat brooding, hunched inside himself, a dark knot of bitterness and rage and suppressed misery. He's hating enough for both of us, Nathan thought.

Then there was tea, and biscuits. Damon refused to eat.

'I should if I were you,' Nathan said. 'My uncle's the best cook in the world.'

He believed he was exaggerating a little, but it was true.

'We ought to call your mother,' Bartlemy said. 'She's concerned about you. But she'll bring the police, and I don't want them quite yet.'

To the three who thought of themselves as his prisoners, that sounded ominous.

Bartlemy pulled up a stool in front of Damon, taking his

face between both hands despite his resistance, forcing him to lift his head. 'No, don't turn away. Look at me. *Look at me.*' And then, as if to himself: 'There's something not right here.'

Nathan was watching, but Ram and Ginger went on eating biscuits. When they had emptied the plate, Bartlemy said: 'You can go now.'

They stared at him, pop-eyed.

'I expect the police will come to see you in due course. You never know. Meanwhile, you'd better take your father back his van.'

I never told him it was my father's van, Ram thought.

'You won't be coming here again.'

They shook their heads eagerly, then nodded.

'You should hurry,' Bartlemy recommended. 'The woods will be dark soon.'

As if it grew dark in the woods before anywhere else, thought Ram, wishing he was as unimaginative as his companion. But even Ginger appeared unsettled as they walked back up the road and groped their way along the woodland track to where they had left the van. They found the doors open and the windscreen shattered, and the undergrowth seemed to have crept nearer, and twitching shadows stalked the edge of their sight.

'I don't like this.' Ginger summed up the feelings of both. 'I don't like it at all. Let's get outta here.'

They brushed the broken glass off the seat, climbed in, and reversed hastily and awkwardly back to the road.

At Thornyhill, Bartlemy told Nathan: 'Call your mother on her mobile. Tell her she can collect you from here in an hour, not before. She will want to bring the Inspector – that's fine – but not till nine-thirty. Mind that: it's important.'

Nathan made the call.

* * *

The daylight was fading as Bartlemy drew the curtains and lit the spellfire. The crystals split and crepitated in the heat; blue-white flames hissed over them, sending ghost-lights and shadows glancing round the room. Twice Damon rose as if to leave, but Hoover rose with him, not growling, not threatening, just there, shaggy and immoveable, blocking his egress, and each time he sat down again. Occasionally he protested: 'You can't keep me here!', but no one bothered to answer and the objection sounded thin even to his own ears. Nathan, at a gesture from his uncle, took a chair well out of the way and stayed there. He felt curious but also oddly uncomfortable, a witness to a scene which ought to be private, like an accidental eavesdropper who overhears a doctor telling a patient he is seriously ill. Bartlemy lit candles on either side of Damon, smelling of strange herbs; the scent made Nathan's head feel fuzzy. At one point, Damon said: 'Not more of this New Age witchcraft garbage. I don't believe in all that shit.'

More? Nathan wondered. *More . . .*

He wanted to ask Bartlemy if Damon really was possessed, but sensed that this was not the time for talking.

Bartlemy seated himself in front of the boy, murmuring something in Atlantean, the secret language of magic. Suddenly, Damon became quiet and still. As the incantation continued his expression emptied, leaving him with the look of a sleepwalker, open-eyed and unseeing. Hoover, his guard duty no longer necessary, retreated to sit beside Nathan. *Damon's hypnotized*, Nathan thought, except his uncle had made none of the moves of the conventional hypnotist. The pale firelight danced over the rug, showing an Oriental design of great complexity, patterns within patterns, glints of vermilion and ruby nestling within coils of beige and blue. Without ever really looking at it Nathan had been familiar with it all his life, but now he seemed to see different shapes flicking in and out of the pattern, runes older than the Orient, symbols of a civilization long gone. Perhaps it was a trick of the fire-glow, but it was almost as if the design had shifted, mutating imperceptibly into new forms, new complexities. By chance or choice Damon's chair was at the centre of a circle; all the radiance of the candles appeared to be concentrated within it, illuminating Damon's face very clearly. Not a cruel face, Nathan reflected, not now, just young and unmarked, cleansed of all feeling.

Bartlemy placed his fingertips gently on the boy's temples, still murmuring the soft cold words of the spell. If it was a spell. It sounded more like a kind of exhortation, a ripple of persuasive phrases insinuating themselves into the blankness of Damon's mind. Presently, Bartlemy began to pull his fingers away, and there was something black attached to them, apparently drawn out of Damon's head, like long strands of clinging vapour which gradually disseminated in the candlelight. More of it came . . . and more . . . Nathan watched in fascinated horror as one great dark clot adhered to Bartlemy's hand like an inky goo, though it seemed to have no more substance than mist.

'What is it?' he ventured, in a whisper.

'An infection,' Bartlemy responded. 'It was clouding his mind, pressing on his thoughts, infiltrating and distorting them. It would inflame the darker aspects of his nature – we all have them – and obscure conscience and moderation. Think of it as a culture of magical bacteria, feeding on his spirit as a sickness feeds on the body. He was perhaps weakened and vulnerable because of his age and problems in his family life – such infections are much less effective when the mind is healthy. Part of him would probably have welcomed the darkness, since it blotted out many things that troubled him.'

'How did it happen?' Nathan asked. 'Could it attack – like – anybody?'

Bartlemy was drawing the last few threads of shadow from Damon's head. When he spoke, he sounded quite matter-of-fact. 'Oh no,' he said. 'It was put there.'

'By whom?'

Something like a shaft of lightning struck the circle. For a millisecond, the whole room seemed to flick into darkness, so that even the spellfire was quenched. The rug scorched and smoked; the curve of the perimeter was burned into the pattern. Damon's glazed stare flashed livid flame. The lightning crawled around his bracelet, which split into two jointed halves and fell to the floor. His mouth opened with a cry of rage in a voice that was not his own – behind him, a huge figure loomed up, shadowy and ominous, leaning forward as if to seize him. The livid fire fled from Damon's gaze to flare briefly in the eyes at his back.

'*Vardé*!' Bartlemy cried. '*Néfia*! *Envarré néan-charne*!'

The figure vanished, imploding into its own lightning. The spellfire blazed and sank. Faint glooms settled gently back into their corners. Except for the scorchmark, the patterns on the rug seemed to fade into their customary obscurity. Bartlemy rose and blew out the candles, returning them to a cupboard at the end of the room. He picked up the bracelet, pocketing it without comment or explanation. Then he cleared the hearth with surprising speed and lit an ordinary fire, despite the summer warmth. Damon sat in his chair with his face blank and his eyes now closed.

'Will he be all right?' Nathan said.

'He will be – himself,' Bartlemy answered. 'It may take him a little time to remember everything he has done. Then he will need help dealing with it. He will have more nightmares than you about what happened in the woods.'

'I shan't have nightmares,' Nathan said. 'I cried, though. I couldn't stop myself.' He felt it was important to say it.

'It was only the pain,' said Bartlemy. 'Crying was natural. It need not trouble you.'

'Is that why people do those things?' Nathan asked after a pause. 'Torture and abuse and stuff . . . Is it an infection in their heads?'

'It can be.' Bartlemy sighed. 'Some are born with their spirits already warped and darkened; we do not know why. Some are damaged by circumstances and invite the infection in. In other cases, it can be put there, as you have seen, though not always by such magics as were used here. There are many forms of the Gift, and all too often it turns to evil. If you have that talent, you don't necessarily need spellpower to control the weak and the willing. Gifted leaders in politics or religion can attract these bacteria – elementals too primitive to have voice or thought, black humours, tiny fragments of living darkness – using them without knowing it, afflicting those under their sway. Sometimes, whole nations can be diseased. But remember, such infection *can* be resisted; without a degree of acceptance, it cannot take hold.'

'Can it – can it be cured?' Nathan said. 'Without the sort of exorcism you did?'

'The only cure is total self-revelation. It is always traumatic, and can scar the spirit for life.'

Nathan considered this. 'But . . . Damon was infected deliberately,' he said. 'By someone with powers like yours.' And: 'What was that – apparition just now?'

'A spirit which had been conjured to instil the infection. The person who did it wanted to be very sure it would take hold.'

'Who was it?'

But Bartlemy was bent over Damon, touching his forehead. Calling his name.

Damon blinked and looked around, vaguely bemused. 'What on earth –'

And then: 'The dog. The dog bit me.'

'I'm afraid so,' Bartlemy admitted.

'What am I doing here?'

'You came to steal something,' Bartlemy explained. 'You brought your father's gun; it's over there against the wall.'

Damon's roving gaze found Nathan, focused. He frowned suddenly, then his face paled into shock. 'I did – I tried to –'

'Yes, you did,' Bartlemy said. 'Happily, you did not succeed. You were not entirely yourself at the time. People are coming soon; someone will take you home. Meanwhile, I think hot chocolate is in order, with a slug of brandy. And something to nibble.'

Nathan followed him into the kitchen, leaving Damon silent and shivering at the fireside.

'Shouldn't we ask him who did it? Who put the bacteria in his mind?'

'It isn't necessary.'

'His father,' Nathan concluded, shocked at the concept. 'It must have been Giles Hackforth, right? He's the one who wants the Grail. It was his own father . . .'

'In a way,' said Bartlemy.

For all her anxiety, Annie obeyed Bartlemy's injunction to delay her arrival at Thornyhill for an hour. As the drive from Ffylde took nearly that, even in a police car with blue light flashing, she didn't actually have to hold herself in check for very long. When she got there she hugged Nathan rather tearily, demanded explanations, and knew immediately, from the look on his face, she wasn't going to get them. Not in front of the inspector, anyway.

Nathan, to his own surprise, found himself playing the whole episode down. Bartlemy hadn't asked it of him, but somehow he felt it was the right thing to do. Whatever anger

he nurtured had withered at the sight of Damon's frozen stillness, his stammering attempt at apology, abruptly cut off
when he realized no words would heal what he had done.
Dimly, Nathan glimpsed the abyss into which Damon was
staring – the knowledge of his own capacity for evil. 'The
dark is in all of us,' Bartlemy had said. 'You and me as well
as Damon. We have to face it, and conquer it. That is the
measure of our strength. When the soul is infected, or dimin-
ished, that is when our demon takes over.'

'It was just a game,' Nathan told Pobjoy. 'A . . . a kind of
joke. It went a bit far.'

'You said Damon kidnapped you.'

'Yes, but – it wasn't meant to be for real. It was just . . .'

'Just a joke?'

Annie threw a sombre look at the kidnapper, but refrained
from joining in. Experience – or instinct – had taught her the
value of non-interference.

'Were you alone in this game?' the inspector asked Damon.

'Yes he was,' Nathan said hastily.

'You're covering up,' Pobjoy said with a trace of bitterness. 'None of you has ever told me the whole truth – about
anything.'

'Consider it simply adolescent high spirits,' Bartlemy
offered. 'Rites of passage.'

'Which?' Pobjoy's tone was arctic.

'Either. Both. It's up to you.' Bartlemy produced his gentlest
smile. 'I expect you've missed your supper. Can I get you
something?'

'No,' Pobjoy said without thanks. 'I'm going to return Mr
Hackforth to his family. I'd like to hear his answers to some
of my questions. He hasn't had much to say for himself so
far. I may also have to take action concerning his illegal possession of a firearm.'

Nathan looked alarmed, but Bartlemy was unruffled.

'Damon is a little overwrought,' he said. 'He may tend to exaggerate what has happened – for effect. Teenagers do like to shock their elders, don't they? Especially those in authority. As for the gun, I understand he took it by mistake. It was in a bag that normally contained a pair of skis.'

'He would be going skiing,' Pobjoy said, 'in a wood in summer.'

As he turned to leave, Annie laid a hand on his arm. 'Thanks,' she said. 'Thanks for everything.' There was nothing left of her old resentment for suspicions past. 'I'm sorry if we've wasted your time.'

But Pobjoy wasn't in a mood to be mollified. 'You always do,' he said.

Nathan saw Hazel that weekend and told her what had happened, but George was with them, and perhaps because of that he curtailed his account, not mentioning the cigarette burns (he hadn't shown those to Annie either). Even so, George was impressed. 'Wow!' he said. 'Cool! I mean, you read about the stuff that goes on in public schools, but I didn't know it happened for real. Sixth-formers kidnapping people, and tying them up, and initiation rituals and so on.'

'It wasn't an initiation ritual.'

'Whatever. Were you awfully scared? I would've been.'

'Nathan's never scared,' Hazel said. Somehow, it didn't sound entirely complimentary. 'You know that.'

'I *was* scared,' Nathan averred. 'Shitless. Damon seemed like he was mad – possessed – as if he didn't care what he did as long as it was bad. That was really scary.'

'Thank God we're at a nice safe boring comprehensive,' George said. 'We just have drugs and sex and ordinary bullying – and I never get any of the drugs or sex. It's pretty dull most of the time. Jason Wicks started an extortion racket last term, but Dale Jorkins told his mum, who's like, *huge*, and does weight-lifting, and she went to see Jason's old man and picked him up with one hand, so we got most of the money back. Jason's bully-cred went through the floor. It was brilliant.'

'You didn't tell me about that,' Nathan said.

'We probably didn't see you,' Hazel pointed out. 'Can I borrow your rugger-shirt?'

'Sure, but – why?'

'I can't find mine, and I – I want to wear a rugger-shirt, that's all. A real one, that's had rugger played in it.' She added, improvising furiously: 'It's a style thing. You wouldn't understand.'

Nathan looked bewildered, but appeared to accept this as part of the inscrutability of female fashions. 'It hasn't been washed.'

'Doesn't matter.'

Later, Hazel took home her trophy, feeling uncomfortable about it, and telling herself a little too often not to be stupid. After all, she had taken an item of his once before, for her great-grandmother, and nothing had happened to him. (That time, the sweatshirt had been recently washed.)

She'd had no problem pinching a hair ornament of Ellen's from her desk at school, but obtaining a 'token' from Jonas had been much more difficult, though unattended by guilt. She had tried abstracting his sweater when he had taken it off at break, but Ellen had seen her, and she'd had to plead a mistake, retreating behind her hair, knowing she sounded unconvincing. Afterwards, she had seen Ellen snickering with her current cronies, and it dawned on her that they thought she wanted to steal the sweater out of unrequited passion, presumably so she could snuggle up to it at night and dream of her beloved. Which wasn't *quite* as bad as the truth but very nearly, since it meant the secret of her affection was out. Now, Ellen and Co. would be looking for telltale signs, the giveaway gestures and expressions that would betray her. And they would find them, Hazel knew, no matter how careful she was. Teenage girls on the track of weakness in a class-mate are more observant than an MI5 surveillance team. She had to do something, quickly.

She had to do the spell.

Desperation made her bold. Jonas had a strip of plaster on his knee after a fall from his bicycle, and she managed to waylay him after basketball to offer a new-lamps-for-old deal. 'You ought to change that,' she said, greatly daring. 'It's dirty. Here – I've got a spare one.'

He stared at her. They'd barely spoken before, and, if he'd thought about her at all, it was as the introverted type who didn't talk much to anyone. He supposed it was part of his newfound popularity, that quiet girls would offer him Elastoplast out of the blue. He said: 'Thanks.'

'I'll get rid of that,' Hazel concluded hastily, snatching the old plaster from his hand. Despite her hidden passion, she didn't want to prolong the encounter. It wasn't exactly roman-tic.

Inevitably one of Ellen's entourage, a lumpy girl known as Fizz, had witnessed the incident and followed Hazel, darkly suspicious, to see if she really did discard the screwed-up plas-ter. She cornered her quarry some ten minutes later in the cloakroom. 'You kept it!' she jeered, the sparkle of glee making her appear, if possible, even less attractive. 'Yeeurrgh! You kept a disgusting bit of icky plaster just 'cause it belonged to Jonas. God, you are so pathetic. Wait till I tell the others about this – they'll laugh themselves sick. Ellen ought to warn him: you might be after his used loo paper next. You know,

168

you're creepy – really creepy. They've probably got a name for people who do things like this. You're the ultimate freako.'

Hazel said nothing. The floor failed to oblige by swallowing her up. She grabbed her jacket and her bag, and fled.

The Saturday, after she left Nathan and George, was taken up with family and other impedimenta. On Sunday, she was finally able to summon Lilliat. It was easy now, she did it without thinking, and this time, with little preparation. The language of the Stone rolled coldly off her tongue. As the image developed in the mirror it seemed to tremble and darken for a moment, as if uncertain what form and colour it should take – then it settled into the high cheekbones and silver tones of the Spirit of Flowers. There was a second when the thought flicked through Hazel's mind: What does she *really* look like?, but she dismissed it. It was too late now for doubts: she had chosen her path, and must go on with it.

'I have the tokens,' she said.

An ethereal hand extended from the mirror and touched the hair clip and the rugger-shirt, hovering over the plaster.

'What is *this*?'

'It was the best I could do,' Hazel said impatiently. The anger at her humiliation in front of her classmates was still with her. 'Jonas had it on a cut. It's got his blood on it – his DNA.'

'Blood is good,' Lilliat said, her upper lip lifting, giving her an almost hungry expression. 'Blood is the ichor of life. But I prefer it in a liquid form.'

'The ick factor,' Hazel muttered.

In the mirror, another face appeared below that of the spirit – Jonas, looking at Hazel with the faint bewilderment he had shown when Hazel offered him a fresh Elastoplast. 'This is the one?' Lilliat asked. 'The boy you love?'

Suddenly, Hazel wasn't sure. Jonas seemed a figure of fantasy, neither attractive, nor desirable, nor inscrutable and mysterious – a passion she clung to because it gave purpose to her life, it gave her a dream to chase, an illusion of depth and feeling. But even if it was a fantasy, she needed it too much to let go of it now.

She said: 'Yes. That's Jonas.'

'And this –' his reflection faded, to be replaced by Ellen Carver, her features pouty with prettiness and spite '– this is the girl you want to destroy?'

'Not *destroy* . . . I just want her out of his life. I mean, I don't want him to care for her any more.'

'It is done,' Lilliat said, smiling.

The surface of the mirror shimmered into nothing – there was just a hole in the air, a space in the very fabric of being. Spirit and reflection disappeared into a whirling, sucking darkness – voices from every corner of the room murmured words in an ancient language, half heard and less than half understood. The hair clip and the plaster flared with a swift blue flame, crisped and vanished. Tiny pulses of power shivered across the floor, and crackled the hairs on Hazel's skin. For a minute, she *felt* like a witch, standing at the core of something unknown and unknowable, sensing the alien magic throb in her fingertips, beat in her blood. In that minute, it was the magic that mattered – the scorn of her classmates was less than the chatter of birds, and all her love for Jonas was gone in a breath. She glimpsed the person she might become, great among the Gifted, immortal among mortals, twisting the threads of her life into the design of her choosing, controlling family, friends, Nathan . . .

The idea of Nathan came as if Lilliat had summoned his presence from the token, pushing it into her thought. Hazel shrank away, flinching from guilt or doubt, and the power fizzled into nothing, and she was herself again, inadequate and alone. In the mirror, the void iced over, and Lilliat was there once more.

'You are afraid,' she said. 'You're afraid of your own power.'

'Will the spell work?' Hazel demanded.

'Maybe.'

'You promised! If it doesn't –'

'What can you do?' The silver laugh mocked her. 'Don't dare to doubt it. Your fear – your faltering – will undermine it. Believe it – want it – *need* it – with your whole body, your whole heart. Give yourself to the magic and it will work for you, and the world is yours.'

'I don't want the world,' Hazel said. 'Jonas is enough for me.'

'Nothing is ever enough,' said Lilliat. 'Now for the final token.' From the mirror her arms reached out, mist-faint and snow-pale.

Hazel snatched the rugger-shirt away, clutching it to her chest. 'Not yet! When I have Jonas – when the spell works . . .'

'The spell is complete,' Lilliat said. 'The price must be paid.' Her hair grew and darkened, overflowing the mirror, streaming through the air like a flood of black water. Her eyes widened, opening onto deeps of midnight. There was no mirror now, no room, only her figure stooping amid the shadows of her endless hair. Hazel screamed – words she had read in her great-grandmother's notes, though she scarcely knew what they portended. '*Envarré! Néfia!* Go! Go now!'

'You rejected the power,' said the spirit who had called herself Lilliat. 'You cannot call on it now. You have neither the strength nor the knowledge. The bargain is made – fulfil your part.' Her hair swirled into a storm, spinning, tugging, while Hazel cowered at its heart. The rugger-shirt was wrenched from her grasp. Then the darkness shrank back into the mirror – there was a splintering noise, and the last wisp of shadow slipped through a crack in the glass. Only the voice of the phantom lingered, whispering, promising. 'Do not regret. You will need me again, very soon. Call, and I will come to you. Call me . . . I will come . . . I will come . . .'

The whisper faded. There was a breath of air that felt chill and smelt faintly salty . . . then only the warm stuffiness of Hazel's bedroom. She sat on the floor, trembling and hugging her knees. Staring and staring at the broken mirror.

It was a long time before she moved.

Inevitably, the kidnapping led to a rapprochement between Nathan and his mother. The barriers were not dissolved but accepted, of necessity on her part; hostilities were over. At Ffylde, Nathan did his best to gloss over the whole incident, saying as little as possible even to Ned Gable. Damon reputedly came in to finish his exams but wasn't seen on the premises at all, leading to rumours he had been expelled. Stories began to circulate about his poker debts, becoming increasingly improbable, pushing them into six figures. Everyone waited hopefully for dramatic developments, but nothing happened. In Eade, Bartlemy dropped into the bookshop and asked Annie to accompany him to the Hackforths. 'They know you. Under the circumstances, I don't think they will refuse to talk to us.'

Annie thought of Selena's face, worn out from the long struggle against her daughter's illness, her son's delinquency. 'Must we?' she said, and then, answering her own question: 'Of course we must. After all, what Damon did wasn't really his fault – was it?'

'Not entirely.'

And, on a note of hope: 'Could you – could you help the girl – Melly-Anne? You know so much about medicines . . .'

'Help – maybe. Cure – no. I cannot perform miracles.'

'Isn't that what magic is for – miracles?'

'I wish it was,' Bartlemy said, a little sadly. 'But magic cannot change the world, only twist it. The Gift, at its most potent, is about power – not the power to do good, but power for its own sake. The mightiest wizard may bend the universe around him, but he cannot stop the sparrow's fall, nor turn a few grains of dust back into a man. Magic is mere force, like electricity. Miracles are beyond explanation.'

'Have you ever seen one?' Annie asked.

'I've seen many. The beauty of the sunset – the strength of the human heart – these are the true miracles. What scientific or magical explanation is there for our pleasure in nature's loveliness – for mercy, kindness, selfless love? We have analysed our world down to the smallest particle, but the answers only pose more questions. As for creation, forensics may tell us how the crime was committed, but not who done it, or to what end. Magic can weave a spell powerful enough to open a door between worlds, but it cannot make those worlds anew, nor restore what has been lost. Keep faith – have hope – and be comforted. Life is full of miracles, though they don't come to order.'

They drove to the Hackforths in Annie's car, arriving just before tea-time.

'We should've called,' Annie said. 'They might be out.'

'They won't be out,' Bartlemy said with the air of one who knew. 'I preferred to take them by surprise.'

Selena greeted them, looking wearier than ever. 'Of course,' she said. 'I suppose . . . I've been expecting you. Is this your lawyer?'

'My *lawyer*?' Annie looked blank.

'Giles thought – Giles said you would take legal action. I can't blame you. Damon told us what he did.'

'I'm a friend,' Bartlemy said. 'I stand to Nathan in the relationship of an uncle. My name is Goodman, Bartlemy Goodman. Your son may have mentioned me.'

'Yes, he . . . he said something . . .'

'May we come in?'

They went in. The dogs rushed forward, welcoming Annie like a long-lost friend, mobbing Bartlemy, who calmed them with a word. They followed him past the kitchen into the drawing room, where a grey-faced Giles sat on a grey-covered sofa. He got up, looking guarded; hands were shaken.

'I'm prepared to pay compensation,' Giles said, rushing into speech. 'If we could just keep the matter out of the courts –'

'We don't want compensation,' Annie said. 'Honestly. I never even thought of it. We just want to talk.'

Hackforth didn't look particularly reassured.

'If I might have a word with you alone,' Bartlemy said, flicking a glance at Annie, who suppressed her curiosity with reluctance.

'We'll get some tea,' she said.

In the end, she steered Selena into the garden, wandering between colour-coordinated banks of flowers, admiring the roses, the shaved lawn, the dubious sculpture in the water feature. 'Barty's really good with homeopathic medicines,' Annie said at last. 'He might have something that would help Melly-Anne. Not – not exactly a magic potion, but – it's all natural stuff, it can't hurt to try it.'

'It's nice of you to think of her,' Selena said with automatic courtesy. 'After Damon . . .' She couldn't bring herself to be more specific.

'Barty says – it wasn't his fault,' Annie said with difficulty.

174

'He thinks Damon was controlled – influenced – by some-one. I expect that's what he's discussing with your husband.'

'You mean, one of his friends? We've never really known who he . . . hangs out with.'

Annie thought of Ram and Ginger. According to Nathan, they had been controlled by Damon, not vice versa. She said: 'Possibly.'

Later, the men joined them for tea. Giles, Annie was pleased to see, appeared less tense, less anxious, almost relaxed. It was Bartlemy in whose manner she detected a faint – a very faint – undercurrent of something she couldn't define – worry, uncertainty, fear. But Bartlemy was never worried or afraid. On the way home she asked him what was wrong, but his response was noncommittal.

'You've found out something,' she accused. 'Something about who was really behind the burglaries, and manipulat-ing Damon. Nathan thinks it was Giles himself, but . . .'

'*Attempted* burglaries,' Bartlemy corrected her. 'Anyway, I only had a suspicion confirmed.'

'What are we going to do about it?'

'Nothing. For now.'

Arriving at school on Monday, Hazel found her worst night-mares coming true. Ellen Carver and her entourage were gath-ered in a little group, talking in gleeful whispers, watching her sideways, sniggering. The snigger spread through the class like a ripple as the whisper passed from mouth to ear, unhin-dered by lessons or the presence of teaching staff. The teachers were divorced from the teenage world, existing on an aloof plane while the real life of the school seethed and festered underneath. If they noticed Hazel was quiet that meant little; she was always quiet, a loner with few close friends who made scant contribution in class. Inside the armour of her silence she thought she died a hundred times that day, stabbed by the giggles, the nudges, the sly remarks, the derisive glances. Those who had been her mates backed off, joining the enemy or simply avoiding her, unwilling to be identified with the pariah. She curled up inside herself like a hedgehog, all prickle, showing no reaction, pulling her hair so far over her face that the gym mistress told her rather sharply to tie it back. Whether Jonas Tyler had heard the story she didn't know – she saw him only at a distance, and he didn't appear to see her – but her faith in the magic was gone. The spell was mere words – words and dreams – the reality was private folly, public shame. She had been stupid, credulous, childish, and now she was paying the price.

It was all Lilliat's fault.

She was leaving school around two, playing truant from her last lesson, when she ran into Jonas. He said: 'Hi,' taking her off guard. She hadn't expected a normal greeting from anyone. She grunted in reply – she couldn't manage *hello*.

They stood for a minute in mutual embarrassment, looking at each other. At least, Jonas looked; Hazel could see little through her hair.

'Thanks for the plaster yesterday,' he went on with youthful tactlessness. 'I'm sorry the others seem to think . . . Well, thanks anyway.'

Hazel gave a shrug which emerged as a twitch. Why on earth was he thanking her for a *plaster*, for God's sake? Perhaps he was mocking her.

She expected him to go away, but he hesitated, shifting his feet.

'They're giving you a bad time, aren't they?'

'I'm all right.' Hazel was gruff.

'Girls can be so bitchy. I don't mean you – you're not like that – but even Ellen . . .'

'I thought she was your girlfriend?'

Jonas fidgeted more than ever. 'Um . . . sort of. Only – I don't like bitches. Of course, she's very pretty – lots of blokes want to go out with her – but she's a bit of a tease. She comes on really sexy and then . . .' He stalled, fumbled, re-started. 'Look, I like you a lot. Honestly. I wish . . . I wish we could talk some time.'

What's happening here? Hazel thought. He's almost asking me out.

This time, it was surprise which paralysed her vocal chords. *The spell must have worked.* Wow.

'The thing is, all my mates would laugh. Maybe we could meet somewhere . . . secret. Get to know each other a bit better. Without anyone finding out . . .'

Wow?

'Romeo and Juliet?' Hazel said. 'That sounds pretty silly to me.'

'They just had family problems, didn't they?' he commented vaguely. 'We've got the whole school to contend with.'

'I don't know . . .' This wasn't working out the way she'd fantasized at all.

'I really do like you.' He reached out, touched her. She found herself shrinking away. 'I bet you're not a tease. I bet if you liked someone . . .'

Hazel gazed into his face and saw the mystery evaporate. He was just a rather shy boy who wanted to get laid. And he thought she was so hooked on him she'd be a pushover. Whether the spell had actually worked or not she never knew. In that instant of disillusion, she felt it didn't really matter.

'I don't like you that much,' she said. 'Sorry.'

She hitched her rucksack further up her shoulder and hurried off, suddenly eager to get away from him. Now, he too would be against her. But her brief glimpse into the shallows of his soul had filled her with panic. The sweet, sensitive persona she had created for him, burdened with unknown sorrows, had disappeared in the glare of reality, leaving an ordinary boy, with ordinary preoccupations – a boy who was hardly worth heartache and dreams, let alone scheming and spells. After all she had borne that day – for his sake, or so she told herself – it was too much. She fled home and shut herself in her room, gazing savagely at the cracked mirror.

She wanted to summon the spirit – the spirit who had lied to her and cheated her, exacting a price she never wished to pay for a spell that had turned sour on her. The bile in her was so strong, the memory of Lilliat's true nature – the darkness behind the veil of flowers – barely daunted her. Without even knowing it, she felt the certainty of power, filling her, driving her, a force all destruction, without principle, incapable of good. 'You said I would call you –' she spoke aloud, pushing herself on, sensing it was foolhardy, knowing it was pointless, but rage gave her the delusion of purpose. 'I'm calling.' And now there were words in her head which she had never even read, tugging at the roots of the air, winging on the wind. '*Santò daiman, santò māna, santò māna maru! Venya! Fia! Vissari!*'

Lilliat's face hovered beneath the surface of the mirror, split in two by the crack, one side silver-eyed and silver-haired, the other all shadow. When she spoke, only half her mouth moved – the half in the light. Hazel fancied she was confused by the crack, and had simply forgotten to move the other half. Her voice came from within; any motion of her features was merely cosmetic.

'What of the spell?' she asked. 'Are you content?'

'No!'

The phantom didn't seem to understand. 'I gave him to you, the one you love. I made him desire you. Isn't that what you wanted?'

'*No*! He just *lusted* after me, because I was there, because he thought I was available. I wanted him to *care*.' I wanted him to be special, the boy in my dreams, not a standard boring male with standard teenage hormones. 'I wanted him to *love* me.'

'He loves you.' Lilliat's half-face went cold. The dark side did not change. 'Love is desire. Desire is love. What else is there?'

'You wouldn't know. You're stupid as well as a liar. It doesn't matter, anyway. It was all for nothing. And now the others – Ellen and her friends – they despise me – everyone despises me – I've become the butt of the whole school. All thanks to you . . .'

'This Ellen – she's the one the boy loved – the one whose token you gave me?'

'Yes. I hate her. I hate her –'

'Hate is good.' One end of Lilliat's mouth remembered to smile. 'Hate is desire. Desire is hate. What else is there?'

'Nothing else,' Hazel said. She was panting as if she had been running, breathless with the emotions that battered and pummelled at her spirit. Hate at least was clear, filling her with a dark burning glow, driving the doubts from her mind. It was easy to hate.

'I granted your wish,' Lilliat was saying. 'The wish of your heart. But . . .'

'It's usual to have three,' Hazel said defiantly. 'I've read the stories.'

Lilliat laughed – half a laugh. The other side of her face was utterly still. 'I cannot be dictated to by *stories*. I owe you nothing: remember that. But maybe – for the sake of your youth, for the sake of your power – I will give you another throw. What do you wish for this girl Ellen?'

'I want her to suffer. I want her to be scorned and reviled. I want her to *hurt*.'

'The wish of your heart?' The question sounded oddly significant, as if it meant more than it said.

'Your spells all go wrong,' Hazel said bitterly. 'It won't work, will it? They never work.'

And: 'Yes. The wish of my heart.'

Afterwards, she thought something changed inside her at those words: feeling became stone, her spirit set in a pattern that could not be undone. But really she knew that was mere self-dramatization, and the change had sneaked up on her, moment by moment, stealing her soul, an atom at a time, turning it to dust.

The pale side of Lilliat's reflection faded first, leaving the dark half somehow more defined, the single eye wide and staring against the waxy skin. There was hunger there, Hazel thought – the hunger she had seen before – and menace. It vanished in a swirl of hair, leaving the splintered glass beaded with water drops. Suddenly, Hazel remembered the head she had seen once, conjured by her great-grandmother, rising from a porcelain basin in the attic above. A white drowned head with eyes deep as the abyss, lifting itself from an inch of river-water . . .

But there was no point in thinking of that now. In any case, Hazel told herself, Lilliat is *my* conjuration, my familiar. Effie Carlow was long gone.

She slept badly that night, troubled not by dreams but waking horrors, dreading school the next day. She wondered about confiding in Nathan, the following weekend, warming herself with his sympathy and partisanship. He would feel for her, he would champion her . . . he would be sorry for her. The thought of his pity gave her an inexplicable shrinking of the heart. After all, wasn't pity the flip-side of contempt? A looking-down on someone, an acknowledgement of their weakness and inferiority. Perhaps Nathan had always considered her inferior – less in cleverness, less in beauty, with no alien powers, no heroic qualities. Why give him the chance to confirm his superiority?

Besides, there was too much she couldn't tell him. About the stupidity of her passion for Jonas (that was how she saw it now), and pocketing the soiled plaster, and conjuring Lilliat, and most of all about the third token, the rugger shirt – the token of her betrayal. 'I'll get it back,' Hazel vowed, trying to convince herself, to make herself feel better. 'Anyway, she took it from me. I would never have given it to her. She took it.' Like Effie more than a year ago, who had made her take hair from Annie's brush and something from Nathan, so she could weave a charm to spy on them. Nothing terrible had happened to them because of that, had it? Annie had fainted once – in London – but that was all. (Anyone could faint in London; the mere idea of it made Hazel swoon.) And even as sleep crept over her mind at last Hazel thought drowsily: 'They're all after Nathan.' Her great-grandmother . . . boys at his school . . . denizens of the spirit-world . . .

. . . all after Nathan.

SEVEN

The Princess and the Peas

It was mid-week before Nathan was summoned for an audience with the abbot. 'It's getting to be a habit,' Ned Gable said. 'What are you going to tell him?'

'I don't know,' Nathan admitted. And, with a flicker of mischief: 'It depends on what he asks me.'

But Father Crowley, as ever, seemed to know almost everything already.

'I fear it's partly my fault,' he said. 'I've known for a long time that Damon was dangerously unstable, but I hadn't realized how close he'd come to genuine psychosis. I'm sorry, Nathan: you had an uncomfortable evening, and I might have prevented it.'

'It was a bit,' Nathan said, mesmerized by the understatement.

The abbot allowed himself a smile. 'More than a bit. You showed great courage under conditions of ultimate stress. Life cannot ask more of anyone.' Nathan began to be embarrassed and, seeing that, Father Crowley moved on. 'Afterwards, too, you seem to have demonstrated amazing self-restraint. I gather you haven't discussed the – er – gory details with your friends here, or made any demands for revenge or punishment. A more extreme reaction on your part would have been perfectly

183

understandable, under the circumstances, yet you appear to have displayed a truly Christian spirit of forgiveness.'

There was the hint of a question in his voice and Nathan, reddening, responded to it. 'It's not like that,' he said, and then stopped. He couldn't possibly take credit for a Christian spirit – the idea made him cringe – but the truth was too difficult to explain.

'Your mother, too – a forceful parent, on occasion – has shown an extraordinary degree of moderation. The Hackforths tell me she has rejected any form of compensation.'

'Mum isn't very materialistic,' Nathan said, and then realized he was passing the responsibility for Christian spirit onto Annie, which was nearly as bad as accepting it himself. 'The thing is, we – we didn't feel it was really Damon's fault.'

'No? Curious.'

There was an expectant silence. Nathan could hold out against physical torture, but not that. The abbot could do expectant silence with a patience and implacability that became, eventually, irresistible.

'He – he wasn't himself.' Nathan struggled into speech. 'When he kidnapped me – when he did those things to me – it was like he was – sort of – mad. Possessed. Not actually possessed, of course, but something like that. My uncle thought he must have been infected – influenced by someone.'

'Your uncle?'

'Uncle Barty. It was his house Damon wanted to rob.' He didn't know if the abbot had heard about the Grail, and hesitated to mention it.

'Ah, yes. Mr . . . Goodman, I believe.' Father Crowley appeared to consult a note on a pad at his elbow. 'I didn't realize he was a relative.'

'He's not really,' Nathan said. 'I just call him uncle. He's, like, a very special family friend. I've known him all my life.'

'I see. And he said Damon was – possessed? Of course, there are those in the church who still believe in the possibility of demonic possession, but it's hardly in line with modern thought. Your uncle was naturally very upset; however –'

'Oh no.' In haste to prevent misunderstanding, Nathan interrupted rather brusquely. 'Uncle Barty isn't like that. He's kind of unflappable. And he didn't say possession, exactly. He says there are these spiritual bacteria, which can invade your mind, and – like – warp your whole personality. Someone like Hitler could do it to huge crowds of people while they listened to his speeches. These bacteria would get into their heads and stop them thinking clearly. Uncle Barty said that's what happened with Damon.'

'In-deed. A most interesting theory. Did he talk to Damon much?'

'Yes, he – Yes.'

'Did he attempt to exorcize these – bacteria? Forgive me, I don't know if I have the correct terminology. You wouldn't exorcize bacteria, would you? Did he administer a spiritual antibiotic?'

'He wanted to help Damon,' Nathan said awkwardly.

'We all want that. Well, this has been quite fascinating, but I'm sure you have classes to attend. Amid all your other preoccupations, I trust you still find time for school work. And . . . continue to exercise self-restraint, if you can. I must say, if you go on like this you may miss being a teenager altogether and emerge overnight into instant adulthood. Like Athene springing fully armed from the brain of Zeus.'

Nathan, slightly baffled by the gentle mockery in the abbot's voice, was unsure if he was teasing or taunting. He stood up to leave, wondering if he had got off lightly, and having to remind himself that actually he hadn't done anything wrong.

As if sensing his confusion, Father Crowley put out his hand. 'Well done,' he said. 'I mean it. The school has cause to be proud of you.'

It's exactly like Harry Potter, whispered an imp at the back of Nathan's mind. With the abbot as Dumbledore . . .

'I should like to meet your uncle some time,' the abbot added.

Although there was no particular emphasis in his tone, Nathan had a feeling it was the most significant remark he had made.

It felt like an age since he had met the princess, though in reality it was less than a fortnight. Term's over soon, Nathan thought, then it'll be easier. He wouldn't have to worry about arousing suspicion in the dormitory, and Annie, though she might get worked up about school bullying, had tended to accept his adventures in other worlds. Possibly she felt they were outside her remit.

Children had wandered into the past and explored the dimensions of magic since the days of E. Nesbitt and *Puck of Pook's Hill*, or so Annie reasoned: it was a vital part of their experience. Children who stayed in the real world, smoking cigarettes and swearing and mimicking the grownups – they were the sad ones, deprived of imagination and the potential to grow. Of course, Nathan was hardly a child any more, and his extracurricular activities were both more tangible, and more hazardous, than those of his predecessors. But it was better than shop-lifting or binge-drinking, or taking drugs or . . . the list of possibilities was endless. Annie had decided long before that alternative universes were a phenomenon she could take in her stride, if she had to, provided Nathan always told her – or Bartlemy – what was going on. And with that thought came the prickle of her conscience, the not-quite-comfortable reminder that she had a secret of her own, a secret she wouldn't share. As always, she began to argue with herself, saying he didn't have to know about his paternity, it would unsettle him, he needed security and stability – winning the debate but not the conflict. Her conscience still niggled her, in the small dark hours, murmuring, accusing. You're afraid, she told herself, and she knew it was true. She was afraid of the power from beyond death that had used and abused her, afraid of its legacy in Nathan, of the doom she sensed or imagined lying ahead of him – the destiny that Bartlemy had said he was born to fulfil. If he didn't know about it, it couldn't happen – that was the questionable logic behind her thinking. And now he had met a princess. Well, a princess should be a nice girl, Annie thought, rather doubtfully. She reviewed the track record of various princesses, in fact and fiction, and was not particularly reassured. Still, every boy met a princess, sooner or later. It was inevitable.

At school, despite the risks, Nathan dreamed. His desire to see Nell was too strong, suborning his sleep; it couldn't wait for the weekend or the holidays. The dream plucked him away out of his dormitory bed and deposited him in the kitchen at Carboneck. Daylight came through the windows, showing the smoke-stains on the ceiling and the general drabness and grubbiness of everything. The princess was sitting at the table shelling peas. She started, dropping a couple of the peas, which rolled across the floor.

'It's you,' she said, on an accusatory note. And then, rather tartly: 'Nice of you to drop in.'

He had bent to retrieve the peas, which, in the way of dropped peas, had completely disappeared.

'I shouldn't bother,' she said. 'There are lots more. You'll find them when you step on them.'

He grinned, pulled up a chair, and sat down beside her, joining in her task.

'I didn't say you could do that,' she said, after a minute.

'I didn't ask. Anyway, you should thank me. I'm helping you.'

'I don't want your help!'

'Why are you so prickly?' he asked, studying her face, which was all little tensions and suppressed feeling. 'I'm sorry I left so abruptly last time. That's just the way it works. I don't have a choice.'

She bit her lip – then emotion took over. 'You've been gone so long! I've been *bursting* to talk to you – waiting and waiting – and you didn't come, and you didn't come –'

'It's been less than two weeks.'

'Six!'

'Oh Lord, I forgot. Our time zones aren't co-tangent –'

'Aren't *what*?'

'Time moves at a different pace in different worlds. I wanted to come sooner, but the dreams just happen. I don't have much influence.' She was counting, he thought. She was counting the weeks. 'I really am sorry.'

The princess digested this, evidently trying to find fault with it. To distract her, Nathan said: 'Where did you get the peas? I thought you didn't have much decent food here.'

'Granny Cleep grows them in her garden. They're early *early* season. We don't really know how she does it – nothing much grows here – but Frim says she has a magic touch.'

'Green fingers,' Nathan nodded. 'Like my uncle. You know, in my world we have a story about a princess and a pea. She goes to bed on a huge pile of mattresses, with a single pea underneath, and she's so delicate and princessly she can still feel it, so she can't sleep properly.'

188

'Like I said,' Nell averred. 'You find them when you tread on them. Or lie on them.'

'It's a test,' Nathan explained. 'To prove she's a true princess.'

'Are you saying I'm not?'

'Don't be idiotic,' Nathan said. 'It's just a story.'

'If I was that sensitive I'd never sleep at all,' the princess snapped. 'My mattress has lumps, not peas. And the whole bed creaks every time I turn over. This palace is falling to bits.'

'I can see that.' Pointedly, Nathan glanced round the kitchen. 'Still, you could at least clean up a bit.'

'We can't get the staff.'

'You could do it yourself.' It was deliberate provocation, and he knew it.

'Prenders says princesses don't do housework,' Nell said frostily. '*However*, you may have noticed I am shelling peas –'

'You've eaten half of them.'

'So have you – and I also scrub floors, and wash clothes, and darn sheets. *You* try cleaning this kitchen. By the time you've got to the end of it, the beginning is dirty again. Prenders and I just gave up. For your information, being a true princess isn't about bossing the servants, or having insomnia because there's a vegetable under the bed. It's about – about –'

'Staying here when it would be easier to leave?' Nathan suggested. 'Standing by your subjects, and the people you love? Punching some poor twerp because he dares to kiss you?'

The anger fled from her face; a smile flickered in its stead. 'I do my best,' she said, half deprecating, half defiant.

'So tell me about it.'

'About what?'

'Everything. Growing up here – the Urdemons – your father. If I'm going to help you fix things, I need to know more about what we have to fix.'

'*Are* we going to fix things?' the princess asked.

'We'll try.'

'There's a legend,' she said, 'it's in several books, but Frim says it's older than the books, as old as the sword itself. One day, a mysterious stranger will come – a prince, or a knight – and his heart will be so pure he'll heal the king at a touch, and end the curse, and he'll be the one man who can lift the sword and subdue the evil in it. Of course, we don't know if my father's the king in the legend. Most of his ancestors tried to wield the sword at some point in their lives, and it attacked them. Men never learn. Kings in Wilderslee have always been pretty unhealthy. Each one must've hoped the legend referred to him. But the curse has got much worse lately, with the demons and everything, so . . .'

'This prince,' Nathan said, 'does he get to marry the princess as well?'

'Naturally.'

'It figures.'

'Are you – are you pure in heart?' she inquired doubtfully.

'No. I'm not a prince or a knight, either. I can't heal your father at a touch and we're going to have real problems with the sword. Apart from that –'

'You're a mysterious stranger,' the princess pointed out. 'One out of four isn't bad. And mysterious strangers are in short supply around here.'

'I think we'd better forget about the legend,' Nathan decided. 'We haven't got the cast.'

'I must say,' Nell remarked, 'you're not dressed very . . . heroically.'

Nathan glanced down. Pyjamas. 'Night clothing,' he explained briefly. 'I'm dreaming: remember? Never mind about that. You were going to tell me more about yourself – and Wilderslee.'

No girl – not even a true princess – can resist it when a boy she likes urges her to talk about herself. The peas were long shelled and still they sat talking while Nell, cautious at first, then more at ease, poured out feelings she didn't know she had, all the turbulence and anger of her youth, the fears she tried to hide, the obstinacy that compelled her to hold on. She told Nathan about the mother she couldn't remember ('My father died too'), and how the king had wanted to marry again, a woman called Agnis famed for her black hair. 'I must have liked her,' Nell said. 'She was pretty, and kind to me. I didn't have Prenders then; she came later. Anyway, there was another man who was in love with Agnis, some baron, and he insulted my father, and there was a quarrel, and that was when papa picked up the sword. Afterwards, Agnis still wished to marry him but he sent her away, he said he would come to her when he was cured. Only of course, he never was. I don't know what happened to her. I was so little, I can't remember any of it very well, but I know I cried and cried when she had gone. It must have been a couple of months later when Prenders arrived. Before, I'd gone around with the other children. Not just the Twymoors and the Yngleveres: there were lots of children in those days, running in and out of the palace. It was all different – bright-coloured paintings, and toys to play with, and ice cream on special occasions. The ice house is still there, but it hasn't been used for years. The marsh was smaller, too, and in summer we would go on picnics, all the way to the woods.' She looked so wistful for a moment that it touched Nathan like a physical pain. 'The Deepwoods are beautiful – the most beautiful in the world.' The glimmer of her smile came and went. 'Perhaps in all the worlds. I'd give anything to go there again.'

'Could we?' Nathan asked.

'It's too dangerous. The marsh has spread – and there are the Urdemons.'

'Perhaps – I could manage something,' Nathan said, suddenly determined. He had transported Kwanji Ley from the prison pits, after all – even if she had ended up in the wrong place. And he had saved Eric, pulling him from Eos into his own world. Maybe, if he concentrated, he could take the princess to the woods her heart craved. He closed his eyes, retreating into his mind, pushing at the walls of thought. He had forgotten how unstable was his tenure in that universe. Too late, he felt the dream receding – heard an exclamation from the princess, anger or shock. He tried to open his eyes, but the lids were weighted, and sleep engulfed him like a wave.

Just when things are really bad, Hazel reflected, that's when you know they're about to get worse. That week at school, they got worse. Jonas was now ranged on the side of the enemy, and Ellen and the Sniggerers put a bag of crumpled plasters in her desk, smeared with red and brown stains which might – or might not – have been felt-tip pen. The next day, the bag contained loo paper, also stained, with a note: *From J.* Fizz, the Chief Sniggerer, leaned across to her in class and whispered: 'That's what he thinks of you. You're just toilet slime. How does *that* feel, lover girl?' And then, to a friend: 'Oh look, she's crying! Her poor little heart is broken . . .'

'I'm not crying,' Hazel muttered. 'It's just that disgusting scent you're wearing which makes my eyes water.'

'Actually, this is *Vampiressa*. It's really exclusive – Ellen got it for me from her mum. She's at the makeup counter in

Boots in Crowford. What do you use – essence of piss?'

'If that's supposed to be wit,' Hazel retorted, 'keep trying.'

She was fighting her corner as best she could, but that afternoon someone stuffed a bottle of yellow fluid in her bag, labelled *Perfume – just for you*. As she took it out, she heard the sniggers, stuttering behind her like grapeshot. Heh – heh – heh – heh . . .

On her way home she ran into Annie.

'Sorry – I wasn't looking. Sorry –'

'That's all right. You know, you ought to get your hair cut. Not short, just . . . different. You've got a pretty face but you never show it.'

'You're the only one who thinks so.'

'Problem with the boys? Or is it school?' Hazel shrugged. 'You and Nathan both. Why don't you come in and have a cup of tea? Tell me all about it – or not, if you don't want to.'

Hazel shook her head, saying something vague about homework and her mother. The little kindness warmed her, but it also made her horribly conscious of her own treachery. Of course, the spell hadn't worked properly with Jonas – lust didn't count as love – and Ellen was still everyone's centre of attention, so maybe nothing would happen with Nathan either. But she couldn't face Annie – Annie who'd always been so nice to her – not after what she'd done. She couldn't face anyone any more. At home, she crawled into her bedroom as into a burrow, and deadened her brain with her personal stereo, and watched *Carrie* on the computer.

On Wednesday, Ellen had the spot.

Most teenagers have spots from time to time, it goes with the territory, but not Ellen Carver. She had the kind of prettiness that's based less on bone structure and shapeliness of feature than accessories like perfect skin and shiny hair – her skin being particularly good, with the smoothness and finish of a rose-petal and the glow of a heroine in a California soap. But on Wednesday there it was, beside her nose, a tiny blister of greenish pus with a fleck of black in the centre like an atom of caviar. The Sniggerers didn't waver in their loyalty, though Fizz, who had several zits of her own, was seen to look at Ellen once or twice with a lingering smugness in her face. Hazel, largely oblivious to the finer points of Ellen's physiognomy, noticed her peering anxiously in a hand mirror during history – a mistake, since the teacher also noticed it, and gave her a detention. Ellen, catching Hazel's eye, glared at her as if she was to blame. A couple of the Sniggerers tagged after her on her way home from school, calling insults and giggling together, and alone in her lair Hazel warmed herself on the thought of Ellen's spot, saying viciously: 'I hope she gets lots of them.'

The next morning, she did. Arriving in the classroom Hazel saw Ellen's henchwomen surrounding her desk as though screening it from view. For once, there was no sniggering; in fact, they ignored Hazel completely. Only when the teacher arrived and they were forced to draw back could she see the cause. Ellen's face had become a bubbling landscape of miniature volcanoes, some heaving and swelling, others exploded into craters that seemed, even at a distance, to be oozing mucus. As the class watched in fascinated horror another one burst and a small white wriggle emerged and dropped onto her desk, where it squirmed into a crack and disappeared. The teacher approached, concerned yet hesitant, evidently worried about catching something. The whispers started. As the day progressed, sinister rumours flew round the school: Hazel overheard someone insisting it was a new strain of sexually-transmitted acne. Jonas was seen leaving a room when Ellen entered. The ranks of the Sniggerers thinned.

Hazel, observing covertly, thought it was the best day she had had in ages – until the doubts slipped in. Supposing it wasn't simply an aggressive case of acne? After all, acne didn't give you maggots. Supposing it was magic . . . 'I don't care if it is,' Hazel told herself. 'It serves her right, the spiteful cow.' But she wasn't as happy about it as she wanted to be, and on Friday, when she got to school, she was nervous. Acne came and went, but with magic, anything could happen.

Ellen arrived just after her. She'd been sent to the doctor's the previous morning but by the time she got there all the spots had burst and she was assured cheerfully that the problem would clear up in a few days. 'Just the usual adolescent stuff. What have you been eating lately?' Ellen's perfect skin now resembled a bomb-site, ridged and pitted and scabbed. Caught off guard by a twinge of fellow-feeling, Hazel found herself hoping the scars would go away.

Then she noticed Ellen's desk. It appeared to be quivering slightly as if in an earth tremor, and a faint humming noise was coming from it. Fleetingly, Hazel thought of the bags of dirty plasters and loo paper left in *her* desk earlier that week. Judgement Day . . . But she didn't feel good about it. Gingerly, Ellen lifted the lid.

The desk was full of flies. There were so many they had almost forced it open – as Ellen raised the top they came out in a huge, black, buzzing explosion, zooming in on her face, her hair, her open mouth. Screaming was a mistake. They filled the room, mobbing the Sniggerers, landing on exposed skin and eyes in great dark clots. Only Hazel was left completely untouched, but no one registered that. The maggots must have crawled into the desk and pupated overnight, but surely not in such numbers – hundreds, maybe thousands of fat shiny flies, swarming over pupil and teacher, feeding off human sweat, tears, saliva . . . *Dear God*, Hazel thought.

Make it stop. Please make it stop. But the flies still streamed out of Ellen's desk like bats from the mouth of hell.

It was much later in the day when they were all disposed of, after the advent of professional exterminators with insecticide sprays and fumigating equipment. Various traumatized students were sent home, but Ellen was still there. Hazel recalled belatedly hearing that she didn't get on with her mother, who was struggling to maintain youth and prettiness and obviously jealous of filial competition. Hazel could imagine such a mother gloating over the ruin of her daughter's looks, and the idea tweaked her conscience – or her heart. She felt she ought to say something, something kind and sympathetic, a sort of apology – without actually acknowledging that it was her fault: that would be fatal. It was what Nathan would do (Nathan had always been her benchmark), only Nathan wouldn't be in this mess. But she couldn't find the right words, and anyway, it was impossible to talk in class. Too many people who might listen, and draw conclusions. Hazel had no intention of betraying herself again. She decided to catch Ellen afterwards, when she was walking home. As long as the Sniggerers were out of the way . . .

But the Sniggerers had found events too much for their allegiance. Ellen sat alone at the back of the school bus. When she got off in Eade Hazel followed her, at a safe distance, trying to look nonchalant, just in case anyone was watching. She knew where Ellen lived and realized she wasn't taking the most direct route, through the middle of the village; instead, she cut down a path towards the river. Hazel headed for the woods when she wanted solitude; she wondered if, for Ellen, the riverbank provided a similar retreat. She passed the pixy-hat roofs of Riverside House, unoccupied for nearly a year now, and wandered down the meadow-path beside the water. It was hot under heavy white clouds, the sort of stifling, midge-haunted heat you get before a summer storm. Clumps of wild flowers grew along the meadow's edge: bladder campion, and mallows, and various worts. She remembered Bartlemy saying long ago that worts were supposed to heal whatever was in their name: woundwort for wounds and so on, though she couldn't help wondering what St John's wort might cure. Bad attacks of sainthood, perhaps? Ahead, she saw Ellen bend down to pick a flower – a white campion – and gaze at it, spinning it between her fingers. The gesture made Hazel like her, though she couldn't have explained why. A few moments later her quarry halted by the stump of a willow tree, deposited her bag on the ground, and sat down beside it idly surveying the river.

The Glyde was tidal, flowing into the sea at Grimstone harbour not far away, but this was a season of little movement in the water, and the stream drifted indolently, carrying a leaf or two towards the bank, swirling a broken twig in a sudden eddy. A dragonfly dipped and drank, making the most of its short life, iridescent even without the sun. Hazel watched it, her footsteps slowing, fishing for phrases she couldn't find. *I'm sorry. I didn't mean it – I didn't know . . .* A long ripple ran through the water, as if below, in the weeds, something stirred. Hazel thought: *It must have been near here they found Great-grandma.*

> *Cloud on the sunset*
> *wave on the tide*
> *death from the deep sea*
> *swims up the Glyde . . .*

The apology was forgotten. She had dropped her rucksack and was running along the path, calling: 'Ellen! Look out! *Look out!*' In front of the willow, the water reared up in a wave, glass-green, translucent, ten feet high – a wave with hands. It curled over the bank, over Ellen, clutching at her with boneless fingers, dragging her down into the river. She struggled, trying to get a grip on tree-root and grass-tuft, but its strength was the strength of the maelstrom, the pull of currents at the ocean's heart. She had no more power to resist than a torn leaf. 'Stop!' Hazel screamed. 'Lilliat!' But there was no Lilliat any more. Only Nenufar the nayad, goddess of the deep. Nenufar whose heart was colder than a fish and whose greed was stronger than the tide – Nenufar who lusted for the Grail and the power it would unlock – Nenufar who would kill without pause, without thought, because human life was less to her than the life of the smallest jelly swimming in the great sea. Hazel groped in her mind for the spellwords she had read in her great-grandmother's book, Commands of dismissal and banishment, but memory failed her. She reached Ellen and managed to seize her arms – felt the straining of her own fragile muscles against the vast sucking force of the water. She too began to slide down the bank . . .

And then the wave withdrew, sinking back into the river, and the clutching hands melted into a frill of foam that settled on the surface for an instant and vanished. All that remained was a ridge of bubbles riding a ripple which sped downstream and was lost in the heavy stillness of the summer afternoon. Hazel dragged Ellen back up the bank; she was wet through, mud-smeared, shivering from the shock.

'What w-was it?' Ellen seemed to have forgotten that this was her enemy, the object of her contempt. 'What *happened*?'

'A freak wave?' Hazel suggested.

'It felt like hands – hands p-pulling me into the water . . .'

'The river current can be very strong,' Hazel offered. 'Maybe it was a what-d'you-call-it – a bore.'

'I wasn't bored.' A little late, Hazel realised Ellen wasn't making a pun. She had obviously never heard of the freak wave which rushes upriver swifter than any tide.

'You ought to get home,' Hazel said. 'You could come to my place – it's nearer. Get dry – have some tea or something.'

Maybe they'd be friends now. She'd saved Ellen's life – even though it was Hazel who'd put her in danger in the first place. (But Ellen didn't know that.)

'No thanks.' Ellen sounded grudging. 'Were you – were you – following me?'

'No.'

'I came here to be quiet, to b-be *on my own*. It's been so awful . . . You were f-following me. You're sick. What do you want – to collect some of my scabs?'

Nothing had changed. She'd felt bad about Ellen, wanted to help, rescued her from the water-spirit – but it made no difference.

Only to me, said a voice in her head.

'Look, I just wanted to say sorry. About everything that's happened. That's all.'

'It's not your fault.'

Hazel looked at her for a second from behind her hair. A strange expression crossed the other girl's face – a shadow of suspicion, a trace element of fear. She drew back a little.

Hazel said: 'I'll walk home with you.'

Ellen was shivering in spasms now, her teeth chattering. The clouds had thickened; thunder rolled far off. Lightning flickered, unobtrusive in the daylight. Rain began to fall in big heavy drops. Soon Hazel was almost as wet as her companion, but when they reached the house, Mrs Carver didn't ask her in. She was an older version of Ellen, with very yellow hair and the pout set in faint lines around her mouth. She fussed over her daughter in a complaining way, as if Ellen had deliberately engendered her own misfortunes to cause trouble for her parent. Hazel was glad to get away despite the weather, hurrying home as fast as she could, to be genuinely fussed over by Lily Bagot in a way she would normally have evaded, given low-calorie hot chocolate because that was all they had, and sat by the fan heater in the living room watching *Neighbours* while she dried out.

On Saturday afternoon Eric Rhindon dropped into the bookshop to have tea with Annie. 'I've been thinking,' Nathan told him. 'There must be *some* way to pick up the Traitor's Sword. After all, you could ward off the gnomons with that herb that smells so bad – *sylpherim* – and white noise, and iron. There's always a way to deal with things, otherwise what would be the point?'

'Spirit in sword is very powerful,' Eric volunteered. 'Much stronger than gnomon. I never hear of anything.'

'If it was a story,' Nathan said, 'there'd be Gauntletts of Protection – something like that.'

'Life isn't like stories,' Annie said. 'It's too untidy.'

'The princess told me there's a legend in her world about a mysterious stranger who lifts the sword and ends the curse on the kingdom. He's a prince or a knight, or whatever. They always are.' He went on: 'I'm a mysterious stranger, but I'd have to cheat for the rest.'

For all her anxiety, Annie managed a faint smile. 'True heroes always cheat,' she said. 'It's the difference between brains and brawn. Anyone can be a hero with pecs.'

'This princess,' Eric asked, 'she is pretty?'

'Ish.' Nathan was carefully noncommittal. 'She's got lots of hair that always needs brushing – it reminds me of Hazel. And she can be quite spiky. But when she smiles . . .' He stopped, uncertain of the words for Nell's smile.

'She is pretty,' Eric nodded, satisfied.

Annie hovered on the verge of saying: *You ought to bring*

her home some time, and sighed. Other mothers have it easy, she decided. She glanced at her son's dark alien face, and felt a sudden pang of fear, because he looked so much like a stranger . . .

That night, Nathan dreamed. He had been sure he would, had felt it with a certainty that came from deep in his spirit, not confidence but knowledge. Perhaps the future, like the past, was something you could remember, if you were able to stretch your mind beyond the confines of the present. Time holds us, drives us, limits us, but there are moments when the spirit breaks free, and can touch infinity. Nathan felt he and the princess belonged together – their lives met and crossed – maybe forever, maybe just for a little while (he didn't want to think about that), but the strength of their fate would bridge the gulf between worlds, and open the unopenable doors. He didn't need to roam the inside of his head, groping for the portal – the patch of wrongness, like interference on a television set. He closed his eyes, and he was there.

There, in this case, being the library. He was standing in the shadows with which the palace – and the library in particular – was abundantly provided. The princess was seated at the table on what seemed to be a pile of books, leaning forward, chin on palm, listening. Frimbolus Quayne sat opposite her, talking with great energy, his dandelion-seed hair quivering in the backdraft from his hand gestures. Daylight had wriggled in somehow, past a shredded banner of curtain, and showed the multiple expressions – sometimes several at once – that flickered over his face. '. . . know nothing about him,' he was saying. 'I've seen him in my workroom – spying on me – hovering around like the phantoms you see with diseases of the liver, all pale and shimmery. I spoke to him, but he didn't say a word. No manners at all! Just stood there gaping like a fish and then faded away.'

'He's been solid enough lately,' said the princess. 'He helped me shell the peas.'

'Very good, those peas. Even Gobbledygoose couldn't spoil them . . .'

'He says he can't help disappearing sometimes. He gets pulled back into his own world.'

'A likely story! Fifteen years ago – before you were born – I found a thief in the king's bedroom, hiding in the wardrobe. Said he'd just popped through from another world. Bumskittles! I daresay if I were up to something nefarious, and got caught out, *I'd* say I was from another world. As good a story as any – it's common knowledge there are other worlds all over the place. The point is – the point *is* – you can't get to them, or *from* them. Not through wardrobes or dreams or spell-windows – trust me. Other worlds are out of bounds: it's an Ultimate Law. Of course, he might just *think* he's from another world. Could be from somewhere else in this one – dreaming out of his body. Might be a scoundrel. Might just be batty.'

At this juncture, Nathan knew he ought to announce himself – he had left it rather late already – but the temptation to eavesdrop a little longer was irresistible. After all, he told himself, rather doubtfully, it could be Frimbolus who was summoning the Urdemons. He must have the necessary magical know-how. If he kept his presence a secret, the old man might yet give himself away.

'He's not batty,' Nell was saying firmly, 'and he's not a scoundrel. I thought he might be the mysterious stranger in the legend.'

'Too much mystery,' said Quayne, 'and could be very strange. Never trust a legend, anyway. Has it occurred to you that if he was *really* from another world he wouldn't look like us? Do you think the human form is universal, let alone multiversal? You think nature can't do better? If this ghostly slubberdegullion of yours was actually from an alternative cosmos, he'd probably have two heads – or no head at all – or merely be a lump of intelligent slime with half a dozen eyes on stalks like a snail. No reason for him to appear as an attractive young man unless he's up to no good.'

'I didn't say he was attractive,' the princess demurred.

Nathan, on the verge of stepping forward, lurked a moment longer.

'Didn't need to,' said Frimbolus. 'It's obvious. Didn't see him too clearly when he came haunting around, but it's written all over you.'

'I don't know what you mean,' Nell said with a sudden access of dignity. 'I'm a princess. I don't go about being attracted to any old young man who turns up, whatever world he's come from.'

'Good for you,' Nathan said, emerging from the shadows. 'You can't be too careful these days.'

The princess started, trying to counteract the effect of her mounting blush with a glow of anger. Frimbolus raised his eyebrows so far up his forehead that they almost disappeared over the top of his skull; wrinkles moved to get out of their way.

The old man recovered first. 'Aha!' he said. 'The world traveller! You may have insinuated yourself into Nell's good graces, but you won't find it so easy with me. I can see through you –'

'I don't think so.' Nathan looked down, and noted with relief that he was completely solid. He had also taken the precaution of going to bed in his clothes.

'Trying to be clever, are we?' Frimbolus responded. 'Think *I'm* going to fall for all this potherguffle about other worlds? If it's the truth, why haven't you got two heads? That's what I want to know.'

'I only need one?' Nathan suggested.

'We have a saying here,' Frimbolus said, with the air of someone who thinks he has scored a point, 'two heads are *better* than one.'

'Not on the same person,' Nathan pointed out. 'They would clutter up your shoulders. We have that saying in our world, which only goes to show how similar it is. After all, parallel universes are supposed to be – parallel.'

'Frizzle my principles! I almost think he knows what he's talking about. Exactly what form of magic do you use to get here?'

'No magic,' Nathan said. 'I just dream.'

'He says it's physics,' the princess interrupted. She didn't like being left out of the conversation.

Frimbolus waved physics away. 'One of the minor sciences. I knew a man once who was obsessed with falling objects. He wanted to know why things fall down instead of up. Call that intellectual research! One day, an apple hit him on the head.'

'Did he discover gravity?' Nathan asked.

'No, but I had to treat him for a mild concussion. After that, he gave up physics to develop a kettle that *tells* you when it's boiling. He was a little eccentric.'

'Without physics,' Nathan inquired, 'how do you know about parallel universes?'

'Logic,' declared Quayne, 'supported by the evidence. In nature, there is never only one of anything. Many leaves on the tree, many trees in the wood, many woods in the country, many countries on the earth. Therefore, it follows that there must be many worlds out there too. My great-great-great-grandfather wrote a treatise on it; I have developed the concept even further. We have infinity and eternity: that's far too much space for only one universe. But each world – like ours – must have its own equilibrium. When universes overlap, their balance is disturbed, and that can only lead to trouble.'

'Do you think the Traitor's Sword could come from another universe?'

Frimbolus' eyebrows soared, plunged, frowned. 'Now, that *is* an idea. Perhaps that is at the root of its malevolence – it's in the wrong world and it wants to go home. And the so-called curse on the kingdom is actually a symptom of disturbance in the balance of nature. It completely vindicates my theory . . . I like it.'

The princess, increasingly piqued at being sidelined, said sceptically: 'How would it get here? Swords don't dream.'

'I'm not sure,' Nathan admitted. 'If it's what I think it is, the sword was sent here for safe-keeping by a very powerful magician in the world it comes from. He wanted to hide it from possible thieves until he needed it, and an alternative universe must have seemed the best place. He . . . he might have had a contact here to help him establish a link. That's what happened in *my* world when something was hidden there.' He was thinking of Josevius Grimling-Thorn, original holder of the Grail.

'How many worlds are we dealing with here?' Frimbolus complained. 'Never mind. According to the stories, the sword was brought to Carboneck by a venerable knight, or alchemist, or both, named Gryphonius Tupper. We don't know precisely how long ago it was – they didn't record time in those days, I'm afraid – but probably several hundred years. Gryphonius was supposed to be holy, and he committed the sword to the care of the kings of Wilderslee, as a God-given charge.'

'What kind of god do you worship here?' Nathan asked.

'The usual kind,' Frimbolus said rather sniffily. 'Invisible, ineffable, doesn't interfere much.'

'Oh,' said Nathan, slightly at a loss. 'One of those.'

'Right,' the princess intervened. 'I've had enough of this. We need to talk –' she seized Nathan's wrist '– and *not* about Alternative Universe Theory, or whatever it is. Frim, I expect you have important work to do. *We* are leaving – before Nathan disappears on me again.'

'You can't possibly go wandering off with a strange young man,' Frimbolus objected. 'Especially when I'm talking to him.'

'I'll do what I please,' Nell announced with sudden haughtiness. 'I'm the princess.'

Frimbolus muttered something about teenagers – a remark common to older generations in all the worlds – but Nathan, borne off into the passageway, didn't catch what it was.

'Let's go somewhere private,' Nell said.

'In a place as empty as this,' Nathan commented, 'that shouldn't be difficult.'

'You'd be surprised,' Nell said darkly. 'Sometimes, either Frim or Prenders seem to be everywhere. Prenders fusses, but Frim's not usually like that. Only just lately . . .'

'You can't blame them,' said Nathan. 'They love you. It's natural they should want to look after you.'

'Do you have to be so *reasonable*?'

Nathan laughed suddenly. 'You sound like Hazel!'

The princess, who was walking briskly along a gallery, stopped abruptly. 'Who's she?'

'My friend,' Nathan said. 'Sort of like a sister. We grew up together.'

Nell looked unconvinced.

'I like her,' he went on. 'I like her a lot. But not the same way I like you.'

He found he was gazing straight into her eyes. Afterwards, he couldn't have said what colour they were, whether they were dark or light, but it seemed to him that her soul gazed back at him. It was a magic moment – a moment when he felt he could do anything. Such moments are rare in anyone's life, and all too often slip away unregarded, but Nathan sensed that instant of power and certainty, and flowed into it. He took her hands, took her gaze, opened his mind and let his spirit stretch out . . . and out . . . The gallery vanished. There was a second that was neither night nor day, dusk nor dawn – and then everything was different.

They were standing in the middle of a wood. The ground sloped gently near the bottom of what seemed to be a shallow valley; it was soft with moss and crunchy with dead leaves. The trees were of every kind and no kind, faintly familiar, subtly different, akin to beech and birch and oak but with traces of maple and *mallorn*, baobab and banyan. It was spring, and the new leaves came in every shade of yellow and green, but those underfoot held more colours than any autumn in our world, their gold deepening to tints of crimson and bronzy purple. If there were flowers Nathan didn't notice them, only the mingled hues of a million leaves. It was, he thought, the woodiest wood he had ever seen. Humans were out of order here and even animals would be intruders, unless they were very small and unobtrusive. Yet it didn't feel unfriendly or dangerous, only wild, with the aloof wildness of a place where people never come.

'The Deepwoods,' the princess said. 'You did it.'

And then, in case he should think her too impressed: 'What about the picnic?'

'Sorry.' Nathan grinned.

'Can't you conjure up some sandwiches?'

'I'm a dreamer, not a magician.'

'Oh well . . .' The princess sighed, then smiled – not quite her usual smile but one with an almost unearthly quality, touched with the wildness of the wood. 'It's wonderful to be here, even if we have nothing to eat. Thank you.'

'Come on then,' said Nathan. 'Let's explore.'

They walked for what seemed like hours, out of the valley and across a low ridge and into another valley, and another – through sun-speckled glades, under low-slung branches, over root-stumps and fallen boughs. In one of the valleys they found a little stream, running downhill between shaggy grasses and deep green waterplants. They drank from it in cupped hands, and ate some wild strawberries which were growing nearby, and sat on the ground side by side, talking little, until sitting became lying, and they were gazing up through the tree-tops at a shifting kaleidoscope of leaf and sky. It wasn't really a picnicky place, Nathan thought, unable to imagine anyone camped here with rug and hamper, eating ham sandwiches and hard-boiled eggs. It was just meant for the trees, and tiny wild things too cunning or too cautious to be seen. He had a feeling he had been here before, or somewhere like it, perhaps in a dream of long ago, but the source of the memory eluded him and he was too happy to search for it. Once, he asked Nell: 'Are we lost?'

'Of course,' she answered.

'I thought you knew this place?'

'Only on the borders. I've never been so far in.'

After a pause, she added: 'Does it matter? When we want to go, I thought you could just – sort of – dream us away.'

'I'll try,' Nathan said. He wasn't at all sure he could recapture the certainty of the moment which had brought them there, but he decided not to worry about it. He was lost in the Deepwoods with the princess, and it didn't matter at all.

He propped himself up on his elbow, looking down at her face, with her eyes half closed against a probing gleam of sunshine and her hair spread out around her, tumbled among the leaves. Then he leaned over and kissed her, a brief, tentative kiss, testing the water. He hadn't done a lot of kissing but it was her reaction which made him hesitant, rather than his own lack of expertise.

'I don't think much of that,' the princess said.

At least she hadn't punched him across the stream in a flash of righteous rage.

Unable to think of anything to say, Nathan turned back to his contemplation of the sky.

'It was awfully quick,' Nell explained. 'I thought kisses were supposed to last longer.'

Nathan started up – then lay back again. 'I was forgetting,' he said, going on the offensive, 'how often you've been kissed.'

'I – beg your pardon?'

'From what I've seen, it's already quite – quite customary for the boys round here to kiss you. I don't really want to join the crowd.'

'Crowd? *CROWD?* How dare you –'

Then he flipped over, laughing at her, warding off a slap that – fortunately – had no magical force behind it.

This time, the kiss went on for quite a while.

The day drew on. They set off again, going in a direction that the princess insisted was west, claiming she could orientate herself by the sun. However, as it was frequently obscured by trees Nathan felt little confidence in her. It didn't trouble him. For the moment, nothing troubled him at all.

There were birds singing somewhere above, hidden among the leaves, disconnected trills and descants piercing the quiet of the wood. They saw pink bluebells and lemon-yellow butterflies and grasshoppers that seemed to be made of grass and stick insects like bits of twig. And every so often there would be a whisk of movement among the branches or a ripple in the autumn carpet, as if some swift small creature had passed by.

'Are there many animals living here?' Nathan asked.

'Not as such,' said the princess. 'There are squirrels and woodmice and other small rodents, and foxes and deer live on the edge, but that's about all. Of course, there are the wood-people, or so they say, but you don't see them very often.'

'Wood-people?'

'Werecreatures. Tree-spooks, impies, brownies, gnomelins. There are supposed to be dryads and fauns and waterfay, too, but that's nearer the mountains; I've never been that way. The trees are taller and darker there, and the ground is uneven and rocky, and there are deep pools and steep-sided dells and hollows hidden under leaves where you can fall in and never get out. Kern Twymoor went there to get the special honey to make the poultice for my father's leg wound. He says he saw a dryad – a wispy little sprite with green hair who ran away when he called to her. Have you ever seen a dryad?'

'I don't think we have them in my world,' Nathan said, 'though they come into stories. Maybe they've all gone. But there's a woodwose at Thornyhill where my uncle lives. We call him Woody.'

'I used to see woses when I was a child,' the princess said. 'They're shy of older humans – I expect we're too big – but they'll talk to children, if you stay very quiet, and still, and wait for them to come to you.'

'Are there . . . many woses here?' Nathan inquired, pointlessly. He already knew the answer.

'Probably,' said Nell. 'But they're very well camouflaged. You don't see them unless they let you.'

Nathan said nothing. He was thinking: *This is where I found Woody. I must have been here many times, even as a baby. I found Woody, and he talked to me, and I dreamed him into my world, because I wanted a special friend to play with.* The arrogance of what he had done, the appalling responsibility filled him with horror. Of course, he had been an infant at the time, acting in innocence, ignorant of his own power or its consequences – but somehow that only made it worse, not just selfish and heartless but terrifying. What else might he have done, in those far-off days of childish self-absorption? What other lives might he have uprooted and stolen? Most recently there was Eric – but Eric had been drowning; without Nathan's impulsive rescue he would have died. And he was happy now, or so it seemed, married to Rowena Thorn, living in a world where he would die of old age after two thousand years of indefinite existence . . .

'The value of a life is not measured by its length,' Bartlemy had told Nathan once – Bartlemy the ageless, who had seen centuries go by, whose oldest friends had died so long ago he couldn't even remember their names. And then, quoting someone, Nathan didn't know who: 'The moment of the yew tree and the moment of the rose are of an equal duration.'

Now, looking at the princess – thrusting the image of Woody to the back of his mind – Nathan understood. This is a rose-moment, he thought. We're from different worlds, thrown together for a while – a little while – until our fates, or whatever you call it, pull us apart. But what we have, no matter how brief, is as important as a lifetime of loving. And he knew he must live the moment – live it with every cell in his body – before it slipped away.

Much later, the princess said: 'I suppose we ought to go home.' She meant that she ought to return to Carboneck, but Nathan took the point.

'I'll try,' he said again, 'but I'm not sure . . .'

They were sprawled on a west-facing bank under a huge

tree whose shimmery leaves hung down in tassels, swaying at the merest hint of a breeze. The princess allowed Nathan to cradle her in one arm, resting her head on his shoulder.

'Not yet,' she said.

Through a gap in the trees they watched the sky-colours change, working their way through sunset before deepening into the blues of evening. A new moon appeard, considerably bigger than ours: the shadowy imprint of great mountain-ranges and oceans of dust meant it really did seem to have a profile, with half-smile, single eye and flattened nose fitted into the curve. Unfamiliar stars came in its train. Nathan guessed one of them would be a spy-crystal for the Grandir, who might be watching them even now, but there was nothing he could do about it so he put the thought aside. The princess asked him about his own world and he told her – about his mother, and Uncle Barty, and the Grail, and some of his adventures last year. He knew they should leave, the princess would be missed, it was time to take her home, if he could, but this was their magic day – the moment of the rose – and neither of them wanted it to end. The evening grew cooler, and Nell snuggled closer, and Nathan put his arms around her, and felt his heart beat faster, and the tickle of her hair against his face.

Somehow, without meaning to, he fell asleep.

EIGHT

Dancing with Demons

Nathan woke in his own bed, wrapped in an afterglow of happiness which lasted about five seconds. He started upright, swearing, hoping his mother wouldn't hear – she still thought he was too young for the stronger four-letter words, at least in the home. *I've left her there*, he thought, *I've left the princess in the Deepwoods on her own. Anything could happen to her* . . . Nell hadn't mentioned any hazards in the woods themselves, but it was a long journey back to the city, even if she could find the way, and there were Urdemons waiting in the marshes – and she would believe he had abandoned her. And if she went the wrong way she might wander towards the mountains, and fall into a dark hollow, and never be seen again. He *must* get back to sleep.

He couldn't.

Since the kidnapping Annie had forgotten her edict about him being grounded, and when in desperation he told her what he had done she suggested they go immediately to consult Bartlemy. 'Maybe he'll have some sort of herbal soporific to *make* me sleep,' Nathan said hopefully. He had tried reaching for the portal in his mind but, as had happened before, it felt oddly blank, like a door closed against

'We'll see.' Privately, Annie was not so sanguine. '
he'll be able to advise you. I'm sure you'll get bac

213

princess very soon, one way or another.'

'I must,' Nathan said tensely.

When they reached Thornyhill, Bartlemy didn't advocate soporifics. 'Drugs induce the wrong kind of sleep,' he explained. 'Even the mildest sedative can affect your dream-patterns. You'd do better to wait for tonight.'

'Herbs aren't drugs,' Nathan objected, 'are they?'

'What do you suppose drugs are made *from*? Think of the opium poppy, the coca plant. A drug is simply a plant that has been rendered down and put through certain chemical processes. The herbal remedy is the drug in its natural state. Happily, most of the remedies that you see nowadays contain herbs or plants that are fairly innocuous and generally legal.'

'What about yours?' Annie asked suspiciously. 'Are they innocuous?'

Bartlemy only smiled.

'Or legal?'

'Never mind that,' Nathan said impatiently. 'What am I going to *do*?' He was haunted by the memory of Kwanji Ley, left in the Eosian desert to die in the poisonous sunlight. Frimbolus had been right: he was no good for the princess. If anything happened to Nell because of him . . .

'Remember the time factor,' Bartlemy said. 'Different worlds move at different speeds. You might go back in a fortnight only to find it has been just a few hours there, or a few minutes.'

'If I have to wait a fortnight,' Nathan said, 'I'll – I'll prob-ably kill myself. Anyway, usually when I go back *more* time had passed there, not less.'

'Then concentrate. Focus on the moment to which you ⸳ to return.'

ave no control –'

do sometimes,' Bartlemy pointed out. 'You took the ⸳ the Deepwoods.'

'Yes, but I don't really kn... *Demons*
ing and thinking . . . There's an... it. I've been think-
work – something sort of opens in... en I can make it
closes, and afterwards I can't analyse it, and then it
what I did that was special . . . It makes me...pin down
so *helpless*. And wicked. I keep doing it – I move stupid,
about it their own world, or between worlds, for my own
selfish amusement – and then someone gets hurt, or dies, and
it's all my fault. When naturalists study animals in the wild
they're not supposed to interfere, even if there's a baby dying
or something really unbearable: it upsets the balance of nature.
But I keep interfering – playing God – and it always goes
wrong. It always goes wrong . . .'

Bartlemy passed him a cup of tea, strangely perfumed,
which he drank absent-mindedly. 'Be easy,' the old man said.
'Understanding will come. Meanwhile, this princess of yours
sounds like a resourceful girl. I'm sure she can look after
herself. She's in a familiar environment, with no immediate
danger. And she appreciates the erratic nature of your visits
– she must realise you would never deliberately abandon her.'

'She may realize it,' Nathan said, 'but she won't believe it –
as a matter of principle. She'll be furious. I don't care about that,
as long as she's all right.' Mellowed by the tea, urgency was slipping away from him. He tried to hold on to it, clinging to his
panic because it was all he could do – without it he felt distanced
from Wilderslee, distanced from Nell, safe and remote in his
own universe. He didn't want remoteness and safety . . .

'Panic achieves nothing,' Bartlemy said, as if hearing his
thoughts. 'What's more, it scrambles the brain – and you need
your brain unscrambled, if you are to be of any use to anyone.
Try to relax, if you can.'

'I can't,' Nathan said. 'Tonight is just too long to wait. Anyway
I'm afraid I'm so wound up I won't sleep. What can I do?'

emy, prosaically, 'with a very dull

'Go to bed,'
book.'

Nathan knew he should talk to Woody

The discovery in the Deepwoods, or call Hazel – she
about him sent him a text message all week – but although
hadn't gained nothing from doing nothing, he still feared any
distraction. Annie stayed to supper at Thornyhill but Nathan
excused himself, for once indifferent to good food, and walked
home alone. At the bookshop there was little to do but worry,
so he kept on walking, through the sleepy Sunday village and
down to the river. Why he went that way he couldn't have
said – he'd always preferred to walk in the woods, but he
might meet Woody there, or even the dwarf, and he wanted
no company that day. Something drew him towards the Glyde,
a tugging at his mind so imperceptible he barely felt it. The
river-path was a popular route for dog-walkers, who would
impinge on his solitude, but he saw none. He flopped down
by the same willow-stump where Ellen Carver had sat, earlier
that week, and plucked a grass-stem, fiddling with it – preoc-
cupation for his hands – while restless thoughts continued to
circle round and round in his head.

But gradually his thoughts slowed. The drowse of a bee
investigating a nearby clump of clover soothed his ears. It
had rained recently but now it was very hot, and a mist
seemed to be rising from the water or the damp ground,
turning the sunshine to a golden haze. The bee-song became
the sound of someone humming, quite close at hand, though
there was nobody there. The water was all but silent,
meandering lazily with the outgoing tide, but there were the
little noises of the river-bank, the plop of a diving frog, the
mute splashing of a duck or moorhen looking for food.
Nathan found himself hearing the echo of the rhyme from
g before.

Dancing with Demons

Reed in the river-pool
weed in the stream
one there a-sleeping
too deep to dream.

Effie Carlow floating in the still water – hadn't it been a Sunday when they found her? A warm, lazy Sunday just like this. His imagination pictured her – a hunk of sodden clothing tide-driven against the bank – an outflung arm, a drifting hand – algae in her hair. And a little further down was Riverside House, where Nenufar the sea-spirit had risen from the water and tried to drown Annie. *Death from the deep sea . . .* Strange to think that violence and pain could come here, where the pace of life was slow-to-stop, and everything was so peaceful, so quiet, save for the river-song running through his head . . .

The humming deepened and changed, becoming the buzz of an engine from somewhere upstream, drawing nearer. Presently a boat came into view, a white motor-launch chugging slowly downriver. Despite its leisurely passage it looked designed for speed, gleaming with luxury and expense. It should have been too big for the Glyde, but somehow it wasn't, and in the hazy sunshine it seemed curiously insubstantial, like a ghost-ship seen through the mist on some haunted coastline far away. Nathan couldn't see who was steering but a woman stood in the bows, a woman as beautiful as the launch, with long pale hair fanning out in a breeze as faint as a sigh. As the boat drew level with Nathan she turned to look at him, and beckoned.

The murmur of the engine didn't stop, but it seemed to him the boat waited. The river flowed on, and the afternoon drifted, but the launch remained motionless, he didn't know how, holding against the current. The fancy came to him that it was about to set off on some wonderful voyage, to seas of emerald teeming with jewelled fish, and islands of coral and palm-trees, and there was room on board for one last passenger, and somehow – because he was there, because of some chance or fate – that one was him. The boat appeared to be close to the bank, and the woman held out her hand, and he knew he had only to jump, and he would land on the deck, and the engine would rev, and he would be speeding downriver to the sea. He was already on his feet when he heard the dog bark.

A man was coming along the path, still some way off, but the dog was running ahead of him – a dog Nathan had seen around the village before, an elderly black Labrador with a greying muzzle. It seemed to be barking at the boat. The engine accelerated, no longer a gentle hum but suddenly harsh, and the woman drew back, and the launch moved on, blurred by the heat-haze, vanishing at last round a bend in the river.

When the man was in earshot Nathan said: 'That was a big boat to see on the Glyde. I'm surprised it was allowed.'

'What boat?'

'The motor-launch that went past just now. Your dog was barking at it.'

'Don't know what made the dog bark: he knows you. There's no boat, lad. You've been dreaming.'

'I do that,' Nathan admitted. He was fussing over the dog, ruffling its ears and tickling it under the chin. He knew he hadn't dreamed. He, of all people, could tell the difference.

'Hot afternoon,' said the walker. Nathan couldn't recall the man's name, but he knew his face, and most of the residents in Eade knew him. 'You dropped off. They've been working you too hard at that school of yours.'

'I expect so,' Nathan said.

He walked home thoughtfully, his mind on something other than the princess.

* * *

Annie didn't return till after dark, and Nathan was in the kitchen making himself a sandwich when he heard the singing. Not the soothing murmur of the river-song but a child's voice, clear and sexless.

> '*The white ship waits by the river-strand*
> *for one who will not go.*
> *The silver witch holds out her hand*
> *and sings the river's flow.*
>
> *Follow the wake of the sea-mew's flight*
> *ride on the white wave's crest;*
> *follow the stars of the ocean night*
> *into the dark of the west.*
>
> *There are stars beneath the rolling wave*
> *that never saw the sky*
> *and burning fish light up the grave*
> *where mermaids go to die.*
>
> *The white ship waits by the river-shore*
> *for one who cannot stay;*
> *the witch will wait a sennight more*
> *to steal your soul away.*'

The song came from the garden. Nathan opened the back door and stared out. For a second he thought he saw a pale figure, child-sized, glimmering in the shadows; but it was gone before he could be certain. He remembered hiding in the kitchen at Thornyhill while his uncle drew the magic circle, and one of the spirits he summoned there, with the face of a child, and a choirboy's voice, and eyes as old as Time.

'Thank you for the warning,' he called out, though he wasn't sure if it *had* been a warning. It might have been a promise.

There was a sound of laughter, clear as a peal of bells, yet afterwards he thought it held a note of malice – a pure silvery malice untouched by conscience or maturity.

Nathan closed the door and went back to his sandwich.

Later, in bed at last, he took his uncle's advice, deciding Walter Scott was dull enough (*The Heart of Midlothian*), besides being full of people speaking Scottish. The print was small, the paragraphs long, the pages thin and crinkly. The words began to shrink and run together; the paper rustled like dead leaves on a forest floor. He was asleep even before he had switched off the light.

But he wasn't in the wood.

There was music coming from somewhere nearby, the kind of music that is played on the lute and tabor, with a piper leading the tune, piping with enough energy to charm a townfull of rats from their holes. Nathan was standing in a courtyard, and the music came from beyond a set of double doors, flung wide onto a great hall or ballroom. People were dancing there, performing the stylized steps and dance-figures that Nathan associated with period films. The room was hung with coloured lanterns and garlands of autumn leaves, and the dancers wore the mediaeval costume of Wilderslee, but richer and more sumptuous, with embroidery on cuff and lapel, borders of fur, and bright jewels peeping out between folds of velvet and silk. He looked for Nell but there was no sign of her, though he was sure this was Carboneck – a different Carboneck from the one he knew, the Carboneck of shadows and decay. Perhaps this was Carboneck in the future, when the curse had gone and Nell had left to marry her pre-ordained prince . . . That day in the woods was all they had had, all they would ever have, and now he was invisible again, the ghost of a thought haunting a party to which he wasn't invited, looking for someone who had gone.

Proceeding down the line of dancers was a man whose face was vaguely familiar, a chubby man with a high colour wearing what Nathan guessed was a doublet, the blue outer sleeves slashed to show red sleeves underneath. Costume of that kind tended to layers, sleeves within sleeves, overskirts, underskirts – perhaps because there was no central heating. He had a crown on his head, not a heavy serious crown but a lightweight coronet like an item of fancy dress. Nathan remembered the sick king lying in the bed with his leg plastered in honey, and realized with a shock that it was the same man. This isn't the future, he thought. This is the past – before the king lifted the Traitor's Sword. If Nell's around, she'll be just a toddler. There was a gallery at the far end of the hall, overlooking the dance floor, and gazing up, he made out a small face peering through the balustrade, but, though he hoped, he couldn't be sure it was her.

The king's dancing partner was a woman with the figure of an egg-timer in a dress which glittered and clung, showing off her tiny waist and the full curves above and below. Most of the ladies wore their hair tucked into tall headdresses or piled up in nets of gold and silver thread, but hers hung down her back in a single thick braid, very long and almost jet-black. Her face was attractive in an earthy sort of way, with broad cheekbones and a sultry mouth. This must be Agnis, Nathan deduced, Agnis whom the king had loved, rejecting her – nobly – until his wound should heal. For a minute, he thought he recognized her, too, though he couldn't recall from where. As he watched, the movement of the dance brought the king round to face her, and he seemed so happy that Nathan, remembering the hollow-eyed invalid in the fourposter bed, felt a stab of pathos.

Someone else was watching from the sidelines – a silent, solitary figure among the chattering courtiers. Instead of gaudy clothing he wore a long shapeless robe of no particular colour, ribbed with darns and blotched with assorted stains –

chemicals, ink, wine, soup. From a cord at his waist was suspended a magnifying glass, a pocket knife, and what looked like a corkscrew. His head was already bald but around it the fringe of his hair was thicker and darker than in later years, flowing over his shoulders, and a drooping moustache gave him a slight look of Don Quixote. He was studying the woman Agnis, and there was an intentness about his expression which Nathan found curiously disturbing. He had always thought Frimbolus Quayne slightly comic; now, he seemed potentially sinister. He didn't like Agnis, Nathan thought. He didn't like her at all. Nathan had never seriously imagined it could be Quayne summoning the Urdemons, but suddenly he wasn't certain.

He wanted to get out of the past, back to the wood and the princess. He tried to wrench his mind away, and the dancers blurred, melting into a dim swirl of colour, and the music ceased, and his spirit landed back in his body with an impact so violent it jerked him wide awake. He opened his eyes on his own bedroom, sat up to switch off the light. When he lay down again, he was sucked back into a quagmire of sleep.

It was a confused night, a night of sleeping and waking, of brief, vivid dream-journeys jumbled together like the visions of delirium, so that afterwards he couldn't remember every detail, or the sequence in which they occurred. When he didn't materialize his experiences were always more surreal, closer to actual dreams. He found himself moving between worlds like a phantom, an awareness that hovered on the periphery of a scene and then fled, reappearing a moment later – a century later, a life-age later – in another place, another cosmos.

He saw the Grandir in his high chamber in Arkatron, where the spy-crystals were suspended in darkness, enabling him to survey the multiverse. He held one globe between his hands, without touching it, and on the ceiling, upside-down, was an image that must be Wilderslee. Nathan made out the causeway across the marshes, and a running figure, and a brown pool heaving with bubbles as something stirred beneath the water. Then he was there, no longer watching from outside but skimming the marsh, and the running figure was a boy with dark hair – he thought it was Roshan Ynglevere – sprinting for the city with one swift backward glance. The brown water bulged, and something burst out – something mud-coloured and slime-coloured, festooned with weed, dripping marsh-ooze, rearing up – and up – and up . . . It was like the slug-creature he had seen in the city only far larger, a giant eyeless worm, its sides frilled with undulating flaps that drove it through the water, its open mouth salivating green-ish froth. It arched above the causeway, lunging at the boy, but he managed a final desperate dash that left the marsh behind, and the danger, and the creature threw back its head, emitting an Urulation of frustrated hunger which carried over the swamp and was borne far away, reaching the Deepwoods as an evil wind that moaned in the branches.

But even as Nathan approached the trees the dream changed, and he was somewhere else. The desert of Ind, on Eos, and the moon was rising – Astrond, the Red Moon of Madness, staining the sands with its dull ruby light. A wild white xaurian like the one he had once ridden wheeled above him; its breast gleamed pale in a roving beam from some-where on the ground. There was a noise like *zzzip*, and a flash. The xaurian jerked abruptly and plummeted earthwards. A voice Nathan thought he recognized said: 'It has served its purpose. I will not risk it interfering again.' Nathan felt a surge of anger and grief, though he couldn't tell if it was *his* xaurian – the xaurian that had saved his life – nor imagine why anyone would wish to kill it.

But his fury went with the dream, and he moved on. He was in a world he had visited before, two or three times, a world all sea. His former visits had shown him a tropical archipelago overwhelmed by a great storm; now, he was near one of the poles, but he knew somehow it was the same place. It was a feature of his dreaming that after a while he could identify instinctively which world he was in. The sea here was a cold deep green, and huge ice floes drifted past, one as big as a whole island, with a cluster of penguins on board. On another, he saw something that gave him a thrill of startled wonder. A mermaid had pulled herself up out of the water and leaned there, supported on her hands, her tail-fin dipping in the sea. But as he drew closer he saw her tail wasn't that of a fish: it was a seal. Her skin was snow-petal white, her eyes dark and large, her long straight hair silvery-grey like seal-fur. He thought: *She's not a mermaid, she's a selkie. A real selkie . . .*

She turned suddenly and slid off the floe back into the sea. He had a fleeting glimpse of her streaking through the water, the light rippling in bewildering patterns along her body – then there was only a seal, diving down into the green deeps.

There were other dreams, other worlds. He was back in Wilderslee, in a small round room with no windows or door. A tower room, he concluded, or a circular dungeon below ground level – a room where something important was kept, or dark deeds were about to take place. In both mediaeval palaces and futuristic skyscrapers, secrets and crimes always seemed to happen in rooms at the very top, or subterranean basements far below. This room was illuminated only by the daylight that filtered through a louver in the roof – or perhaps there were a couple of tiles missing and, it being Carboneck, no one had climbed up to repair them. He could make out a pedestal in the centre of the chamber, and a long chest on top, heavy with ironwork. He couldn't lift it – he had neither substance nor form – but from the shape it was easy to guess what it contained.

Suddenly, a section of the wall slid back with the grinding

noise of stone on stone, and a light came in. An oil lamp, held aloft by an unsteady hand, and followed by a face – the king, no longer in party mode, looking both anxious and daring, like a schoolboy egged on by his fellows to some questionable act. The woman Agnis came behind him, in a dress even more clinging than the one she had worn at the ball, her black hair loosened and falling nearly to her waist. She seemed to be hanging back, hesitant or afraid, and in the shadow of her hair her expression looked surreptitious and sly.

'Is it here?' she whispered, glancing from side to side. 'The spirit-guardian – is it here?'

'It's in the sword.' The king didn't whisper, but his voice was stiff with tension.

'Will we see it? How does it show itself?'

'I don't know.' The king approached the chest, setting the lamp down on the pedestal beside it. 'I've – I've never actually *seen* the sword.'

'But it's your family heirloom!' Surprise made her forget to whisper. 'You said your father –'

'He brought me here when I was a boy – showed me the chest – but he wouldn't open it. He said best not. We guard it; we don't need to see it. Some things should be left alone.' He was staring at the chest as if he agreed with his parent.

'Weren't you ever curious?' Agnis said in the accents of Pandora.

'Not really. It's a sword – brings bad luck – you can't even touch it. Not a good idea to be too curious about that. Are you sure you –'

'Yes.' Agnis sounded resolute. 'I just want to *see* it. Only once. I won't marry you with some dark mystery hanging over us. Anyway, how do you know it's still there?'

'Of course it's there. Where would it go?'

'Somebody might have stolen it.'

'Not possible. I told you –'

'With all this secrecy and security,' Agnis said, 'your ancestors must've been worried about thieves.'

'Don't think they were trying to keep anyone *out*,' the king said unhappily. 'More like something *in*.'

'I'll believe it when I see it,' Agnis declared stubbornly. 'Come on, Wilbert: open the chest.'

The king fumbled in his doublet and produced two keys hung on a chain round his neck. He took it off, and jabbed the larger key at the lock, though his hand was trembling so much it took at least a minute before he could slot it in. It turned very smoothly for a key that couldn't have been used in a generation or more. Agnis leaned forward, nervous and eager, her lips parted in the breathlessness of anticipation. But it was the king who raised the lid, lifting the lamp so they could see inside.

'There it is.'

The sword lay on a bed of velvet, completely encased in the scabbard the Grandir had made for it. Even the hilt was covered with a leather guard which seemed to be fastened to the sheath by a strap with metal rivets. Nothing could be seen of the blade within. Nathan had been sure this was the weapon Romandos had forged, in another world, another age, but here was confirmation. This was the Sword of Straw – and in the unseen blade the spirit slept, dreaming its dreams of freedom and vengeance, waking at a touch.

'Take it out!' Agnis hissed.

'Are you mad? I told you –'

'You don't have to actually handle it, silly. Lift it out in the scabbard and unfasten that leather thing so we can take a proper look. You can't chicken out now we've got this far. As it is, the scabbard could be empty. We're here to check.'

It's not empty, Nathan thought. The sword was in there,

226

with its occupant. He could sense the spirit even in its sleep.

The king still hesitated, plainly reluctant, but Agnis alternately pestered and cajoled, and Nathan knew he would give in. (Of course he knew – this was the past, Nell's past, ten years before he left her in the Deepwoods. There would be no surprises.)

At last the king said: 'All right, I will, but shut the door. We *must* be private.'

Now it was her turn to falter, looking round at the windowless walls. 'I'd rather not. You know how I am about closed-in places. Supposing we were shut in? You said yourself this room is a family secret. That stone must be virtually sound-proof: we could call and call and no one would hear us. No one would come. We might starve to death in here.'

Eventually, the king agreed to leave the door open. He lifted the scabbard out of the chest – Nathan felt the spirit stirring, sensed the changing pattern of its slumber. The blade seemed to be nearly four feet long and very heavy: the king staggered under the weight of it. He rested the point on the floor and inserted the smaller key into what looked like one of the rivets on the connecting strap. Even though he had never seen it before, it was clear he had been given precise instructions, though Nathan couldn't help questioning the logic of that. If you weren't meant to touch the sword, why pass on the details of how to gain access to it? He suspected Bartlemy would say it had something to do with human nature.

With the lock released, the strap sprang free. The king took hold of the scabbard lower down, and carefully prised the leather guard off the hilt. It gleamed with a dim blue sheen; Nathan remembered it from earlier dreams. No gems were set there. Apart from the lustre of the metal there was nothing else to distinguish it.

'It doesn't look all that special to me.' There was a note

227

of disappointment in Agnis' tone. Her awed whisper had long gone. 'What about the spirit guardian? Where is it?'

It's there, Nathan thought. *Don't disturb it.*

'In the sword,' the king said. Now, it was his turn to lower his voice. 'Like I told you.'

'How do you mean, *in* the sword? I don't see –'

'I don't know, and I don't want to know.'

'Couldn't you just draw the blade a little way? Hold it through your sleeve or something.'

'You can't do that,' the king explained. 'The spell on it doesn't allow cheating. You can hold it through the scabbard: that's all. My great-grandfather was the last man to draw it – he wore gloves. The Duke of Quilp had challenged him to single combat, I forget why; we weren't on very good terms with Quilp at the time. One of the king's ministers suggested he use this – thought it would give him an edge, sort of thing. The Duke was the best swordsman this side of the Deepwoods.' He fell silent for a moment.

'What happened?' Agnis prompted.

'Not exactly sure. No witnesses except the Duke, and he wouldn't talk about it. My great-grandfather was killed, with his minister, and the Duke's second. Quilp was wounded in the shoulder or the side – forget which – it crippled him, he never fought again.' So much for the Gauntletts of Protection, Nathan thought. 'After that, my grandfather made this room, sealed the chest inside. Out of harm's way. The Traitor's Sword won't be lifted, except by the right man.'

'But who's the right man,' Agnis mused, staring down at the exposed hilt, 'and how will he know?'

'A hero, the legend says. Or a traitor. Depends which story you read. As for how he'll know . . .'

'It might be you,' Agnis said, and her voice was very sweet, and her gaze slid sideways to meet his.

'I'm no hero. Got to be pure in heart for that – ha! No traitor either.'

'You're a hero to me.' Her sultry mouth curved into a wide pussycat smile. Only cats don't smile, Nathan reflected, but that's how they'd look if they did.

She's evil, he tried to tell the king, forgetting this was the past, and it could not be changed, and he had no voice to speak or warn him. Even though Nell had liked her, she was evil. No one would have pushed matters this far out of mere curiosity . . .

'That's enough,' the king said, with a sudden stab at regal authority. 'I'm putting it back.' He tried to replace the leather guard on the hilt, but his fingers fumbled, still shaking with nerves.

There was a sound from outside – footsteps on stone, drawing nearer. The echoing footsteps of metal-shod feet. Agnis turned, pressing a hand to her breast. (Was there a flash of triumph in her eyes?) The king started, clutching the scabbard.

A man strode in – a big man, much bigger than the king, with a beard that jutted aggressively and eyebrows to match. Nathan noticed his iron-tipped boots, a glimpse of chain-mail under his tabard, a longsword at his side. 'Agnis!' he said sharply. 'Where have you been? Slipping away like this – letting Wilbert inveigle you up here – What is this anyway? A secret room? A seduction chamber?' His face, naturally ruddy, grew still redder with outrage.

The king bristled. 'My intentions towards your sister are perfectly honour–'

(Sister, Nathan noted. Nell got it wrong. Not a rival in love – an irate brother. He was as dark as Agnis, dressed partly in black, and Nathan couldn't help thinking of him as the Black Knight.)

'You'll never marry her!' the intruder was saying. 'The

spineless ruler of a petty kingdom – a one-city state with a few acres of farmland tacked on. No warriors – only peasants, merchants, *shopkeepers* – a king who wants to eat well and sleep deep instead of fight and conquer. You're not a king – you're not even a man! Agnis can do better for herself – better for *me* –'

'Get out of here!' The king's grip tightened on the scabbard; Nathan saw the whitening of his knuckles.

'I love him!' Agnis announced dramatically.

Her brother drew his sword. Nathan saw the king was unarmed, save for the deadly contents of the sheath. Agnis had taken a step back, as if seeking protection, placing him between her and any danger of attack. 'I won't be sacrificed to your ambition!' she told her brother. 'Wilbert, help me! *Please!*'

'I have no weapon –'

His assailant gave a derisive laugh, reminiscent of Damon Hackforth. 'You have a sword between your hands, yet you say you are weaponless. There speaks both a fool and a coward!'

They've set him up, Nathan thought. They're in it together – it's obvious . . .

'Defend yourself, or die!' the Black Knight cried, whirling his own sword in a great arc.

It's a bluff, Nathan hazarded. They wouldn't dare kill him like this. It's a bluff to make him draw . . . His heart would have been in his mouth if either organ had been tangible. He forgot all about not interfering – if he had known how, he would have changed history. But he could only watch.

The Traitor's Sword came out of its scabbard with a sound like tearing silk. The blade seemed to be edged with blue fire, but beneath the sheen of the metal Nathan thought he saw shadows move, and two red gleams that slid down the shaft. Then the sword leaped from the king's hand, parried the attacking blow, and took off the Black Knight's head with a single stroke. It shot across the room, bouncing against the stonework like a ball, jets of blood spouting from severed arteries and spraying in all directions as it rolled. Floor and walls were spattered; one side of Agnis' skirt was drenched. She screamed with genuine emotion this time – screamed and screamed, clutching her own head as if she feared to lose that too. Her brother's body stood for a second as though taken by surprise and uncertain what to do, then it crashed to the ground. The sword swept round the room, hovered briefly within inches of Agnis' neck, then sheared off her hair at the nape and moved on. She fell to the ground, sobbing and shriek- ing in alternate spasms. The king had shrunk back against the pedestal. 'No!' he gasped. 'I didn't mean it! I couldn't –'

The blade plunged into his thigh.

Nathan awoke moments later, panting from the horror of it, a cold sweat on his forehead. His limbs slowly relaxed but his thoughts were racing. *They planned it together, Agnis and her brother. From what he said, they weren't from Wilderslee. I expect he hoped the sword would kill the king so he could take over the kingdom. But the Black Knight was killed instead – they didn't plan for that – and the king saw through Agnis and sent her away.* Or did he? He had seemed fairly besotted, and not particularly perceptive. Maybe he really *had* refused to marry her out of nobility, because of the wound. Perhaps it went right up to the groin and he was unable to have more children: that would explain it. Nell had had a close shave. She might have been saddled with the ultimate wicked stepmother.

And then: *I wonder . . . I wonder if Agnis could be behind the Urdemons?*

He lay back, still tormented with worry about the princess, trying to sleep and failing, his mind spinning with unresolved problems. In the end, he was forced to read more Walter

Scott, drifting off just before dawn into a darkness without even the glimmer of a dream.

That week saw the end of the summer term at Ffylde. Hazel had to struggle through two more weeks, but Nathan finished on Wednesday, although, racked by the demands of his other life, he could barely contain himself even that long. The abbot didn't summon him again, but went out of his way to talk to Annie, when she came to collect him, reducing her to a mush of embarrassment and pride with his praise for Nathan's sterling qualities. Nathan's classmates, too, wanted to give him a heroic send-off, but he managed to dissuade them, threatening Ned Gable with dire consequences if anyone so much as slapped him on the back. Damon Hackforth hadn't been seen in school again, but Annie said she had had a letter of apology from his parents, drafted she guessed by Selena, which had moved her so much she shed a tear.

'I suppose I can't complain about how little you tell me,' she said. 'I gather from Father Crowley you didn't say much to anyone. He said you showed commendable restraint – that was the phrase – and great magnanimity. I blushed so red I wanted the floor to swallow me up. It's awful being a proud mother. I just hope you'll never be restrained and magnanimous again.'

'I'll do my best,' Nathan grinned. With school finally over, he felt some of the tension leaving him. From tonight, he could dream at leisure . . .

'He seemed very intrigued by Uncle Barty,' Annie was saying. 'The abbot, I mean. He asked a lot of questions about him. They ought to meet some time. I think they'd get on, don't you?'

'Mm.'

Nathan's mind was elsewhere.

There was no song in the garden that night, though he had half expected it. With all his anxiety about the princess, and the Traitor's Sword, he hadn't forgotten the ghostly motor-launch, or the child-spirit's elusive warning.

The white ship waits by the river-shore . . .

The memory of the words sent a faint chill over his skin, though the weather was warm.

He went to bed thinking about Agnis, and whether it could be she who was controlling the Urdemons, and what it was about her that was vaguely familiar. The long black hair reminded him of Nenufar the sea-spirit, whom he had seen only briefly in the magic circle, wearing another woman's face. But Annie had seen her in another form, with a river-fall of hair and eyes deep as the Pit . . . Could they be two aspects of the same spirit? But no: one was mortal, one phantom, and they were in separate worlds, separate dreams. Of course, *this* world wasn't a dream – or was it? Increasingly, he was beginning to wonder which was the dream, which the reality. He was tossed between worlds like a storm-spun leaf, and each mirrored the one before, with parallel stories, parallel histories, myths and magics that intertwined across the gulf of time and space. There were no two-headed aliens, only humans, moving through the same old routine of drama and tragedy, passion and destruction. Modern science had taught him that throughout the multiverse there were other Nathans, other Annies. The princess was a different edition of Hazel, livelier, more confident, with a longer tangle of hair and a sweeter smile – a Hazel to fall in love with – but still, somehow, Hazel, best of his friends. And Frimbolus – Frimbolus was Bartlemy, with his lore-books and his poultices, like and unlike, a counterpart, a reverse image. If he waited long enough, he might meet George (surely not Roshan?), Ned, Damon . . . Familiar people behind unfamiliar faces, pattern duplicating pattern, world reflecting world. He could wander infinity living a multitude of lives, endlessly new, endlessly different, always the same. His head reeled at the thought.

He found he was falling asleep and – for once – forced himself back to wakefulness, fearful that the morass of philosophy might infect his dreams. With such thoughts in his head, who knew where he might end up. *Focus*, Bartlemy had said. *Focus on the moment to which you wish to return.*

It wasn't difficult to concentrate on the princess, and that day in the woods . . .

He slept.

When he opened his eyes, the sun was rising. The light came streaming through the lacework of twig and leaf, foundering in a thicket, slipping though chinks in the scanty spring canopy, casting a muddle of tiny shadows which danced across the woodland floor and were lost in the debris of last year's autumn. He saw the princess beside him, still sleeping – he knew a sudden hope that she had never known he had gone. He waited for the dawn to wake her, watching as the whole sky lightened, listening to the morning song of the birds. A small golden squirrel played peekaboo round a tree-trunk, then scurried down to the ground and vanished into the wood with a whisk of its tail. It occurred to Nathan that Nell wasn't where he had left her: the cover was deeper here, and the tree that shaded them was different, with twigs splayed into fans and crumpled leaves only half unwrapped from their buds. He wondered how long it had been till his return, and whether Nell was angry, or hungry, or both; but at least she was safe. That was all that mattered.

Her eyelids stirred and lifted; she stared up at him, blinking.

'You came back! You *did* come back! Nathan – Nathan –' There was a moment when she was hugging him and hugging him, half crying with relief – then the hug became the grip of fury, fingers clenching on his arms, and she was shaking him, or trying to, sobbing accusations. 'You left me – you *left* me – how could you? It's been a whole day – a day and a night – I looked for you – I waited and waited – I was all on my own –'

'I'm sorry,' he said. 'I couldn't help it. I fell asleep, and when I woke up I was in my own world. I'd never deliberately abandon you – you must believe that. It's been worse for me – no, I don't mean that, but longer – four days. I kept trying to get back to you, but whenever I dreamed, I was in the wrong place, or the wrong time. Nell –'

'I didn't say you could call me Nell!'

He smiled – a mistake. She tried to shake him again, snarling with rage and frustration. He caught hold of her arms to restrain her, hoping to calm her down.

'You brought me here – you managed that – so *why* didn't you get back? Don't tell me you can't control it – I'm sick of that one. You can when you want to. You dodge in and out of universes, spirit people off somewhere, then disappear when it suits you –'

'It didn't suit me,' he said, being rational, sensing too late that rationality wasn't what she wanted. 'If I could choose, I'd never leave you. You know that.'

'Do I?' She subsided into a sulk – just a small one, since she wasn't good at sulking. 'How can I trust you, when you come and go like this – with no warning, no word? How can I ever trust you?'

There was no answer to that, but he knew he had to find one, even if it was the wrong answer. 'You can't,' he said. 'I can't trust myself. Sometimes I'll leave – no warning, no word – that's how it is. But you can trust your heart, and mine. My heart will never leave you.'

She gazed at him with eyes scrunched up against the sun. 'That's a beautiful line,' she said, trying to be cynical. 'Frim would probably say you were silver-tongued. Do they teach you to talk like that, in your world?'

'No,' he said. 'It comes naturally.'

She gave a shaky laugh – and everything was all right again, or as all right as it could be.

'You're quite clever,' he remarked, 'for a princess.'

'Princesses are supposed to be clever.'

'Not in my world. They just have to look pretty, and wave at the crowd, and do things for charity.'

'Even in my world most princesses do that,' she said. 'Only not me. At Carboneck, I haven't much of a crowd to wave at. And according to Roshan, I'm only *quite* pretty.'

'He was wrong,' Nathan said airily. 'You're not pretty at all.'

Her gaze slitted.

'But you *are* beautiful.'

'You're doing it again,' she said. 'Saying the right thing.'

'I know. I've been practising.'

'On who?'

After a while, they began to talk about practical matters – how to get back to Carboneck, and what the princess had done the previous day, and whether they could find anything to eat. Left on her own, Nell had been befriended by a wood-wose, who had shown her another stream where she could drink and found her some more wild strawberries and a few nuts from a squirrel's hoard. 'But I ate them all,' she said. 'There weren't many, and I was starving. I still am.' Nathan knew he wasn't hungry, but he found his stomach yearned in sympathy. 'The wose said it was *this* way, towards the road to the city. I was sort of heading in that direction before I stopped to go to sleep.'

'Good,' Nathan said. 'I think we should start walking.'

'Can't you just –'

'I daren't try. I might disappear again. Or spirit you off to my world.'

'I shouldn't mind,' Nell said.

'I thought it was your princessly duty to stay in Wilderslee?'

'Yes, but – I could go to your world just for a visit, couldn't I? You could dream that.'

'The problem,' Nathan said, 'as always, would be bringing you back.'

There was no path to follow, only the vague indications of the woodwose. 'We go southeast,' the princess said. 'Now the sun's up, it's easy. You just find a shadow and work out the angle.'

'The sun moves,' Nathan pointed out, 'and the slope deflects the shadows. Also, it's early in the year, so . . .'

'It's this way, all right?' Nell said. 'Unless you have a better idea.'

They had been walking for a couple of hours when they came to a steep bank which plunged abruptly into a narrow valley. They scrambled down with some difficulty, often slithering several yards in a flurry of dead leaves. At the bottom they came upon the road – a mere track, long unused, hidden in a tunnel of trees. But it was heartening to find it at last – to be treading a route that was clearly marked. Nathan apologized to the princess for doubting her, putting her in a good mood, and they set off rather more briskly, heading due east now, which Nell assured him was the way to Carboneck. She had no recollection of the road but insisted that wasn't relevant, since the picnics of her childhood were so long ago. After a mile or two the valley opened out, and the trees thinned, and they joined another, much wider track, grass-grown and pitted with wheel-ruts. A sunken stone at the verge was carved with a double arrow, pointing one way to Quilp, the other to Wilderslee.

'See?' the princess said buoyantly. 'I told you so. I think I remember this bit.'

As they walked, Nathan told her about his latest dreams – the Traitor's Sword, Agnis, the Black Knight.

'I didn't remember it was her *brother*,' Nell said, and: 'I *liked* her. I really did. How could I have liked a – a deceiver, a scheming spy?'

'Young children don't have very good judgement,' Nathan said diffidently, realizing too late he sounded patronizing. 'I expect you were lonely – your mother was dead, and your nanny came later. It made you vulnerable. Anyway, your father liked her too. Maybe it was a spell.'

'Maybe.'

'Was she foreign?'

'Depends what you mean by that. There are lots of little kingdoms in these parts, all close together. We don't really think of our neighbours as foreign; foreign means people from a really long way away, towards the coast, or beyond the Deepwoods. But Agnis wasn't from Wilderslee; I'm pretty sure about that.'

'So the brother was planning a takeover,' Nathan deduced. 'The king would be killed in such a way that it would seem to be his own fault; you were just a child; he would get himself installed as regent or protector with no battles to upset anybody, and move on to the next conquest. Politics.'

'Instead of which,' the princess said, '*he* was the one who got himself killed, my father was only wounded, and Agnis was sent away. She could have been queen, but she didn't even get that. She must have been choking on her own bile.'

'And then the Urdemons came.'

'That was a couple of years later.'

'It's still too much of a coincidence. Anyhow, she would've needed time to cook up a new plot. An infestation of demons would take a while to arrange. She's behind it all somehow: I'm sure of it. She still wants to be the ruler of Wilderslee, one way or another.'

'If you're right,' Nell said pensively, 'then she's defeated her own object. At the rate we're going, there won't be anything left to rule.'

By midday they had left the woods behind and the road was winding among bare hills criss-crossed with dry-stone walls. They passed the occasional roofless cottage or the skeleton of a barn, and stopped to drink from a well whose creaking chain and leaky bucket indicated it had been long abandoned. A knot of sheep grazing nearby paused to stare at them. They were led by a huge black ram with a helmet of twisted horns, a feral eye and the fleece of an unkempt yak. As they finished it charged at them, but they vaulted a low wall and ran away across the fields, back to the road.

'There used to be many farms here,' the princess said, 'but they've all gone now.'

They were both increasingly hungry, but there was nothing to eat.

In the afternoon the weather changed. A thin veil of cloud drew across the sky, shutting out the sun. The wind grew chill. Nell was getting blisters and they paused to rest, but not for long; sitting still was too cold for comfort.

'When we get home,' the princess said, meaning *her* home, 'I'm going to have Prenders bathe my feet, and rub them with oil, and I'm not going to walk anywhere for at least a week. But first, I'm going to eat the biggest dinner in the world.'

They kept on walking. Both were tired, but they didn't dare rest again: they were too anxious to reach Carboneck before nightfall.

Once, the princess said: 'Whose bright idea was it, to spend a day in the Deepwoods?'

'Yours,' said Nathan. 'I think.'

It was raining when they reached the marshes, a misty, drizzly, grizzly kind of rain that a depressed climate can keep up for hours. The horizon had dissolved into cloud, and the twin hills of Carboneck seemed to be floating above the wetlands, ghost-faint in the greyness of the afternoon and very far away. The road became a causeway, supported at intervals on wooden piles, some sagged or fallen, leaving yawning gaps, or stretches where the ground looked solid but wasn't, needing only the pressure of a footstep to induce collapse. On either side the broken pools straggled into the distance, interspersed with reed-clumps and patches of boggy earth. There were no trees, but the bulrushes grew very tall, bending in the passage of the wind. Nathan remembered his dream of the swamp, and Roshan – or whoever it was – fleeing from the giant worm. (Maybe he had been trying to search for the princess.)

'The Urdemons live here,' Nell said. 'They don't need acts of magic to summon them. They hear if you try to cross.'

'How did the people manage to leave the city?'

'It's all right if the sun shines. They don't like the sun.'

'We could wait,' Nathan offered. 'It might stop raining.'

'It won't,' the princess sighed.

And, after a pause: 'I'm famished.'

'Are you afraid?' Nathan asked her. Just checking.

'Yes.'

'Good. So'm I.' He took her hand. 'Let's go then.'

They went carefully along the causeway, trying as far as possible to follow recent cart-tracks, in the hope that where the ground would support a cart, it would support them. But no cart had passed for many months, and what tracks there were had almost gone. The rain persisted, turning the earth to mud, and their progress was very slow, and they got wetter, and colder, and Nell began to shiver. 'We could run for it,' Nathan said, when at last the city started to draw near.

'No. The demons hear everything. Any vibration – running footsteps – will bring them out. I think . . . they haven't heard us because of the rain. The sound of it on the ground – on the water – must drown us out. As long as we move quietly . . .'

They went on. A little further ahead, Nathan felt the earth give beneath him. He sprang back just in time, while a whole section of the road caved in, subsiding with a muddy *flump* into the pool below. There was only a narrow lip of causeway remaining on the edge of the hole, slippery and treacherous in the wet. Nathan seized the princess' hand again and dragged her along it, though she almost fell twice. 'They'll have heard that,' he said as the path widened. 'Now, we run.'

She didn't argue. She was wearing a dress she'd long outgrown, the skirt well above the ankle, torn by the walk through the Deepwoods into a ragged finish that would have looked stylish in twenty-first century England. She didn't have to kilt it up, though the sodden material hampered her, and she paused to rip it further up her legs. Then she ran, kicking off her shoes, bare feet gripping more surely on the damp ground. Nathan followed, staying just behind her, listening as he ran. He knew the sound from his dream – that deep bubbling, gurgling noise, and then the surge of water as the thing heaved itself out of the swamp . . .

'Run!' he screamed to Nell. 'Don't look back! *Run!*'

She looked back anyway, stumbled, got up. Her face was very pale.

'I'll deal with it!' he cried, pushing her onward. '*Run!*'

In that moment, she believed him. She had seen him in phantom-form, outfacing another demon – she knew he could do it. She trusted him – his strength, his courage, his unknown powers. She ran . . .

Nathan swung round to confront the demon.

It was the one from his dream, a monster of slime, its massive neck curving towards him, greenish sputum drooling from its toothless jaw. It was solid, and he was solid, and he knew there was nothing he could do about it at all. He hadn't even picked up a stick to defend himself. Why hadn't he thought to go to bed with a weapon of some kind? Stupid, stupid . . .

Too late now.

The mouth came rushing down on him, opening wider – wider – he saw the network of huge blood vessels plunging into the tunnel of its throat. He stammered the words of his uncle's spell, but he had not that Gift, and whatever had once empowered him was gone. The stench of demonbreath overwhelmed him; bony gums gripped his waist. He was thrashing about in darkness, plunging his hands into a thick ooze of saliva, feeling the moist texture of its tongue. He didn't know if he screamed, but no one would hear.

Then daylight flared as he was spat out, ejected upwards into the air as an animal might do with a recalcitrant morsel, tossing it up to swallow it whole. Below, the jaws stretched into a giant gape – the glutinous tongue heaved – he was tumbling helplessly into the wet red channel of its gorge . . .

NINE

The White Ship

He woke up.

Relief washed over him in a great wave – a relief so intense it left him feeling slightly sick. He was in his own bed, in his own room. His clothes were sticky with sweat and possibly urine, but he was intact. Safe. Reaction set in – his teeth began to chatter – he got up and tottered to the bathroom, tugged at the lightswitch. It took a moment for his vision to adapt, but then he saw. He was covered in greenish mucus – his torso, hands, arms – it must be all over the bed too. He doubled up over the loo and retched violently.

Annie came in shortly after, roused by the sound of surreptitious washing – not a noise she was accustomed to hearing in the small hours. She found Nathan simultaneously running a bath and trying to dunk his clothes in the sink. 'What is that?' Annie gazed at the scum in horror, shrinking from the smell of it. 'Have you been in the river? I thought you'd gone to bed. You had a princess to rescue . . .'

'I rescued her,' he said. 'I think. If she ran like hell . . .'

Suddenly, she saw he was crying. She hugged him instantly, getting the stuff on her pyjamas, coaxing him to laugh weakly at the thought of still more washing. 'We'll put it all in the machine,' she said. 'Don't worry about it. Is it on the sheets too?' She wondered if it was vomit, except that there was so much of it, and the smell was wrong.

'I couldn't see in the dark. 'Spect so.'

'It's okay. It's okay now.' He was still shuddering. He'd stripped to the waist and she thought irrelevantly how tall he'd become, shooting up in the manner of teenagers. Too tall for his body – stretched out – ribs jutting through his skin. She hugged him tighter. What would Bartlemy recommend? 'I've got some of your uncle's hot chocolate mixture.'

'Sounds good.'

She made hot chocolate for them both, adding brandy from the bottle she had bought for cooking last Christmas. Then Nathan told her, not about the white ship and the beckoning woman – that didn't seem important now – but everything else, everything he could remember, all about finding the princess in the Deepwoods again, and Agnis and the Black Knight, and what had happened on the causeway. He wasn't either proud of what he had done or ashamed of it, he just needed to talk it out. As he talked some of the horror passed out of him, into his words, into his story, becoming a separate thing, so he could distance himself from it, see it in perspective. Like Bartlemy's spiritual bacteria, he thought: they had been inside him, like an illness, a nausea in his stomach, a darkness on his heart. But mere words – no spell, just the simple mechanics of communication – carried away the infection, or some of it, transmitting it into the ether. He waited for Annie's reaction, for the anger born of fear, the inevitable recriminations. Of course, even if she grounded him for the entire school holidays, she couldn't control where he went in his sleep.

But Annie didn't look angry. She sat there in silence, listening, while the skin formed on her chocolate. Even when he stopped speaking she seemed to listen, her face set in stillness, though she had gone very pale. She was thinking: He's an adult now. He runs into danger – terrible danger – and there's nothing I can do. I can't protect him any more, I can't tell him *Don't play with matches: you'll get burned – Don't run into the road: you'll be knocked down* – all that parent-child stuff is over. He knows the risks – he makes a choice – he's gone beyond my reach. Behind her stillness the panic started to spiral out of control, so she wanted to yell at him, and yell at him, getting through somehow with combined impact of noise and rage. Sound and fury. *Sound and fury.* She knew it wouldn't do any good. This is the worst part, she thought. Being a parent was wonderful – magical – exasperating – scary – but *this* was the worst part. The part where you had to let go.

She picked up a teaspoon and began to peel the skin off her chocolate. 'I don't know what to say. I don't want you to do these things – get into these situations – but that isn't important any more. What I feel isn't important . . .'

'It's important, but –'

She made a tiny gesture, brushing his protest away. 'You're grown up now – grown so far up I can barely reach the top of your head. What you do is up to you. I hoped you'd be a child a little longer, but . . . that hasn't happened. I just want you to know – oh, the usual clichés. I'm here for you, always. I'm here to listen to your problems, make you chocolate, feed you – wash demon-spit off your clothes. I've tried to teach you things – courtesy, consideration, values – but the rest is for you. Who you become – how you live – *if* you live –' She stopped, looking down, fingers squeezing the mug.

'I thought you'd shout at me,' he said awkwardly.

'I wanted to. But what's the point? It wouldn't change anything.'

'Thank you.' Dimly, he sensed what she was going through, sensed her struggle and her generosity, though he didn't really understand. 'You're the best mum ever.' And, with a touch of gêne: 'I love you.'

Annie sniffed damply and achieved a wan smile. 'How awfully American we sound,' she said. 'You know English people don't use the L-word. What we feel for each other is just . . . assumed. Unless it's wartime, and you're going to the Front, or whatever.'

'*Avé Caesar*,' Nathan said with a slightly lop-sided grin. '*Nos morituri te salutamus.*'

The traditional greeting of the gladiators: We who are about to die salute you . . .

Annie shivered – and tried to turn it into a shrug. 'You stay here,' she said. 'I'll go change your bed. This chocolate's gone far too scummy to drink.'

While she was upstairs, he made himself some toast, spreading it lavishly with butter and home-made jam. The aftermath of terror had left him in need of calories. As he sat down to eat he heard the singing, faint but clear in the dark of the garden.

> '*Follow the flight of the albatross*
> *over the midnight sea.*
> *Follow the road tide-turned, wave-tossed;*
> *the white ship waits – for thee!*'

When Annie came back downstairs the toast was uneaten and Nathan's expression was strange and faraway. But that was fairly standard, she thought.

'Did you hear something?' she said. 'I thought there was someone singing, just outside. Bit weird, at this time of night.'

'I missed it,' Nathan said. 'I must have my bath.'

The next day, he texted Hazel twice and left a message on her voicemail, all without eliciting any response. Of course, she must be still in school, possibly too busy to answer, but he wanted to see her – wanted it badly – though he didn't try to analyse why. He would have to wait till the afternoon, when he could go to her home. In the meantime, he walked over to Thornyhill. On the way, he looked out for Woody, but there was no sign of him. At the manor, he found Bartlemy in the kitchen, giving breakfast to the dwarf. At least, it was morning so the meal must be breakfast; it looked like crispy fried woodlice, but Nathan was sure that was wrong.

'Ye been staying out o' trouble?' Login Nambrok asked.

'Not really,' Nathan admitted.

'Ah, well. There's some are born to it, come what may.' Nambrok polished off the last of whatever it was he was eating. 'There's trouble around, I'm thinking. I ha' seen things, down by the river. Ye dinna want to be going that way.'

'What did you see?' Bartlemy inquired.

'The white ship. O' course, it were different in my day, wi' sails and that, and the oars dipping, though you never saw a body there to do the rowing. But this one, it must a had one o' those devil-machines in it, growling softly, softly, like yon hound might if he were getting angered. Any road, it were the white ship. They used to say it would be waiting for the lucky one, the chosen one, down by the sea-shore. It would wait out its time – five nights or seven, I dinna recall – and if ye came, it would carry ye away to the Isles o' the Blest, beyond the setting sun. That were said to be the land o' the Shining Ones, the Fair Folk, the Good People – but I dinna trust any man who glows in the dark. Anyhow, the Isles are gone now, if they were ever there, and it don't seem healthy to me, to have a bit of an old legend lingering on, all dressed up new.'

'I've heard that legend,' Bartlemy said. 'But there are many boats on the river. The one you saw sounds ordinary enough.'

The dwarf grunted and slid from his chair, departing without thanks through the back door and into the woods. Nathan sat down on another chair, waiting for his smell to follow him. 'Does he come here much?' he asked.

'When he's hungry,' Bartlemy said, 'if my cooking is to his taste. The dwarfish palate is different from ours.'

'What *was* that he was eating?'

'His breakfast. How about yours? Bacon and eggs?'

'Yes please. Uncle Barty, I've seen a white ship on the Glyde, a motor launch. There was a man from the village walking his dog, but he didn't see it at all, though the dog barked. What does it mean?'

'I don't know.' Bartlemy looked thoughtful. 'But Nambrok was right about one thing: it isn't natural when part of an old legend long past its sell-by date turns up in new clothes. Avoid it.'

Nathan nodded – he didn't think it was necessary to mention the beckoning woman, or the song in the garden – and launched into the tale of his overnight adventures. It was easier in the telling, the second time. Already the horror of it was slipping away from him, relegated to the dream-world from whence it came. He didn't know if that was good or bad; when peril is no longer immediate, fear can be swiftly forgotten, and then, grown rash or careless, you stray into the danger zone again. In one way at least, Nathan was determined to learn from his mistakes.

'I should have had a weapon,' he told Bartlemy. 'I ought to go to bed better equipped – take a kitchen knife or something – but I don't know how to guarantee I can dream it with me.'

'It depends what you take,' Bartlemy said. 'I will give it some thought. There is also the matter of the king's leg wound. You asked me if I could come up with a cure.'

'Can you?' Nathan's face brightened with sudden hope.

'It's difficult. The wound itself is obviously straightforward enough, but the fact that it doesn't heal is clearly due to some magical influence, probably the work of the spirit trapped in the blade. There is only one way to heal an injury like that.'

'How?' Nathan demanded eagerly.

'You must touch the wound with the weapon that made it. It's an ancient spell and, I suspect, applies throughout the multiverse. In the cause of the infection you will find its cure. In modern medicine you may see the equivalent in the principle of vaccination. Science and magic are not that far apart. Both work with nature, one way or another.'

'But nobody can lay a finger on the sword!'

'I said it was difficult. There will be a way – there's always a way – but you will have to find it for yourself. Meanwhile, I will give you a lotion for the king to ease his suffering, and a cordial to act as a restorative. There is little magic in either, but the lotion should make him more comfortable, and the cordial with provide nourishment and encourage healing sleep. Both are in crystal containers, which should pass the portal. I have no experience of inter-cosmic transportation, but crystal is pure, and much used in magic. I trust it will serve our purpose.'

'Thanks,' Nathan said. 'But what about a weapon of my own? Do you think there's something . . . ?'

'What weapon would you like?' Bartlemy asked.

'A Kalashnikov,' Nathan said promptly. 'But I don't suppose it would pass the portal, even if I knew where to get one. It's just that I like the idea of blasting that Urdemon into pulp. Flying pulp,' he concluded, forming a mental picture.

'Remember, the creature is an elemental, and its substance is unstable. The pulp would only re-form, possibly into something even more unpleasant.'

Nathan's mental picture changed for the worse, and he abandoned it.

'I think you would do better to find your weapon in Wilderslee,' Bartlemy said. 'There are things you may be allowed to carry with you in your dreaming, but I suspect a gun would be . . . out of order. So to speak.'

'Whose order? Allowed by whom?'

'That's the catch.'

Nathan gave a sigh of resignation. There were too many unanswerable questions out there, and he didn't want to think about them right now. 'I hoped you would have a suitable weapon,' he said. 'Like . . . an antique dagger, or a magic sword.'

'I have only a slice and a frying pan and several kitchen implements,' Bartlemy said, setting a plate of bacon and eggs in front of Nathan. 'The magic sword is in Carboneck.'

Nathan began to eat, and the taste of the food – eggs scrambled into fluffiness, bacon all crisped and curling round the edges, mushrooms oozing black juice – dispelled the last shreds of nightmare, and he was normal again, a normal boy eating a normal breakfast, with no alternative universes to spoil his appetite. Bartlemy smiled to himself, and put his pan in the sink. His magic was not in swords.

Annie had left the washing till morning, since the washing machine was noisy and given to violent paroxysms which shook the little house like an earth tremor, and her bedroom was over the kitchen and thus directly above the epicentre. Once Nathan had gone out she crammed the sheets and clothes in, holding her breath from the stench of slime, getting it on her hands, her forearms, even – she caught her reflection in the window – a daub on her face. Yuk, she thought in teen-speak, shuddering. She knew it was the fate of mothers, particularly mothers of sons, to do endless washing; apparently, it was what motherhood was all about. But it wasn't supposed to include getting covered in stinking green spittle from otherworld demons. Nathan might be eating his way back to normality but for Annie, normality had gone down the drain. *Along with the demonspittle*, she thought, trying to switch on the tap to clean her hands without getting that, too, smeared in sputum.

The shop was open but with the washing machine rattling into action she didn't hear anyone come in, nor the light knock on the connecting door.

'Am I bothering you?' said a familiar voice – the voice of someone who was accustomed to bothering people, and didn't much care.

DCI Pobjoy.

'Oh – it's you,' Annie said, caught off-guard. 'Sorry . . . I'm just trying to –'

'What have you got on your hands?'

'Stuff,' Annie said. 'Nothing really. Just . . . slimy . . . stuff.'

'It stinks.' Pobjoy switched on the tap for her. 'What on earth –'

'Look,' Annie said, too strained and too weary to improvise, 'I could lie to you, and you might believe me, but it's too much effort. Or I could tell you the truth, and you wouldn't believe me, so it would be pointless. Much better to just let the subject drop. Thanks for doing the tap. Could you turn up the cold a bit, please?'

He adjusted it accordingly. This wasn't a professional visit – he'd made an excuse to himself to drop by, to see if she was all right, and her son was all right, a bit of community relations – but his policeman's senses were twitching. He couldn't help pressing the matter.

'Has it got something to do with Nathan?' Nathan didn't

necessarily cause trouble, he knew, but trouble followed him, for some reason, spreading out from him in ripples that disrupted everything in his vicinity. Besides, Pobjoy was a copper: his instinct was to blame the teenager.

'Actually,' Annie said, 'it's the spit from a giant worm-thing that tried to eat him.'

'Very funny.'

'I said you wouldn't believe me.'

'There aren't a lot of giant man-eating worms in Eade,' Pobjoy said, going with the joke. He'd been told he needed to work on his sense of humour.

Suddenly, he remembered the bizarre incident at Crowford Comprehensive which a colleague had mentioned to him. Something about a plague of flies . . .

'It wasn't from round here,' Annie said matter-of-factly. She knew she should stop now, before he decided she was a total fruitcake. She didn't want him to think of her as some batty New Age freak. When Nathan had been kidnapped he'd been kind, in an understated way, or at least strong – someone she could rely on. Like Michael . . . Not a good train of thought.

'Last year,' she said, 'you must have realized there were odd things happening here, things you couldn't explain.'

'A robbery and three murders?'

'I don't mean criminal things – not just criminal, anyway. How did a man die of drowning in the middle of a wood with no water nearby? What became of the woman masquerading as Rianna Sardou? – you never found a trace of her. Who was the dwarf involved in the robbery? Why was everyone *really* after the Grimthorn Grail?'

'There are always loose ends in any investigation.' There had been too many in this one. It still nagged at him. 'If you know something –'

'I know everything,' Annie said. 'But there's no point in my telling you. It's like the giant man-eating worm. You wouldn't believe me.' Why was she doing this?

'I never had you down as one of those black-magic may-the-force-be-with-us types,' he said awkwardly. 'Are you going to tell me it was all due to ley-lines and phases of the moon?'

'I wouldn't recognise a ley-line unless it was drawn on the road,' Annie said. 'Sorry. I'm stupid today. Forget it.'

She was biting her lip, wishing she hadn't spoken, wishing he hadn't caught her when she was vulnerable, desperate, angry – angry at no one and nothing, needed someone on whom to vent her anger.

'If you say so.'

Her hands were clean now, though the smell still clung. She made an effort to compose herself, turned to face him. 'Would you like some coffee?' But he had gone.

Pobjoy lunched at the pub on a pork pie and a pint, listening to the gossip, automatically sifting it for anything of interest. There wasn't much. A forthcoming cricket match, Eade versus Chizzledown, a rumour that Lily Bagot was engaged, although someone pointed out she had yet to divorce Dave (there followed a few reminiscences of Dave Bagot, who had left the village and wasn't missed), a report that Riverside House had at last found a purchaser. 'Well, I wouldn't have it,' opined an elderly resident. 'Not if you paid me. Place is bound to be haunted, after what happened. That Mike Addison . . .'

''Twasn't his fault,' said another. 'It was that woman what got hold of him. Made herself look like his wife, didn't she? And they say it was her what did the killing – he didn't know about it till after the fact. Partial she was to drowning people, seeing as how she came from the river. Nothing good ever came up the Glyde.'

'What d'you mean, she came from the river?' Pobjoy asked, inserting himself without preamble into the conversation.

They looked at him, then at their drinks. They knew who he was.

He bought a round.

'She was a river gipsy,' said the second man, 'so I heard. But the Glyde's had a bad reputation for centuries. There'd be pirates and raiders sailing up from Grimstone a matter of three or four hundred years ago. And then there were the smugglers, in Georgian times. They'd have fights between rival gangs, or kill anyone they thought had betrayed them, and plenty of bodies would come floating on the tide. There used to be a rhyme about it – I've seen it in a book somewhere.

Death from the deep sea
floats up the Glyde.

There was a lot more work for a copper round here, in the old days. Of course, they didn't have coppers then – just the customs officers, Excise men they were called, and they weren't too popular. Much like now, when they won't even let you bring back a few bottles from Cally without making a fuss.'

'But the woman,' Pobjoy interceded, 'what do they say about her?'

'She went back to the river from which she came, that's the story. There's some as say she was a loralilly, not a real woman at all, but that's fairytales: we don't believe in that stuff no more. Still, she wasn't seen in these parts again, that's true enough. And you lot never caught up with her, did you?'

Pobjoy didn't answer – partly because he didn't want to discuss the shortcomings of the police, but mostly because he was wondering what a loralilly was.

Later, when the regulars had trickled away, he had a chat with the landlord.

'There's always been a bit of witchcraft in Eade,' he said. 'I don't mean all that trendy Wicca business, dancing on a hilltop in the nuddy and getting in touch with nature: you've got to go to Brighton for that. No, I mean the old stuff, the bad stuff. It was the Carlows, mostly. They burnt one of 'em, back in the sixteenth century. No point in putting her on the ducking stool: the Carlows always floated. Their power came from the river, or so folk said.'

'Effie Carlow drowned,' Pobjoy reminded him. 'Her power can't have been up to much.'

'I can't answer that one,' the landlord admitted. 'Maybe the river had done with her – but you know how it is with these tales: people will twist anything to fit the plot. I don't believe in all that rubbish myself, but there were some said Effie was a witch. She certainly had an evil eye, though I don't know there was any magic in it! Funny thing, I've heard talk about her great-granddaughter, just lately.'

'Hazel Bagot?' Pobjoy said sharply. He remembered her very well.

'That's the one. Quiet kid, untidy-looking. Got picked on at school or something – you know how kids are – and there was a bit of an incident. Shelley Carver's girl found her desk full of flies – no one knew where they came from. Pretty girl, Ellen, like her mum, but a bit tarty. Still, they all look that way now. Anyway, seems Ellen got spooked, thought it was something to do with Hazel. Witchcraft in the family and all that. Good thing, too: they might treat her with a bit more respect from now on. Shelley was in here the other night, heard her talking about it. Said something else, too. Ellen used to like going down by the river – probably wanted to sit quiet, get away from her mum. Now, she won't go near it. Don't suppose there's any connection . . . still, it's a funny thing.'

I should have paid more attention to the river, Pobjoy thought. Effie drowned in the Glyde, the German drowned in the wood, Addison and his wife lived at Riverside House. A river runs through it . . . (He'd heard the phrase somewhere, though he couldn't recall where.) He didn't believe in all this folklore stuff, naturally, but sometimes new crimes had old histories. Technically, the murderer was caught, the case closed. But not for him . . .

'Been a new boat there, last few days,' the landlord was saying. 'Big motor launch, so I'm told. Some see it, some don't. You don't get many like that on the Glyde.'

'Could it be the river-gipsies?' Pobjoy asked.

'Wouldn't know about that. They say it's pretty fancy, ocean-going craft, not exactly a gipsy barge. But there's a woman on board.'

'Did anyone recognise her?'

'Couldn't say. But she's the only one they've seen. No crew. Only the woman.'

When Pobjoy left the pub, the afternoon was hot and stuffy. He headed for the river path, 'just to look,' he told himself. Just to check. He was off-duty, gnawing the ends of old plots; he seemed to have no life outside his work. He'd dated a paramedic recently, met at the site of a road accident, but it hadn't lasted long. And something always drew him back to Eade. He liked Annie – he really liked her – though she'd acted rather strange that morning. (What *was* that green stuff? River-scum?) And he had unfinished business here.

There was a thick white mist lying in strands across the meadows, obliterating the river. It wasn't thick enough to be dangerous – he could see several yards ahead – but it made everything pale and ghostly. Under such conditions, he thought, you could understand how the stories started, tales of phantoms and loralillies (he must find out what they were) which would appear from the river and disappear apparently by magic. A tree brushed past him, twig-fingers clutching at his arm; a more fanciful person might have turned it into something else.

Annie, for instance – she was the fanciful type. Not silly-fanciful, despite her conversation that morning, but perhaps . . . an overactive imagination. She would know what a loralilly was . . .

The white silence of the fog had become a faint murmur, like the thrum of insect wings, or the shushing of the river. There was a moment when he almost thought it was a song, the sound of someone humming . . . then he realized it must be an engine, its vibration soft as a purr in the throat of a sleepy cat. It drew nearer, and he saw the prow of a launch, dim in the mist, a white motor launch with no visible crew, only a single figure standing in the bows. A woman. He stopped to stare, and she reached out to him, her long arms pale as foam on the sea.

'I know you,' she said, and though her voice was very quiet it woke strange echoes in his head. 'You've been looking for me. You've been looking for me for a long time. But you're not the one . . . you're not the one I'm waiting for.'

The launch moved on, vanishing into a veil of mist. Afterwards, he thought she was fair-haired, but he wasn't sure. She might have been dark, dark as Rianna Sardou, with eyes as black as the ocean-depths. He was a detective, a trained observer, yet he couldn't describe her, he couldn't pin her down. She had come and gone like a phantom, like a loralilly . . .

At the bookshop, Annie had just made tea.

She looked surprised to see him again – surprised and pleased. He was pleased she was pleased, but he didn't know how to show it. He accepted a cup with added sugar and propped one buttock on the edge of her desk.

'What's a loralilly?' he asked.

'A loralilly?' Annie frowned, puzzled. 'Oh – you mean a loreley: is that it? A kind of siren, a water-spirit . . .'

'Maybe.'

'In legends, they sit on rocky islands, serenading passing sailors. The sailors are so enchanted by their song they come too close to the rocks, and their ships are broken, and they drown. Not exactly good citizens, loreleys. Were you planning to arrest one?'

This was the Annie he liked, sensible, down-to-earth, despite her imagination. He was glad she wasn't talking about giant worms any more. Of course, she must have been joking – she was joking now, in a gentle, teasing sort of way. A sense of humour was a good thing: he must develop one some time.

'Somebody mentioned them in the pub,' he said. 'How come everyone knows about these things except me?'

'It depends what books you read when you were a child,' Annie said. 'Most of us get through Hans Andersen, the Brothers Grimm, the Chronicles of Narnia . . . Tolkien, Alan Garner, Roger Launcelyn Green. What did you read?'

'Sherlock Holmes.'

'Good stuff,' Annie said. 'I read those too. But if you're going to go chasing loreleys, you've got some catching up to do. Let me know if you want background reading.'

'Thanks, but I don't have the time.' He had odd evenings in front of the telly, but he wasn't going to start reading fantasy. God knows where that would lead.

He thought of telling her about the motor launch, and the mysterious woman, but the incident had unsettled him in ways he didn't want to discuss, and he let it go. He almost thought he'd imagined it, only imagination wasn't his thing. He believed in evidence, and instinct – instinct honed by experience – not the wild speculations of an erratic fancy. Forensic science could tell you almost everything these days . . . except the secrets of the human heart, the strange pathways of the mind.

When he had finished his tea he left almost as abruptly as before, afraid to find himself talking too much about loralillies, and man-eating worms, as if such things really existed.

Nathan was waiting at the bus stop when Hazel came home from school. For a second her face lit up – then something in her expression fogged, as if she were deliberately withdrawing from him.

'You're mad at me,' he said, 'because I haven't been round lately. I'm sorry.'

She shrugged. 'You had other things to do.'

'I shouldn't have done. You're my best friend. I didn't mean to take you for granted.'

'Of course we take each other for granted,' she said. 'People do.'

At her house they retreated to the bedroom, though Nathan thought Hazel seemed oddly reluctant to admit him. She had run out of coke and didn't seem to have any new music she was eager to play for him. He said: 'What happened to your mirror?' and she shrugged again, but her gaze slid sideways, avoiding his.

'Accident,' she said.

'You should be more careful,' he said, picking up the candle-stump from the clutter of her dressing-table. 'There's so much guff in here, if you knocked this over you could easily start a fire.'

'I'm careful,' she snapped. 'Don't fuss.'

Presently, she began to relax a little, and he related the saga of his adventures – the Deepwoods, the woses, his feelings for the princess, his close encounter with the Urdemon. She was excited by the news of woses like Woody and impressed by the demon, but didn't appear very enthused by his descriptions of the princess, announcing unexpectedly: 'I'm a republican.' He asked what had been happening to her, but in an automatic way, or so she told herself, without pressing her, or intuiting that something was wrong. Eventually, she made an excuse about homework, and said he would have to go. Since Hazel never bothered about homework, always avoiding doing tomorrow what she could put off from today, Nathan was both unhappy and unconvinced. He knew she didn't want him and decided it had to be all his fault, picking at his nebulous guilt like a scab all the way down the street. Without really noticing where he was going, he found himself on the path to the river.

In her room, Hazel lit the candle-stump and glared into the broken mirror, muttering the liturgy of summoning. Nothing happened. She tried again, speaking louder and more forcefully, still without result. Then she groped for Effie's notebook and began leafing hastily through it, looking for words of conjuration and Command, wishing she'd read it more carefully beforehand. Finding a page headed *Incantation to Bind a Recalcitrant Spirit* she began to read, stumbling occasionally over the pronunciation, ignoring the footnotes about protection and precautions. Clouds slid across the mirror, diverging on the crack, so the two halves didn't match. Briefly she glimpsed as if through smoke a ship with white sails, and a single figure at the helm with blowing hair and pointed ears; it could have been man or woman. Then the ship changed, becoming a modern cruiser, and the figure was Lilliat, smiling her silver smile. '*Mi-venya!*' Hazel ordered. '*Té nimrrao, su vier ti-nimrrassé!*'

Lilliat turned, so she was gazing straight at Hazel. Her face altered and darkened; her eyes grew wide; the smile parted to show the pointed teeth of a predator. Her outstretched hand crackled with power which came rippling through the mirror-crack like the whiplash of an electric eel. Hazel jumped back, but not fast enough, not far enough – in the confines of her room she had no space to manoeuvre. The impact sent her sprawling, the tail-end of the lash catching her face, leaving a savage burn across her cheek. As she fell, her head collided with the bedstead, and when she hit the floor she was unconscious.

The mist crept through the village, draining it of colour and substance, turning it into a phantom village of insubstantial buildings and people who loomed up suddenly and then vanished without a word spoken. Sound was either muffled or carried strangely: footsteps might be heard, apparently close by, with no visible feet to keep them company, or there would be a raised voice – a call – and when you approached, no one would be there. A few cars crawled along the road, their lights gleaming out for a minute and then fading into the fog. People dived into the pub, the deli, the bookshop, needing to talk about it, telling each other they'd never known it so bad – you couldn't see more than a couple of yards in front of your face – attributing it variously to the unnaturally wet summer, global warming, or the new mobile phone mast erected controversially close to the church. Somewhere up above the sun was still shining, but all that could be seen of it, now and then, was a smudge of brightness that failed to penetrate the mist-veil.

The fog lay thickest over the water-meadows and along the river. Nathan walked slowly, lost in a trance, his mind as blank as the blankness around him. He had forgotten why he was going that way, if there had ever been a reason, but it didn't matter. He moved like a zombie in a pale, empty world. Sometimes, a spectral tree passed him by, shadow-faint although it might only be a few feet away. Presently, he saw he had reached the river. The tide was high and he could make out the water lapping just below the border of the path, and the ripples running downstream as the current changed. Without making any conscious decision he stopped, close to the willow-stump, waiting. A tiny niggle of thought disturbed the paralysis of his brain, straining to remind him of something, urging him to some unspecified action, but he wouldn't or couldn't respond. His mental processes had shut down; there was nothing in his head but the mist, and the waiting.

A shape emerged through the brume, drifting towards him. For an instant he thought it was an elf-ship like the ones in stories, with swan-neck prow and carven wings, then even as it drew nearer it seemed to shrink, and he saw it *was* a swan, its neck curved, its wings half furled, floating with the current. It sailed past him and disappeared almost immediately, white in the whiteness of the fog. With its disappearance he felt as if whatever he was waiting for had come and gone, and he turned to retrace his steps along the path.

This time, there was no drowsy humming, and the engine was so quiet he could barely hear it, merely a faint throb in the background. But the song was very close, the pure, sexless voice piercing the mist in his head, not a warning but a guide.

> 'Follow the foam of the dolphin's run
> over the pathless deeps;
> there in dark without moon or sun
> there where the kraken sleeps
>
> where the bones of long-lost galleons rot –
> the desert under sea –
> there the goddess decks her grot
> with mermaids' eyes – for thee!'

Nathan no longer heard the words, or hearing, no longer understood. The verse had become a part of the spell, one strand among many, entwining his thought, weaving him into the net. He saw the woman leaning towards him, over the rail of the boat, and in her hands she held his rugger-shirt, the one he had lent Hazel, and somehow that decided him, if there was anything left to decide.

'This is yours,' she said, 'isn't it?' He nodded. 'Come to me, and you can have it back. Come on board. There is room for just one more.'

The launch appeared empty, save for her, but he didn't doubt or question. She stretched out her hand – he stretched out his – they almost touched. Then he jumped, vaulting the rail somehow, landing lightly on the deck – so lightly the boat hardly tilted. The mist flowed over him and through him; it was bitter cold, as if it had blown straight from some polar waste, but he didn't shiver. The woman smiled, and her teeth glittered like points of ice, and her slanting eyes were moon-silver and shadow-black. She held out the rugger-shirt.

'Put this on. You must be cold.'

He was wearing a long-sleeved T-shirt, but he put it on over the top.

'Don't take it off,' she said, 'even to sleep.'

The river bank slipped away, and there was only the mist.

'What is this ship?' he asked, not out of real curiosity, more for something to say.

'It's mine,' she said. 'One of many. All ships come to me, in the end.'

'Where are we going?'

'My home.'

He was very tired – so tired he could barely lift his eyelids. He thought he had been wide awake a moment earlier, yet he felt as if he had been tired for a long time, fighting sleep, desperate to give in. The woman took him aft, where steps led down to the cabins. He saw no one at the wheel, no hand on the throttle, yet the boat held to her course. The woman showed him into a cabin with a wide bed, deep soft pillows, a quilt like a drift of snow. He tumbled thankfully into the embrace of pillow and quilt, heard the closing of the door as the woman left.

But he couldn't sleep, not yet. He wanted to sleep – sleep was bearing down on him like a great weight – but there was something wrong, a germ of discomfort in the welcoming softness of the bed. Of course: he still had his shoes on. He loosened the laces with clumsy fingers, wriggled his feet out of them, and lay down again. But there was a lump digging into his back: his rugger-shirt had rucked up under his arms. He pulled it off and dropped it on the floor, forgetting or disregarding the woman's injunction. Now at last sleep would come . . .

Hazel didn't know how long she had been unconscious: she only hoped it wasn't long. She stood up, fighting dizziness. Her head ached and her cheek burned, but that wasn't important now. Her brain, functioning in slow motion, hung on grimly to a single train of thought. Lilliat-Nenufar – a boat – boats meant water – the river. *The river*.

She was out of her room, out of the house, running down the street, stumbling and bumping into people in the fog. It was beginning to clear now, thinning in the heat of the sun, separating into ragged curtains that drifted out over the meadow, hung around for a while, and then evaporated into nothingness. By the time she reached the river path there was sunlight ahead of her, wan and pale at first but growing brighter, growing warmer. The school didn't insist on much sport and she was panting for breath, but she kept going. As she neared the bank she called out Nathan's name, her voice a croak. There was no reason for him to have come this way but she knew he had – knew it with the certainty that always precedes something terrible. The path was empty; the sun sparkled on the water. The dread darkened inside her.

She went on downriver, further than she had ever been before, walking, running, walking. A swan came out of a reed-clump and waddled towards her, hissing; she had never seen a swan on the Glyde. With its neck extended it was up to her chest, and it seemed very aggressive – perhaps it was protecting a nest. She shouted at it, waving her arms, until it backed down and let her pass. A little further on she saw something wedged against the bank. There was a moment when her stomach clenched, remembering Effie, but she got a stick, and nudged it closer, until she could fish it out of the water. It was a shoe, a lace-up trainer. She recognised the zig-zag pattern on the side at once.

It was Nathan's.

Someone was calling him. He didn't want to wake up but he knew he must; the call wasn't loud, but it was compelling, its pull as strong as gravity. He groped his way through muffling folds of sleep – through the veils of space and time – into the spinning star-dark of another world. And all the while the voice was calling, calling. When he came to himself at last the voice was there, near at hand, no longer insistent but cool and quiet.

'Nathan.'

He opened his eyes. There was a face looking down at him – a face all beauty and arrogance, power and pride, with a mouth that might have been sculpted in steel and a cold deep gaze softened now by some alien emotion. The skin was both dark and golden, the black hair shone with a lustre that was almost green, almost blue. The customary hood was thrown back, the mask discarded. The Grandir – ruler of Eos, lord of a dying universe, watcher over more than a dozen worlds. A man whose schemes were too deep to penetrate, whose purposes too lofty for comprehension. Looking down at Nathan with something like concern in his face.

'I almost lost you,' he said. 'The werewoman is skilled, for her kind, and your mind is limited. You know so little . . . so little. She has gone, but she will return. She senses the pattern, and the power. The time has almost come, but you still have much to do. I cannot always protect you. I can reach into your thought – open the portal – but only if you let me. Had you kept wearing the garment she bespelled . . . but fortunately, I was able to induce you to remove it. My influence over you is wayward, but the sleep she put on you allowed me through. Be calm: there is no more need to fear.'

'I'm not afraid,' Nathan said. It was true – though there was a shivering deep inside him that was almost like fear. He was aware that he was lying on a bed or couch, under a coverlet, in a room with soft lighting; but he saw only the Grandir.

'It is well. You must have wondered why the gnomons didn't come, but the enchanted mist befuddled their senses, and there was a noise in the spellsong which they cannot endure, though no mortal ear could hear it. Forgive me: I had thought they would prove more effective guardians.'

'The gnomons?' Nathan remembered the unearthly swarm, only half solid and invisible in his world, which could invade the human mind, draining thought, bringing madness.

He said: 'I thought they protected the Grail.'

'For centuries that was their task,' the Grandir explained. 'But I sent others to watch over you and your mother. They are Ozmosees: they can move between worlds. They appeared adequate for my purpose. But your danger increases – and I did not expect you to be so reckless. That moment with the Urdemon . . .'

'Was it you who saved me?'

'Both times. But at the second confrontation the creature had more than marsh-power – there was something else lending it substance . . . I was barely in time. Do not take such a risk again. You have only one act to perform in Wilderslee: the rest is distraction.'

'But . . . what act? What –'

'You will know. The act must be involuntary, or the pattern will be disturbed. The Urdemon is merely a diversion, no matter how perilous. Avoid it.'

'It's a bit difficult,' Nathan said. 'There are rather a lot of them.'

'No. There is only one, though it has many forms. It slept under the marsh for five thousand years before it was disturbed. Now, it is angry, hungry, and very confused. Let it stay that way.' Nathan tried to sit up, full of eager questions, and found himself gently but firmly restrained. 'Sleep now. Return to your own world. There may be a time when we can talk, but it is not yet. Remember: you must take more care. I cannot . . . always . . . protect . . .'

The voice faded, and he was falling once more into the star-dark, the sleep-channel between the worlds. For a minute he resisted, fearing to find himself back on the white ship, reduced to an automaton, his brain fogged with magic . . . *She has gone*, the Grandir had said. Remembering that, he let go, feeling safe and thankful, slipping away into unconsciousness . . .

This time, it was Annie who roused him, a look of relief on her face. (He was getting to know that look much too well.) He was in his own bed, and his mother was shaking him, and Hazel stood behind her holding a sodden trainer in one hand.

'Do you think,' Annie said when they were downstairs, 'you could manage to spend twenty-four hours without being kidnapped, or getting yourself coated in demonspit, or losing your shoes in the river so people think you've drowned, or –'

'I'll do my best.' He turned to Hazel, who was still clutching his shoe. 'Did you find the other one?'

'No.'

'Damn. Those are my favourites. Let's go look for it.'

As they walked along the river bank, Hazel told him what she had done. All about her crush on Jonas Tyler, and Ellen and the Sniggerers – Lilliat, the tokens, the rugger-shirt. He said he forgave her – forgiving was easy – but she knew that afterwards, when he thought about it, a tiny germ of distrust would remain, perhaps never to be eradicated. She was his best friend, and she had let him down, in the worst way, betraying him for a price, a reward, for her own advantage. He said: 'I let you down too. I wasn't there for you' – but they both knew that was a little thing, compared to her treachery. Her sentences got shorter, her tone more gruff, the more he tried to reassure her.

'At least we know Nenufar is back,' he said, resorting to practical matters. 'I mean, she's gone now, but it's just a strategic retreat. She's obviously obsessed with the whole Grail thing, and she thinks I'm part of it.'

'Aren't you?'

'I suppose so.' He couldn't talk about his meeting with the Grandir: it had touched him too deeply, stirring feelings – instincts – too private to express, too complex to define. A silence fell between them of things unsaid, and Hazel, inevitably, thought she knew what it meant, and made no attempt to break it.

'We ought to discuss things with Uncle Barty,' Nathan said eventually. 'He could help you with the magic business. He's a wizard, after all.'

'I don't need help. Not going to try it again.'

'You never know,' Nathan persisted. 'It might come in useful. It could be cool, to be a witch. I wish I'd seen those girls in your class, when the flies went for them.'

'Not funny,' Hazel said.

'Sorry – I know you're upset – but – but – stop agonising over it.' He meant, what she'd done to him. 'It's history now. Let's just forget it.'

'You're being *kind*,' she said furiously. 'I knew you'd be kind. I can't stand it.'

'Sorry . . .'

'Friends should be equals. We're not equals. You're cleverer than me – more attractive – more popular – and *nice*. How am I supposed to forget all that? Just by – by being there, you're shoving it down my throat. Then I do something terrible to you – really terrible – and you *forgive* me. Why don't you shout at me, and swear, and call me names?'

'Sorry.'

'And stop saying sorry. It's worse than nice – it's *wet*.'

'All right. All right. You're a rotten deceitful little cow who sold out your dearest friend to a manipulative evil spirit, just to – to win the love of a boy who wasn't worth it. I'm so hurt by that I don't want to talk about it, and I'm trying to blame myself because it's more bearable that way, and I'm not going to punish you because – because I can't think of any punishment awful enough. Satisfied?'

'Not really,' she said, 'but it's an improvement.'

They walked on without further conversation. Nathan was still looking for his shoe.

'I'm not wet,' he said at last, 'am I?'

'A bit,' Hazel lied. 'Like, when you say sorry a lot, and forgive people, and keep acting nice when any normal person would be totally vile. You could try being mean sometimes.'

'I'll work on it,' Nathan promised.

And then: 'We're not going to find that shoe. How about you buy me a new pair? It's your fault I lost them.'

Hazel said something which sounded like *umph*.

'They were very expensive,' Nathan added, with what he hoped was an evil smile.

Hazel said something which sounded like *shit*.

They walked back to the village, side by side.

TEN

Elemental Powers

For over a week, Nathan didn't dream. It was as if some controlling power – perhaps the Grandir, perhaps a dream-ometer deep in his psyche – decided he needed a respite, a period of normality in which to recoup his strength and restore his nervous system. He did the usual teenage things, slightly limited by the fact that his term had ended sooner than Crowford Comprehensive – lay in late every morning, played cricket with George and his mates after school, went shopping with Hazel for new trainers, borrowed George's brother's new computer game, Ultimate World Domination, and went to level one first time. He climbed Chizzledown Hill with Eric and gazed at the strange chalk symbol cut deep into the turf – an arc bisected by a straight line, enclosed within a circle – which the exile said was an emblem of great magical importance on Eos, though what it imported he didn't know. And Annie took Nathan, Hazel, and George to Corleone's, the upmarket pizza restaurant which had just opened in Eade, reputedly in response to the needs of all the wealthy Londoners who were moving into the area. Normal service has resumed, Nathan thought. If he *had* any dreams, they were the ordinary kind, and stayed in his sleep where they belonged.

The only one of which he could remember anything – and

that not much – was about the motor launch: the woman in the bows had turned into Halmé, bridesister of the Grandir and the legendary beauty of her time, wearing a white bathrobe as she had done when he first met her. She was just unfastening it when he heard the princess, running along the river bank and calling to him – or was it Hazel, waving a dripping trainer? When he turned back Halmé had reverted to the phantom, pale Lilliat, dark Nenufar – and Nenufar became Agnis – and Agnis became someone else – and when he awoke he thought: *That's it* . . . but the dream fled from him and he couldn't recall whom it was Agnis had become. He thought about Wilderslee – Nellwyn – the Grandir – in the periods between sleeping and waking, and went to bed in his clothes with the crystal phials in an inner pocket; but it was the summer holidays, and for a little while at least, he was able to relax, and be just Nathan.

Hazel was persuaded to confide in Bartlemy, and began to visit Thornyhill on her own, discussing her experiments in magic, her great-grandmother's legacy, her private fears and doubts.

'It was all a cheat,' she said. 'The power felt as if it came from me but it didn't, it came from Lilliat, and the spell didn't make Jonas love me –'

'You can't *make* anyone love you,' Bartlemy said, 'with or without magic.'

'It was nothing but illusions and lies,' Hazel went on. 'Lilliat – Nenufar – Rianna Sardou – they're just faces, identities she takes on and off like clothes. I bet the real spirit looks quite different – if she *has* a face at all. She could be just a – a kind of entity, like Nathan's elemental in the sword. She used me – and I let her. I knew really it was using, I knew I was being stupid, but I did it anyway. And now I know I *can* do things – call up spirits . . . I don't want to try again but I'm so afraid I will.'

'Believe it or not,' Bartlemy said, 'I do understand. I understand very well. I was born with the Gift, in an age when wizards were commonplace, though mostly charlatans, and there were spirits who used me, for a little while. Then I learned to use them. But like you I distrusted the feeling of power – the high – the rush – whatever you would call it. I distrusted the desire to use that power, to manipulate other human beings. And so having learned to control the power, I had to learn to control *myself*. That is the important lesson. You know already that it must be learned, so you're half way there.'

'How old are you?' Hazel blurted out. 'Sorry – that was rude – but you said *in an age when wizards were commonplace* . . .'

'Old enough,' Bartlemy responded, with the hint of a smile.

'Great-grandma said she was two hundred – three hundred – something impossible. Are you –?'

'I'm older than that. An effect of the Gift – sometimes. Do you wish for long life?'

'N-no, I don't think so. It would be scary. The world changes all the time, and it might be difficult to keep up. And you'd be so lonely. Your friends would die, and you'd just go on, and on, all by yourself. I wouldn't like that. Death is scary too, but it's *natural*. Are you . . . lonely?'

'Let us say I am alone. I have lost many that I loved, and had more time than most for missing them. But there are always new friends to care for – and I have Hoover.'

'Is he old too?' Hazel contemplated the dog with fresh interest. He put his chin on her lap and gazed wistfully at the scone she was eating.

'Enough of the personal questions. Hoover's very sensitive about his age.'

'He doesn't look sensitive,' Hazel objected.

'Back to the matter in hand. We know you have the Gift,

so you *must* learn how it works. It will be your choice what to do with it – you may never try another spell – but it's vital no spirit is able to use you again. I can teach you to control the power, but self-control you must learn on your own.'

'Do *you* do much magic?' Hazel asked, a little shyly. 'Nathan and I watched you draw the circle that time, and summon spirits, but I've never seen you do anything else.'

'I just cook,' Bartlemy said, and his eyes twinkled blue and innocent as a baby's. 'Food and drink is the best magic. It gives strength to the body – warms the heart – cheers the spirit. The most potent spells happen in the kitchen.'

'I'm not much good at cooking,' Hazel said.

'Maybe it's time to learn.'

Ten days had passed without adventure or horror, and Nathan was growing restless. He felt he had been given a brief period of leave before the final battle, a lull before the storm, but now he wanted to get back to Wilderslee and finish what he had begun – even though he wasn't sure how. The future seemed to loom over him like a great dark cloud, its sagging belly heavy with rain, rumbling with thunder, the leading edge of the storm only a footstep ahead of him. He had to take that step, take it now, before the suspense became too much for him and the feeling of imminent doom overwhelmed him. Waiting is always worse than doing, or so he had heard. He didn't want to wait any longer.

In bed that night he reached for the portal, behind closed eyes, stretching out into the wide dim spaces of his mind. But there was light there – a hidden light, felt but not seen, coming from somewhere else – light pushing against the portal – a sudden ray of brilliance streaming through a chink in the blur of the doorway. For an instant, as he plunged into the tunnel of stars, he was irradiated, lit up like a comet, tumbling through the blackness of another world in a trail of blazing sparks. It was an experience like no other – it would be long before he tried to describe it, a lifetime before he would forget. Afterwards he was strengthened, somehow empowered, as if the light in passing through him had left a glimmer of its splendour deep in the kernel of his soul.

When at last he was back in himself, he half expected to see his body glowing, as when he had seen off the Urdemon outside the palace in Carboneck. But he looked ordinary enough, and he wasn't in Wilderslee, with a demon to challenge. He was back on Eos, facing a door that looked vaguely familiar, with his hand already on the bell panel. The door opened, and there stood a man with braided beard and three-quarter mask, his hands ungloved. Osskva. Osskva Rodolfin Petanax.

Nathan thought: Bugger. What am I doing here?

'Well, well,' Osskva said. 'You leave from the central salon, but return by the door. It is nice to see some of the old courtesies preserved.'

'I didn't mean to offend you,' Nathan found himself saying, in the formal speech of Arkatron. 'I can't –'

'You can't predict your arrival or departure. I believe you mentioned that. Come in. You are looking rather less ghostly this time.'

Nathan took a seat on a curving sofa near the cakestand-fountain where the water circulated endlessly, rippling down the glasswork and sending mirror-glows dancing across the ceiling. There was daylight beyond the window-screens but Osskva removed his mask and, in deference to Nathan's solidity, offered him a drink which both smelled and tasted like floral tea. A tiny bowl of pale green crystals proved to be a kind of sweetener; Nathan added several to his cup.

'We talked about the Sangreal,' Osskva observed, 'on your previous visit. I gather it remains in your world, supposedly for safe-keeping. What did you come to talk about now?'

'I don't know,' Nathan admitted. 'Last time, I thought I had to tell you about Kwanji – that's why I was here – but . . .'

The old man studied him thoughtfully with those amethyst-blue eyes; perhaps it was their colour that made them appear at once penetrating and profound, windows onto a great depth of soul. 'You have done many things since last we met,' he said. 'I think you have grown, though not in height. Welcome back, Nathan Ward. You told me you tried to help Kwanjira, and I believe you spoke the truth: a first level practor is not easily deceived. In return, I will help you, if I can.'

Nathan didn't respond – the floral drink was hot, and he had scalded his throat. 'Indeed, I probably would anyway,' Osskva continued, 'since your presence here – so near the end of my world – is obviously of enormous significance, even if I have no idea what that significance is. One like me should know when he is touched by fate, or he is not worth the name of magus.'

'Thank you,' Nathan said, recovering, 'but I'm not sure what to ask.'

'What is on your mind?'

'The sword. The Sword of *stroar*. In the world where it's being kept, they call it the Traitor's Sword.'

'It has been called that here, too. Do you know its history?'

'Romandos made it – the first Grandir,' Nathan said promptly. 'But he was killed with it, by his friend, Lugair. It might have been treachery and murder, but it might have been a sacrifice. It mayn't be important – it was awfully long ago – but . . . I should like to know what really happened.'

'Romandos . . . Few have heard that name, even now. Where did you get it?'

'In a dream. It's like . . . I can enter other worlds at any point in their time. I'm not restricted to dreaming things in chrono-logical order. I saw Romandos, forging the sword, and Lugair came in to talk to him. It was in a cavern hung with green stalactites.'

'I have heard of that place,' Osskva said, his voice almost a sigh. 'Some say it was on Gabirone, some say Alquàrin. It hardly matters now: they are all gone, eaten by the contamination in a few hundred years. Did you see . . . the killing?'

'No.'

'Evidently your dreams are censored; it would be interesting to learn by whom.' Nathan didn't comment. 'I will tell you what I can, since this may be what you came for. It isn't much, I'm afraid. In this world, it has become a crime to invent or embroider a story; therefore, when no accurate records remain, stories are seldom told, and the nucleus of truth in a myth or legend can be lost, along with the fantasy. The law was made by the previous Grandir, no doubt for the best of reasons, but I have often deplored it. Privately, at least. Grandirs do not brook criticism.'

'About Romandos . . . ?' Nathan said, hoping to stick to the point.

'Romandos . . . As is traditional in the ruling family, he had a sister. Only the present Grandir is childless: normally, children were born before magical longevity rendered both parents sterile. Have your dreams ever shown you Halmé, bridesister to our current ruler?' Nathan nodded. 'I too have seen her. They say she is the most beautiful of women. Of course, that is said in every generation, of one girl or more. Nonetheless, Halmé is – exceptional. Romandos' sister, Imagen, was such another, or so it is written. He wedded her – it had long been the custom, in families Gifted with the greatest powers, in order to maintain the superiority of their lineage.'

'In my world,' Nathan said, 'we think incest in unhealthy. For the children, I mean. Too much inbreeding is supposed to make people stupid.'

Osskva smiled. 'A strange idea,' he said. 'Mate intelligence with intelligence, power with power, and the children will be more powerful and intelligent than their parents. That is nature.'

'Genetics doesn't work that way with us,' Nathan said. 'We think variety is good.'

'Your world must be very primitive,' Osskva remarked. Maybe Nathan imagined the hint of condescension.

'*My* world isn't about to self-destruct,' he said.

'That is all too true. Forgive me if I offended you. We were talking of Romandos, and Imagen. He loved her, and accepted her love, without questioning its depth or its meaning. We know that from writings of his which survive. They had three sons and a daughter: the eldest boy inherited his rule. But Imagen had long been close to his friend Lugair, though whether she had given him her body is not known. No account of hers endures, and the Hall of Voices, where the witnesses of history left their words, preserved forever in undying echoes – that was destroyed in war more than an age ago. Of one thing we can be certain from other records of the time, Lugair loved Imagen – loved her so much that his affection for his friend was destroyed, and only bitter envy remained. He came from a family nearly as powerful as that of the Grandir; he was ambitious, ruthless, greedy. Exactly why he killed we do not know – he may have hoped to seize power, or fooled himself it *was* a sacrifice – but Romandos' heir discovered him, and snatched up the sword which Lugair had let fall, and cast it at him. Unhappily, Imagen came between them, and so she was slain, and Lugair was executed later. It was considered fortunate that there were the children to carry on the purity of Romandos' line. It is said, the present Grandir is moulded in his image.'

'But –' Nathan said, and stopped. He had seen the ghost of the past in the Grandir's face, and it was not Romandos.

'What if – what if the heir had been the son of Lugair?'

'Unthinkable.' Osskva all but shuddered. 'To corrupt the blood of the ruling family would be a terrible crime. The taint, remember, could never be erased. The present Grandir's right to rule might even be called into question.'

'Isn't it a bit late for that?' Nathan said. 'After all, there isn't much left to rule over.'

'You do not understand. The Great Spell – the spell which may yet save those of us who are left – was initiated by Romandos. His blood dripped from the sword, and filled the cup. The one who completes that spell *must* have the same blood, or the magic may be distorted. It is one of many reasons why I could not do it. The sorcerer who starts the spell must finish it – he or one of his descendants, genetically almost identical. There are laws that cannot be cheated. The sacrifice, too . . .'

'Must there be a sacrifice?' Nathan asked.

'There is always a sacrifice,' Osskva said, and the sentence fell heavily on the air, as if written in stone.

Nathan woke abruptly, jerked back into his own universe by he knew not what, with the stony echo of those words still in his ears. His frustration at being unable to enter Wilderslee was forgotten; unanswered questions crowded into his head. Did the Grandir know the truth about his ancestry, and if so, had he deliberately sent Nathan to find out? No – Nathan had opened the portal himself, on both his visits to Osskva; whatever fate or hazard had guided him, the Grandir wasn't part of it. And how far would it affect any attempt at performing the Great Spell, if the magus in charge wasn't a full blood descendant of its originator? He's descended directly from Imagen, Nathan reasoned; surely that would be enough. He couldn't believe Osskva's theory about incest guaranteeing genetic supremacy – even if the biology was different in the world of Eos. 'It's like

Hitler and all that stuff about the Aryans,' he concluded. 'Hitler was stupid and wrong – Osskva is clever and wrong – it's still wrong. Mixing genes is good for you.' (It sounded a little like an advertising slogan for a better, more tolerant world.) Whoever made the Ultimate Laws could not possibly have intended to encourage controlled breeding and the arrogant dominion of a single race – or a single family . . .

Nathan thought of the Grandir as he had first seen him in his semicircular study, a man whose very back view had presence, whose thought-waves were so powerful they could distort the planet's magnetic field. An autocrat, a dictator, lord of a billion suns and star systems beyond count – the same man who had leant over him, naked without his mask, an expression on his face that might have been concern. But the physiognomy of his kind was unlike ours, with fractional differences in proportion and feature, even in muscular movement, which meant expressions could not be easily read. Nathan touched the phials which were still tucked inside his sleeveless jacket, and turned on his side, pushing thought away, reaching not for the portal but for a rest from both doubts and dreams. Sleep came soft-footed, so he barely noticed it, drawing a kindly veil over the world.

When the veil drew back he was in Wilderslee. Once again, he was standing in front of a door. The door was at the end of a passage, dim not with the gloom of night but the habitual gloom of the palace, the tapestried, cobwebbed, ill-lit gloom of a place where no one ever opened the curtains or cleaned the windows. The door added to the effect, being made of dark wood and carved into a complex maze of geometric shapes, squares and triangles and diamonds. The long curved door-handle was of iron, or something like it, black from lack of polishing. Nathan decided to dispense with knocking. He pushed the handle down and went in.

He was in a bedchamber – the king's bedchamber. There was the massive four-poster with its laminated drapes, the high ceiling festooned with tassels of dust, the windows muffled in a moth-fodder of shredded velvet and brocade. A single casement was open to light and air. The king was slewed against the pillows with his nightcap awry and an embroidered bedgown bunched and scrunched around him. Having seen him recently as a younger man, Nathan was shocked afresh by the change: his plump face had sagged like molten wax, his eyes were scalloped with paunchy shadows. To his right, Frimbolus Quayne was holding his wrist, frowning at a turnip-watch on a short chain. To his left, the princess was perched on the edge of the bed, stroking his other hand. When Nathan came in she looked up, and such a radiance lit her face it almost took his breath away. She dropped her father's hand and jumped up, running towards him.

'Nathan! I was so afraid – I was afraid you –'

But she didn't fling her arms around him, not this time. Presumably the presence of her father and Quayne inhibited her. She stopped just in front of him, her eyes filled with liquid light, grabbed his wrist and drew him towards the dais.

'Father, this is Nathan, the one I told you about. He's saved me twice now. I think he's the mysterious stranger we've been waiting for.'

'Depending on which legend you've been reading lately,' said Frimbolus. 'Humphellump! I heard, young man, you'd been eaten by an Urdemon. Thought it was too good to be true.'

'Sorry,' Nathan said, risking a grin.

'For one thing, never known an Urdemon to actually eat anyone. There've been plenty of rumours, but no eyewitness evidence. It would've been a bit of a first.'

'No it wouldn't,' Nell said sharply. 'No eyewitness – I was looking the other way. Father . . .'

Nathan saw King Wilbert's hand on offer, and shook it carefully. It felt limp and slightly clammy, the hand of a sick man. 'Good to meet you,' he said. His voice was faint and whispery. 'Thank you for protecting Nellwyn. Good man.'

'If he hadn't dragged her off to the Deepwoods she wouldn't have needed protecting,' Frimbolus said, evidently determined to find fault. 'What's more, in my day young men didn't take young girls to the woods for *protection* – they usually had something quite different in mind. Ha!'

'I *asked* him to take me!' Nell fumed. 'And he behaved like a perfect gentleman!'

'He did?' Frimbolus looked scornful. 'Spineless young fool!'

'Well, except for . . .'

'Except for what?'

'Nothing. Nothing that's any of your business, anyway.' Nell assumed her haughtiest princess-look.

Nathan thought of the kiss (several kisses) with a twinge of guilt which he decided almost immediately was a waste of time.

'Furthermore,' Frimbolus resumed, rivalling the princess in loftiness, 'if young what's-his-name here is the mysterious stranger who's going to perform a miracle cure on his Maj, what about it? He just touched the king, and I don't see anything miraculous happening yet, do you?'

'I don't do miracles,' Nathan said hastily. 'I never said I did. But I brought these.' He extricated the crystal phials from inside his jacket. 'My uncle made this stuff. He's a wizard – sometimes – and good with herbs and things. The balm's to go on the wound – he says it won't cure it, but it should make it more comfortable. And this is just a medicine, to – to help the king relax and sleep well.'

Frimbolus unstoppered the phials one at a time, sniffing their contents, his eyebrows leaping up and down on his forehead like acrobatic caterpillars. 'Doesn't smell very miraculous to me.' He was peering closely at the salve.

'I told you, it isn't meant to. But . . .' Nathan hesitated.

'Yes?' Nell said encouragingly. 'Have you got an idea?'

'My uncle says magical wounds can only be cured with the weapon that made them.'

Frimbolus glanced up quickly, caterpillar-brows frozen in mid-leap. 'That's true,' he averred, 'or so they say. I never thought of it. Blinkus! I've been an imbecile. All these years, and it takes a jumped-up whippersnapper from another world to tell me something I've known all along. But handling the sword . . .'

'No,' said the king. His voice croaked on the word; his face was crumpled with agitation.

'If no one can touch it . . .' The princess looked doubtful, hopeful, vaguely beseeching.

Nathan knew he was on the receiving end of her plea. 'We can keep it in the scabbard,' he said, 'and uncover the hilt. Like –' *Like when you showed it to Agnis*, he was about to tell the king, when he realised the concept of his spying on people in dreams wasn't going to recommend him to anyone. (Nell had resented it from the start.) And in view of what had happened that time, it would have been an unfortunate reminder.

'You know . . . about the scabbard?' Wilbert had seized his sleeve, and was gazing up into his face. 'You are young for a magician. Shows I'm getting old – when even wizards start looking young to me.'

'I'm not a wizard,' Nathan said. 'That's my uncle. But I do know about the sword. Is it still in the secret room?'

The king nodded. 'Got to stay there. Best place. Couldn't bear it if Nell . . . if anything happened . . .'

'Nell can stay out of the way,' Frimbolus said briskly. 'We'll have the Prendergoose lock her in her room.'

Nell's eyes gave a creditable imitation of shooting lightning-bolts at him. 'You – will – not! Anyway,' she added, her tone reverting to normal, 'my room doesn't have a lock. It rusted when the roof leaked, and now it's broken.'

'In that case you can go to the kitchen and help Prendergoose with dinner.'

The palace evidently didn't run to dungeons, Nathan deduced – although of course it was castles which had dungeons, not palaces. The argument escalated when Thyrma Prendergoose herself arrived, carrying a basin of water for washing the king's leg-wound. On being introduced to Nathan she gave him a glare of undisguised hostility before rounding on the princess, in a rare alliance with Frimbolus. If they *were* going to do something with that terrible sword – which she for one thought was a pointless exercise, potentially disastrous for all concerned – her Nell wasn't going to be anywhere near it. Everyone knew it was utterly evil – it would jump around by itself, slashing people's heads off . . . She turned pale at the mere idea, making an odd gulping noise in her throat so that for a moment Nathan thought she was actually going to be sick. Nell took advantage of the pause, drawing herself up to her full height and then a bit more, donning an expression of regal authority.

'I should not have to remind you that I am the princess,' she said. 'In a time of national crisis, a princess doesn't hide in the cupboard. She doesn't run away and allow her – her *servants* to face danger for her.' Mrs Prendergoose bridled at being called a servant; Frimbolus' eyebrows leaped. 'This is my father – this is my kingdom – and I'm staying. Anyway, I have faith in Nathan. You yourself said he was right, Frim. Why don't you have the courage to trust him all the way?'

The dispute sputtered on, but Nathan, knowing Nell's obstinacy, wasn't surprised when she won her point. The king might have put up more resistance, but Nathan's unexplained knowledge of all the circumstances surrounding the Traitor's Sword filled him with an almost religious awe, and although he did much sleeve-clutching, he allowed himself to be overruled by his daughter. As for Nathan, he was inclined to object to her participation, but the thought of what Hazel would have said in the same situation kept him quiet.

Eventually the king unbuttoned his nightshirt to reveal the keys which still hung around his neck. He waved Frimbolus and Mrs Prendergoose away, urging Nell to come nearer, mumbling instructions into her ear. The nurse kept up a muttered stream of objection in the background; Quayne, meanwhile, was bundling his sleeves above the elbow, preparatory to removing the royal bandages. When the king had finished speaking he subsided back onto the pillows, his face grey in the daylight. Nell looked at Frimbolus, then Nathan. 'Do we do it now?' she asked.

It was Nathan who said: 'Yes.'

As he had guessed, the secret room was at the top of a tower – or rather a turret, a tall slender structure that sprouted from one corner of the many-cornered palace like an ectopic limb. Inside, it seemed to be filled almost entirely with a precipitous staircase which spiralled round the central column until it came to an abrupt end beside a door leading back into the main building. In front was a blank wall. Like the rest of the palace, it was constructed of intersecting stone blocks, slightly irregular in size and shape. The princess studied them carefully, biting her lip in concentration, while Nathan held the oil-lamp so the light fell on the area. Then Nell ran her hand over the uneven surface. 'Papa says it's around the sixth block, counting down from the ceiling. There's supposed to be an indentation which you can feel but not see, cut in the shape of a crown. The stone's all pitted . . . I can't feel anything special.'

'Shall I try?' Nathan offered.

'No. This is my job.' He thought she was going to say *I'm the princess* yet again, but she didn't. It was something she needed to assert, he realized, perhaps because of the bleakness of her everyday life, perhaps to remind herself of the duties which bound her. I have a father who is chronically sick, a kingdom under a curse, absentee subjects and Urdemons in the backyard – no pretty dresses, no parties, no fun – but *I'm the princess*, so it's all right.

He felt as if she'd said it, even though she hadn't.

What Nell actually said was: 'Got it.'

She touched the spot with her fingertip, pressing lightly, murmuring a key word which Nathan didn't hear. The wall creaked into action immediately, shifting back a few inches and then sliding laboriously aside. Beyond, the secret room looked dim and dusty, the hole in the roof admitting only a sliver of light. Nathan knew a sudden fear that the Black Knight's body would still be there, a headless skeleton in rusted armour and a few rags of clothing, with its skull grinning from across the floor – but evidently it had been removed. Gingerly, the princess stepped through the doorway. Nathan came behind her, carrying the lamp, his other hand resting automatically on her waist.

'There it is,' she said, indicating the plinth. Nathan didn't point out that he'd seen it all before.

She fiddled with the larger key, while he tried to direct the light onto the clasp of the chest. The oil-lamp was unhelpful, its all-round glow too diffuse for direction, blurring detail instead of highlighting it, while the shadows of Nell's fingers obliterated precisely the section she was trying to see. Nathan thought he could have done with a pocket-torch as well as a Kalashnikov. Eventually, she managed it – he heard the scrape of the key turning, lifted the lamp so they could see into the chest.

The sword lay there, once more locked into its scabbard. Nathan sensed the presence of the sleeping spirit as something imminent, subtly menacing, a cloud on the horizon of a clear sky.

Nell, unconsciously echoing Agnis, said: 'Should we see – anything?'

'Not if we want to live.'

They stared down at it for a long minute – the scabbard with its unseen contents, heirloom of centuries, seat of the family curse – silent with a kind of awe, thinking of its doom-laden history, its potential for death. Nathan swung round so the lamplight reached the wall; he saw the splatter-stains, ten years old, where the Black Knight's blood had jetted from his severed head. They appeared unnaturally recent, still vividly red. The princess gave a gasp of horror, and pointed to the floor where they had walked, smeared with more ugly stains.

'They look fresh,' she said.

'Magic,' Nathan suggested. 'If the wound doesn't heal, maybe the bloodstains don't fade. Perhaps Agnis' hair never grew again.'

The princess was trembling. 'I wish we didn't have to do this.'

'At least we're doing it for a good reason. Not because we want to fight some stupid duel, or are plotting to take over the country. Here, hold this.' He passed her the lamp.

She took it, startled but unresisting. 'What –?'

'I'll need both hands to carry the sword.'

'*You're* not going to –'

'Yes I am. I'm the mysterious stranger.'

'It belongs to my family – it's my responsibility – I'm –'

'And don't say *I'm the princess*. You say that much too often. It's getting to be a bore.'

'You obnoxious – ill-mannered – *peasant*!' Nell's fears were dissipating in the melting-pot of indignation and rage. 'You have no idea –'

Nathan kissed her, very quickly, partly because some instinct told him it was the right move, mostly because he wanted to. 'This is *my* job,' he said.

Anger vanished instantly, allowing fear to return. 'I don't like it.'

'Nor do I.'

He reached into the chest before he had more time to worry about it, seized the scabbard with a firmness which belied his nerves, and picked it up. It wasn't quite as heavy as he had expected; he realized that if you held it by the hilt it was the sheer length which would make it awkward. But it was his sense of the spirit within which jolted him – the nearness of it, the tension in the blade, the evil that only half slumbered under his hand. For a second, he almost dropped the sword.

'What is it?' On a reflex, the princess moved to support it.

'*Don't*. Don't touch it – not even the scabbard. It's –'

'Why not?'

'The spirit in there – I can feel it. It's sleeping – if spirits sleep – but it's going to wake up. Soon.'

'We can't do this. It's too dangerous.'

Her protest steadied him. 'Yes, we can. We must.'

In the king's bedchamber, Frimbolus had exposed the wound, cleaned it, and applied some of Bartlemy's salve. 'It does feel a little easier,' the king was saying. 'Less tight and sore.' Some of the pain-lines faded from his face.

Then he saw Nathan with the sword.

'You got it,' said Frimbolus, for once out of expostulations.

The king's pallid cheek had become a shade paler. Mrs Prendergoose backed away a step, her gaze fixed on Nathan's burden like a rabbit mesmerized by a snake.

'Nell,' she said, 'you must leave now. *Leave.*' Her tone was insistent, husky with terror.

'It would be wise,' said Frimbolus.

'I have to unlock the scabbard.' The princess took out the smaller key. Nathan lifted the sword like an offering, holding it by the shaft. Nobody argued with the princess any more – none of them spoke at all. It was so quiet you could hear the sound of a very small key sliding into a very small lock, and the tiny click as it turned. The leather guard came loose; Nathan, grasping the sheath in one hand, peeled it away from the hilt. He could see it clearly now, closer far than in his dream. He had always assumed the pommel was plain, without gemstone or ornament, but now he made out a design incised into the metal, the lines as thin as scratches, all but invisible. It looked similar to the pattern around the rim of the Grail. He bent nearer, forgetting caution, and Frimbolus' soft admonition broke the silence.

'Remember: don't touch it.'

Nathan straightened, and approached the bed. He could feel the spirit stirring now – a dark, seething essence straining at both scabbard and sword. It felt a little like holding a bottle of champagne which has just been violently shaken and will explode at the slightest nudge. He looked down at the deadly wound, flesh torn from flesh, still red and raw inside but rucked along the edge with the scabs of unsuccessful healing. Here and there, daubs of Bartlemy's lotion had gathered like milky tears. It went deep into the groin, vanishing under the king's nightshirt.

'What do I do?' he whispered. It was one of those moments when you have to whisper – a loud word might split the air. 'Just . . . lay the hilt on the wound? Is there a spell – something I should say?'

'I haven't a clue,' said Frimbolus brightly. 'This was your idea.'

Nathan glanced up at him, seeking inspiration – saw the king's haunted stare, fear and hope in his eyes – saw Nell's anxious face – Mrs Prendergoose, flabby with terror, her cheeks white as her linen, her mouth a hole without a scream. He wondered fleetingly why, out of all of them, she was the one whose reaction was most extreme. And then – maybe it was the proximity of the sword, infecting him with its alien power – suddenly everything was very clear. He stepped back, not touching the king – not yet – and when he spoke, his voice was sharp and commanding.

'Nell, pull off that wimple.'

'*What!*'

'Your nurse – pull off her wimple.'

Mrs Prendergoose was clutching the headdress without which, presumably, she had never been seen. Nell ran to her, plucked her dress. 'Nathan . . .'

'*Pull it off.*'

Nell reached up, doubtfully, even as Mrs Prendergoose flinched back. The linen unravelled – her hair came loose – hair once black, now streaked with grey – sheared off at the neck in a sword-straight line. 'Agnis,' said Nathan.

'Prendergoose!' Frimbolus' shout was loud with fury, more than half at himself. 'Why didn't I see? You must have becharmed us all – re-shaped your very features – but I should have seen, I should have known. When Agnis Embernet first came to the court there was gossip – rumours of occult ceremonies – black magic – cantrips to bewitch the king. I distrusted

Agnis – I detested Thyrma – I should have *known* –'

The king had turned his gaze from Nathan to the woman who had been his daughter's nurse. 'Agnis . . . It can't be . . . Agnis?'

The face of Mrs Prendergoose began to change, muscles tightening, cheeks lifting, eyes and mouth slipping back into place – tiny changes that reassembled her features into those of Agnis Embernet. An older Agnis, the sullen pout become vicious, the earthiness toughened into grit.

'When I first saw Agnis I thought she looked like someone,' Nathan said. 'I just couldn't remember who. But –'

'You took everything from me.' The woman ignored Nathan, Quayne, the princess, staring only at the king. 'My brother's life – all our plans – all our dreams. The sword was supposed to go for *you* – then I would have married you, nursed you out of this world, and Wilderslee would have been ours. We could have ruled twenty kingdoms like this, been the greatest king and queen in the history of this age . . . Instead, my brother was slain – you sent me away – I had nothing left. *Nothing.* I swore then I would destroy you – you and your petty realm – wipe you off the face of the earth – and I have. I have! Look at you – a helpless invalid in a mouldering palace above a city deserted by everyone –'

'Deserted?' The king latched on to the word, his expression fuddled with bewilderment and pain.

'Oh yes! They wouldn't tell you – they wanted to protect you – but your subjects have gone. There's only a handful left – grass grows in the streets – the houses are full of ghosts. You're king of a graveyard – a graveyard where even the corpses have moved out. A king without subjects, a deluded fool ruling in a void. May you rot!'

'It was you calling the Urdemons,' Nell said, the hurt clear in her face. 'It was, wasn't it? All the time I thought it was me – and it was you. I believed you cared for me, I thought . . .' She was fighting the tears, unable to go on.

Agnis looked at her as if there was a kink in her hatred, a knot which couldn't be unravelled. 'I told you to leave, didn't I? *Didn't I*? You were a sweet little girl – I never wanted to harm you. If you hadn't been so stubborn, if you'd gone to your cousins . . . but it's too late now. You stayed – I have no choice – you'll die with the rest of them.'

'Nonsense!' said Frimbolus with rare coherence. 'No one's going to die. The demons are mere illusion –'

'There's only one,' Nathan said, 'but it isn't an illusion.'

'Clever of you.' Agnis' mouth made the shape of a smile, but there was no joy in it, only a kind of gloating. 'It had slept in the depths of a bog for three thousand years, but I woke it up. I spread the marsh for it to dwell in and its Urulation sounded over the city, driving the people away. It took those forms it could remember – I tried to teach it new ones, but it hasn't much imagination. Like all elementals it's drawn to acts of magic – and the aura of the sword. I haven't let it feed often; it doesn't need to, save for pleasure. But I've learnt how to make it stronger, hungrier, more solid – to meld my substance with its spirit – to make one being, one Urdemon with the mind and power of a witch, sharing its appetite, filling its belly. I don't know how you got away last time, but it won't happen again. I wanted the suffering to go on a little longer, I was enjoying it so much, but now – now I shall feed on you all, and swell and swell to the size of a behemoth, and doze in the marshes to keep Wilderslee a desert forever.'

There was a short, stunned silence. In a minute, Nathan thought, she'll give an evil cackle. But she isn't funny; she's real. And the demon's real. And I can wake up, but the others can't . . .

'Mad,' Frimbolus said abruptly. 'Barking. Absolutely barking.'

He grabbed her by the arm, but she shook him off, backing towards the open window. 'You can't stop me!' Contempt seethed in her voice. 'You're a scientist, not a magician. And Nell – all she can do is make mud-pies and untangle her hair. The boy can't draw the sword – no one can draw the sword.' For an instant, as her gaze flickered towards it, the spectre of an old terror blanched her cheek. But only for an instant. 'This is my revenge – and it's almost complete! *Venya urdaiman – venya daiman-glaure! Fiassé! Fiassé! Enfirmi!*'

The daylight darkened behind her. The sound of the Urulation was the howling of winds and wolves, the screeching of ravening harpies. The king reached for his daughter, clasping her hand – Frimbolus drew closer – Nathan moved round the bed, gripping the scabbard, with some vague notion of protecting them, though he didn't know how. Outside the window, something like a cloud was thickening rapidly, growing blacker, growing denser, pouring into the room like smoke. In the smoke shapes formed and dissolved . . . baleful eyes, jagged fangs, an ogre's face, a scaly paw, things with claws and horns and tusks. The shadow-shapes swirled around Agnis as she stood in the attitude of a voodoo priestess, arms outstretched, head thrown back, her throat bulging with effort as the words hissed from between her lips. '*Uvalmi! Invardé! Enfirmi!*'

The darkness condensed into a ribbon of vapour which streamed into her mouth. Her neck arched to an impossible extent, bending her into a bow – her muscles billowed to improbable size – limbs writhed – her whole body seemed to flow together into one amorphous lump. Nathan was briefly grateful they couldn't see what was happening to her face. The room was filled with the rotting odours of the swamp – slime oozed across the floor. Then the quivering mass of unformed flesh erupted upwards into the familiar slug-creature, smaller than the one in the marsh but far too big for the room. This time it had remembered to provide itself with teeth – a jagged collection that appeared to be all incisors, some almost the length of Nathan's arm. The green saliva not only frothed it steamed, huge drops burning holes in what was left of the carpet.

Frimbolus said: 'Definitely . . . not . . . an illusion.'

The princess said: 'Papa,' but she looked at Nathan.

Nathan looked at the sword.

The Traitor's Sword. The Sword of Straw. It was all he had. He felt the spirit waking in the blade, wrestling against the spells that bound it there. The monster that faced him was nothing to the power trapped under his hand . . .

Now was the time to make a choice – the choice – the only choice.

He thought at lightspeed: I'm not the one. I'm not a knight or a hero, I'm not pure in heart, I don't do miracle cures. The blood of the Grandir doesn't flow in my veins.

He thought: It'll kill me but maybe Nell will be spared . . .

The slug-monster lunged towards them, squelching across the floor, its blind head eclipsed by a gape full of teeth.

Nathan's hand closed on the hilt.

The sword came out of its sheath with a sort of silken scream. The blade was edged with blue fire, but under the sheen shadows moved, and two red gleams slid down the shaft. Nathan swung the sword or the sword swung him – he wasn't sure which – slashing across the Urdemon's mouth, shaving the points off a row of teeth with less effort than cutting grass. The poisonous saliva bubbled along the blade and evaporated instantly into nothing, as if it could not endure the metal's temper. Nathan slashed and slashed again, half terrified, half exultant, slicing great chunks out of the vast wormy body, until what was left collapsed in a shuddering heap of blood and gluten and pus. Then the whole mess gave a great heave

– shrank inwards – and a wisp of darkness trailed through the window, its lonely Urulation dying away in the direction of the marsh.

The bits that remained on the floor looked horribly like what you might get if a human body was attacked by a psychotic bacon-slicer. Nathan looked and looked away, suddenly sick, too overcome to notice anything else.

'The sword.' It was Nell. 'It hasn't . . . it didn't . . .'

'You *are* the one,' said Frimbolus.

The hilt was still in Nathan's hand, the tip of the blade resting on the ground. The blood on it, like the venom, smoked and vanished as if scorched out of existence. Nathan could feel the spirit reaching out to him, all power and rage, yet he knew somehow it could not touch him. He was in control.

He didn't understand any of it.

Nell tried to cling to him, but he pushed her away, afraid she would inadvertently brush against the sword. Then he went back to the bed. The king was trying to pull himself upright, a painful eagerness in his face. Nathan laid the blade the length of the wound running from ankle to groin, and up into the stomach: inch for inch, it was a perfect match. He said: 'Heal,' because he felt he had to say something, and that was the best he could do. The king's shoulders twitched – he made a small whimpering noise. Slowly, the wound began to close. As Nathan lifted the sword clear the flesh knitted, scabbed, itched, flaked into smoothness.

'I'm cured!' Wilbert said. Forgetting modesty, he hitched up his nightshirt and bedgown still further, exposing his repaired body to all and sundry. 'Nell – Frim – I'm cured!'

'Yes, Maj,' said Frimbolus. 'Pull your clothes down.'

Some time later, when the king had been left to sleep off the excitement with a dose of Bartlemy's sedative – in another room, due to the body parts on his bedchamber floor – Nell and Nathan repaired to the kitchen. They were both starving, and it seemed like a good place to talk. The sword was back in its scabbard, but Nathan carried it with him.

'I think,' he said, 'I'm supposed to take it back with me. It isn't the responsibility of your family any more.'

'What will you do with it?'

'Leave it with my uncle. He'll keep it safe. He seems to be collecting these things.'

'That must be quite a collection,' Nell said.

She heated some thick soup – the kind with lots of barley and limp, unidentifiable vegetables. It had been made by Mrs Prendergoose, which meant it both smelled and tasted uninspiring, but they were too hungry to object to either the flavour or the cook.

'Do you think the Urdemon will come back?' Nathan asked.

'Frim says not. Agnis conjured it, and she's dead, so . . . It'll go back to sleep at the bottom of a bog for another few thousand years, and the marsh will dry up around it, and people will come back to the city . . .'

'And the kingdom will prosper and everyone will live happily ever after,' Nathan supplied.

'Mm.'

There was a pregnant pause – a pause so pregnant it was practically giving birth.

Nell said: 'Will you ever come back?'

'I – don't know.'

'In the story,' her manner was carefully detached, 'the hero marries the princess. It's customary.'

'In my world,' Nathan said, 'we'd be too young to get married.' He knew he wasn't doing this right, but he didn't think there was a right way to do it.

'We're not in your world,' Nell retorted.

'That's just it. *I* am. I mean, I'm here now, but here isn't where I belong. I've done what I was meant to do, and now I've got to go home. I don't know if I'll be able to dream myself back any more. I want to – I really want to – but even if I could, it's not going to go anywhere, is it? You and I – it'll always be hopeless. Maybe it's best to say goodbye now. Get it over with.'

'Not yet,' the princess pleaded, abandoning the dregs of her soup. 'You could dream yourself back just one more time. We could go for a picnic again – a real picnic, with sandwiches and lemonade – and explore the Deepwoods all the way to the mountains, and see dryads, and waterfay. We can't say goodbye so soon. You have to come – promise me. You have to.'

'I'll try,' Nathan said. He must come back, he knew, just once, but not for the princess.

There was a further pause, no longer pregnant, merely uncomfortable.

Nathan felt an unfamiliar sensation twisting inside him – it wasn't physical but it *felt* physical, like the onset of an illness – a squeezing at his heart, a knotting in his stomach. Somewhere ahead he glimpsed rashes, fever, sleepless nights. He thought: 'Is this love?' The L-word, Annie had called it, shying away from overuse. He could say it now, he could tell the princess *I love you*, and the word would be out there forever, a word that would bridge the gulf between worlds, a bond from soul to soul that could never be broken. With that word, Nell would hold on to his memory – the thought of him, the dream of him – and though a hundred princes came to woo her, all their wooing would be in vain. He could say the word and kiss her again – he *deeply* wanted to kiss her – and go home on a flood of happiness and unhappiness, a bittersweet magical moment never to be repeated, never forgotten.

Or he could go with the word unsaid, and she would see him as a hero who had come and gone in a dream, doing his heroic duty and going his heroic way, leaving her with only a tiny pang to remember him by. Her feelings would fade, withering in a late frost, ready to bloom again another day, for another boy. He didn't want to think of her with someone else – he wanted the bittersweet magic that is stronger than any spell – but . . .

But . . .

The pause stretched out, and stretched out, until neither of them knew what to do with it.

'I'm tired,' Nathan said at last. 'I'd better take the sword and lie down somewhere.'

'My room,' said the princess.

The tower bedroom with its cosy bed, and the crescent moon carved on the pelmet . . . He lay down on the coverlet, hands folded on the sword-hilt like a crusader in effigy, resting on a marble tomb. The princess sat beside him. 'Do you mind if I stay?'

''Course not.'

Presently, he moved over and she curled up along the edge of the bed – there was just enough space – and he took one hand off the sword to stroke her hair, all long and thick and tangly, and they fell asleep together.

It seemed a life-age later when he awoke in his own bed, with the sun shining through the curtains, and the leather-bound sword digging into his ribs, and a strand of hair still wound around his fingers.

EPILOGUE

Autumn Leaves

Another time, another world. Having dozed late, exhausted by the night's activities, Nathan was in the kitchen eating a lunch appropriate for a demon-slayer – cornflakes with chocolate sauce. He had been talking both between and during mouthfuls, while Annie, too horrified and too riveted even to nibble a sandwich, sat propped on her elbows listening.

'Are you going to see the princess again?' she asked at last.

'I don't think so. I need to dream myself back there, just one more time – there's something I have to do – but it won't be to see Nell. We'd only have to say goodbye all over again. What's the point?'

'But you like her,' Annie said, probing gently. 'You like her a lot . . . don't you?'

'Mm. That's just it. I nearly said it – you know, the L-word?' He scanned his mother's face for signs of shock, but failed to find them. 'Only I suddenly saw, if I said it, that would make the whole thing real. It would be, like, this big tragic romance – Romeo and Juliet – we come from different worlds, we can't ever be together, but our love will somehow unite us – that sort of thing. If I said it, Nell would always remember me – remember me saying it – maybe it would stop her loving someone else. I never knew how powerful words are, till then. Because I didn't say it, our – what we felt – was just a passing affection, something she can put behind her. She deserves to love some guy in her world – to live happily ever after. She'll think of me . . . like someone in a dream. No big deal. After all, it *was* just a dream, really. Best to keep it that way.'

'So you do – L-word – her?' Annie said.

Nathan ummed an affirmative. 'She's the most wonderful . . . We argued a lot, but that was wonderful too. She made me feel I could do anything, *be* anything. I could be the hero she wanted – fight demons, cure the king. Do you . . . d'you think I just did those things to impress her? That would be awfully silly.'

'It's natural,' Annie said. 'But even if you did, you'll learn as you get older it's *what* you do that counts, not why you do it. We have all sorts of reasons for doing things, some good, some less so, but it's your actions that make you who you are.'

'Was I right,' Nathan asked, 'not to say it? The L-word, I mean.'

'Yes,' Annie said. 'I think you were right.'

Later, she drove him to Thornyhill, with the sword on the back seat of the Beetle, bundled in an old blanket.

'I thought we could hide it here,' Nathan told his uncle. 'With the Grail.'

'I see,' Bartlemy said. 'I'm not sure that's a good idea, but there are no obvious alternatives, so . . . You'd better put it in the secret cupboard yourself; I hope it's big enough. I would prefer not to touch it, even sealed in the scabbard and wrapped in a blanket. I can feel the aura of its inhabitant even now.'

'I still don't understand why it let *me* touch it,' Nathan said.

'Fate,' Bartlemy suggested, flicking a glance at Annie which she pretended not to notice. 'You are part of a pattern, the whole of which we cannot yet see. No doubt clarification will come, in due course.'

He took Nathan to the chimney-piece in the living room, and showed him how to operate the hidden catch to open the door. There was a small package already inside, anonymous in brown paper. Nathan wedged the sword in beside it – there was only just enough space. He felt the moment should somehow be more dramatic, more ceremonial, a ritual concealment of a weapon of great significance – but it wasn't.

'Supposing I got kidnapped again?' he said. 'Now I know where it is, I might tell someone.'

Bartlemy smiled. 'I'm not worried.'

'Could I stay here one night?' Nathan went on, changing the subject. 'In the week. I need to do something – dream something – and it would be easier here.'

'Of course.'

It took Nathan two days to find Woody – or rather, to let Woody find him, sitting on a log with a packet of Smarties for a lure. He'd forgotten about the wose's penchant for Smarties, but Hazel reminded him. Woody perched on the log at his side, picking out the green ones, while Nathan told him about Wilderslee, and the Deepwoods. That night, the wose came to Thornyhill Manor, avoiding Hoover – he was nervous of dogs – by climbing through the bedroom window. He settled down to sleep beside Nathan, evidently ill-at-ease in the strange surroundings (Nathan knew he would never have come to the bookshop), his twiglet body scrunched up on top of the quilt, his knotty fingers twined with Nathan's.

Nathan didn't say: *I've never done this before.* He wasn't even sure he could, but he hoped, if Woody believed in him, something in his spirit wouldn't allow him to let the wood-wose down.

When Woody appeared to be sleeping, he fumbled for the portal, trying to focus on his destination without losing contact with his companion. It was horribly complicated – afterwards, he thought it was like trying to do exams in three different subjects at once. He was concentrating so hard that as the channel opened it felt as if the world turned inside out, or he turned inside out, and there was a rush of nausea even though he had lost touch with his stomach, and the reeling vertigo of an endless fall. But somehow, though his hand was somewhere else, or nowhere at all, it was still entwined with Woody's. He landed in his own body, on the ground, with an impact so hard he was winded. But there were trees – autumn trees, orange and gold and crimson and pink – and sun sparkling through the leaves, making leopard-patterns on the woodland floor. And Woody was beside him.

They walked for a while, when Nathan got his breath back, through the many-coloured forest, with the leaves falling slowly around them, and winged seedpods whirring by like tiny shuttlecocks, and spiders spinning their shimmery webs, and the whisk of squirrel-tails vanishing in a flurry of foliage. After a while they halted in a clearing with a moss-grown tree-stump surrounded by toadstools – small brown ones like miniature umbrellas, and big red ones with white spots, and green ones with purple frills, and three tiers of yellow bracket fungus sprouting from the bole. Beyond in a net of interlocking branches a dark strange eye was watching, wary and curious.

Nathan said: 'You'd better go.'

Woody didn't hug him, because woses don't hug. He said: 'Goodbye,' and 'Say goodbye to Hazel,' and 'I'll miss the Smarties.'

Then he was gone.

Nathan went on walking by himself. It had been early

spring when he was there with Nell, and he wondered how much time had passed since. One summer, or two, or a hundred years. Nell could be dead and gone now, another princess sleeping in the carved bed. The thought made his heart shiver. Then he heard voices – laughing, chatting, calling – somewhere not far away. He went towards them, cautiously, halting at the crest of a rise, dropping to his stomach to see but not be seen. The ground fell steeply in front of him, and in the dell below a group of people were having a picnic. It was a very sumptuous picnic, with two big hampers and a low table littered with plates and bottles and glasses, bowls of nuts and berries, platters of cured meat and sandwiches cut into assorted shapes. There were perhaps half a dozen picnickers with a couple of servants to look after them, but Nathan only noticed one person. Nell.

She looked, he thought, a little – a very little – older, maybe sixteen. Her hair was woven into braids and twisted up in a complicated mass on the crown of her head. She wore earrings that dangled and glittered, and a dress of some silky material with no darns or patches, kilted up to show another dress underneath. The Nell I knew, he thought, only wore one dress at a time – but layers were evidently still in fashion in Wilderslee. She wasn't as chatty or as noisy as some of her companions, but from the way they turned to her every so often it was clear she was the important one, the centre of attention. No longer the ragged princess of a forgotten city but a princess with a court and courtiers, with jewels and clothes and admirers – a princess who might sleep (badly) on a pea but would certainly never shell one. She talked a great deal to the young man beside her, a young man with hair the colour of copper-beech leaves and cinnamon freckles on his arms, though Nathan couldn't see his face. Nell was smiling often, the lovely smile he remembered so well. He was glad she wasn't old, or dead, but somehow it stabbed him. *She looks happy . . . really happy . . .*

He watched for a few minutes then slithered back down the slope, trying to make as little noise as possible. He went on through the woods until the picnic was out of earshot, wondering why it should hurt so much, that Nell was happy, and wore two dresses at once, and would never shell peas again.

The dream ended without his noticing it, fading into darkness in the way of dreams, and when he awoke, a bit of the darkness was still there, like a bruise on his spirit.

Downstairs the kitchen was full of breakfast smells, but he wasn't hungry.

'A broken heart,' said Bartlemy. 'I see. There is no food for that, not even chocolate, though many would disagree. First love – first pain – isn't the worst, but the trouble is, you don't know it at the time.'

'I didn't say I was in love,' Nathan responded. Certain confidences had gone no further than his mother.

'In that case,' Bartlemy said, unperturbed, 'what would you like for breakfast?'

Nathan stiffened his sinews, or possibly his upper lip.

'Scrambled eggs, please.'

Hazel was there, a few days later, when Bartlemy had the unexpected visitor. A tall man – or such was the impression he gave – with silver hair receding from the double arch of his brow and very piercing eyes. He wore a black flapping raincoat and a high collar which proclaimed his calling. 'You'd better go,' Bartlemy said to Hazel. 'We'll talk tomorrow.'

She went, conscious of that sharp glance, like a laser boring into her back.

Bartlemy turned to his uninvited guest. 'Zakharion.'

'Bartoliman.'

'Do come in.'

As they entered the living room Hoover rose, hackles bristling, his normally buoyant tail very still. 'Sit,' Bartlemy said quietly, presumably to the dog.

The men sat too, in a careful fashion, their attitude neither tense nor relaxed, but somewhere in between.

'No doubt you were expecting me,' said the visitor, whom Hazel had thought unexpected.

Bartlemy made a noncommittal response. He was stroking Hoover's head, pulling one floppy ear between his fingers. The dog, taking his cue from his master, looked calm but alert.

'I thought it was time we met,' the stranger continued.

'We have met many times.'

'My dear Bartoliman, let's not be pedantic. You and I have been – shall we say, in competition? – for a long, long while. However, we have not had a . . . *rapprochement* since – was it Damascus, or Samarkand?'

'I wouldn't have called that a *rapprochement*,' Bartlemy said. 'But my French is a little rusty.'

The visitor chose to ignore that. 'I had no idea you had buried yourself down here. A beautiful part of the country – very quiet after all your travels. The kind of place where nothing ever happens. I imagine that was what attracted you. Quite a coincidence that I too should have found myself in the area.'

'Coincidence?' Bartlemy queried.

'Perhaps. Of course, I have a position of importance – I am a man of some stature on a national level. Whereas you –'

'You were always interested in importance and stature,' Bartlemy said.

'What is it you're calling yourself these days? Goodman, isn't it? A modest title.'

'Aspirational.'

'Hmm. Let's not waste time fencing with each other. I infer the same thing drew us both to these parts. I don't suppose you would consider – joining forces? Together, we might be able to put the object – or objects – in question to good use. Our combined skills –'

'I wouldn't presume,' Bartlemy said, picking his words, 'to combine my skills with yours.'

There was a silence – a significant sort of silence, the kind that says more than speech.

'I expect you'll be moving on now,' Bartlemy said.

'Moving on?'

'Leaving the school. You must have done all you can there. A man of your talents will always be in quest of pastures new, I'm sure.'

'Indeed.' The visitor arranged his hands very deliberately on the arms of the chair. He had beautiful hands; Velazques might have wanted to paint them. According to some sources, he had. 'However, I have no immediate plans for departure.'

'It would be wise. Consider your reputation. There is Giles Hackforth, a man in need of a crusade. If he were to make inquiries . . .'

'My dear fellow, there is nothing into which he could inquire. Still, you may have a point. If the – er – battle is lost, a prudent man will leave the field while he is still in one piece. Is that what you are trying to tell me?'

'The battle is neither lost nor won,' said Bartlemy. 'In fact, it has barely got started. But there are too many forces in the field, none of them on the same side. It's already untidy. Were you to – bow out of the lists, it would thin the crowd a little.'

'I will bear that in mind. It is true that my present situation has begun to pall. A school is a very limited bailiwick for a man of ambition. Nonetheless . . . what of the boy?'

'Which boy? Your school is full of them.'

'The boy who dreams,' the visitor said. 'Nathan Ward.'

'I'll look after him – as far as possible.'

'Your ideals, Bartoliman! Always getting in the way. Such an unusual boy. He fell asleep in my study once and disappeared completely. I could have done something with a boy like that. Once in control of his mind . . . Well, we'll let it go. You've never been enthusiastic about mind-control, I know that. Cookery – such a waste of your talents. Yet you don't even offer me a biscuit – an unexpected discourtesy.'

'Not really,' Bartlemy said.

'Ah. We don't break bread together. How traditional you are. Since no refreshment is forthcoming, I had better leave. One small thing.'

'No.'

'Bartoliman, don't jump down my throat! The boy Damon had a bracelet – he stole it from me, I'm afraid. Distressing to find such lax morals in the child of caring parents from a privileged environment. I wondered if he left it here?'

'Yes,' said Bartlemy, 'and no, you can't have it. A strabythmic amulet, I believe. You didn't seriously imagine I would return it to you?'

'You never know.' The visitor rose to depart. 'People can grow careless in old age, and you're considerably older than me, if you will forgive me for mentioning it. The amulet is valuable – look after it. Whatever you do with the boy.'

When he had gone Bartlemy turned to Hoover. 'That, Rukush,' he said, 'is why I don't use my Gift, any more than is absolutely essential. But I fear – I very much fear – things are going to get more essential from now on.'

It was perhaps a fortnight later when Chief Inspector Pobjoy dropped in. Although he did so with a casual air, Bartlemy was not deceived. No visitor to Thornyhill was ever casual – the house was too far off the beaten track for that – and nothing Pobjoy did was completely unplanned.

'Stay to lunch,' Bartlemy said, taking acceptance for granted. The inspector might well have timed his visit with lunch in mind: it was just before noon.

They had omelettes flavoured with herbs and molten cheese, and a salad of watercress and other leaves which Pobjoy didn't recognize. But then, he had had few encounters with salad in any form.

'I would offer you a glass of wine,' Bartlemy said, 'but I assume you're driving.'

Pobjoy had thought he would find it difficult to describe his experience with the woman in the motor-launch – this was the first time he had mentioned it to anyone – but somehow, under the influence of the omelette, it was easy to open up.

'She seemed to know me,' he said, 'but I'd never met her before. She didn't resemble the computer image we made up for the Sardou woman, but I thought . . .'

'What did she look like?'

'I . . . Fair. Dark. I *don't know*. It's ridiculous, but . . . Of course, that was the day of the fog. It made everything a little . . . surreal. In the pub, I'd picked up a rumour that our suspect was a river-gipsy, but I've never heard of any round here. And then . . .'

'And then?'

Pobjoy hesitated, lingering over his omelette. 'I had a strange conversation with Annie – Mrs Ward – earlier that day. She's very fanciful, isn't she?'

'No,' said Bartlemy.

'I mean . . . quirky, jokey . . . She said some things – funny things – as if they were serious.'

'Such as?'

'I don't recall specifics.' He wasn't going to mention giant man-eating worms. 'But – she talked about what happened last year as if . . . it might have a supernatural explanation.'

'It might well,' Bartlemy said. 'When you have eliminated the impossible, as Holmes would say.'

'It wouldn't stand up in court,' Pobjoy said. 'Mind you, I read him when I was a boy – great stories, but nothing to do with real police work. I don't believe in the supernatural. No evidence.' He felt comforted, hearing himself say that. Evidence was something solid to hold on to.

'Conan Doyle did,' Bartlemy said mildly.

'He was a writer. They'll believe anything.' Pobjoy was dismissive.

'Indeed. You might say, it's their job.'

'I suppose so.' Pobjoy clearly had a problem thinking of writing as a job. 'So – are you going to tell me that woman last summer didn't escape, she *dematerialized* – and the river's haunted – and those people were drowned by a ghost?' He made his voice as scornful as he could to conceal his own doubts.

'Not at all,' said Bartlemy. 'Have some blackcurrant champagne sorbet.'

'I don't think – all right. Thank you.'

There was an interlude in which omelette plates disappeared and were replaced by green glass bowls with scoops of purple-black ice.

'Well,' Pobjoy said when they'd finished, 'won't you tell

me *something*? Tell me it's real – tell me it's nonsense – tell me *I'm* being fanciful.'

'I would never dream of telling you what to think,' Bartlemy said. 'That's up to you.'

'No advice?'

'Not really. Advice is the one gift you can give people that they never actually want. Should I give any, I always keep the receipt, so they can send it back when it doesn't fit.'

But Pobjoy wasn't in a mood to cultivate his sense of humour. 'Did you ever find out if there was someone behind your latest burglary attempt?' he went on. 'The Hackforth connection, for instance? That kid Damon – a nasty piece of work. He was mixed up in it somehow, wasn't he? A yob is a yob no matter what his family background.'

'I don't suppose you'll be having any trouble with him in the future,' Bartlemy said with his usual tranquillity. 'If there was any connection with – let us say – a criminal element, it has been dissolved.'

'I thought Damon *was* the criminal element,' Pobjoy said bluntly. 'That type doesn't change – trust me. His dad was protecting him – his dad and the school. The abbot didn't want a stain on his spotless Christian reputation, I daresay. I hear he's moving on.'

'Really? Where did you hear that?'

'The ACC had it from someone – he didn't say who. Probably one of his political chums. I infer promotion is in the air – an archbishopric, if that's what they call it, or a bigger abbey, or maybe they're moving him up to senior seraphim. Whatever the next step is for an abbot.'

'I wish him luck,' Bartlemy murmured thoughtfully. 'Of one sort or another.'

As the inspector rose to leave, there was a sound from the kitchen. Hoover pricked his ears; Bartlemy opened the adjoining door. For an instant, Pobjoy glimpsed the intruder – a very short figure, swarthy, whiskery, raggedly dressed. He had met a dwarf once before – a good citizen, working in the film industry – but this dwarf was different. This was a dwarf who looked as if he belonged in a story, the kind of story with giant man-eating worms, and witches, and loralillies.

Bartlemy said to him: 'Help yourself,' though he didn't specify to what.

Pobjoy left with a sense of well-being in his stomach and a growing unease in his head.

That evening, Bartlemy walked in the garden, watching the shadows grow longer and the light of the setting sun tangle with the leaves. The woodwose had gone, but the dwarf stayed. Nathan and Hazel, in their different ways, had each loved and lost, fought battles major and minor, grown a little further up. A policeman was beginning to see that there was a world beyond the scientific evidence, a world the laws of man could not touch. It was progress, of a kind. Bartlemy saw life as endlessly varying, expanding, diversifying, going somewhere, though he didn't know where, constantly moving, never arriving, driven by a purpose which he had to hope was good, because all the centuries had taught him was that only the hopeful heart survives. But maybe we must make our own good, he thought, if we can. The light ebbed, and darkness flowed towards him, and he went inside to the mingled scents of his kitchen, letting tomorrow take care of itself, leaving the great unanswered questions in the garden where they belonged.

A Sorcerer's Treason

Book One of the Isavalta Trilogy

Sarah Zettel

When lighthouse-keeper Bridget Lederle rescues an oddly dressed, tattooed stranger from the storm-tossed Lake Superior he tells her he is from another world, a world in which she is a great magical force. Only she can save the Dowager Empress, currently under threat from her poisonous daughter-in-law. For a woman with nothing to lose, it's an attractive offer. But when Bridget arrives in Isavalta she finds nothing is quite as he promised her . . .

'This engaging and vivid slice of fantasy will keep fans of Robin Hobb more than happy'   *SFX*

'A sumptuous tale of subtle magic, malevolent sorcery and twisted loyalties – you won't regret venturing into Sarah Zettel's world.'   SARA DOUGLASS

'Zettel's first fantasy novel is a triumph of storytelling. Rich, compelling and exciting, this could be the best fantasy debut in years.'   JONATHAN WEIR, *Amazon*

ISBN: 0-00-711400-1